NOT A SPARROW FALLS

not a sparrow falls

Linda Nichols

Minneapolis, Minnesota

Published by Bethany House Publishers
11400 Hampshire Avenue South
Bloomington, Minnesota 55438

Bethany House Publishers is a division of
Baker Publishing Group, Grand Rapids, Michigan.

Printed in the United States of America

ISBN 978-0-7642-0747-1

The Library of Congress has cataloged the original edition as follows:

Nichols, Linda.
    Not a sparrow falls / by Linda Nichols.
       p.   cm.
    ISBN 0–7642–2755–6
    ISBN 0–7642–2727–0 (pbk.)
    1. Single fathers—Fiction. 2. Problem families—Fiction. 3. Alexandria (Va.)—Fiction.
4. Young women—Fiction. I. Title.
    PS3564.I2745 N67   2002
    813'.54—dc21   2002006085

To Ron and Laurel Pentecost

and the people of Clover Creek Bible Fellowship,

who showed me the Christ of Calvary

who still changes lives.

ABOUT THE AUTHOR

Linda Nichols, a graduate of the University of Washington, is a novelist with a unique gift for touching readers' hearts with her stories. *Not a Sparrow Falls,* her bestselling debut novel for the Christian fiction market, was a 2003 Christy Awards finalist in the Contemporary category. Linda and her family make their home in Tacoma, Washington.

ACKNOWLEDGMENTS

Many people gave me information and help for this book. Thank you all for your patience and time.

J. W. Gregg Meister answered general questions about Presbyterian church government, as well as Keith Wulff, Coordinator of Research Services for the Presbyterian Church (U.S.A.).

Lt. Daniel Pierce of the Fairfax County Sheriff's Department and Richard Folsom of the Nelson County Sheriff's Department helped with information on law enforcement.

Phillip Payne, Commonwealth Attorney for Nelson County, Virginia, patiently answered questions regarding legal matters, as did Debbie Giles at the same office. My husband, Ken, was also very helpful to me in clarifying the criminal justice process.

Thanks also to the Virginia Department of Corrections for their information on prisons.

I also want to thank my mother and all my Virginia relatives. In addition to loving me all these years, you answered my questions and helped with my research for this book.

As always, I'm indebted to Jo Ann Jensen, Sherrie Holmes, Sherry Maiura, and Mae Lou Larson for their encouragement and critiques, as well as Bethany Maines, Kathryn Galbraith, Bill DeWitt, and Debbie Macomber. You are more than writing partners; you are friends. I would also like to thank Bridget Honan and the Wednesday night group for supporting me and encouraging me to keep on writing.

As I wrote this book, my devotional life and my writing life became beautifully intertwined. The sermons of Jim Cymbala and the music of the Brooklyn Tabernacle Choir, principles from *Experiencing God* by Henry Blackaby, as well as insights from the leadership and people of Clover Creek Bible Fellowship wove into the tapestry of this story.

I'd also like to thank my father for always believing in me and encouraging me.

It has been a privilege to work with all the professionals at Bethany House Publishers. Thanks to Barb Lilland and Sharon Asmus for their insightful and gracious editing, as well as to everyone else who contributed to this book. I'm truly grateful to each one of you. You do your jobs with excellence.

A truly generous person is one who gives to those who can't return the favor. Nicholas Sparks has done that for me.

Finally, I would like to thank Theresa Park, my agent and friend. Not only have you represented me with skill, intelligence, and dedication, but always with my best interests at heart. You encouraged and believed in me when things looked dark. I will never forget.

prologue

HATTIE DIDN'T KNOW EXACTLY WHAT she was praying for. Or who. All she knew was that it had awakened her, this hard stirring, like a wooden spoon working and mixing up her insides. Years ago she might have ignored it and gone on back to sleep. Thought it was something not settling in her stomach, or some troubling of her dreams. But she had learned better. After eighty-some years of listening to the Spirit of the Lord, she'd finally gotten acquainted with His ways.

She lay under the heavy layer of quilts and felt the chill of the room on her face. Time was, she might have slipped to her knees by her bedside, prayed silently in the dark so as not to wake Alvin. But Alvin had been gone for twenty years now, and she was so crippled up with arthritis she couldn't even get herself out of the bed, let alone kneel on the hard wooden floor. The Lord knew.

"Dear Jesus," she whispered. "Somebody's in trouble. You know who it is. You know what they need." She prayed on and on and didn't look at the clock, but by the time she felt a clearing in her spirit, yellow slats of weak winter sunlight were coming through the blinds and falling across her bed. She'd barely slept a wink, but it didn't matter. At her age daytime and nighttime were one and the same. Sleep a little here, a little there, and she suspected that death would come along about like that. One day she would doze off in her chair and wake up in glory.

She heard a clatter from the direction of the kitchen. The back door creaked open and closed.

"It's me, Miss Hattie."

"Good morning, Martha," she called back. Her own voice sounded quavery and old, even to her.

She heard the floorboards creak, and she followed Martha's movements in her mind. Another door opened and closed. Martha was hanging up her coat. Metal on metal—the stove door opening. Then the sound of newspaper crackling and the clunk of stovewood on the sides of the grate as Martha made a fire. Hattie smiled. It would have been easier for Martha to flip on the heat, but she knew how Hattie liked a fire in the stove. Metal on metal again as the stove door closed. More footsteps, and in a moment Martha's face was beaming over her. Her cheekbones were high, as if cut from some dark stone, and her eyes were almost black. As usual, her pretty mouth was curved into a smile. Martha was pretty and smart enough to have gone out into the world and done something important instead of taking care of an old lady. Hattie wondered if she was satisfied being a home health aide. She never asked Martha, though, afraid she'd put an idea into her head, and some morning another aide would come through the door instead of her friend.

They went through their morning routine. Martha helped her dress, combed out her plait and rebraided it, wound it into a bun, and stuck it down with four hairpins.

"I didn't poke you, did I, Miss Hattie?"

"No, darling, but it wouldn't matter if you had. I'm not tender headed," she answered and tried to help as best she could as Martha helped her to the bathroom and dressed her. She leaned forward while Martha buttoned up her dress and lifted her twisted feet as Martha worked them into her Hush Puppies and laced them up. Martha hummed. Hattie watched her hands, so quick and gentle.

As blessed as she was to have someone to care for her, she wished again she could do more for herself. She was used to doing for others, not having them do for her. The faces of loved ones came into her mind. She couldn't do anything for them either. She could only pray. She felt a heaviness settle under her breast, but almost instantly she realized the truth. Praying was doing something. It accomplished more than she ever could have, even when her own hands had been quick and her legs strong.

Martha helped Hattie into her chair, wheeled her into the kitchen, and parked her at the table. Hattie watched as Martha went about making their breakfast. She was singing, as usual. This morning it was "His Eye Is on the Sparrow."

"Would you like some sausage and gravy with your eggs this morning, Miss Hattie?"

Hattie answered yes and thanked her.

Martha put the sausage on to fry, then opened up the flour bin and shook a few cups of flour into the chipped mixing bowl. Hattie had never measured anything either. Martha added baking powder, salt, cut in some Crisco, then poured in milk. She mixed with her bare clean hands, just like Hattie always had. It took a touch to know when the dough was the right consistency. You couldn't tell just by looking. Martha shaped it into a mound, dusted the top with flour, and rolled it flat with a clean glass.

"We'll just have hoecake instead of biscuits this morning, Miss Hattie, if that's all right with you."

"That would be just fine, Martha," Hattie answered but with only half her attention, for she was distracted again. She felt the burden return, the same pressure that had awakened her last night, only stronger now, and this time the call to pray came with a picture. She closed her eyes, and a scene appeared on that dark screen behind them.

She saw a sheep alone in the desert. It lay on bloodied sand. Its neck was torn, and it was too stunned and wounded to cry out. A wolf was circling, teeth bared, eager to finish it off.

Hattie felt a flash of anger, and words, loud and fervent, tumbled from her mouth. "Father, the enemy wants to destroy a child of yours. This one is hurt, Lord, with no one to help but you." She'd been reading the book of Daniel last night before sleeping, and suddenly it seemed to be no accident. "Lord, you were the fourth man in the fiery furnace where the king threw your three servants, and not even a hair on their heads was singed. Father, when Daniel was put into that lions' den, you sent your angel to shut the mouths of the lions, and he was delivered. Not a scratch on him."

"*Yes*, Lord," Martha called out, agreeing in prayer from her post by the stove. "*Nothing* is too hard for you."

"You're the same now as you were then," Hattie cried. "Show us your power, Lord. Rescue this child of yours."

"*Yes*, Lord," Martha agreed again.

Hattie heard an egg crack against the side of the skillet, then sizzle as it hit the hot grease.

"Your heart is tender, Jesus, and your arm is *mighty* to save," Martha declared.

Hattie's eyes were still closed, but the picture on the dark screen began to change. A shadow moved between the injured sheep and the predator. As the figure became clear she could see it was someone young and strong and clothed in a dress so white it was blinding in the desert sun. It was her, she realized as the face came into view. She reached toward a beautiful golden scabbard strapped to her waist and pulled out a bright, gleaming sword. The blade flashed in the glaring sunlight and sliced the air as she threatened the wolf. He bared his teeth again, and his yellow eyes glowed with hatred as he slunk back into the shadow of the rocks. She watched for a few more moments, but the image began to break up, chunks of it dissolving into splashes of color and light.

Hattie opened her eyes. Martha turned the eggs, slid them onto a plate, opened the screeching oven door, and brought out the golden hoecake. Hattie felt the tension drain from her. She was worn out, as though she'd fought a battle.

Martha drained the sausage, and when they were each seated at the table with a hot cup of coffee and their breakfasts before them, Martha spoke, nodding as if she had just decided something. "I feel like the Lord heard our prayer," she said. "He's moving."

Hattie nodded, too. Her spirit had cleared. She was hungry. "Pass that damson jelly over here, if you please."

"Yes, ma'am," Martha said, waiting until Hattie had a good hold of the jar before letting it go.

Hattie ate until she was full, thankful she could still manage a fork. When they were finished, Martha wheeled her chair over by the stove. The fire was burning hot, crackling when Martha opened the door to add another stick of wood. The room was warm. Hattie felt herself become drowsy. Martha began singing again as she started on the dishes. "I've got a feeling everything's gonna be all right."

Hattie smiled in satisfaction, closed her eyes, and drifted off.

≈ *one* ≈

"WILL THAT BE ALL FOR you, then?" The cashier, an old man with bifocals and a droopy gray moustache, gave her a curious look, but nothing more. Mary Bridget Washburn smiled just a little, not having to pretend to be timid, and cast her eyes down at the array of cough and cold preparations on the counter in front of her.

"It's the flu," she lied. "Whole family's laid out with it—my husband and children. I'm doctoring my mama and daddy, too." She fingered the driver's license in her pocket, one of the many Jonah had paid the fellow in Charlottesville to make for her. Sometimes they asked for ID when you bought this much stuff, even if you were paying cash.

"Um-um." He shook his head. "You don't look old enough to be married, let alone have children."

Mary was thinking of what to say, but then realized he wasn't expecting an answer. He rang up the sale and loaded the bottles into a bag.

She just nodded and knew that once again her silky blond hair and wide blue eyes had done the trick. "Be twenty-five next birthday," she said, the only truthful thing she'd told the poor man in the whole conversation.

"Um-um," he repeated again. "Don't look a day over seventeen."

She held her breath until he had handed her the change from her hundred.

"I thank you," she said, forcing herself to look up. He looked right at her now, as if he'd suddenly realized what she was up to. She didn't let on, just flashed him another smile. She felt the familiar surge of relief as the bells on the door jingled behind her; then she aimed for the sidewalk and looked for the truck, which was there for a change. Usually she had to kill time waiting for Dwayne to get back from his runs to the agricultural supply and hardware stores, but this time he was waiting for her. It was a good thing, for it was cold, even for Virginia in October. It would freeze again as soon as the sun set.

Dwayne flicked his cigarette out the window and started the engine as she put the sack of cold preparations in the back, along with the bottles of antifreeze and drain cleaner and the two big tanks of anhydrous ammonia. She tried not to think about what they would become. She'd seen a picture once in school of a fellow who'd been on methamphetamine. First picture was normal. Next picture looked to be about ten years later, the third one taken when he was an old man.

"These photos," the DARE officer had said, "were taken six months apart. That's what meth does to you."

Mary put that thought out of her mind. Tried to, at least. She climbed into the passenger side, and thankfully, Dwayne didn't speak, just grunted and shifted the truck into gear, pulled out onto the street, and then aimed for the bypass and home. *Home*, she thought with a shudder. A rusting singlewide where they ate and slept, and an old, falling-down smokehouse out back where Jonah made the candy, as Dwayne called it. She closed her eyes and tried to ignore the voice that asked her, louder and louder each day, what she was doing here.

It's not my fault, she argued with it. *I'm making out best I know how.* She certainly hadn't graduated from high school, set down her cap and gown, and decided to begin her career in meth production. No. Like her grandmother used to say, it had been like boiling a frog, a gradual and easy turning up the heat until the water was rolling up all around her, and here she still sat. She reviewed the steps that had gotten her here. The good reasons she'd had to leave home with Jonah and take his offer of easy money. But as she justified her actions, she could hear her mama's voice, gentle but stern, cautioning even from the grave that there was no right way to do a wrong thing.

If Mama were here, everything would still be right. Or at least not as bad wrong as it had become. But Mama was dead, and Papa was gone, her brother and sisters scattered. And she was here.

For the time being, anyway. Over the last five years she'd lived more places than she could count. They'd been like nomads, picking up and moving on every time the law got to sniffing around. Sometimes their timing was bad, and Jonah or Dwayne would get picked up. They'd do jail time, then get out and be back at it again. She'd never gotten caught. Just lucky, she guessed. She supposed she could have left during one of their jail sentences. She could leave now, for that matter.

She wasn't a prisoner. Exactly. She could easily walk away any number of times during the course of a day, slip out the back door of one of the pharmacies or hardware stores while Dwayne waited out front in the pickup. Head for the bus station while he was making a sale. But where would she go? And what would she do once she got there? She couldn't go home again, and even the thought of home—the word calling up the image of the old white clapboard house nestled in the hollow—brought a sharp stab of pain. She couldn't go home. It wasn't just an hour away, but a lifetime. No, after what she'd done and become, she couldn't go there. And she had no money to start out anywhere else.

The promised profits had never been delivered. She asked for money now and then. Dwayne would say ask Jonah, and Jonah would dole it out a twenty at a time. That was not counting the hundred-dollar bill Dwayne handed her every time she went into a pharmacy to buy cold medicine or diet pills. They must know that if she ever got her hands on anything larger, she would be off and gone.

And then what? she asked herself wearily. She had no education. No skills besides buying ingredients for meth, and she was afraid of what would happen if she lived on the streets. That pressure had already started. The men who came to transact business with Dwayne were giving her looks, not to mention Dwayne himself.

Jonah, though, the one she'd run off with, hardly even noticed her anymore. The earth could open up and swallow her, for all he was concerned. He was always out in the shed cooking candy, and even when he was present physically, he was in a world of his own. But then, that was nothing new.

Jonah had always been different. He wasn't like the other boys around home who lived for football and hunting. He'd never had any patience for their foolishness, their big cars, their silly social games, and he hadn't minded saying so. When she remembered Jonah, the image that appeared was his back disappearing into the woods. That seemed to be how she'd most often glimpsed him—mysterious and slightly out of touch, like someone born in the wrong century. Jonah, silent and intense, roaming over the hills and hollows, coming back with pockets full of arrowheads, ginseng plants with roots neatly wrapped in his handkerchief, a handful of sparkling rocks carefully picked from the red dirt. His best friend had been that great-uncle of his who lived in the cabin up on the ridgetop. That old man's hands had been thick as leather from all the stings he'd gotten through his years of keeping bees, but he'd made the best sourwood honey you could ever hope to taste. It was sweet and fragrant and a clear light amber. Jonah had gotten his solitary ways from him.

He looked like him, too, the shadow of the old man appearing in the young. Both had the same rough-hewn features, reminding her of the mountains they loved. Both had high, broad foreheads, sharp cheeks, and broad, sharp-angled jaws. Like his uncle's, Jonah's face was plain and straight, just as if it had been cut from stone. Even his eyes were like the mountain's gray granite, and just like those rocks, they were flecked with little bits of white.

Jonah's movements had alway been easy and fluid, amazingly graceful for such a tall, lanky man. He'd moved through the woods silently and quickly, or stood still, only his eyes moving, watching some creature, taking note of whatever had changed since the last time he'd passed through. He knew the location of every beehive and squirrel's nest. There was nothing on that mountain he didn't see.

"He's peculiar," her father would say flatly, watching with narrowed eyes whenever Jonah passed by. She twisted her mouth into a bitter smile. If Papa had thought Jonah was peculiar then, she wondered what he would say about him now.

He probably wouldn't even recognize him. Jonah's skin had become pasty white, his face gaunt and haggard. And it wasn't just his body that had changed. It was as if his personality, that indefinable thing that made Jonah himself, had been slowly eaten away, edged out an inch at a time by his bitterness and the steadily increasing diet of methamphetamine. She had a sudden vision of Jonah's soul looking like a piece of Swiss cheese. Whoever lived in his body now was paranoid and wild in the head. He'd go off about nothing at all, typical of the hardcore meth user he'd become.

Dwayne prided himself that he only used occasionally, but Mary knew that's how it had started with Jonah, too. She used some milder things from time to time, but nothing really touched that empty spot inside of her. Whenever she wondered why she bothered to restrain herself, a quick look at Jonah reminded her.

He went through the same cycle over and over again. Get high, higher, higher, using a little more each time, becoming crazier and crazier. He would yell and scream and see things, and that phase could go on for days, even weeks. Then he'd come down with a crash, sometimes having a few hours or minutes of sanity as he plummeted, finally sleeping for days, almost comatose. He would wake up hungry for more, and off he'd go again.

She'd heard about a man in New Mexico who'd been tweaking— at the peak of the cycle of highs. He'd become convinced his son was possessed and had cut off the boy's head and tossed it out the window of his truck. Lately Jonah had been having those kinds of paranoid fits, staring at her and Dwayne, then suddenly going silent, as if voices inside his head were saying things that scared even him. She was afraid of him and had gone to hiding the knives and razors, anything he could use to hurt himself or someone else. Last week he'd burst into the living room of the trailer, shotgun raised to his shoulder, talking about somebody stealing his brain.

"Give me that thing before you kill somebody," Dwayne had said, wrenching the gun away from Jonah, who'd stared at him, wild-eyed and panting, his sharp features even more pronounced since he'd lost weight. "Here." Dwayne had handed the gun to her. "You better keep ahold of that. Jonah's been sampling too much of the product. Getting into the candy a little too often."

She'd taken the gun, and as soon as she felt the smooth stock under her hand, the realization had come to her like a long awaited dawn. Dwayne trusted her. But then, just as if he'd read her mind, he settled himself onto the broken-down couch beside her, lifted one of those tattooed hams of his, and rested it around her shoulders. She'd done her best not to flinch.

"There was an old boy down in Boone's Mill tried to cheat us out of some money a while back," he said conversationally. "Know what happened to him?"

She shook her head and pretended to be uninterested.

"Somebody doused him with gasoline and set him afire while he was sleeping."

She hadn't responded. It was probably just more of his foolishness. That was just Dwayne. Always bragging. But Jonah. Well, these days there was no telling what Jonah might do. She hadn't said anything after that, just pointed her eyes toward the television, but the little spark of hope had died out just the same.

She'd gone to her room after a while, when all the traffic started coming in and out, when the music started pounding the walls. She'd read a magazine for a while and then finally fallen asleep. Around five in the morning she'd gotten up to go to the bathroom. Everyone had finally gone home, and someone had turned off the stereo. She could hear Dwayne snoring from the couch. She headed back to her room, but Dwayne roused himself, got up, and followed her down the hall. She hurried into her bedroom, pressed the door quietly until it latched, then hooked the pitiful lock. Not that it would do much good if he decided to come in. He lumbered closer, and she heard him pause outside the door. She had held her breath, and after a few minutes the floor creaked, and she heard his bedroom door open and shut. But it wouldn't be long. She had rested her forehead against the bedroom door that night and tried to pray, but no words would come.

Now she turned her face toward the truck window, barely taking note of the beauty of the mountains, the flaming leaves on the trees. How was it that her life had become such a dry, hot desert? A canyon of stone and dust where every turn just led her farther in instead of out into grassy valleys with shady trees and quiet ponds.

She felt weary all the way to her bones. She leaned her head against the window glass.

Who was she, really? Surely not this person she'd become. She tried to remember the last time she'd caught a glimpse of her real self. She focused her thoughts, not playing with the idea, but really wanting to remember, and her mind went to a place she'd tried hard not to visit. She was twelve years old. Her little-girl face beamed back at her from memory's hiding place. Her teeth were a shade too big for her features, her hair silky white, spilling down around her shoulders. Her legs were thin and still bruised from play, her shining eyes lit with a light that hadn't yet gone out. Mary Bridget smiled, remembering the high point of that year. She had memorized one hundred verses in Sunday school and won a brand-new white leather Bible with her name embossed on the front in curly golden letters.

The scene shifted. Another tableau came into focus, and she was with her mama at Grandma's, snapping beans and going over those verses. She could almost smell the fragrance of Grandma's kitchen—a mix of coffee and biscuits and apples and woodsmoke and whatever she was cooking for supper. She could almost hear the energetic hissing of the pressure cooker, the murmur of their conversation, the creaking of their chairs, the strains of Grandma's gospel music in the background.

Mama and Grandma had both come to the church the night she'd been awarded her Bible. She stared straight ahead, and instead of the dusty dash of the truck she saw the two of them, starched and pressed, sitting in the front row, their pride beaming toward her so strongly she could still feel its warmth. She held on to the bittersweet picture as long as she could, but after a few moments it faded.

She stared bleakly out the smudged window of the truck. Where had that girl gone? What had happened to change her? It was a question she never allowed herself to ask. And the only reason she was asking now was the gnawing, growling torment that had come upon her lately. Something in her that she'd managed to keep sleeping all these years was coming awake, twisting and struggling to be free. And it hurt. She hadn't felt such misery since the first days, since that first morning when she'd awakened next to Jonah and realized what she'd done. Shame had spread through her chest and stomach, like something cold and poisonous. It had felt so bad she hadn't thought she could live. So she had learned how to make it go away.

You just didn't think, that was all. You just kept your face pointed straight ahead and you didn't think, and you didn't feel, and you just did the next thing, and whenever something made you feel bad, you looked away, or closed the cover, or turned it off, or found something to distract you.

But she must be wearing out or the presence getting stronger, because it wasn't working any longer. More and more, when she was lying on her bed almost asleep, when she was staring out the window, her mind unguarded, that presence would come, that voice would speak. *Who are you?* it would ask. *Whose are you?* And when it did, that little girl's face would appear in memory, and Mary couldn't tell if she was being taunted or beckoned back to something still possible.

Was it possible? Did that person still exist inside her somewhere, or was she lost forever? As the question echoed, long forgotten words came to her mind. They suddenly seemed right, a perfect description of what her life had become. She closed her eyes and whispered them to herself. "Fearfulness and trembling are come upon me, and horror hath overwhelmed me. . . ."

There was more to it, but she couldn't remember. All the way home she repeated the first part, trying to recall the rest of the verse. Finally, as Dwayne turned the truck off the highway onto the snaking back roads, the rest of the passage came to her. "Oh, that I had the wings of a dove!" she whispered. "I would fly away and be at rest."

"Fly away and be at rest," she repeated to herself as they turned onto the long dirt drive up to the trailer. "Fly away and be at rest," she whispered as she gazed at the meth trash mounds in the ditch— mountains of empty antifreeze and drain cleaner containers, spent cans of lantern fuel. She murmured the words over and over again, and somehow, by the time the truck pulled up in front of the rusted trailer and shuddered to a stop, something had changed. They had become a plan rather than a prayer.

✌ *two* ✌

SHE KNEW ENOUGH TO BIDE her time. A day went by, then another, then a week, then two. Finally, when all the necessary pieces came together, it took her a few minutes to realize that this was it. The chance she'd been waiting for.

She and Dwayne spent another long day visiting stores to buy ingredients. They drove up to the ragged trailer about six o'clock. Jonah came out of the smokehouse just long enough to get what he needed, then went back to work. Mary Bridget went into the kitchen. She washed up the dirty dishes, threw out the empty beer cans. When Dwayne went out to the truck and came back with two quarts of home brew, her heart thumped. This was her chance.

"I did some business in Franklin County today." Dwayne grinned and sniffed the cap of the bottle. "A mild fragrance with just a hint of battery acid and the tiniest aftertaste of lead pipe."

Mary Bridget laughed like he'd said something clever. She took the chickens she'd bought yesterday from the refrigerator and breathed another prayer of thanksgiving that she hadn't cooked them. She made a big, heavy meal—fried chicken and biscuits and gravy—the kind of meal where Dwayne always ate three times what even he needed, then fell asleep on the couch while watching TV.

She finished the dishes, even sat down beside him and watched television—show after show. Dwayne swigged from the bottle every minute or two. Finally, just when she was losing hope in her plan, his head lolled back, and he started snoring.

She sat there for a minute, making sure he was out, then slipped out from under his arm and forced herself to walk down the hall just as normally as possible. It wouldn't do to have him wake up and find her tiptoeing around. She checked her watch. She had about an hour before the cars would start pulling in. Evening shoppers looking to buy what they needed. She went into the bathroom and looked out the window. It was dark, but she could see a sliver of light edging past the black plastic over the window in the smokehouse. She quietly went back into the hall. Dwayne was still sawing logs.

Jonah's door wasn't locked. He never slept in his room. In fact, he never slept at all, and she prayed he kept the money here instead of with him in the makeshift lab. She glanced toward the living room one more time, then turned the bedroom doorknob and went inside.

It looked like a bomb had exploded. The bed was unmade, and there was a strong smell of dirty clothes. Jonah had given up bathing some time ago, and she'd noticed little bloody scabs on his arms where he'd taken to picking at them. She wrinkled her nose and thanked God she would get used to the odor in a minute. There was money everywhere. Tens and twenties balled up on the top of the dresser, with wadded-up receipts and coins strewn among them. She glanced past them, knowing there must be a bigger pile somewhere. They took in thousands every day, and she knew for a fact Jonah hadn't marched into the bank and opened an account. She looked through a drawer or two and found only gray underwear and socks and a snake's nest of old dungarees and T-shirts.

She heard the dogs start baying, and her heart thumped. She went to the window and peered out. The lights were still on in the shed, and she didn't see a thing or hear a sound other than their hoarse cries. Sometimes they went off like that, and there was no telling why. Perhaps a raccoon or a possum had passed by in the night. She eased open the bedroom door, craned her neck, and looked down the hall. Dwayne was still snoring.

The fright galvanized her to more speed. She became methodical in her search, opened and closed each drawer quickly and quietly, went to the closet and looked underneath the pile of dirty clothes and the smelly boots and shoes. Finally she had searched the whole room. Nothing. The money wasn't here. She leaned against the wall, then slumped down onto the dirty carpet and felt like dissolving into tears. She covered her face.

"Help me, God," she prayed, not missing the irony. She had to get out of here, though. That was all there was to it. The money had to be with Jonah out back. She opened her eyes and wondered how she could get him away from the smokehouse. She stared straight ahead, not seeing the messy room, trying to come up with an answer, but as she stared, her attention was snagged by something. Between the yellowed box spring and mattress was an edge of green paper. She crawled to the bed and gingerly pulled it out. It was a hundred-dollar bill. She hauled up the mattress, and sure enough, there it was. The stash of money, piles of raggedly banded bills nearly covering the entire box spring. She stared for a second longer, then took the green duffel and began raking it in. She jammed in the wads of hundreds and fifties until the zipper was stretched tight. Might as well be hung for a sheep as a lamb.

She hoisted up the bag, and not wanting to risk passing Dwayne by exiting through the front door, she went into the bathroom. She opened the window and tossed out the duffel bag and her backpack. She climbed out herself, dropped onto the soft ground underneath the window, then lowered it slowly. She carefully crept toward the truck, opened the door as quietly as she could, and shoved the duffel across the gearshift to the passenger seat. She was just easing herself in, hoping the truck would compression-start as she coasted down the hill and wondering what she would do if it didn't, when the dogs started up again. Her heart froze, not beating at all for a second, then thumping down hard and taking off racing.

A slice of light cut through the darkness as Jonah threw open the door of the smokehouse. He blinked, hair and eyes wild. He had the shotgun on his shoulder again, and the flashlight lurched wildly over the yard, finally coming to rest on her in the driver's seat of the truck. Mary took a deep breath and decided to go down fighting.

"Turn that blamed thing off of me before I go blind."

The light continued to blaze for a moment, then swung down toward her feet. She could see him, awful and frightening, framed in the light of the shed, and even though it terrified her to do so, she began walking toward him, for the last thing she wanted was for him to come to her and see the duffel on the seat beside her. As she drew closer she could see that his sharp face was gaunt, and he was biting his lip and moving his jaw around in that strange way he'd taken since he'd started using. She got closer and could smell the odor even before she saw the array of Mason jars, Pyrex glasses, and tubing on the tables behind him. She tried not to breathe. It smelled like fingernail polish remover, only a hundred times stronger. She planted herself in front of him and spoke before he could ask her a question.

"Give me the truck keys," she demanded, keeping her voice calm and sure.

"What for?" His eyes were thin circles of gray around black discs.

"I need to run to town." She purposely made herself sound impatient.

He stared at her suspiciously, his jaw working. His hand started picking at the scab on his arm. The top came off, and it began to bleed.

"Well, for mercy's sake." She made a sound of irritation. "I need something. Some feminine products."

"Oh." Jonah looked perplexed.

"Give me the keys," she demanded again.

He stared at her for a minute, tilted his head.

"The keys," she said again, and finally he dug in his pocket and handed them over.

She held out her hand, suddenly inspired. "And some money."

Jonah set aside the shotgun and took out his wallet. "Here." He handed her a twenty, and the door was closing in her face before she could even reply.

She ran after that, heart thumping in her throat. She climbed into the pickup and shifted it into neutral, praying that Dwayne was still passed out on the couch. She coasted down the hill without the lights, hoping she wouldn't run into the gully, and didn't shut the door and start the engine until the road leveled off and she had no choice.

It was just after two o'clock in the morning when she pulled into the parking lot of the twenty-four-hour Wal-Mart in Charlottesville. She sat for a moment, thinking; then when her plan was made, she went inside and bought a pair of earrings, some lipstick, and a bottle of dark brown hair dye.

She went into the bathroom and colored her hair, mopping the drips from her neck and shoulders with paper towels, ignoring the curious looks from the one salesclerk who came in to do her business and left without a word. Mary didn't speak, just applied the dye, ignoring the pain that shot through her when she saw the corn-tassel hair becoming the color of mud. She did the best she could to dry it afterward, ducking her head to catch the air from the little wall-mounted dryer. She quit before it was fully dry, but combed it down straight onto her shoulders. It felt thick and sticky, as if she hadn't done a good job of rinsing it. She leaned forward and examined her face, already somewhat unfamiliar.

Adding the dangly earrings made her look even more foreign, and by the time she outlined her lips with the dark lipstick and made up her eyes, another person stared back at her from the mirror. Now she was ready. No one would recognize her like this, and with as many IDs as this fellow made for students at the college, there was no way he would remember her as a former customer. No way he would connect her with Jonah.

She drove Dwayne's truck toward the school and cruised slowly up and down the streets. There it was. That was the apartment building. She breathed a prayer of thanks, though she felt odd again praying about such a thing. She justified herself. Without identification she couldn't get a job, and if she worked under her own name or one of her aliases, it would be like leaving a trail of bread crumbs leading Jonah to whatever hiding place she was able to find.

She set the brake on the truck and made her way through the concrete maze of the apartment complex. She found the bank of mailboxes and counted on the hope that she would recognize the fellow's name when she saw it. She'd looked through the whole first row when the thought occurred to her that he might have moved. After all, it had been two years since she'd last used his services. Her stomach tightened into a knot but then relaxed when she saw it: Eric Whitley.

Reassured, she went back to the truck to sleep awhile. She tried, but her nerves felt as if they were strung tight. Finally she dozed off. When she woke again it was nearly eight o'clock. She made her way to Eric's apartment at the back of the complex and rapped on the door. Nothing happened, so she rapped again, louder this time, and was rewarded by a shuffling sound and the bark of a dog.

She cleared her throat and composed herself, trying to remember what Eric had looked like. Tall and thin, she remembered, not at all what she'd expected for a forger. He looked as though he could be one of the professors at the school and acted like it, too. Quiet and studious, with a scraggly red beard and thinning hair. But she, of all people, knew there was no telling what circumstances had led him to this life. She shifted her weight and leaned forward as the door opened.

It was a child, not more than four or five, a little girl with blond hair that could use a good shampoo and combing. She was wearing skimpy little pajamas and looked cold. The dog was one of those like the queen of England had, with short stumpy legs. He thrust his head at Mary Bridget and shifted the girl aside.

"Hey," Mary Bridget said, holding her hand out to the dog. He sniffed it and pushed a cold, wet nose into her palm. "Is your mama or daddy awake?"

The little girl didn't answer. Just rubbed a calf with her foot. The dog was trying to get out. Mary Bridget caught his collar, and seeming to lose interest, the little girl drifted away from the door. Not knowing what else to do, Mary stepped inside and closed the door behind her.

The apartment was messy but not as bad as she was used to. The pressboard tables were littered with pop cans and beer cans, brimming ashtrays, and a couple of plates of last night's pizza. A newspaper and some of the little girl's clothing littered the floor. There had been no children the last time she'd come here. She was certain of that.

The little girl went back to the couch and pulled a baby blanket over her bare legs. The television was tuned to cartoons.

"Where's your mama?" Mary asked her again, feeling a sharp sympathy for the little child sitting here all alone, probably hungry. But actually, she had to admit, the child didn't look scared or ill-treated. It was probably her own pains she was grieving, she told herself.

"Mama's sleeping," the child said.

"What's your name?"

"Brittany."

"Do you go to school, Brittany?"

"Sometimes." She lifted a shoulder. "When Mama wakes up in time."

Mary Bridget called herself to task. Remembered her mission. She wasn't a social worker. The truck was parked out front for anybody to see if they cared to, and although he wouldn't be calling the police, there was no doubt in her mind that Jonah would come looking for her as soon as he came down from his high. Or send Dwayne. She didn't have time to spare looking after other people's children. "Where's your papa?" she asked, moving on to business.

The little girl lifted a shoulder again and seemed to know exactly what to say to seal Mary's fate. "I'm hungry," she stated, and then waited, as if she knew what would follow.

Mary sighed deeply, then rose. She peered down the hall. All the doors were firmly shut. She went toward the kitchen. She hesitated a moment, feeling a little strange about rummaging around another woman's cupboards, but maybe she could find a box of cereal and pour the child's milk. Then her conscience would be clear and she could go back to the truck and wait. The little girl watched her, quiet and solemn. Mary sighed again, flipped on the light, and looked in the cupboards. No cereal. No food at all except a few cans of vegetables and a jar of Tang. She opened the refrigerator. There were some eggs, and the breadbox contained two dry heels of bread. She debated for another minute. Taking over somebody else's kitchen wasn't exactly good etiquette, but that seemed like a silly point, all things considered. Besides, the child was hungry.

She scrambled the eggs and used the stale bread to fry up some French toast, which she served with butter and brown sugar, since there was no syrup. She mixed up the Tang, which would have to take the place of milk. Other mornings of scouring the cupboards for something to feed her brothers and sisters, of making meals from bits and pieces, came back to her in sharp relief. She shoved those memories aside and focused her attention on the child.

They conversed between bites, and when the girl had eaten all she wanted and had gone back to watching cartoons, Mary Bridget finished the remains of the breakfast. She washed the plate and thought she might as well do the rest of the sinkful of dishes, her years of enforced homemaking coming back to her again. She came back to reality when the child reappeared, pointing toward the hall. "There's Mama," she said.

The woman stood in the hallway and blinked a few times. She had short brown hair, six or seven earrings in one ear, and none in the other. The belly under the white T-shirt was swollen with the last stages of pregnancy. She didn't seem offended or even puzzled at finding Mary in her kitchen, as if having strangers underfoot wasn't an unfamiliar occurrence. "Who are you?" she finally asked, pulling her robe closed.

Mary had her mouth open to answer truthfully, then remembered why she was there. It wouldn't do to identify herself. She hadn't thought about what name to use, but the minute she spoke, it came out, almost by itself. And afterward it seemed right that Mama's name had sprung from her mouth. Fitting that every time she spoke it, she would be reminded of how far she'd slipped from the person she should have become. It would be a cruel reminder of the truth of who she was—and who she was not. "My name is Bridget," she said. "Bridget Collins. But everyone calls me Bridie."

Eric eventually emerged from the bedroom. He made the new driver's license, went on the Internet and, with a few clicks, had

Mama's social security number. He threw in the card at no extra charge.

Mary Bridget unzipped the duffel and, as inconspicuously as she could, peeled off four one-hundred-dollar bills from the first bundle she grabbed, then handed them over. The driver's license was still hot from the laminator, and the face that was framed in the picture was strange. Her own, yet not her own, and the name felt the same way. "Bridie." She repeated it firmly and told herself to get used to it. This was who she was now. "Bridie Collins."

Eric asked no questions. The woman spoke hardly at all. "You know your way around the kitchen" was all she said by way of thanks.

"My mama was sick for a long time when I was growing up. I did most of the housekeeping."

"She die?" the woman asked, almost casually.

Mary didn't answer for a moment. Why did strangers think they deserved to know everything about you? She finally nodded, remembering her father's terse instructions that she tell her brother and sisters that their mother had died. *"I've got to go to work,"* he'd said. *"You'll handle it better than I would, anyway."*

Their business transacted, Mary said good-bye to the child, thanked Eric, and got as far as the door. "You won't tell anyone?" she asked, turning back.

"I wouldn't stay in business long if I did," Eric answered in his oddly gentle voice.

On impulse Mary rummaged in the duffel again, then crossed to the woman and thrust another hundred dollars into her hand. "Here. Buy something for the children," she said and turned away before the woman could answer.

Eric said nothing. The child said nothing. Not even the woman acknowledged the gift. Mary Bridget glanced back one last time as she left them, gaunt and quiet, watching her from the couch.

The truck found its final resting place behind a huge magnolia in the Piggly Wiggly parking lot. She took the registration from the glove box and shoved it into her backpack. Not that it would do much good. They could trace the truck through the license plates, but she didn't have the time or the tools to mess with removing them. She left the keys in the ignition, hoping someone would steal it. What wasn't there couldn't be tracked. She walked across the street to the Greyhound bus station, annoyed at herself for worrying about Dwayne and Jonah. It was like she was mama to the whole sorry world.

"Where to, miss?" the attendant asked when it was her turn at the counter.

Mary Bridget hoisted up her backpack and gripped the duffel, her hands shaking from fear and hunger and fatigue.

She shook her head and wanted to say anywhere, but that wouldn't do. She needed to be calm and sure and not do or say anything that would cause him to remember her. She read the destination of the next departing coach from the board behind the clerk's head, and when she spoke it was with a firm, sure voice. "Alexandria," she said.

"That'll be twenty-two dollars," he said, and Mary put two twenties into his outstretched hand.

He handed her the ticket and change, and she ducked her head and walked out to the departure area. She boarded, not daring even to look around until the bus had started up and rattled its way onto the highway. She looked out the window for an hour or so and didn't see any familiar vehicles, and finally, when the rolling hills gave way to flat green pastures, she used her backpack for a pillow, closed her eyes, and fell into an uneasy sleep.

It must have been the bus stopping that woke her. She sat up, groggy, and looked around, peered out the window, and read the sign. Culpeper. Everyone around her seemed to be in motion. Some leaving, some getting on. She wondered if she had time to get out and use the bathroom and buy herself some food. She reached beneath her legs to take another fifty from the duffel and her hand closed on empty air. She felt as if somebody had hit her hard in the stomach. She looked down, then knelt on the dirty bus floor and looked underneath the seat. Then the one in front of her and the one behind. Nothing. It was gone. She sat for a moment, clutching her stomach, then excused her way to the front of the bus.

"Pardon me, sir."

The bus driver turned a kind face toward her.

"Did you see someone get off with a green duffel bag?"

He didn't answer, just gave her an incredulous look and gestured toward the knots of people in and around the terminal, all equipped with some kind of knapsack or duffel.

She nodded and vowed she would not cry. She would not be sick. She went back to her seat and sat there until her breathing slowed down. Until she thought of what she should do next.

This was an unforeseen complication. She had been counting on that money to take her someplace far away. Alexandria was to have been a temporary stop until she could make her plans. But now it looked as if it would be the end of the line for her as well as the Greyhound. Her mind went over the problem, and it didn't take long to reach a solution. If she couldn't put a continent between herself and Jonah, even a state or two, then she had to make sure he wasn't in a position to follow her. She nodded slightly with resolution and hardened her heart, then unzipped the pocket of her backpack and took out the change from the hundred she'd used to buy the hair dye. That and the change from the bus ticket was the only money she had left. She shoved it into her pocket and made her way to the front of the bus again.

"Do I have time to make a telephone call?"

"Received." Walter Hinkley set the half-eaten sandwich aside with a sigh and shifted the cruiser into drive. Some folks didn't have enough to do with their time, or they wouldn't make such a fuss about drug paraphernalia being found in an abandoned pickup truck. Charlottesville might have been a sleepy little town when Thomas Jefferson lived here, but nowadays finding a drug kit was hardly an event worth interrupting his lunch break.

He drove toward the Piggly Wiggly just the same, taking a bite of his ham and cheese every time he hit a red light. He could have put on the siren and lights, but there was no sense getting everybody excited.

There he was. The store manager was hovering by the abandoned pickup like a worried hen. Walter shook his head and got his eyeroll out of the way before he emerged from the car. Ned Pearson was a law-enforcement wannabe, one of those people who probably never missed an episode of *America's Most Wanted* or *Cops*. Even though his day job was managing the grocery store, at heart he was a crime stopper and he policed the Piggly Wiggly beat for all he was worth. Nearly every day Walter got a call about minors trying to buy alcohol or cigarettes. This was the big time for Ned.

Walter pulled to a stop, brushed at his chin to make sure there were no crumbs. "Hey," he called out as he opened the door.

"Just take a look here." Ned pointed toward the back of the truck, obviously excited. His combed-over hair was blowing around in the stiff wind and Walter suppressed a smile.

"What have we got?" he asked, walking toward it.

"Just take a look at that."

Ned pointed toward the back of the truck, and Walter peered inside the canopy. There was a fifty-gallon tank, stained blue around the valve—a tip-off that it contained anhydrous ammonia instead of propane.

"I read about this in the *Police Beat* column and I think this is a crime scene. I'm fairly sure of it."

"Um-hum," Walter said, keeping his voice level and his face straight. Ned was probably right, and this was a serious situation. It wasn't Ned's fault he reminded Walter of Barney Fife. "Go back into the store," he said calmly. "Call for the hazardous materials team. Tell them we have a possible meth lab."

Ned's short legs were trotting away before Walter had even gotten the words out. He smiled again. He was being safe rather than sorry, actually. The jug of anhydrous was dangerous, of course, but it didn't look as though they'd actually cooked meth in the truck. He checked anyway. He'd seen enough labs in the trunks of cars to know anything was possible. He opened the passenger door, flipped open the glove box, and glanced around the cab. Nothing there except the keys, swinging slightly, still in the ignition. Just like he'd thought, the lab was somewhere else.

He stopped for a minute and frowned. Why would somebody go off and leave a perfectly good truck with keys in the ignition and incriminating evidence in the back? He shook his head. There was no telling. Drug dealers weren't the most intelligent species on the planet. That much was for certain.

He went back to his car and called in the plates. In a minute the dispatcher came back. Owner was one Dwayne Heslop, the address a rural box out in an adjoining county. He asked to be patched through to the Nelson County sheriff's office, then gave them the address. He had no doubt they'd find a full-blown operation out in the woods somewhere.

"We just got a tip for this address," the sheriff's dispatcher told him. "They're probably already there."

"Is that right?"

"Yes, sir. A woman. Anonymous. Somebody not happy with daddy."

"I guess not. All right, then." Walter signed off. Well, that solved one mystery. Hell hath no fury, he mused, and washed down the last bite of sandwich with a slurp of cold coffee while he waited for the HazMat team.

❧

The Greyhound bus groaned into the Alexandria station around five o'clock. Mary Bridget took a city bus headed for downtown and picked a stop at random. King Street. She stepped off the bus, leaving behind the smell of stale diesel, feeling wrinkled and sticky and exhausted and cold clear down to her bones. She did nothing for a moment except stare. Alexandria wasn't what she had expected. It was an old town of red-brick and cobbles. And lots of rich people. She could tell by the new, expensive cars lining the streets and the immaculately restored buildings. Crowds on their way home from work surged past her on the sidewalk like a river around a rock. She moved off to the side and stood under the eaves of a restaurant. She was exhausted, and her brain stalled, thinking about what she should do. For lack of a better idea, she began to walk. The lights were going out in the office buildings, her own reflection staring back at her from the tinted windows. She walked faster past the restaurants, which she could tell were expensive. Her stomach growled. She ignored it and kept walking.

There was a pharmacy on the corner. She stepped in and felt the warm air envelop her like a blanket. She bought two packs of peanut butter crackers and a diet soda. She paid and shoved the change back into the pocket of her blue jeans. She thought about asking a question but didn't know where to begin. She had nowhere to go, no job, no money to speak of, though she hadn't taken a good count. And the chief problem was, she couldn't think straight to make a plan. She was so tired. So weary. She went back outside and started walking again. There didn't seem to be any hotels other than the Hilton and Sheraton. Nothing she could afford. The backpack was heavy, and she felt a knot of pain tightening between her shoulder blades.

She kept walking, made a turn or two, and soon noticed the buildings around her were homes instead of businesses. Pretty brick row houses. The lights glowed golden out of their windows and she imagined what the people inside were doing. Husbands and wives greeting each other after a day at work, playing with children, starting supper. It began to rain. She quickened her pace and opened her crackers, ate one package, then the other, and wished she'd bought more. When she was finished she put the wrappers in her pocket.

She slowed her pace, and despair caught up to her. The rain was falling in earnest now, dripping down her scalp. She hoped the hair dye didn't run. Finally she stopped and asked herself the obvious question. Where, exactly, did she think she was going? She knew no one. She had no destination. She wiped her eyes—not that it did much good—then sat down on the curb, right there on the pavement, and bent her head onto her knee. She cried, trying her best to be quiet and not get herself arrested or hauled off to a mental hospital, although that didn't seem altogether bad at this moment. At least there would be food and a warm bed. She gulped and sobbed until she'd let it all out. When she was finished, she felt a little better. She lifted her head and tried to dry her eyes on the sleeve of her wet jacket. The lights had come on in the building across the street while she was having her little pity party.

It wasn't anything fancy, just a plain square of red-brick. Steps on each side of the narrow porch led to two glossy dark green doors. The windows were old-fashioned squares of glass, and a lamp burned brightly behind each one. It was a church. Knox Presbyterian, the sign said. She rose and went toward it. Mama and Grandma had been Baptists, but right now a Hindu temple would have been all right as long as the doors were unlocked.

The door opened when she turned the knob. There didn't seem to be anyone around. It smelled old and pleasantly musty, like her grandma's closet. Closing the door quietly behind her, she stood there for a moment, her own breathing and sniffling the only sounds. She took a step. The wooden floors creaked under her feet, and her wet tennis shoes squeaked. She crossed toward the sanctuary and peeked inside. It was old. Even she could tell that much. It had pews inside little boxes that were carefully painted white. The floor was covered with red carpet. The lights she had seen from outside were hurricane lamps twinkling on each windowsill. She looked for a dim corner and found one. She walked toward it and went inside the pew. Taking off her coat so she wouldn't get the cushion wet, she sat down and tried to gather her thoughts. It was no good. Her body would not go another inch, and she felt so sleepy she could barely keep her eyes open. Using her backpack as a pillow, she lay down, pulled the damp jacket over her shoulders, and went to sleep.

Jonah blinked once. Twice. His eyes hurt as they darted around his room trying to catch up to his thoughts. The picks were coming out of his skin again. He could feel them. Little shards of ice, little crystals pointing up out of his pores. He picked one out, then another.

His heart raced as he looked under the mattress and realized what this meant—she'd run off and taken his brain.

He tried to lick his lips, but his mouth was too dry. He needed a drink. He picked at another sliver. He needed a drink of water; then he could think what to do about finding Mary and getting his brain back. He needed his gun so he could go after it. He dropped the mattress, picked up the twelve-gauge from where he'd leaned it against the wall, and opened the door. But he'd no sooner swung it open than there was shouting and running and he found himself on the floor with someone's knee in his back. He tried to speak but couldn't get the words out. Somebody was pulling him, roughly, through the trailer. They grabbed his hands and tied them up behind him. They were taking him to the seat of eternal judgment.

He started screaming then. His doom was sealed. He would go to hell without his brain. The Bible was clear about that.

There were more of them on him then, and he tried to get away but couldn't. One had an arm around his throat and pulled it so tight he lost his breath.

"What in the world was he screaming about?" a voice was asking when he came to. His face was on a car seat, his arms fastened tight behind him, but the door was open. As long as that door was open, there was hope, even though the demons were standing guard outside.

"Something about some woman who stole his brain," another voice answered. "He has to find her, or he'll go to hell for eternity."

"Lord, have mercy," the first one said. "They'll have fun with him at the jail." They both laughed.

Jonah thought about screaming for help but realized it would do no good. They had him now, and there was nothing for it. He summoned all his strength and aimed himself for the open door. He threw himself out, knocking one of his captors over in the process. He almost got away, but then somebody tackled him and he was on his face in the dirt.

"Good grief, he's strong as an ox," he heard. Then the arm came around his throat again and everything went black.

⋄ *three* ⋄

One Year Later

ALASDAIR ROBERT MACPHERSON HELD HIMSELF still and straight, as his father had taught him to do in church. Only his eyes moved when he glanced toward the windows. It was a gray day. Foggy and dim, in spite of the dancing flames of the hurricane lamps on the windowsills. The organ murmured the prelude. He lowered his gaze and inspected the cuffs of his pants, breaking at exactly the correct point on his shining black wing tips. He closed his eyes and rested his hands on his legs, which were tensed, as if for action.

Suddenly, and who knew why, he was reminded of the legend of the fisher king, that mythic man who had been struck by a sword and left with a wound in his thigh that would never heal. He opened his eyes and looked at his own leg as if he might see a spreading blot. Of course he did not. He saw only his hands resting on his knees, and the only stain was the one on the middle finger of his right hand from the old Waterman fountain pen he couldn't bear to part with. He raised his head and stared at the altar cloth, but even there the uninvited tableau was projected. He could almost see the injured knight, too wounded to live, yet unable to die. He felt a throb of pain in his chest, as if someone had bumped a bruise. He frowned and refocused his attention.

Bodies and paper scuffled as the choir filed in, took their places, and opened their books. Their bright red robes created an atmosphere of cheer in contrast to the music they'd selected. It was Bach, full of power and mourning. He closed his eyes again and tried to occupy his mind, but without his will, the music washed over him. He bowed his head, felt relieved when the piece was finished, and even more relieved to hear the voice of the worship leader come clear and strong through the sound system. "The grace of the Lord Jesus Christ be with you all."

"And also with you." He looked up and answered automatically, his voice blending with those around him.

"This is the day that the Lord has made," she declared.

"Let us rejoice and be glad in it."

"Let us pray."

He bowed his head again.

"Almighty God, to whom all hearts are open, all desires known, and from whom no secrets are hidden," she began.

He detached himself from her words. His eyes drifted open, and her voice became background. He gazed around him at the sea of people. Their heads were tipped down, topped in varying shades and lengths of Anglo-Saxon hair. The prayer finished and their heads tipped back up, faces bland. Blank. Waiting to have something written on them.

There was his daughter. She was beginning to look like Anna. She had that same porcelain fragility. She'd begun to act like her, as well. She sat aloof, alone, beside a knot of whispering girls. He watched her and felt something break loose within him, falling down, bouncing hollowly against the inside of his chest and abdomen as it rattled past. Another chunk. Another small piece of what used to be solid and firm, filling him up. He readjusted his body, as if that would bring his mind under control, and could hear his father reminding him that questions, though understandable, were not commendable.

The prayer was over. The worship leader stepped down, her robes flowing around her as she moved. The choir rose again and began the hymn. "I Lay My Sins on Jesus."

The worship leader stood again, led the Confession, the Pardon, the Peace. That was the accepted order. First the confession. Then pardon and peace. He wondered what would happen if a clot of unbelief lodged itself in the channel of faith. If the movement through those places stopped. He knew the answer. There would be pain. Searing. Almost beyond imagination. Then a slow numbing—a deadly lack of feeling spreading through the body as living flesh blanched and died.

He frowned again, coughed slightly into his fist. When had his mind become a highwayman, lying in wait to ambush him? Bring every thought captive to the obedience of Christ, he instructed himself.

The congregation stood. They recited the Gloria Patri. They were seated. The lector read the Prayer for Illumination. The first reading was given. Then the second. Another hymn. The choir shut their books and moved off the dais smoothly, without so much as a dropped paper. He sat still for another moment, and gradually the movement around him stopped. Everyone readied themselves. Hymnbooks were put away, papers stuffed in pew boxes, skirts and jackets rearranged. A few coughs, the sound of a child whimpering and being stilled; then they were settled, quiet and ready. They all waited expectantly to receive some illumination, some insight, a reason to get up in the morning, to put one foot before the other, to draw the next breath. It was time for the sermon.

He rose from his seat and made his way to the pulpit.

"Overcoming Emotions That Destroy." Lorna read the title of Alasdair's sermon and felt a lurch of pain at the irony. She put the bulletin in the drawer beside the telephone in her brother's house.

"It has *not* been two years," Fiona insisted with professorial finality as she put the lid on the plastic container.

"It's been *at least* two, if not longer," Winifred corrected firmly. "I'm afraid you're mistaken."

Winifred was right, but Lorna knew better than to interject. Even at thirty-five she was still the youngest, barely an adult in their minds. Her vote was hardly enough to tip the scales in a clash between the two elders. When Fiona and Winifred argued, it was like Zeus and Apollo doing battle, she thought, and immediately knew her father, rest his soul, would not have approved of the analogy. *"Two heathen deities that should never cross the tongue of a Presbyterian,"* she could almost hear him intone, and she immediately changed the analogy to Wesley and Calvin.

Her brother was reminding her more and more of their father since Anna had died. More than two years ago, no matter what anyone said. She felt a stirring of unease and didn't know which thought had brought it on—Father's memory, her brother's personality change, or Anna's death.

"Lower your voice," Winifred cautioned, ending the argument with her word conveniently last. "Alasdair's study is just upstairs, and you know how noise carries through the heating vents."

Fiona gave a slight nod, rinsed her hands at the sink, and dried them on a paper towel. "Well, regardless," she said, her voice barely above a whisper. "It's time some permanent arrangements were made in regard to his household. I don't know what stops him. He carries on well enough in other areas."

It was true, Lorna thought as she opened the refrigerator and made room for this week's meals. In fact, no one but her seemed to think there was anything amiss with Alasdair at all. Even his reactions in the days just after Anna's death had seemed exemplary, the model of how a Christian should face tragedy. She hadn't been there when the police had come with news of the accident. By the time she'd arrived, Alasdair was returning from having identified the body. Even then he'd been in control. It was she who had collapsed. Even Fiona and Winifred, who had never been particularly close to Anna, had been stunned into weeks of tearful silence. Alasdair alone had displayed the proper mix of sadness and faith, unlike her own anguish or Samantha's wild anger.

She remembered crying out to God when her brother had told her. "Why?" she had wailed. "Why?" It had actually been a prayer, but Alasdair had taken it upon himself to answer her.

"Shall not the judge of all the earth do right?" he had demanded. The words were correct, but the hoarseness of his voice and the darkening of his eyes had told the truth.

Alasdair had made all the decisions during that horrible time, asking his sisters for help only in caring for the children. He had arranged matters without consultation, opting for a private interment instead of a service. He'd dispatched the flowers to local nursing homes and hospitals and had his secretary field condolence calls and send thank-you notes for the ever present casseroles. Yes, in the matter of Anna's death Alasdair had performed as efficiently as he'd always done in all areas of life. As was his habit, he had surveyed the situation and met its requirements. She only wondered what the effort had cost him.

She stopped her shuffling of plasticware, shocked at what she was feeling toward her brother. Irritation. No, anger. A surge of shame engulfed it. Alasdair had been through a horrendous ordeal—losing the wife he'd loved, then trying to deal with the newborn twins and the eleven-year-old daughter she'd left behind. Everyone dealt with grief in his or her own way, she remembered, paraphrasing what the associate pastor had told her when she'd confided her concerns.

Alasdair would someday be himself again, and for a moment the person he had been flashed across the screen of her memory. She remembered him as a boy, kindhearted to a fault and passionate in his defense of the underdog. The worst punishment he'd ever received had been for fighting at school, for defending her from perpetual teasing about her weight, a fact he had never divulged to Father and forbade her to reveal. *"It doesn't matter,"* he'd told her, sparing her the humiliation of repeating the names they had called her.

She remembered his intensity, his fire. He had loved with all his being and had given himself completely to whatever he did. She remembered watching him run, and oddly that image became the sum of all he had lost. His body had moved with such fluid ease, cutting through air like butter, feet and legs seeming to flow just above the surface of the earth instead of pounding onto it, his face a picture of joy and abandon.

She thought about the man her brother had become and knew the truth, whether anyone else would acknowledge it or not. Something was wrong. Something was gone. Something precious had been lost. She felt a pang of sadness and hoped this new person hadn't taken up permanent residence in Alasdair's body.

"Well, what have we?" Winifred queried, and Lorna turned her attention back to the contents of the refrigerator.

"The week's meals are done," she answered, glad for the distraction. She slid the last plastic container into the refrigerator.

"Pantry and refrigerator are stocked, and Samantha's lunch money is in the envelopes," Fiona put in.

Lorna glanced at the bulletin board where five envelopes, labeled Monday through Friday, were stuck with a thumbtack.

"Did you put in a quarter for ice cream?" she asked, knowing the answer.

"Ice cream is unnecessary," Winifred said. "It will only keep her from eating properly. Besides," she added, giving Lorna a sidelong look, "we wouldn't want her to get plump."

Lorna's face heated up, but she didn't answer back. She would have added the quarter. But then, it hadn't been up to her.

The telephone rang, and Winifred answered quickly. Fiona dried her hands on the towel and leaned back against the counter in exhaustion. "So we've done the meals and started the laundry."

"I cleaned a little yesterday," Lorna put in.

Winifred hung up the phone and turned toward them, her face grim. "That was the baby-sitter."

"Not again!" Lorna closed her eyes and shook her head.

"Yes, again. She says she feels as if she's coming down with something."

"What are we going to do?" Fiona's voice sounded as weary as Lorna felt.

"Tomorrow is Alasdair's day off," Winifred pointed out. "I suppose he'll just have to manage."

"It's not just that." Fiona shook her head, pulled out one of the kitchen chairs, and dropped into it. "It's everything. I don't know how much longer we can keep this up." Her voice sounded defeated. It was the closest any of them had ever come to complaining.

"It wouldn't hurt the rest of the congregation to do more." Winifred's face drew into bitter lines.

"I doubt if they even realize there's a need," Lorna said. "The machine continues to hum along."

Winifred frowned at her, and Lorna flushed. She should keep her opinions to herself. Her sisters were justifiably proud of Alasdair. Who wouldn't be? He had taken the medium-sized congregation his father had passed down to him and turned it into a nationwide organization of daily radio broadcasts, a monthly magazine, conferences, seminars, and books on every subject in Christendom. He was even editing his own study Bible. She was proud of him, too, she told herself, as if someone had argued the point. Still, the nagging awareness returned that there was something out of place. Something not as it should be.

His sermons were still well researched and interesting, dynamically delivered, though perhaps a shade intense. Angry was the word she wanted to use, but then again, she had always been overly sensitive. She smiled gently, remembering the early days of Alasdair's ministry. Having been accustomed to her father's rather remote style, the congregation had drunk in Alasdair's personal care. He had preached with passion and gentleness, sat at many a deathbed and sickbed, comforting, counseling, praying.

But then some board member had had the bright idea of beginning a radio broadcast. One thing had led to another, and soon Alasdair was a speaker in great demand. Eventually his days on the circuit outnumbered his days at home. That was when Bill Wright had moved into the gap. She felt a rush of affection as the earnest, homely face of their former associate pastor appeared in her mind. When someone's child was in the hospital, it was Bill who had gone and prayed with them. When a marriage was falling apart, it was Bill who had helped mend the pieces. She recalled tearful hours she had spent in that process herself, Bill's kind and steady voice like a line tossed across the frothing waves toward her outstretched hand.

For the first time she wondered if the heavy burden of ministry was what had driven Bill away. The longer she considered it, the more probable it seemed. There was no way the church could hire a third pastor to help the assistant. At Bill's new church, he would have the same duties, but with an associate to help him. She felt a twist of regret that he'd been so unappreciated, and a twinge of worry when she thought of what might happen now that he was gone.

"This morning I heard someone say that Alasdair's healing process would be complete when he married again." Fiona's voice brought Lorna out of her reverie.

Winifred snorted. "I'm sure there would be plenty of applicants for that position."

"I suppose," Fiona said, smiling. Almost at once, though, her pretty face clouded. "By the way, I heard a rumor that disturbed me."

"What was it?" Winifred demanded.

"That there's a movement afoot."

"What kind of movement?" Winifred asked, seeming only slightly interested.

Lorna understood why word of rumors didn't bring an immediate panic. The three of them were veterans of their father's years of ministry. These so-called movements could be motivated by the slightest of disturbances, from unhappiness with the color of the carpeting in the Sunday school rooms to major doctrinal concerns. They could be anything from a quick shower to a devastating hurricane. She waited for Fiona to elaborate, the clenching of her stomach her only premonition.

"A movement to have Alasdair replaced."

Her stomach twisted. This was a gale force wind.

"Piffle," Winifred dismissed. "Who told you that?"

"Ruth Anderson said she heard it from Edgar Willis."

Winifred frowned, and with reason. Edgar Willis was one of the ruling elders, the senior ruling elder, as a matter of fact. "If it's true, I lay it at Bill Wright's feet. He should never have left."

Lorna thought perhaps they should be grateful Bill had stayed as long as he had, picking up pieces and smoothing the path for Alasdair.

"I'm sure there's nothing to it, though," Winifred dismissed. "Just the usual gossip."

Fiona didn't answer, just lifted one of her exquisitely shaped eyebrows.

Lorna took a deep breath and tried to ignore her feeling of foreboding. She closed the refrigerator door and went to the sink to perform her final ritual. Neither of her sisters ever scrubbed it, and the food scraps in the drainer and yellow stains on the porcelain made the kitchen look even more grim and neglected than usual. She emptied the drain trap into the garbage, then shook the green cleanser and watched the granules turn dark as they hit the wet sink. She felt a frustration she couldn't name, and suddenly she was angry with Winifred and Fiona. And she was angry with Alasdair as well, she realized with a shock.

"What were you two arguing about?" Alasdair's voice behind Lorna startled her, and oddly, instead of banishing her thoughts, the little surge of adrenaline from his appearance only increased their force. Her brother picked up the empty coffeepot and reached around her to fill it at the faucet.

Winifred looked stricken, probably wondering how long he had been listening and trying to remember what she'd said. Alasdair didn't even look at her. He reached up to get the filter and coffee from the cupboard.

"I can't remember," Fiona said, laughing. "You know us."

Suddenly Lorna was hot, as if someone had lit a little fire in her chest. Why did no one in this family ever tell the truth?

"They were arguing about how long it's been since Anna died," she blurted out. "How long has it been, Alasdair? Surely you know."

Winifred's jaw dropped. Fiona's eyes widened. Even Lorna was shocked, though the words had come from her own mouth. Alasdair stopped his coffee preparations and looked at her. For just a moment his eyes seemed unveiled, and she glimpsed the churning froth behind them.

"I don't remember exactly." He turned away.

"Really, Lorna," Winifred reproached under her breath. Fiona said nothing, just became very interested in the contents of her purse. Alasdair went back to his coffee preparations. He did not look up again. Lorna began scrubbing and rinsing the sink with hot energy, and when she was finished, she turned her irritation toward the countertops, cluttered with a week's worth of debris.

There were phone messages, a schoolbook of Samantha's, a clean, empty baby bottle, two dirty spoons, a yellow writing tablet, a cracked mug full of pens and pencils, two letters addressed to the Reverend Alasdair MacPherson, John Knox Presbyterian Church, 922 Fairfax Street, Alexandria, Virginia, one from B. Henry, 33 Harrison Street, Richmond, Virginia, another with the Old English Italic letterhead of the United Presbyterian Church denomination headquarters in the same city, both neatly sliced open along their folds. One small glove, looking lost without its mate.

The entire house needed a good going-over. She should take down the curtains over the sink and give them a wash. They were awful—gold things with brown rickrack and a fringe of little orange balls around the bottom. In fact, everything was awful. The wallpaper was dark—a pattern of orange and brown mushrooms against a green background. The cupboards were dark and outdated. The paneling on the bottom half of the walls was dark. All in all, the room gave the effect of moldering decay and depression. And Lorna had to admit it had been that way even when Anna was alive.

"I'm going to finish reviewing tonight's sermon." Alasdair flipped the switch on the coffeemaker and it began to gurgle. He looked each of them in the eye. "As always, I thank you for all your help." His face was once again wiped smooth of any expression.

Lorna shook her head and felt frustration mixed with a searing sadness as she thought of her sister-in-law's legacy: a small brass marker in the churchyard next door, a perpetual collection of brown-tipped potted plants with limp ribbons at the bank of the Potomac beneath the Woodrow Wilson Bridge, three motherless children, and a husband who became more untouchable each day. Her mouth opened, once again without her conscious intention, and she spoke, the words fueled by this unfamiliar emotion.

"Anna died October fifteenth, two years ago. This is the twenty-fourth of October. That makes it two years, one week, and two days."

No one spoke. Alasdair turned back and stared at her for a moment. She was half afraid of his anger, half hoping for it, but when he spoke his voice was steady, his face expressionless except for those desolate eyes. "Well, then. There you have it. Argument settled." He turned and left the room.

Fiona and Winifred gave her disapproving looks behind his back. She started to call out, hesitated, then followed him. She reached the hallway as he came to the stairs. She opened her mouth to speak, to apologize, but something stopped her.

Alasdair had stopped at the bottom step, his hand on the banister, head bowed. His shoulders were rounded and she wasn't sure if he was praying, weeping, or simply gathering strength. She felt a strong whip of shame at her cruelty. She opened her mouth again, but once more something stopped her.

No, a still, small voice corrected. *Leave him.*

She nodded, blinking back tears. Alasdair raised his head. His shoulders rose and fell with a deep breath. He climbed the stairs. She watched until he disappeared from sight, then returned to the kitchen where her sisters awaited.

"What in the world was that about?" Winifred demanded, furious.

"Really, Lorna. I should think you'd want him to put it behind him," Fiona added gently.

Lorna had no answer. She felt very ashamed of herself. Her anger had fizzled out like a wet sparkler. What *had* she been thinking? What *was* she trying to prove?

Her sisters shunned further conversation with her, turned as if by mutual agreement, and began to gather up their coats and purses. An old method of controlling her and as effective as always.

"I'll stay until evening service," Lorna said, feeling miserable and guilty.

"I've got to arrange for the nursery," Winifred protested, as if Lorna had shamed her. Her sister hated being bested in the competition of who could help the most.

"That's fine. You go," Lorna soothed. "I'll just be here when the babies wake, and I'll keep an eye on Samantha."

"That sounds fine." Fiona checked her watch and pulled her coat closed, buttoned it with a firm hand that allowed no slipping and sliding. "Come along, Winifred. I've papers to grade."

Winifred reluctantly agreed, the two sisters made their exit, and Lorna felt the flood of relief that she always did when they left her. There was something about their mere presence that made her feel ignorant and inept. She poured Alasdair's coffee into the carafe, put the teakettle on for herself, then went upstairs to check on Samantha.

Her door was open a crack, and a thin slice of light shone along the dark hall carpet. Lorna pushed it open quietly so as not to disturb her niece at her studies, but Samantha wasn't at her desk. Her schoolbooks looked untouched, still in a pristine stack. She pushed the door open all the way. Samantha wasn't there at all. She must have slipped out again.

Lorna sighed and wondered if she should alert Alasdair. She looked around at the room before closing the door. There were new posters on the wall—of rock bands—some of them ominous-looking. The vanity was covered with lipstick and eye makeup, the sparkly kind that sold for a dollar in the pharmacy. She'd noticed Samantha's attempts in that direction lately and wished she could help. She was such a pretty child. Brown hair, pink cheeks, and those fine, even features she'd gotten from her mother. Lorna wished she felt more capable of helping her niece with the practical matters of womanhood, but her own adolescence seemd light-years away. Besides, Samantha didn't seem to be listening to anyone's advice these days. It was as if the sweet child who had been her niece was gone. Lorna felt the loss as sharply as another death. The strangeness of her role with these children assaulted her again. She lived in that gray region between mother and aunt. For the first year of the twins' lives, she had been the one who cared for them. She had stayed at night for a while and then begun arriving before they arose each morning. They were her treasures, especially the babies. They were like her own. In fact, she often imagined they were. She rocked them, fed them, worried over them. The cruelty of her situation cut her again. Michael's unfaithfulness and financial debacle had rocked more then her little world. Her small share of the debts not discharged in bankrupty had put an end to her surrogate mothering. Now she spent days at one job and nights at another instead of being here, caring for the children who felt so much like her own. She took a moment to release her anger, to forgive him again.

Lorna closed Samantha's door, then paused outside the twins' room. She didn't hear a sound. She crept back down the stairs, not really breathing again until she reached the kitchen, and just caught the kettle before it began to whistle.

She took down the teapot, ran the water until it was finally hot, then filled it and took out the tin of tea. She emptied the pot, added the tea, and poured the boiling water over the leaves. While she waited for it to brew, she made the usual telephone calls. She located Samantha on the second one—the home of that poor boy with all the earrings who never looked anyone in the eye. What kind of radar did these unhappy children have that allowed them to find each other?

"Come home, please," she said pleasantly, but was rewarded by a sullen reply. "Shall I call your father to the telephone?" she was forced to threaten. This time the line disconnected. She sighed, replaced the telephone, and made another halfhearted stab at cleaning off the counter.

She picked up the empty bottle and started to put it away, then reconsidered and took out another. She filled both with milk and set them in the door of the refrigerator, ready to warm when the babies woke. They were two years old and really should be weaned and potty trained. But there were only so many hours in the day, and for her, eight of them were spent at the secretary's desk at John Knox School and four nights a week processing film at the Kodak plant. She had bills to pay. She half smiled at the irony of the understatement, then checked her watch. She was due there at three o'clock in the morning, as a matter of fact, and really should go home and get some sleep.

She went back to her tidying. She put the yellow pad in the drawer under the telephone and gathered up the scattered messages, glancing at them briefly to see if any were urgent or hadn't been answered. There were six from various committee members and parishioners regarding classes needing teachers, families needing counseling, people with questions only Alasdair could answer.

And one from Mrs. Tronsett at Knox School. Lorna frowned. Mrs. Tronsett was the principal. The message had been received late Friday. *Please call regarding Samantha* was all it said in the sitter's loopy handwriting. That brought on another spasm of worry, and Lorna spent a few moments thinking about Samantha's problems.

She sighed and picked up the last piece of debris—yet another telephone message. This one from someone named Bob Henry with a long-distance number. She frowned and remembered why the name sounded familiar. B. Henry had been the name on the letter she'd seen earlier.

Lorna retrieved it, along with the one from denomination head-quarters. She turned them over and inspected the backs of the enve-lopes, then placed them both down on the counter very gently, as if they contained explosives that might go off in her hand.

She took the glove and added it to the load of dirty clothes in the washer and started them washing, took Samantha's schoolbook upstairs and set it on her desk, returned to the kitchen and washed the two spoons, dried them and put them away, all the while taking side-long glances at the two letters. Then for the third time that day she did something for which she had no explanation. Certainly no justification. She picked up the first one—the one with the United Presbyterian Church logo. She unfolded it and began to read. She wasn't halfway through before her puzzlement turned to apprehension.

Dear Reverend MacPherson,

Even though I've never had the pleasure of meeting you, I greet you as the apostle John greeted the church at Thyatira in Revelation, chapter two, verse nineteen. "I know thy works, and charity, and service, and faith, and thy patience." You, like they, have poured out your life in service to the Gospel, and your sterling reputation is known to all.

It has not escaped my attention that it has been just over two years since your wife, Anne, passed on to her eternal reward.

Lorna shook her head. The least he could do was get Anna's name right.

> *I am aware that a grief of such magnitude extends its shadow to the farthest reaches of one's soul and circle of influence. And though we are exhorted to run with diligence the race marked out for us, there may come times when rest is called for.*

This was ominous. Her stomach clutched, but she read on quickly.

> *Though you have carried out your responsibilities with the strength only Christ can provide, the cost of doing so may be great, not only to you, but to your family and congregation as well.*

Lorna frowned as she deciphered the roundabout phrasing, and her pulse picked up as the message became clear.

> *As overseer, not only of the sheep, but of those who shepherd them, I would appreciate an opportunity to dialogue with you regarding your needs and those of your congregation. It is no shame to allow oneself a temporary respite, and I must confess my motives are not entirely unselfish. The services of a man of your singular talents would be coveted by many here at denominational headquarters.*
>
> *Sincerely,*
> *Your co-laborer in the harvest,*
> *Gerald Whiteman,*
> *President*

Lorna sank into a chair and dropped the hand that held the letter onto the table. Her brother was being summoned. There was no other interpretation. She'd known the situation was bad, but not this bad. She took three or four deep breaths and finally calmed herself enough to think. Determined to hear all the bad news at once, she took the second letter out and read it as well. It was dated the same day as Gerald Whiteman's.

Al,

I can't believe you've let the inmates take over the asylum. Gerry got a letter from a few strays from your flock, bleating that you've lost your zip. Maybe it's not too late to sidetrack him, but we need to make a plan. Call me.

Bob

It was signed with a flourish. Lorna squinted her eyes at the far wall and finally remembered Bob Henry. He'd been in seminary with Alasdair but had withdrawn before graduation and was now obviously in the inner circle at the administrative offices in Richmond.

She put both letters back into their envelopes and carefully placed them where she had found them. She'd forgotten all about the tea. It was black as tar. She poured it out, then sat down at the table again and tried to think.

So. The rumors were true. Those who were unhappy with Alasdair were taking advantage of Bill's leaving to make a move against him, and it was no mystery why they were going in through the back door. If Alasdair were reassigned rather than being asked to leave, the damage would be contained. There would be no rancor, no name-calling, no angry MacPherson loyalists leaving the church and taking their tithes with them.

Without wanting to, she recalled the tittle-tattle she'd heard. It always got around. They were saying that Alasdair was more interested in his empire than his church. More concerned with writing books about apologetics than shepherding the flock that had been entrusted to him. *"If I want to hear my pastor's voice I turn on the radio,"* one had quipped at the last congregational meeting. *"His office door is always closed."*

"I feel pulled in too many directions," Alasdair had confided to her after the meeting was over. She had thought of a hundred things to say. Perhaps you should readjust your priorities. Maybe they need you, Alasdair. You are their spiritual leader, after all. She tried to remember what she *had* said and remembered with a grimace that she had offered him a cup of tea and changed the subject.

That wouldn't do now. There would be no avoiding this. No changing the subject this time. Still, for all the urgency, her mind was blank. The only thing she could think to do was pray. She dropped her head, more in dejection than reverence.

"Oh, Father," she began, then faltered and stopped.

Her sisters were right. She was slow-witted, not quick and smart. After all, she had never gone into the world, never done anything important. Fiona and Winifred would know what to say, how to help.

"Oh, Father," she repeated, "help my brother. Help Samantha. I don't even know how to pray." But the thought had scarcely dawned before a verse of Scripture she'd learned long ago popped into her mind. *"The Spirit himself intercedes for us with groans that words cannot express."* She thought about that for a moment, took heart and a deep breath, then went on.

"You work in ways we cannot see," she finally managed to wring out. "Make a way through this problem for Alasdair. Ease his burdens, Lord. Heal his heart."

She felt as if she ought to at least offer the Lord a few suggestions as to how He might accomplish the task. Fiona would have a list of them, she was sure. She thought of her—intelligent, teaching her classes at the university, so smart and quick. She could call her.

No, said a quiet voice.

Winifred, then. Winifred, who could organize anyone to do anything, even if she pulled them along by the ear.

No. She felt the blank wall of refusal again.

"Oh, Lord," she whispered. "Surely someone must do something."

You are someone, the voice said, bypassing her ear.

She felt a stir of something. Fear.

"I'm not . . ." She paused, and any number of adjectives competed to fill in the blank. Smart enough, quick enough, brave enough.

I am, though, the voice answered back, implacable.

"You are," she agreed, but the sentiment didn't seem to reach to her stomach, which was still twisting.

I can use you, the voice insisted. *May I?*

"Anytime or anywhere," she whispered back, her heart sinking. "I only wish you had more to work with." But then she remembered a sermon her brother had preached years before, before the darkness settled. He'd said God uses ordinary people, fallible and imperfect, to accomplish His purposes. God writes straight with crooked lines, he had reminded them. She covered her face with her hands.

"If you can use anyone, Lord, maybe you can use me," she said. She suddenly remembered David, the shepherd boy, the one God chose to be king, the one who had battled the giant Goliath. "Everyone who watches will know that it is not by the sword or the spear that the Lord saves; for the battle is the Lord's," she recited from memory. She nodded. Of course. She saw now why He had chosen her. She held out her hands on the table, open.

"If you can use anyone, Lord, you can use me." She repeated the words, this time with faith, but even as she said them, she remembered Samantha's troubles, her brother, walking though wounded, the motherless babies. The thoughts felt like small sharp darts aimed at her weak resolve.

"If you can use anyone, Lord, you can use me," she repeated again, stubborn now. He could prevail, even against darkness this thick. For that is what the light loves to do. Pour through the darkness and clear away the shadows.

She had a sudden blinding image, almost a vision, it was so real. Of Alasdair, face open and smiling. Of Samantha, playing and laughing like a child again. Of the twins, being loved and cared for.

Then the voice, in a final benediction, delivered one last message. *I'm going to do this,* it pronounced. *And you may help.*

"Thank you, Lord," she exclaimed, and no sooner had she finished speaking than one of the babies cried, sounding hoarse and congested; then the other's voice joined in. The front door slammed, and Samantha came in and stomped up the stairs. Lorna rose and hurried up after her, wondering what would happen next, from which direction reinforcements would arrive.

❧ *four* ❧

MARY BRIDGET ROUNDED THE BEND *in the gravel road, and there it was. Home. A white clapboard house with a sloping tin roof, wide front porch, glossy boxwoods, and huge pink and red azaleas nestled up against its foundation. Farther out on the wide, cool lawn were two big oaks, dogwood and redbud underneath, and off to the side a stand of white pines. Beyond it were the misty blue mountains. She stepped onto the graveled driveway. The screen door screeched open, and she strained to make out the face of the one who stood there. It was familiar and loved. Her hesitant steps quickened into a run.*

She startled awake and stared into the dim light of her room. It took a moment to orient herself. She was here in Alexandria in the apartment she shared with Carmen. This was home now. She sat up and checked the clock, felt gooseflesh rise on her arms from the chill in the air. It was nearly seven. She turned off the alarm, which would have gone off in just minutes, pulled her housecoat from the foot of the bed, stood up, and put it on. There. That was better. She slid into her slippers, opened her bedroom door quietly, and stepped into the hall. Carmen's door was closed. She went to the living room window and peeked through the slit in the curtains. Newlee's car was gone. She let the curtain drop and breathed a sigh of relief. It made her nervous having him around, even though she knew there was no way an Alexandria police officer would know about a drug raid over a year ago in a different part of the state. No way he could know about the one who'd gotten away.

During those tense first days, she'd searched until she'd found a newsstand that carried the *Charlottesville Daily Progress* and had scanned it religiously. There had been nothing that first day, and she hadn't known whether to feel relieved or terrified. She thought she saw Jonah everywhere. She would glimpse an angular jaw disappearing into a crowd, whip her head around, and see that it belonged to someone else. She would catch the sound of a similar voice, and her heart would freeze. See a long, lean body coming toward her in a familiar lope, and her tongue would stick to the roof of her mouth. Even after she knew the truth. That Jonah couldn't come after her.

The article she'd waited for had finally appeared. It had actually been three days. It had only seemed like an eternity. It was a pretty big spread, in fact. "Drug Enforcement Task Force's Efforts Yield Results," the headline had announced. The story had gone on to say that the Nelson County Sheriff and Virginia State Police were working on busting meth labs and targeting the places dealers bought their ingredients. She'd darted through the two-page story until she'd found what she was looking for. There, along with a mention of several other raids, were two beautiful paragraphs about an anonymous tip that had led to the shutdown of a huge lab, location right on target. There was even a photo of the rusty trailer and falling-down shack. She'd held her breath until she read the article twice and ascertained that Jonah and Dwayne had both been arrested, though Dwayne had been picked up downtown trying to sell to an undercover cop. Figured.

She'd clipped that article and put it in her Bible, which served mostly as a safe deposit box these days. She reread it occasionally, but only when her fears got the best of her, for at other times it filled her with remorse.

You did what you had to do, she reminded herself, but it was thin comfort. She could only imagine what torment prison would be for a man like Jonah—someone who couldn't breathe in the city, who had to be traipsing through the woods to feel alive.

That Jonah doesn't exist anymore, she told herself. *The Jonah you knew is not the man who's locked up.* She could barely remember the old Jonah. She tried to recall him now, and her mind peeled back the layers of years. He'd been raw, roughhewn, inscrutable, and remote, but his passion for the land had burned like a pure, hot flame. He would have been perfectly happy to find some fold in time and step through to long-ago days. To live without cars and factories and people polluting his mountains.

His differences had been the fuel for her infatuation with him. She'd been fascinated with him for as long as she could remember. In junior high she'd frequently walked up the road past his house, hoping to catch a glimpse of him. Most days she'd had to be content to look at the pie-eyed cows grazing the sloping pastures, the fields of mountain cabbage, the orchards full of apple trees.

When she did find him, they went walking through the woods— actually Jonah strode and she scrambled to keep up. He didn't chatter like everybody else, but when he spoke it was usually something worth hearing. He knew all about the plants and trees and animals and their ways, and he had a good solid common sense about him. But he didn't play the games of polite society; that much was for certain.

"That boy's downright unfriendly. It must be his mother's side of the family coming out. She was a Crawford, you know," Mary's aunt Brenda would say, lifting her chin and taking that little sniff. *"And crazy as a coot, besides."*

Which had irritated Mary no end. It wasn't right how everybody talked about his family, saying they were sorry and no-account. It wasn't Jonah's fault his papa couldn't keep a job or that his mother had whatever problems she had.

She supposed she and Jonah were two lost souls and that's why they'd finally ended up together. Their families had certainly met similar fates. Jonah's mother and father had divorced, and the bank repossessed their house. One of his brothers went into the navy. The other moved to Lynchburg and took a job at a furniture store. Jonah had already been living with his old uncle. He was working at the towel mill, but they'd gone to laying off, and Jonah was last hired. But he probably could have even survived all of that if his uncle hadn't died. Joshua Porter had gone out to feed his birds, broken his hip, and gotten pneumonia. And after that it just seemed as if Jonah didn't care anymore. That's when he'd started on the drugs. That's when he'd set out to be as bad as he could be.

She'd known all of that when she'd run off with him, of course, but she couldn't exactly afford to be choosy. Jonah had offered her a way out of what had become an intolerable situation. She shook her head now at the bitter irony. Out of the frying pan.

Well, she was safe now. He couldn't come after her. Nor could he watch the sun come up over the mountains, or hear rain pelt the leaves, or smell that loamy smell after a good drenching.

She hardened herself and reviewed the facts. Jonah hadn't seen a sunrise in years. He'd been too busy cooking meth. Besides, this Jonah, the meth-eaten Jonah who existed in reality rather than some girlish fantasy, likely wanted to kill her, she reminded herself, and she felt the familiar chill of fear.

She did her best to shake it off and made her way to the kitchen, put on a pot of coffee, dropped a piece of bread in the toaster, then sat down at the table. Carmen was proud of that table, yellow Formica with chrome all around the sides. She'd gotten it for fifty dollars at a garage sale. "I could sell it for four times that—any day of the week, Bridie." She smiled, thinking about the way Carmen's Brooklyn tongue tried to curl around her name.

Bridie, she realized. She thought of herself as Bridie now. She had finally eased her way into her new persona, though it had been like a game at first. Whenever she was faced with a decision, she would ask herself, "What would Mama do?" and then do it. When a customer at the Bag and Save got testy, she would ask herself, "What would Mama say?" and unfailingly her words would come out kind and patient. She even turned without hesitation when someone called out the name. She had everybody fooled. Everyone thought she was a kind, sweet, innocent girl from the hills of Virginia.

"Act a way long enough and it'll become who you really are," her grandmother had been fond of saying, and for a moment a tiny hope flared inside her heart. It flickered out before she could warm herself by it, though. Jonah wasn't the only one who'd changed. She knew the truth. She might talk like Mama, act like Mama, even think like Mama, but the shadow of Mary Bridget Washburn still trailed along behind her wherever she went.

There was a curl of paper beside Carmen's cigarette case. She picked it up. It was a strip of pictures from one of those booths that snap four or five shots in a row. She smiled. There was Carmen, big eyes and dark bubble of hair, wide smile and white, even teeth. Behind her Newlee stood guard, looking like a soldier with his crew cut and steady eyes. She felt a stab of loneliness, dropped the pictures back down onto the table as if they'd burned her, then got up to take a shower. She was clear into the hallway before she heard the spring of the toaster and remembered her breakfast. She left it, showered, dressed, and caught the early bus to work, not even taking a cup of coffee after she'd gone to the trouble to make it.

❧ *five* ❧

ALASDAIR SKIRTED THE PATCHES OF ice on the walkway, barely visible in the dusk, and slowed his pace. It wouldn't do for him to fall and break a bone. Then what would happen to the children? He picked up the soggy *Washington Post* lying on the brick walkway and retrieved the mail spilling from the letter box. He barely took note of it. His mind was on this month's column for his magazine, which he had just mailed, and the subject of his next series of radio broadcasts. That would be tonight's project, as well as going over the publisher's contracts for the study Bible. He also had a speaking engagement coming up in December. He felt as if they were all spinning plates, and he was the circus performer. He gave the first one a twist, then made his way down the line, coming back to the beginning just as the momentum was failing and the china beginning to tipple. The secret was to keep moving, he told himself.

He turned the key and let himself in. Samantha was waiting in the dark hallway, though it took him a moment to make out her shape. She thrust Bonnie at him even before he could take off his coat.

"She's been whining for an hour." Her voice sounded angry and defiant.

He took Bonnie and handed Samantha the mail, which she promptly tossed onto the stairs. A few envelopes slid through the railing to the floor. He decided not to make an issue of it. "Where's Lorna?" he asked.

"She took Cam to the doctor."

Alasdair nodded and felt a twinge of concern. Cameron had been running a fever for days now. A surge of appreciation for Lorna filled his heart. She had given up her only afternoon off to help him with the children. What would he do without her? He shifted Bonnie higher onto his shoulder. Her little face felt hot against his own. She was becoming ill, too. He closed his eyes and took a deep breath.

"All right," he soothed. "First things first. All things decently and in order."

He aimed himself up the stairs toward the bedroom, his daughter struggling against his arms, still whining. He eased her gently onto the bed and took off his coat. Bonnie slid on her stomach to the edge of the bed. He caught and righted her just as she began to pitch down. Finally he had her right side up and on the floor. He led her to her own room, changed her diaper and wiped her nose, then took her small hand in his, and they toddled back down the stairs to the kitchen. He put her in the playpen and gave her a few toys. Samantha was sitting on the couch watching television. He sat down beside her, since there was no other furniture, and patted her knee. He attempted conversation.

"Thank you for watching Bonnie. Do you have homework you should be doing?"

She pulled her leg away and didn't answer. His fault. He shouldn't have combined his praise with nagging.

He tried again. "How was your day?"

Samantha didn't answer, just pushed a button on the remote control that changed the station and landed on *Jerry Springer*.

He stared at her for a moment. When had they become enemies? He sighed. "Find something else to watch, Samantha, or better yet, turn it off. This is unsuitable for a twelve-year-old child."

She ignored him and stared straight ahead. He frowned and leaned toward her. She was wearing makeup. Quite a lot of it, mostly clumped around her eyes. He had never given permission for that. "Samantha—" he began.

"I'm thirteen." She punched the remote again. The news this time, a report of a fatal collision between a car and a semitrailer.

"Turn it off," he said sharply, his voice rising.

She stared at him coldly, tossed down the remote control, and stalked off. He turned off the television himself and was about to call her back to deal with her disrespect, but Bonnie began to cry, and the telephone rang. He debated for a moment, then went to the phone.

The caller ID said anonymous. It could be a solicitor. It could be someone complaining about the choice of hymns last Sunday. Or it could be someone in the congregation who needed him. *And what help can you offer?* a familiar, hateful voice whispered. He clenched his teeth and picked up the receiver.

"Man, I was beginning to wonder if you still existed."

Alasdair felt irritation well up as soon as he recognized the voice, familiar again from the number of messages left in recent weeks. He forced himself to be polite. "How are you, Bob?"

"Good," Bob Henry answered quickly. "Better than you. Why don't you return my calls?"

"I appreciate your offer of help, but this is something I'm going to have to face on my own." No tricks, he thought to himself, remembering the maneuvering and subterfuge Bob had specialized in, even in college. Behind him Bonnie let out a pitiful, wavering cry of high-pitched misery. He turned toward her. She was rubbing her nose and forehead with a tiny hand.

The front door opened and closed. Alasdair leaned around the corner. It was Lorna with a miserable-looking Cameron on her hip. She smiled and waved. Alasdair held up a hand in greeting, then pointed back toward the playpen with a look of apology.

Lorna nodded and headed toward the crying child. "It's the flu and nothing to be done for it," she whispered as she passed him.

Of course. He shut his eyes briefly, but it had no effect on Bob Henry's voice rasping on in his ear.

"I don't think you understand, Alasdair, how things are. The wheel's squeaking pretty loud and Whiteman's as serious as a heart attack."

"This situation has nothing to do with Gerald Whiteman. I serve at the pleasure of this congregation and the presbytery."

"Or not," Bob pointed out. "And they've contacted Gerry and asked him to get involved. You'd better be glad he *doesn't* bump it back down to the presbytery. If he does, there's not much I can do. And what were you thinking, telling him you couldn't meet with him?"

"My schedule won't allow it."

"Give me a break!" Bob erupted.

Alasdair said nothing. He took off his glasses and rubbed the bridge of his nose.

"Now listen," Bob continued. "I know you're an upfront kind of guy, but playing it straight isn't going to work this time. I might be able to help you if you'd tell me what's going on."

The doorbell rang again. The babies were still wailing. Alasdair replaced his glasses. "Bob, I've got to go. You've caught me at a busy time. I'll consider what you've said."

Bob let out a frustrated sigh. "You do that, pal. You've got my number."

Yes, he certainly did.

Alasdair hung up the phone, not even saying good-bye, and went to the door. The bulb in the hallway burned dim and yellow, as if weary of beating back the gloom. He made a note to replace it with a stronger wattage. His legs felt heavy, but he picked them up and put them down just the same. Samantha came back down the stairs, passed him without speaking, and after a moment he heard her voice mingle with Lorna's in the kitchen. The twins had stopped crying.

He stopped before the door and looked out the peephole. Blinked, leaned forward, and looked again. Four of the nine elders of the church were crammed between the potted Norfolk Island pine and the wrought-iron railing. Alasdair stepped back, opened the door, and quickly checked his watch. "Did I forget a meeting?"

"No, Pastor." The most senior member, in every sense of the word, Edgar Willis, stepped forward. His white hair flew in the wind and he looked frail enough to blow away, were it not for the triumvirate that flanked him—the Big Three, Lorna called them. They were the power brokers. They looked grim. And determined.

"We have a matter to discuss with you. Of some urgency, but I suppose we should have called first," Edgar admitted.

"Please come in." Alasdair took another step back from the door as they passed him. He ushered them into the formal living room, used only for such purposes, then excused himself for a moment and went to the kitchen.

The babies were both in their high chairs and eating a banana, most of which was being rubbed on the sides of their faces and in their hair. Lorna was opening a can of soup. Bonnie's nose was running again, but at least she'd stopped crying.

"I'm sorry," he said to Lorna, "I wasn't expecting them." Not entirely true, but he hadn't been expecting them today. That much was right.

"That's all right, dear—what happened to Tuesday's casserole?"

"I forgot to thaw it out."

"That's all right," Lorna repeated and patted his arm. "It doesn't matter. You go on to your meeting. Do you know what it's about?" She looked worried.

He felt another surge of affection for her and a throb of anger at the scoundrel who had abandoned her after fifteen years of marriage. He shook his head. "I'm sure it's nothing." He felt the pressure under his eyes, took off his glasses again and massaged them. He left her looking worried and headed back to the living room.

"Feed my sheep." The words materialized from nowhere and landed in his ear. He took a deep breath, replaced his glasses, and entered the room. The air felt stiff, and he imagined he could feel it crackling as he passed through it. He pulled one of his great-grandmother's Chippendale chairs from the corner and sat down facing the half circle they'd formed. It held his back straight. He rested both palms on his thighs and waited for them to speak.

"Reverend MacPherson," Edgar began, "we should have come to you sooner."

Alasdair said nothing. He took note of who had been invited to the meeting and who had not. His four staunchest supporters— MacPherson devotees who would endorse the family cat if put forth for nomination—were noticeably absent, as was the newest member of the elder team, still an unknown quantity.

Edgar cleared his throat. The Big Three shifted uncomfortably in their chairs beside him. "We had hoped to avoid this kind of confrontation," he said.

Alasdair remained silent. Edgar opened his briefcase and pulled out a piece of paper. His agenda, Alasdair realized. He felt a churning mixture of anger and fear. He kept his face impassive.

"We've received letters from several church members. Telephone calls from more. Some have come in person. The congregation is not happy," Edgar said bluntly.

"And your solution to that state of affairs was to prevail on the president of the General Assembly to offer me a job in Richmond."

Edgar's face flushed, and the others shifted in their seats. A direct hit. "Perhaps we should have come to you first," Edgar murmured.

Alasdair kept his voice steady with an effort. "Yes, I think you should have."

Edgar sat up a little straighter. "Well, regardless, we're coming to you now. As I said, there have been complaints. Many of them."

"Is there a problem with my sermons?"

"Not when you're here to deliver them."

He ignored the barb. "What, then?"

"The shepherding. Or the lack thereof."

"I beg your pardon?"

"I'm sorry, Pastor," Edgar said. "But it's true. Since Pastor Wright left there's been no shepherding at all."

"Then hire his replacement instead of dragging your feet as you have been." The words came out harsher than he'd meant.

"There's no money for a replacement."

Alasdair stared at Edgar, incredulous. Perhaps he hadn't been following finances as closely as he should have in recent months, but no money to replace a previously funded position? "How can that be?" he demanded when he found his voice.

"Giving is down. Significantly." Edgar nodded toward one of his compatriots, who flipped the latch on his briefcase as if on cue and handed Edgar a sheaf of papers.

"Here are last week's figures." Edgar passed the papers to him. "The General Fund offering is down twenty-five percent from the budgeted amount, as is Faith Missions and Benevolence. We've had to shuffle budget categories to cover existing expenses."

"That's perfectly ridiculous," Alasdair sputtered. "The sanctuary is full every Sunday."

"Full of visitors who have heard you on the radio and drop a five-dollar bill into the plate when the offering comes around."

"They support the radio broadcasts."

"Well and good." Edgar's tone became hard. "But it's not the radio audience you've been given charge over, which brings us to the next point."

Alasdair felt the scene take on an appearance of unreality. Frail Edgar Willis was giving him a dressing down. Edgar's face was dangerously red, little dabs of spittle on the corners of his mouth. He'd had a heart attack last year. This kind of agitation couldn't be good for him.

"A significant number of the congregation feel that your best efforts are expended elsewhere," Edgar continued with energy, heart and voice apparently in tip-top condition. "Their needs are not being met, and they resent paying your salary so that you might further your career. Perhaps being the greatest apologist since C. S. Lewis is a fine personal ambition, but it hardly qualifies you to lead a local church."

A flare of anger swept through Alasdair like a tongue of flame. Fear seemed to evaporate in its heat. He stood up, almost knocking over the chair. "Those were not my words. If you're going to pick a fight with me, at least fight fair." The comparison the *Washington Post* had made in their feature article on him a few years ago had mortified him then, as well as now.

Edgar sniffed, folded his hands, and pressed his thin lips together. "At any rate, the situation is untenable." The room fell silent.

Alasdair breathed deeply for a moment, crossed to the mantel, rested his hand on it, and gathered in his anger. "Would you like me to take a cut in pay?" he raised his head to ask.

"I'm afraid that won't do," Edgar said, too quickly to have even considered the offer.

They'd already made up their minds, Alasdair realized. They hadn't come to discuss. They'd come to inform. "It sounds as if you're asking me to resign," he said. "Is that what you're doing? Without any discussion at all? In this underhanded way? Where are the rest of the elders? Why isn't this being discussed at the regular session meeting with everyone present and able to voice their opinions?"

"You know exactly what will happen if this matter is brought up officially. Sides will form, and the congregation will split down the middle. All ministries will halt while war is waged. Besides, would you have responded any differently if we'd gone through proper channels?" Edgar demanded. "Gerald Whiteman called me this morning and said you'd refused to even meet with him. Why should we think you would have listened to our appeal? You can be stubborn, Pastor. And intimidating."

"You should have come to me," Alasdair repeated. "This is all wrong."

"We're coming to you now. Will you change? Will you drop your radio programs and speaking engagements, cut back your writing schedule, and lead the congregation?"

"That's an outrageous demand."

"It's the one we're making, nonetheless." Edgar closed his lips tightly, primly.

Alasdair felt a rush of heat to his face, and suddenly this had nothing whatever to do with the work of the Lord. Heart thumping, blood singing, lungs sweeping air in and out, he felt as if some warring tribe had just tossed over the head of one of his generals. As if he'd topped the ridge to see his village burning and enemy hordes making off with plunder.

"I. Will. Not. Resign." His breath came in pants, as if he delivered blows instead of merely words.

Edgar Willis blinked. "Will you give up your outside ministries?"

"I will not."

Sutton tightened his jaw. "Do you want to split the church? Is that what you want?"

"If the church splits, it will be your doing, not mine."

Sutton frowned. "People have left, Pastor. More have announced their intention to do so. It's up to you. We can do this the way that would be most edifying to the Lord, or we can tear the church to pieces by drawing battle lines."

He could not lose his church. That was simply not an option. "I will not resign," he repeated.

Smith sighed. Sedgewick shut his briefcase.

The telephone rang. Stopped. Samantha appeared, her face defiant, her voice sounding afraid.

"Telephone for you," she said. "It's *supposedly* urgent."

His visitors stood and silently made their way to the door.

"It won't end here," Edgar said, and Alasdair wasn't sure if it was a promise or a threat. "It's the Lord's church, not yours."

He shut the door on the callers and went into the kitchen to answer the telephone.

"Yes."

"Hello, Reverend MacPherson. This is Lois Tronsett."

"Yes," he repeated.

"I'm Samantha's principal."

He didn't respond at all this time. All the available space in his mind was occupied by what had just taken place. There was no room just now for his daughter's academic problems.

Lois Tronsett paused, then steamed ahead.

"I'm concerned about Samantha," she said bluntly.

"What's your concern?"

"There was trouble at school today."

The babies began banging their spoons. He put a finger in his ear. Lorna must have heard. She came in and removed the children from their chairs and took them away.

"What kind of trouble?" he managed to respond.

"A boy was involved, but my concerns are deeper than this one event. I'd like to talk to you in person."

"What about a boy?" Alasdair's pulse skidded and thudded in his ear.

"Some kissing behind a tree during lunch break, but it's the big picture I'm worried about. Samantha's withdrawn from the other girls. Isolated. I think she might benefit from some counseling."

He flashed back to his father, eyes steady, voice sure. *"The Word of God, properly interpreted and applied, is sufficient for every circumstance of faith and life."*

"I'd like to sit down and talk to you in more detail." She came at him again, sounding determined.

"I'll call you tomorrow from my office," he said, still trying to take in what she'd said. "I'll have a better idea of my schedule with my calendar before me."

That seemed to satisfy her. Alasdair hung up the telephone and stood there for a moment. His anger was morphing into a different sensation. A strange sensation. It was as if his feet were fixed to the floor, but a great hand had a grip on his head and was pulling. He could feel himself grow thinner and thinner as it pulled, and he wondered when he would be stretched so thin he would simply pull apart.

He walked back into the living room and slumped down onto the sofa. He stared at the wall, past his mother's gilt-framed botanical prints and the china plates, past the faded wallpaper. He sat there for some time, doing nothing, thinking nothing. Simply staring at the wall as if some writing might appear on it with a divine message for him. He gave a short laugh.

"What is it?" It was Lorna, leaning over him. Her face was worried. He hadn't noticed her come in.

"Mene, mene, tekel, upharsin."

Her eyes grew wide. "Alasdair, you're frightening me."

"I'm sorry." He turned away from the blank wall and focused on his sister's face, rubbing away at his headache. "It's from the book of Daniel," he explained. "It was the writing on the wall."

She didn't ask what it meant. He wondered if she knew what the divine message to the king had been: *You have been weighed in the balance and found wanting.* For the first time he identified with the pagan king in the story instead of with the prophet of the Lord.

"Alasdair," she began, and he waited for his sister to soothe him.

To dispense one of her usual remedies, and he wondered which one she would reach for this time. "You're tired, that's all. You'll feel better when you've had a good night's sleep." Or perhaps, "When we find the right sitter things will calm down." Or maybe, "Things will be better after Easter or Advent or Lent," or whatever event was closest on the calendar. What she actually said surprised him, though. He, who had lost the ability to be surprised.

"I've prayed," she stated simply. Her face was calm, though heavy with love and pain.

He didn't have the heart to point out what he had learned through bitter trial. Prayers weren't always answered. "Something will·work out," he said instead, even though he didn't believe it.

"I think it already has," she answered, "we just don't know it yet."

❧ six ❧

"FOR HEAVEN'S SAKE, LORNA, WHAT was so important you had to call us out on a weekday?" Winifred unbuttoned her coat and hung it neatly over the back of the restaurant chair. "I'm missing a planning meeting for the Christmas bazaar, and heaven knows what they'll decide with no one to herd them." The waitress materialized at her elbow, and Winifred gave her an irritated look, as if the woman had violated some etiquette by offering her a menu. "I'll have the chef's salad and coffee," she said without taking the menu from her hand. "Decaf with cream."

"Thank you," Lorna supplied as the waitress turned to leave, but she must not have heard.

"Well?" Winifred persisted. "What's this about?"

"Wait until Fiona gets here," Lorna said, bracing herself for more of Winifred's displeasure. "I'll tell both of you at once."

Winifred frowned and checked her watch, heaved a huge sigh, then gave the restaurant a sweeping glance. "Whatever made you choose this place?"

"I'm sorry," Lorna answered automatically. Actually, she'd spent quite a while selecting the little café, but she knew Winifred had been in mourning for fifteen years, since her favorite lunch spot, Honora's Tea Room, had become a sushi bar.

Winifred gave her head a small shake and reached a hand up to smooth her hair.

Lorna pulled her coat back up around her shoulders. It was colder than usual for this time of year. She turned away from her sister's irritated face and looked out the tinted-glass window. The sun had tried valiantly to make an appearance all day but had never quite overcome the low-hanging clouds. The streets were throbbing with the evening traffic as people surged from the King Street metrorail station to homes in the suburbs. Tomorrow morning the process would reverse itself as everyone headed back into D.C. to work.

She looked past the cars to the neighborhood itself, to the brick row houses and shops, some of which had been here since before the American Revolution, to the winter-bare trees lining the cobbled sidewalks. The streets gleamed slick with rain, and the antique street-lights glowed steadily in the gathering dusk.

She had once thought she would step out onto these streets and follow them to adventure and excitement, but somehow she'd never managed to get very far from the gate of the parsonage. She'd taken the first two years of college at George Mason but couldn't seem to settle on a major. When Michael had come along and offered to marry her, it had seemed the right thing to do. But even then she'd only moved a few blocks away from home. She had thought they would have children and settle in, but the Lord had never seen fit to bless. Perhaps it was just as well, considering.

She still had trouble believing what Michael had done, though she lived with the consequences of it every day. He had taken all their savings, bled the equity from their home, taken out credit cards and run them up to their limits—all without a word to her. To buy into some real-estate investment scheme. Unfortunately, he'd made enough profits to incur a hefty tax liability before the venture had collapsed. He'd lost it all, and before she'd even taken that fact in, he'd announced he'd found someone else. The property settlement had amounted to dividing the bills—the ones that weren't discharged in the bankruptcy.

She felt a familiar shame at being deserted and guilt when she thought of the money she owed. If not for that, she could quit her jobs and help Alasdair with the children full-time. She couldn't count the number of times she'd prayed for God to clear the way for her to do just that, but so far that prayer hadn't been answered. A small thought nibbled at her awareness—that the request had more to do with her need than the children's.

Alasdair would welcome it, she was sure. He had offered to have her move into the guest room. She had been greatly tempted but had refused. As much as she would have liked to stay close to the children, she felt a stop, a sharp conviction. It would be so easy but not right. She had the feeling, as seductive as the temptation might be, that it would be stealing. Taking something that wasn't hers and holding it so closely it smothered. She wondered, with a hollow sense of guilt, how much her preoccupation with her brother's family had contributed to the ending of her marriage. Nothing excused what Michael had done. But had she cleared the path toward his sin, opened the gate for him, and waved good-bye? Would he have been able to fly so far off course if she had been connected to him? She didn't know. She sat for a moment in the company of that bitter regret, then forcibly rearranged her thoughts. She had much to be grateful for. The small room she rented from a teacher at the school more than met her needs, considering she was rarely home. And she was thankful for her jobs.

She brightened when she thought of her work at the school. She loved being there, even if she was just a secretary. Every day she got to see the children come in and out. She knew their names, she visited their classrooms and helped with art projects when things weren't busy in the office. She would have done it for free. The paycheck was an added bonus. And her job at the film processing plant paid very well. The work wasn't hard. It was even interesting, in a way. Four nights a week she looked at frozen moments of other people's lives. Frame by frame they passed before her.

A familiar thought accused that she had gone nowhere, accomplished nothing with her own life. *Look at you,* it said. *Thirty-five years old and what have you done?*

Winifred heaved another great sigh and shifted restlessly in her chair, bringing Lorna back to the present situation. Fortunately Fiona blew in the door with a gust of wet wind at that very moment and wound her way through the maze of closely packed tables to join them. She took her seat and arranged herself.

"Well?" Fiona demanded, not as rudely as Winifred, but in her usual no-nonsense manner.

"It's Alasdair," Lorna said.

"What about him?" Winifred snapped.

"Leave her alone, Winifred. Just organize your thoughts, Lorna," Fiona encouraged, speaking a little slower than normal.

Lorna felt a hot surge of exasperation. "He got a letter from the president," she said.

"Of the United States?" Winifred was incredulous.

"Of the General Assembly Council," Lorna corrected, keeping her voice level. "Offering him a job."

Both sisters frowned, sensing trouble. Their puzzlement turned to comprehension as she continued. "There was another letter from an acquaintance of Alasdair's—Bob Henry. He works for Gerald Whiteman now. He said there'd been complaints. That the job offer is an end run around a pulpit war."

"I knew this was coming," Fiona announced, sounding triumphant.

Winifred's face hardened. "I'd like to know who started it."

"It doesn't matter," Fiona rebutted quickly, but looking grim as well. All three of them knew how these things worked. Their father had ridden out several coup attempts. No one emerged unscathed.

"That's not all," Lorna continued. "Last night Edgar Willis and the Big Three showed up. Complete with balance sheets. They said the congregation was unhappy that they weren't being shepherded since Bill left, that Alasdair was unapproachable and intimidating. They asked for his resignation."

"No!" Fiona's face was shocked.

"Yes." Lorna nodded.

"What did Alasdair do?" Winifred demanded.

"He refused. Quite decisively." She saw again his eyes, suddenly as hard and lifeless as granite. "I don't think they'll go to the congregation just yet. They were concerned about a split."

"They'll probably go back to President Whiteman and press harder from that end," Winifred predicted.

"Alasdair won't take the job at headquarters," Fiona said, shaking her head. "He says a pastor's job is to preach, not shuffle paper and count beans."

"He may live to eat those words," Winifred pointed out flatly.

"I can't think a move to Richmond would be in anyone's best interest," Lorna said. "The children have had enough upsets. What they need now is stability."

"Samantha is struggling as it is," Winifred agreed.

"And how would Alasdair get on without his family?" Lorna asked. "By himself, without anyone at all to love the children." Her eyes were beginning to tear up just at the thought.

"Alasdair's leaving is out of the question," Winifred pronounced. "There's always been a MacPherson behind the pulpit of Knox Presbyterian. Great-great-grandfather Hamish, and then Great-grandfather Dougal, Grandfather Seamus. Father, of course—"

"And now Alasdair stands to be the last in a long line," Fiona finished.

Winifred gave Lorna a hard look. "I wish you'd said something sooner."

Lorna thought about defending herself, but Winifred spoke again before she had a chance to formulate her thoughts.

"Perhaps we could tell him to quit his other involvements."

"For heaven's sake, Winifred," Fiona objected. "Alasdair is a grown man. He's not our baby brother any longer. Besides, you know how headstrong he is."

"Well, if he doesn't mend his ways, he's going to lose his job," Winifred pointed out. "Perhaps he'll just have to do what we tell him."

"I'll give the matter some thought," Fiona said. "Then we shall talk to him." Winifred nodded in agreement, the matter settled as far as they were concerned.

Lorna felt relief to have the problem out of her hands, but then just as quickly she remembered her strange commission the day she had prayed. The feeling that *she* had been chosen to help her brother, not her competent sisters. Ah, well. That notion had probably been just been one of her flights of fancy. She was perfectly content to support any solution to Alasdair's problems, from whatever direction it came.

The food arrived, and Winifred and Fiona began talking about other things—Winifred about the Christmas bazaar the Women's Fellowship would be sponsoring, Fiona about her upcoming bid for the chair of the History Department at George Mason. When they were finished, the two of them rose with one accord. Lorna followed suit.

"By the way," Winifred said, "the sitter made it official."

"They quit nearly as quickly as we can hire them," Fiona said grimly. "The children are just going to have to go to a day care. I can't keep on taking time to interview and check references."

"I'll do it," Lorna offered quickly. "I'll call the paper and have them put the ad back in. Perhaps this time will be different," she said, but not really believing it. It was hard to find competent help willing to work for any wage, much less what her brother could pay.

"We might as well go to the Bag and Save since we're all here," Winifred said. "We can shop for Thanksgiving dinner."

Fiona nodded agreeably. "I need cat food."

"There is a solution to this," Winifred assured Fiona.

"I'll be thinking," Fiona agreed. "We'll compare notes in a day or two." And Lorna, following behind them, thought she might as well not have been there at all.

Bridie shoved the ten-pound sack of potatoes toward Jeremy, the bag boy, and turned her attention toward the three sisters. She usually enjoyed their weekly trip to the Bag and Save. They were so prim and proper, and they squeezed a nickel until the buffalo hollered, as her grandmother used to say. She felt a sharp pain at the thought of her grandmother but put it quickly aside. She had managed to survive by dividing her life into strict categories. The past existed only in some distant world, and she tried to give it a certain unreality, to think of it like a book she'd read or a movie she'd seen and loved long ago. Keep your mind where your behind is; that was her motto. And right now her behind was here, in check-out stand number three at the Bag and Save in Alexandria, Virginia.

She counted her blessings again. She had a little money put away. She had a home. She had a friend in Carmen. Sort of. And Jonah hadn't come looking for her. Yet. She felt the little chill that thought always brought with it, though she could reassure herself as often as she wanted. She had sat at Carmen's computer every day at first and now at least twice a week, visiting the Virginia Department of Corrections Web site. She clicked on the button for On-Line Inmate Locator, searched for Porter, Jonah. Each time she would check the columns. Status: Active. Custody: Security Level 2. And the one that would calm her the most: Release date, which was still far enough away that she didn't need to worry. She would have to face that someday, she told herself. There was no telling what he had become in prison, and he'd been scary enough to begin with. Eventually she would need to put a lot more miles between herself and Jonah. But not today.

She took a deep breath and blinked her eyes to make the thought of him dissipate, then focused back on the sisters. The one in front of her, the oldest one, now she was a corker. Winifred Graham. Red hair salted with gray and a mouth puckered up as tight as her purse strings. Married to an accountant. Three grown daughters, two married and living out of state, the youngest one gone to college just last month. In Montreal. Bridie wondered if there was a pattern there. She chided herself for her cattiness and greeted her, as usual, speaking first.

"How are you today, Mrs. Graham?" she asked.

"Very well, thank you, Bridie," she answered back, as always. Mrs. Graham unfailingly called her by her first name, but never suggested that Bridie should call her Winifred. Bridie smiled at her and weighed the sweet potatoes, scanned the bag of mini-marshmallows, the green beans, the can of fried onion rings, the cream of mushroom soup, the two packages of brown-and-serve rolls, and the turkey—a twenty pounder.

"You planning a big Thanksgiving dinner?" Bridie asked, violating the company policy not to ask customers about their purchases.

"It ain't none of your business, Bridie," Winslow had told her more

than once. *"And don't you go frowning and sniffing when folks buy liquor. If they got ID, that's all that's your concern."*

Bridie hadn't said anything then, and she didn't say anything when she scanned a six-pack, either. She supposed, considering her history, she was straining at a gnat and swallowing a camel. Still, she had her reasons. She'd seen firsthand the damage alcohol could do, and for a second her ribs felt sore just from remembering.

"Yes, these groceries are for Thanksgiving dinner." Winifred—Mrs. Graham—nodded with a slight air of offense, as if Bridie had indeed broken some rule of polite society.

Bridie flushed, scanned the celery and carrots, and vowed to keep her mouth shut from now on. She looked past the first two sisters back to her favorite. Lorna was obviously younger than the other two, a little shy, with a sweetness that was genuine, not the phony kind that set your teeth on edge. She was pretty and plump with a heart-shaped face and soft brown hair framing it. And it was funny. Even though their whole relationship had taken place across a check-out stand at the Bag and Save, Bridie had the feeling Lorna could have been a friend if their lives had been different. "How are you doing today, Lorna?" she asked.

"I'm just fine, Bridie." Lorna was unloading her purse onto the check-out stand. A wadded-up tissue joined a set of keys and a check-book.

"What are you looking for, Lorna?" the other sister, Fiona, asked, with an overly patient tone that said volumes.

"I had a coupon for that onion soup. I just know it."

Winifred rolled her eyes and exchanged a glance with Fiona.

Bridie felt a little surge of anger on Lorna's behalf, reached into her drawer, and found an extra. "I've got it here." She scanned it quickly and watched the computer take off the discount.

"What are your holiday plans, Bridie?" the middle sister asked. She was pretty, with hair a darker shade of red than Winifred's and fine, delicate features. She'd told Bridie she was a professor at George Mason—ancient history or something. Her husband was a doctor. No kids. But she was nice and had a slightly shorter poker up her back than Winifred. When Bridie had called her Mrs. Larkin, she'd insisted on Fiona instead.

"Oh, I'll probably spend it here," she answered.

"Surely they'll give you time off to go to services?" Winifred asked.

Bridie murmured, noncommittal. Winslow would really get hot under the collar if he found out she was discussing religion with a customer, even if they'd been the one to bring it up. "Is that all for you today?" she asked the sisters, her finger poised over the Total key. Fiona nodded. Winifred nodded. Lorna looked disturbed, as though she was trying to get something out, but it seemed as if her mouth automatically closed when either of her sisters' opened.

"That will be all, thank you," Winifred said.

Bridie pushed Total with a flourish and read the sum. "That's one hundred twenty-two dollars and nineteen cents."

"How shall we divide this?" Winifred asked her sisters.

"Pay out of household, and we'll make it right later," Fiona suggested.

"That sounds fine," Winifred agreed, then both sisters looked at Lorna expectantly. She nodded and went fishing in her purse again. Fiona and Winifred exchanged another glance.

Bridie helped Jeremy finish the bagging, and seeing the makings for the holiday dinner gave her another feeling of emptiness. When she looked up, Lorna had apparently found her checkbook and was gazing square at her, an expression of compassion and concern on her kind face. Bridie flushed. She'd been wearing her heart on her sleeve again and had gotten caught. She flashed Lorna a bright smile, then repeated the total. Lorna nodded and filled in the amount.

The sisters always paid for the groceries with a presigned check from the account of Alasdair MacPherson. It was a constant entertainment to Bridie to concoct stories about who this Alasdair MacPherson was. Perhaps an old, crippled father. Maybe a young man, their cousin or brother, struck down in his prime. In a wheelchair. A veteran. She never asked, though. It was more fun to wonder. Another of her silly little games.

Lorna handed over the check; then with her hand poised over her wallet, she asked Bridie the same question she always did. "Do you want to see Alasdair's identification?"

Bridie didn't know what possessed her, but this time, instead of waving her away and shaking her head as always, she had a sudden yen to see what this Alasdair MacPherson looked like. "Let me take a glance at it. If you don't mind," she added to placate their surprised expressions.

"Certainly." Lorna recovered and produced the identification, an expired Virginia driver's license. The picture was sort of dark, but Bridie brought it up to the light on her check stand and took a good look. He was a young man. That was the first surprise. And handsome, but fierce and stern looking, as though he'd just heard somebody whispering in church. He had brown hair that was combed back from a high forehead, dark blue eyes, a hawklike nose, a square chin, and a nice mouth, but serious and lying in a flat line, as if it never had curved up at the corners. Bridie made the little crossed lines on the top of the check and scribbled some numbers and letters on them, but it was just for show. She'd just had a curious spell, but now it was over.

"Thank you," she said. "Manager's having a hissy fit this week. He'll be over it by next time." She handed the card back and loaded the last sack into the cart, embarrassed at her nosiness. "There you go," she said. "I'll see you next week." The two older sisters said good-bye and steered the cart toward the exit, but Lorna stood as if planted. She leaned forward, took a breath, then closed her mouth. Bridie could see the next customer in line fidgeting from the corner of her eye. Lorna didn't budge.

"Will there be anything else, then?" she asked.

"What are you doing for Thanksgiving?" Lorna blurted out. "I was wondering . . . I mean, would you like to join us for dinner?"

Bridie's face burned, and she felt as humiliated as if she'd been caught with her hand in the till. Now she understood. Lorna was feeling sorry for her. She answered, hearing her own voice over the wet slush of the pulse in her ears. "Thank you, but no," she said. "I'm sorry. I can't do that."

Lorna's sweet face looked as though Bridie had dashed a glass of cold water into it, and suddenly it was she who was feeling sorry for Lorna.

"Oh, I see," Lorna said. "Of course. You probably have other plans."

Bridie didn't say one way or the other. "Good-bye," she said, feeling miserable.

The other two sisters looked back. They had gotten as far as Carmen's check stand and were waiting, obviously impatient.

"Lorna," Winifred called to her sister, annoyed. "Let's go."

"I'll tell you what," Lorna said brightly, compounding Bridie's misery by giving her hand a little pat, as if to show there were no hard feelings. "I'll leave you the telephone number just in case you change your mind. You can leave a message here." She tore off part of the grocery receipt, scribbled something on the back, and pressed the scrap of paper into Birdie's hand. Bridie was just opening her mouth to say she was sorry, that she hadn't meant to be rude, but Lorna turned and was gone. Bridie stared after her for a minute and was tempted to go chasing after the sisters.

"I'd love to come to your house for supper," she wanted to say, but she knew inside with a hollow finality that that would never happen. She fingered the paper. She would never go inside the houses of decent people and eat at their tables. She would stay right here at the Bag and Save and tend to her business. That was all she could expect. That was the best life had to offer, she thought, shoving the receipt into the pocket of her smock. She turned to the next customer, gave him a greeting, and began to scan his groceries. That was the best life had to offer, she repeated again. For the likes of her.

Carmen Figueroa glanced across the check stand toward Bridie working in the next lane. It was hard to believe it had been a year, and she still remembered how different Bridie had looked the first time she'd seen her. Skinny as a rail, in a dress that had to have come from the thrift shop, a bad dye job, nails chewed down to a bloody quick, and if that had been all there was to her, Carmen probably never would have made the offer. But something about the new checker's eyes had snagged the quick once-over. They were big, china-doll blue, and not exactly pleading. That would be saying too much. But when she'd come up to Carmen and spoken in that soft voice of hers with the accent that stretched out all the middles of her words and rounded off the ends, her eyes had lit up with hope like somebody striking a match in a dark room.

"Are you the one who posted the notice in the lunchroom about needing a roommate?" she'd asked.

Carmen had sighed. "Yeah, that's me all right." And that was how it had happened. A year ago. Huh. Now the pretty hair, which Carmen could tell from the roots would be a very light blond, was still covered with brown, but a light golden brown, and Carmen had talked her into a rinse instead of permanent dye. And Bridie had finally put on enough weight so that it didn't hurt to look at her anymore. Last month she'd told Carmen she was going to quit biting her nails, and she did, just like that. They'd had manicures to celebrate, even though Carmen had had to talk her into it. Bridie never spent anything on frills. Carmen even had to convince her it was okay to buy a new outfit every now and then.

Carmen still itched to give her a makeover. She had such a pretty smile, and with her pink cheeks and creamy skin she'd be gorgeous if she let her hair go back to blond. An easy job with a little help from Clairol number 87. But no matter how much Carmen argued, she couldn't convince her. Bridie's mouth would clamp shut, and her eyes sort of hooded over like Carmen's cat's.

"No," she'd say, and the way she said it, you'd think Carmen had suggested being launched into space instead of just coloring her hair. Weird. Anyway, that was just one more piece of evidence. Something was hinky somewhere. She couldn't say exactly what or even why she thought so. Just that somehow Bridie's insides and outside didn't seem to match.

Bridie must have felt Carmen's eyes on her back. As soon as she finished bagging up the church ladies' order, she turned around and flashed Carmen a smile.

"Are you going out with Newlee tonight?" she asked, her voice casual.

Carmen gave her a sharp look. Bridie smiled back, all inno-cence.

"Dinner in," she said. "But you don't need to be gone. Stay and eat with us." She tossed out the invitation, half meaning it and half just wanting to see what Bridie would say.

"Oh, that's all right," she answered quickly. "There's a movie I've been wanting to see." She turned away, and Carmen couldn't see her face.

"Suit yourself," she said to Bridie's back, but she wasn't fooled. It was just as she figured. This had nothing to do with any movie. Bridie made herself scarce whenever Newlee came around. Something about him gave Bridie the bejeebers, and Carmen was pretty sure it was the fact that he was a cop. In fact, she thought, grinning just at the idea, if she didn't know better, she'd swear that Bridie was on the lam.

She frowned and stared into space. She'd been joking, but what if? Huh. Bridie had all the marks. Showed up out of nowhere. Talked all the time about the old home place but clammed up whenever you asked for specifics. There was the way she'd looked at first, as if she'd been chained in a closet for the last year. Put that together with her freakiness around Newlee, and it fit. Who knows, maybe she'd robbed a bank or something.

A forty-pound bag of dog food crashed onto her conveyor and snapped her to attention. It was the big biker dude. "Hey, Larry," she greeted him.

"Hi, Carmen," he nodded. "I'll take a carton of Camel hard-packs, too."

"Coming up," she said, locked her till, and went to the cigarette case, glancing at Bridie on the way.

Nah. No way she'd robbed a bank. She was just weird. After all, Winslow, a store manager without a kindhearted bone in his body, would have checked her references. A big-eyed look wouldn't have cut it with him. He said Bridie'd been a checker at some grocery store in the sticks—one of those places where they have to bring in the mail on horseback. But, then again, maybe Winslow *hadn't* checked her references. Bridie had shown up the week two other checkers had quit, and they'd been pretty desperate for help. Winslow probably would have hired anybody who could work a cash register and had a pulse.

Carmen got Larry's Camels, totaled his order, then closed her lane behind him. It was time for her break, and she headed out the door for a smoke, giving her roommate a wink and a smile on her way out. Whatever.

There was something wrong with this picture, but it wasn't her job to figure it out. She pulled out her cigarettes, checked her watch, and calculated how long until she got off, putting the matter of Bridie's past out of her mind. If something about her roommate was out of whack, the truth would come out eventually. It always did. She lit up and started thinking about what to fix Newlee for dinner.

Bridie hung her smock in her locker and, for no reason she could think of, transferred the paper with Lorna's telephone number to her coat pocket. Somehow just feeling her fingers around it reminded her of who she had been once upon a time. She punched out and went down the narrow stairs from the lunchroom. She was glad, for once, that Carmen had a date with Newlee. She didn't feel like talking to anyone. She would have to find somewhere else to hang out for a few hours, but that was all right. She supposed she could go to the movie like she'd said. She headed out of the Bag and Save, then just stood there for a minute. The brick sidewalks were slick with rain, and a few of the cars splashing past her on the narrow streets had turned on their lights.

She liked Alexandria. It wasn't home, but it was nice. Old and pretty. Everything was orderly and square. Gardens were neatly contained behind the wrought-iron fences, shops tidy, and everything built of solid, red Virginia brick. The old-fashioned streetlights made glowing circles on the street.

She started walking. She looked at the shop windows as she passed them, glanced into Le Gaulois, the snooty French restaurant, passed its garden where tables were set under a grape arbor that would be leafy and romantic come summertime. She went by the bar and grill, the stationery shop, the fancy boutiques. The trees, neatly boxed into squares of brick-lined earth, were bare but would be covered with pretty twinkling lights in just a few weeks. There were dogwood, redbud, flowering magnolia, and cherry, all asleep now.

She inspected the windows of the flower shop, the city office building, the courthouse, Gadsby's Tavern, the old inn where everyone ate sitting at the same table. She pulled her coat around her chin, and without even being aware that she'd given the order, her feet took her toward the old church. She turned onto Fairfax Street, away from the bustling traffic, past the brick row houses with their shuttered windows.

There it was, rising up in front of her, stark and beautiful, stately and peaceful. Established 1788, said the plaque on the sidewalk in front. She didn't know why she loved that old church, but the square angles, the solidness of it made her feel safe and protected. Since the first day it had been a refuge.

She didn't go inside right away. Instead, she slipped around the side of the building. She followed the narrow walkway that led to the churchyard in the back, went past the hollies, under the arbor of winter-dead cherry trees, past the mounded and mulched flower beds. The bricks under her feet were so old they were stained almost black.

She stopped. Stood still for a moment, just looking. There they were. The graves. Some were crypts, others strange-looking table-like tombstones sitting up above the ground. The grass was neatly trimmed around them.

These were people, she realized, people who had lived and breathed and loved, and now they were gone. Their lives were finished, time closing over the space they'd left, filling it in, only these stones remaining.

She stopped in front of her favorite marker, not even needing to transpose the strange *f*'s into *s*'s, as she had at first. She almost knew it by heart, she had read it so often.

> *Erected to the memory of Eleanor, wife of Mr. Daniel Wren, who departed this life on the Day of April 22 in the year of our Lord 1798, aged 32 years.*
>
> *"And I heard a voice from heaven saying unto me, Write, Blessed are the dead which die in the Lord from henceforth: Yea, saith the Spirit, that they may rest from their labours; and their works do follow them."*
> *Revelation, XIV Verse XIII.*

She loved that part. About resting from their labors and having their works follow them. How nice that would be. To have good works that would follow you into a sweet eternal rest instead of memories that tore at your heels like angry dogs.

> *This stone was placed over her by order of her disconsolate husband, who was left with two children to lament her loss, John and William Wren, three years old. . . .*

The rest was worn away. She stood there for a moment, savored the sweetness and felt the pang of loss. The disconsolate husband, the tender children. She blinked. It was cold, and her feet were growing numb. She turned and went back to the church's front door.

She opened it, stepped inside, and closed her eyes. She smelled the years, the faint musty aroma of old hymnbooks and Bibles. She opened her eyes. Took in the visitors' table, the little books and pamphlets: "Save our Organ," "About Knox Presbyterian Meeting House." A bulletin board hung on the wall beside the table. It was decorated with a picture of a bird falling from its nest, and scraps of paper in odd shapes and sizes, written by different hands, were tacked beneath it. "Not a Sparrow Falls to the Ground Without Your Father Seeing," said the caption. Bridie read a few of the notes. "Pray for my mother's biopsy," one said. "My husband has been out of work for six months," said another. "I would like to see my father before he dies. Pray he can forgive me."

Bridie's throat tightened. She sniffed and stepped inside the now familiar sanctuary. It was starkly beautiful. Its wood floors were burnished to a high gloss and covered by a threadbare crimson runner. Simple rectangular box pews with swinging doors and wooden trim had been painted white so many times the finish was glossy and thick. The windows were made of shimmery old glass, and on each sill sat a hurricane lamp. One day while she had been sitting here, the caretaker had come inside and lit them with a long wooden match. It had made her happy for a moment to see the flames glowing, their reflections twinkling in the windows, remembering how they had cheered her on that first lonely day. She exhaled a long sigh of air now, swung open the door of her pew—the one on the far side in the back of the sanctuary. She entered it and sat down. She closed her eyes and wasn't aware of how much time had passed. In fact, she might have drifted off to sleep for a moment or two, but her eyes snapped open when she heard the door in the narthex open and close.

She stood and was preparing to dart out the back door, but she paused when she saw who had come in. She could see the person framed in the open doorway. A young woman. No, it was a child, a girl, thin, with long brown hair. And something about her expression was heart-achingly familiar. It was a combination of loss and forlorn despair. Bridie watched her pull a scrap of paper from the pocket of her coat and stick it on the bulletin board under the picture of the falling sparrow. She stood in front of the board for a moment. Her shoulders slumped downward, and Bridie almost called out to her, but something stopped her. Wasn't everyone entitled to a little privacy? she asked herself. She was an interloper here, and besides, what did she have to offer the child? Whatever the girl needed was beyond her ability to provide. Still, her heart ached, and suddenly she was remembering the girl she had been, a girl who had watched her life and home unravel in ways she would never have predicted. For just a moment that girl from the past blurred into the girl before her.

"Oh, that I had the wings of a dove! I would fly away and be at rest," Bridie whispered to herself.

The child couldn't have heard her—that was ridiculous—but she lifted her head just as Bridie spoke. She looked into the dark sanctuary, then quickly turned and went back out the way she'd come, the door flapping loudly behind her. Bridie crossed to the window to see where she went. There she was. She cut across the piece of lawn between the church and a tall square of red-brick next door. The door opened, and a woman came out onto the porch. Bridie frowned and narrowed her eyes. Something about her was familiar. She was medium height, plump, and when she turned, Bridie felt a shock of recognition. The woman's kind face was filled with concern. She said something, then ushered the girl inside and closed the door. Almost stunned, Bridie turned back toward the sanctuary. It was Lorna. And that must be the place to which she'd invited Bridie for dinner this Thanksgiving. That little girl's home.

Bridie fingered the receipt in her coat pocket, the one Lorna had written the telephone number on. She walked slowly toward the bulletin board, dreading what would come, but knowing she had to look. Afraid somehow that reading the child's note would seal her fate. She couldn't help herself, though. The defeated slump of the girl's shoulders and the familiar sense of sadness she carried seemed to Bridie like a hand going up amidst churning waves. There was no way she could ignore it. She took a deep breath and stepped toward the bulletin board, located the piece of paper that hadn't been there before. There it was. A piece of lined paper like children carried to school, the letters formed in neatly penciled cursive. "Help me, God," it said.

Bridie felt her heart sink. If it had been nearly anything else, some specific malaise, like God help me to pass my math test, or God please don't let my kitten die, she could have whispered a quick prayer of agreement and walked away. But this, well, this was something too vague and troubling to ignore. Help me, God? Why, that could mean anything, could take in any possibility from illness to abuse. Bridie heaved another sigh, stepped out of the church into the cold night. The lights inside the house next door were on, but barely. It had a cold, forsaken look that made Bridie feel sorry she'd come near here today. She turned and walked back toward the town center. She stopped at the theater, bought a ticket for the romantic comedy that was playing. She went inside and sat through the feature, but the plot was thin, and the laughter seemed empty. When the show was over she walked home. When she got to their apartment on the shabby back street, she was relieved to find both Carmen and Newlee gone. With a feeling of resignation, she went to the telephone before she had even hung up her coat.

"Could I speak to Lorna?" she asked when a man answered, and she thought immediately of the stern face of Alasdair MacPherson.

"Just a moment, please," he said. Bridie heard a scuffling and then Lorna's voice.

"Lorna, this is Bridie Collins from the Bag and Save."

"Oh!" She sounded pleased. "It's good to hear from you."

"Is the dinner invitation still open?" Bridie asked, more than halfway hoping Lorna would say no for some reason. Then she could hang up and go on about her business, conscience clear. She would have done all she could.

"Oh, we would love to have you," Lorna almost sang out in delight.

"What can I bring?" Bridie asked, her doom decided.

"Nothing but yourself. Dinner will be at two, but we'd love to have you join us for church if you'd like."

"That'd be fine," Bridie said, suppressing a sigh. Lorna gave her directions she didn't need, and finally Bridie hung up the phone. She had the feeling she had just tipped the first in a long line of dominoes.

❧ *seven* ❧

BOB RAPPED SHARPLY ON THE mahogany door and examined his gleaming cordovans while he waited.

"Come in." Whiteman's voice was smooth and sonorous. He probably practiced. Bob ran his hand over his hair out of habit, even though he'd cut it short. He moved his neck around, adjusted his tie, and went inside.

"Good morning, Mr. President." Bob said, careful with his tone. Too obsequious and Whiteman would suspect his motives. Too casual and he'd be branded an upstart. But then again, in this hierarchy anybody whose bones didn't creak when he changed chairs was an upstart. A little new blood was what this group needed, he thought, and not for the first time. A few well-placed funerals.

"Sit down, Bob."

Bob settled himself on the chair, set his leather portfolio on his knees, and waited. He aimed his face forward, composed it into a solemn expression.

Whiteman leaned over and opened the bottom right-hand drawer of his desk—the trouble drawer. He took out a manila file folder and set it on his desk, then started drumming his fingers across it. Bob read the tab—he'd gotten really good at reading upside down. *John Knox—Elder Correspondence.*

"I received another letter this morning from the elders of the Alexandria church," Whiteman said. "Their pastor was a classmate of yours."

"Alasdair MacPherson," Bob supplied. "The latest in a long line of MacPhersons to pastor that particular church," he put in, just to show he was paying attention. "I called him again, as you requested, and this time I was able to speak to him."

"And?"

Bob shook his head. "He still didn't seem to be amenable to meeting with you, sir."

Whiteman's jaw flexed. He nodded and picked up the piece of stationery. Bob was careful not to reach for it until Whiteman extended it. Bob scanned its contents. Same old song.

> *Dear President Whiteman,*
>   *It is with great regret that we feel the need to contact you again.*

Sure it is, Bob thought. These types weren't happy unless they were stirring things up. He remembered his own miserable childhood as a pastor's son. His father was always too busy for his family, but no matter how hard he worked, the church people were never happy.

> *The situation about which we sought your counsel as not improved. Indeed, when we met with our pastor as you suggested, he absolutely refused to comply with our requests, which we felt were quite reasonable. The situation leaves us with few appealing options.*
>   *We could, of course, proceed with the dissolution of the ministerial relationship by calling a congregational meeting to ask for Reverend MacPherson's resignation, and then petition the presbytery to enforce it. However, as we stated in our previous letter, we fear such an approach might cause disruption to vital ministries as well as possible harm to his reputation.*

Bob made the translation. If they put it to a vote, the church would divide up and giving would go even further down the toilet. A situation to be avoided at all costs.

> *However, should you see fit to encourage Reverend MacPherson to take an administrative assignment, we feel the Lord's work could be carried on without hindrance.*

The Lord's work. Yeah. Everybody's top priority. Bob set down the letter.

"Well, what do you think?" Whiteman's silver hair was smoothed back, and his thick gray brows were drawn together. Bob wondered if Whiteman combed and sprayed them. He wouldn't put it past him.

"Interesting," Bob said, not committing himself until he saw which way the wind was blowing. There was a right answer here, and he was determined to find it. "As I said, Reverend MacPherson didn't seem eager to talk." *At least to me,* he added to himself, knowing that Alasdair had never particularly cared for him. And he knew why.

MacPherson was one of those unbendable types. He had a straightjacket morality that was painful even to witness. In fact, Bob remembered with just a small remnant of emotion, he held MacPherson responsible for his own less than stellar grade in Hermeneutics.

"I'm not asking you to give me the answers," he'd pleaded after Alasdair had gotten an A from the course. *"Just tell me the questions that were on the final. That's not cheating,"* he'd pointed out. *"You're just . . . uh . . . directing my studies."*

But Alasdair had shaken his head and said something Bob thought of as vintage MacPherson. *"It wouldn't be fitting,"* or something like that. So Bob had plodded along and barely passed, grieving his father once again. Not that it had mattered in the long run. He'd dropped out of seminary and transferred to the state school. Took journalism for a while and seemed to have a talent for nosing out a story, then switched to public relations when his dad had scratched up this job for him. Of course, being the denomination's PR hack didn't exactly put him on the Pulitzer track. The most exciting thing he wrote was the monthly newsletter, but one of these days he'd break out. His novel was halfway finished.

"I am disturbed by the situation," Whiteman intoned, bringing Bob's attention back to the present. "Ordinarily this matter should be dealt with by the congregation and the presbytery. However, they do have a point. Since Reverend MacPherson has a national ministry, the good name of the entire denomination is at stake, which is why I've called you in."

Bob nodded seriously.

"I'm also concerned about MacPherson," Whiteman continued. "Now that I've become aware of his struggles, I feel I can't simply turn my back on the situation. After careful consideration, I think the Knox ruling elders could be right. Perhaps a change of duties might be spiritually revitalizing for him."

Bob nodded, his mind racing, trying to orient himself. *What does Gerry want?* he asked himself. That was easy. Right now Gerry wanted to get appointed to a second term as president. And what did he need to get that? Also easy. He needed the endorsement of the members of the General Assembly Council. Everyone knew the vote by the whole assembly at the annual meeting was a rubber stamp. The herd voted yes to whoever the council recommended, and they'd be deciding who would get the nod in the next few months. He tried to connect those dots to the present situation. How did the MacPherson mess fit into all of that?

He reviewed the facts. John Knox Presbyterian was one of the oldest churches on the East Coast, and right now they weren't happy campers. For the last few quarters the big donors had aimed their contributions toward the denomination's general fund instead of to their local congregation. There were important and influential men in that church. One was actually on the General Assembly Council, and the others had connections. If Gerry made their problem go away, they might be inclined to throw him their support. And if Gerry was reappointed, Bob would keep his job for another four years.

"I'd like you to look through the vacant posts here at headquarters," Whiteman continued. "Find something suitable to offer MacPherson. Perhaps if we had a specific position, he'd take the offer more seriously."

"I'll get right on it, sir." Bob started to stand, then hesitated. Things could get ugly. MacPherson was no pushover. If he wouldn't even meet with Gerry, what made Whiteman think he'd give up his church at his suggestion, shuffle off to the mailroom, or whatever, just because it would be more convenient for everyone concerned?

"Something's troubling you, Bob?"

He had to be careful here. "Sometimes those with the deepest problems are the least likely to see their true situation," he offered.

Whiteman nodded.

"Denial can run deep."

Whiteman sighed and gave a small shake of his head. "I wish we could somehow convince him that it would be in his best interest to cooperate. I can understand his reluctance to leave, though," Whiteman mused. "The Alexandria church is a sophisticated, well-educated congregation, located in a metropolitan area. With congregational and elder support, there would be no financial problems. I'm almost tempted to take it myself," he said with a little laugh.

Bob nodded solemnly, not letting his excitement show on his face. The future had just fanned itself out for him like a handful of aces and kings. He saw Alasdair taking some administrative position, the Alexandria movers and shakers aiming votes in Gerry's direction out of gratitude. And after that, whichever way things went led to a happy ending. If Whiteman got the presidency, no problem. If he didn't, he could assume the Alexandria throne, an option Bob would point out to him at the right time.

"Perhaps I should go to Alexandria and speak to MacPherson in person," Bob offered.

Whiteman nodded slowly, gave a half shrug. "Perhaps."

Bob kept quiet. He knew there was more coming. Gerry kept thinking and steepling.

"Let's prepare thoroughly," he finally said. "I'd like to try to resolve this with as little disturbance as possible, and it would help if we *knew* more about the situation before we plunged in. Angels fearing to tread, and such. We really should corroborate the church's complaints rather than rely on gossip," he said.

Bob could have burst into song. "We certainly should," he agreed. "I'll do some investigating before I call on him."

Whiteman nodded. "I'll phone the elders and tell them to postpone any action for the time being."

Bob handed the letter back to Whiteman and said his good-byes, satisfied as a cat. His feet slid noiselessly on the carpeted hallway as he exited. He hit the button for the elevator and bounced on the balls of his feet. He was going to go to Alexandria and come back with a signed resignation in his hand. Problem solved. He just needed to dig up some dirt on MacPherson. A stick to run him off with.

His general belief was that everyone had a naughty secret or two, but if he had to come up with a possible exception, it would have been Alasdair MacPherson. But then, he told himself, the dirt didn't have to be on MacPherson himself. This kind of operation was like lobbing grenades. Anything that landed close would cause some damage, and he didn't have to prove anything in a court of law, just get him to sign on the dotted line.

He reviewed what he knew about MacPherson and family. There were the sisters. He remembered them well. One was pretty and smart, one was a battle-axe, one was a chubby, mousy little thing who wouldn't say boo if you stepped on her. Probably nothing there, but he'd ask around. There was the dead wife. He wouldn't be able to get his hands on any medical records, but he could get the death certificate and request a copy of the accident report. Maybe there'd been a six-pack on the seat beside her. He could only hope. The babies were a bust, but the older kid definitely had possibilities.

He smoothed his tie, and his eyes narrowed as he stared at the shiny metal doors, feeling the excitement he always felt when he was on the trail of a story. He would give it his best try. Turn over a few rocks and see what skittered out.

❧ *eight* ❧

BRIDIE MERGED INTO THE THIN crowd of Thanksgiving worshipers. Everyone must be at home cooking their turkeys. There was a bottleneck at the door of the sanctuary where an old man was handing out bulletins and personally directing each person to their seat. She waited patiently and looked up to find herself in front of the bulletin board that had started all this trouble. There was the baby bird. There was the promise that God took notice when it plummeted to the ground. She felt her mouth tighten and turn down at the corners.

A nice thought, but evidence in her life seemed to be piling up to the contrary. She thought of the empty spot her mother had left, remembered the way the family had come unstrung. It was more than remembering. She saw it again on some Technicolor wide screen of her mind: Mama's illness and death, then Papa starting up with the drinking, followed quickly by overdue bills, empty cupboards, and eventually tirades and violence. Finally she saw the state welfare workers as they loaded Jimmy, Bethie, and Christy into the white van with the seal of the Commonwealth of Virginia stamped on the side, only leaving her behind because she'd just turned eighteen. They'd trundled them off to a receiving home, not even answering her desperate protests that she could take care of them, that she'd been doing it for the last two years.

She remembered again the hearings, the relatives who acted as though they were doing her family a favor to split up their children and parcel them out. She had done her best to convince the judge that she was responsible enough to care for them. She'd rattled off the homemaking skills she'd honed since Mama had died—doing the laundry, cooking, cleaning, shopping, making sure they all got to school with paper and pencils, lunches, and warm clothes, nursing them when they were sick, making Christmases and birthdays out of nothing. She could keep on taking care of them; in fact, she could do it better now that she didn't need to be afraid of Papa.

Grandma had pleaded for the children as well. *"Let me have them,"* she'd begged. *"Don't take them away from here. It's the only home they know."* But the judge had decided she was too old and her health too poor. *"Why haven't you taken them before now?"* he'd demanded, and Bridie had driven the last nail into her coffin when she'd admitted that she'd hidden the truth from her grandmother. She'd felt she could bear Papa's meanness as long as he kept it away from the younger ones. And somehow she'd known this very thing would happen if anyone knew the truth about their family's state. They would stop being a family. And that's just what had happened.

The judge had decided that a fresh start was what the two younger girls needed. A fresh start in South Carolina with private schools and tennis lessons. Bridie felt a familiar surge of bitterness and wondered bleakly how her sisters were doing with Aunt Brenda for a mother. She wondered where Jimmy had landed after he'd turned eighteen and left Uncle Roy's. She closed her eyes and willed the thoughts away. They were too hard to bear.

She opened them and looked at the bulletin board again, this time bitterness hitting her with a hard little thump as she read the promise of the Father's care. It was a lie. There were some people God watched over and some He didn't. Some were on their own. He wasn't watching over the likes of her, and that was just as well, considering some of the things she'd done. Maybe He cared more for sparrows than people. Especially people like her.

"Excuse me." Someone jostled her elbow, and she realized she had stopped still, her body frozen with her thoughts. She caught up to the others, entered the sanctuary, and sat down in a back pew. After a minute she felt herself settle down. This church, her familiar place, had a calming influence on her rough-edged thoughts. She ran her gaze over the warm red carpet, the shimmering windows, the globes of the hurricane lamps on the sills. The altar was banked with red and gold chrysanthemums twined with ivy this morning, and the organ was playing something pretty. She tried to remember the last time she'd been to church on Thanksgiving. The last time she'd been to church at all.

She closed her eyes and could almost see Grandma, Mama, herself, and her brother and sisters in a squeaky-clean and pressed row. Papa had never come to church, but the rest of them had gone every Sunday, at least until Mama got sick. To church and to Grandma's afterward for dinner. She could almost see her mother's pretty golden hair and smiling face as she helped Grandma set the table, could almost hear Grandma singing.

She opened her eyes and made herself look hard around her. She wasn't back home. She was here, and it did no good to dwell on what was gone. What wasn't coming back. She focused her attention back on the service. The minister was rising and walking to the pulpit.

She frowned and took a closer look. Well, for mercy's sake. She looked down at her bulletin, and sure enough, there on the inside page was the pastor's name: Alasdair MacPherson. She gave her head a little shake and kept staring as he took his place behind the podium. Yes, it was him all right, in the flesh this time instead of a darkened image on an expired driver's license. There was the disappointed dash of a mouth, the same hawk nose, the same combed-back hair. The same severe look, as if he was displeased, as if they had all let him down somehow. He grasped the sides of the pulpit and began to pray.

"Lord God, how wonderful your care for us, how boundless your merciful love. On this day of Thanksgiving we thank you for your most gracious gift. To ransom a slave, you gave away your son." His mouth was moving, but his face stayed stiff and hard. And his voice, low and even, didn't quite match up with the words he was speaking, which seemed like they should have been shouted if you really believed them.

Bridie tried to pay attention during the sermon, which was something about people having an obligation to be thankful and not waiting until they felt happy about their circumstances. The congregation sat

listening, their faces looking set and determined, like they were taking a beating. When the service was over, she saw different emotions
flicker across them. Some looked relieved, others disappointed, still
others angry. She supposed she could understand why. His words had
felt heavy and burdensome, and everything, especially faith, seemed
more complicated and confusing after he'd spoken.

She followed the crowd out, then escaped to the ladies' lounge,
fiddled around for fifteen minutes or so until she couldn't put it off
any longer, then squared her shoulders, stepped outside, and took
aim for the parsonage.

It was a red-brick house, like nearly every other house in the
city of Alexandria, but set farther back on the street than the other
homes on the block. It was surrounded by a boxwood hedge, but not
the glossy green, pungently fragrant boxwoods she was used to back
home. These were spindly, old, dying things, needing to be put out of
their misery. And trees were nice, she thought, stepping over clumps
of rotted leaves on the walkway, but there was such a thing as too
many. She wondered if any light got through those windows when
the trees were in full leaf. The closer she got to the house, the more
she got the feeling that it was bearing down on her.

She was being silly. She adjusted her purse, careful not to knock
over the scrawny-looking potted pine next to her on the porch, then
stepped up to the black door, not about to be cowed by a pile of wood
and bricks.

What exactly are you doing here? she asked herself, nonetheless.
Saving some child when you can't even save yourself? And from what?
Nothing, that's what.

She had another strong temptation to leave. To catch the bus back
home, then call Lorna and give the excuse that she'd been called in
to work. But the image returned of the girl tacking the paper to the
bulletin board, the defeated slump of her shoulders, the despairing
set of her face. Bridie squared her own shoulders, took three long
breaths, and rang the bell.

You could tell a lot about a person by how they welcomed a stranger, Bridie thought as she went through all the polite formalities. She set her face in the shape of a smile, took off her coat, greeted the ones she knew, and met the ones she didn't, but her mind was somewhere else. Grandma always had extra places set at Sunday dinner. Sometimes the guests were strangers, sometimes the lonely, sometimes a missionary family just passing through. Whoever came was welcomed warmly.

Now she was the guest, and Bridie felt a sharp sense of being out of place. She should have brought a gift—a plant or something. She could almost hear Mama asking her where she'd left her manners. Not that Lorna's sisters were exhibiting many.

Winifred looked puzzled when Lorna presented her, frowning slightly.

"You remember Bridie," Lorna prompted.

"From the grocery," Winifred acknowledged briefly before returning to the conversation she was having with her husband about who should sit where.

Fiona was pleasant enough. Gave her a nice smile and said, "Happy to see you again."

Alasdair MacPherson greeted her, shook her hand, then wandered around as though he was in a fog. The girl—Samantha, she learned—was nowhere to be seen.

Poor Lorna was trying to juggle the two babies and put the finishing touches on dinner. Bridie was only too happy to help. She loved babies and hadn't held or played with one in years. And to be honest, it looked as though these poor little tykes could use some attention. They were clean and looked well-fed, but something about their knee-clinging whininess made Bridie wonder if anybody had time for them. Lorna said they were ill-tempered because they'd been sick.

Bridie asked if she could help in the kitchen, and Lorna, her sweet face flushed from the heat of the oven, asked if she would feed the children. Bridie said of course, then put them in their high chairs, cut up some turkey, and added a dollop of mashed potatoes and a few green beans. After they had eaten all they wanted and had taken to playing with their food, she took them out of their chairs, wiped their faces and hands, and took them into the bare little sitting room.

She played shape sorter with the boy, Cameron. He was big-eyed and missed nothing but didn't speak. Bonnie, the little girl, jabbered like a magpie. Bridie helped Lorna change the babies' diapers and put them into their cribs for a nap. Then they washed up, and Lorna called the others to dinner. The older girl, who was her reason for coming, finally appeared then, trundling down the stairs. She was older than Bridie had thought at first, though it could have been all the makeup she was wearing that created the impression. She was going through a growth spurt most likely, looking a little too tall for her clothes. She wore a black skirt and a long-sleeved black sweater. Her hair was long, curly, and a golden brown. She had a pretty, delicate face, but her eyes looked hollow and tired, like a soldier who'd been on the battlefield too long and seen things no one should see.

"Shall we sit?" Lorna asked, flustered.

Bridie smiled and nodded, followed the line to the table. It was no wonder Lorna had taken to bringing in outsiders to cheer things up. Fiona and Winifred's husbands hardly said a word, just sort of hovered around, reminding her of how people acted after a funeral, like folks who don't quite know what's expected of them.

She stood awkwardly while the sisters had another discussion about seating. Apparently Lorna's idea of putting her between the reverend and Samantha wasn't suiting everybody.

"Calvin is left-handed, Lorna," Winifred said with barely contained irritation. "You know he has to sit on the end."

Bridie inspected the dining room while they argued. It was dark and dim in here, too. The smell of the food and the pretty dishes on the damask tablecloth made a spot of cheer, but all in all, it was but a drop in the river. The bulbs in the lights gleamed low and yellow, as if they were depressed, too weary to shine very brightly. The windows were covered with heavy curtains. It was a shame, for the house could have been beautiful with a lighter hand. The floor under her feet was shiny hardwood, and the woodwork that surrounded all the doors and windows was polished mahogany. But the walls were covered with a drab wallpaper. Bridie squinted and made out small daisies on a faded orange background.

The reverend cleared his throat and the sisters stopped arguing. Bodies shuffled behind chairs. Calvin took the end seat. She took the next one, and Samantha took the place to her right.

"Shall we pray?" the reverend asked, his voice deep and resonant. "Father, we thank you for all your good gifts," he said, and Bridie took the opportunity to inspect him. He was a big man and tall. His clothes were well cut, and he was perfectly groomed. He would be handsome if he learned how to smile.

"Amen," he said when the prayer was finished.

"Amen," she murmured with the others. They all sat down and began passing food around.

She took some of everything, then handed the bowls and platters to Samantha. She made a few attempts at conversation.

"Where do you go to school? What grade are you in?" Samantha gave monosyllabic replies, and Bridie wished she could ask what was really on her mind. *Why are you so sad, little girl? Who has done this to you, and why?*

"Please help me," Samantha's note had said.

I'm here, she wanted to answer. *Just tell me what to do.*

But Samantha just kept her eyes on her plate, her voice expressionless, and after a moment or two Bridie saw the ridiculousness of her mission.

Who did she think she was, after all? She almost laughed out loud at the absurdity of it all. She, Mary Bridget Washburn, who would be sitting in prison right now if the truth were known, was here to save somebody. She gave a little disgusted shake of her head and focused back on the dinnertime conversation that was spurting and halting around her like a car running out of gas.

"Where are you from, Miss—er, Collins?" Reverend MacPherson asked her, taking off his glasses and rubbing his eyes. He set his glasses on the sideboard, and she couldn't help wondering if he would be looking for them later. He looked at her, and she noticed his eyes. They were dark smoky blue. As if he'd read her mind he looked deliberately at the sideboard, picked up his glasses, and put them back on.

"Charlotte, North Carolina," she lied, picking a place she had visited enough to fib about intelligently.

"Ah." He nodded and gave her a relaxing of his features that passed for a smile. "Lovely country. Do you still have family there?"

"My grandmother," she said, again telling a partial truth. "She's all the family I have left in the area. My mother passed away." And Bridie might have imagined it, but some little wave of emotion went all around the table, fluttered across each face, but then was taken back in just as quickly as it had appeared.

"Oh," Lorna murmured sympathetically. "How old were you?"

"Sixteen," she answered.

"And your father?" Lorna asked.

"I don't know where he is," Bridie said, which was the truth.

There was an awkward pause.

"How long have you been coming to our fellowship?" the reverend asked, smoothly moving the subject toward safer ground.

"This morning was my first visit." She didn't count the times she'd come there alone to sit and think. That wasn't what he meant.

"I hope you'll come again and let us know if we can be of service in any way," he invited.

"Thank you," she answered, not intending to darken the door again, but she had to admit he seemed sincere.

She felt a flash of shame that she'd had the man already tried and convicted, thinking that whatever ailed the child was the fault of the father. But now that she was looking close up, she wasn't sure. It seemed more likely that whatever was ailing the child was ailing the father also, though she wasn't sure what had led her to that conclusion. It couldn't be his clothes, for they were perfectly appointed. Dark suit, white shirt heavy with starch, crease in his pants so sharp it could cut. His face was cleanly shaven, his hair neatly barbered and combed. Only two things about him were less than perfect. There was one little piece of hair that didn't want to stay with the others. It kept falling down onto his forehead. And the fingers of his right hand were stained with ink.

So what made her think he was ailing? Perhaps it was his mood. He seemed dark under his calm. She wondered if that had anything to do with the fact that there was no Mrs. Alasdair MacPherson.

She looked around and watched everyone eat, since that seemed to be the end of the conversation. The sisters all took tiny, precise bites and rearranged what was left of their food after each one, tidying it up into neat little mounds, lining up all the stray pieces of turkey, making a nice little square of the mashed potatoes and dressing, bringing stray green beans back into the fold. The reverend didn't do that. He ate neatly and quickly, but as if he didn't taste a thing. His mind seemed to be on someone or something else far away.

Bridie knew she had lovely table manners. Lord knows, she'd had it drilled into her. Sit up straight. Use your proper fork. Take little bites. Chew with your mouth closed like a lady. Just because you're from the country doesn't mean you have to act like a bumpkin. She took a small sip of her water, used the salad fork to spear a piece of lettuce, broke off a small piece of her roll, buttered and ate it.

Finally the meal was over. The reverend excused himself and went to his study. The sisters gathered up their things, leaving Lorna to do the dishes.

"The sitter you interviewed turned down the job," Winifred said. "I might have guessed." She seemed unable to leave before she delivered one more jab at Lorna.

"I'll see if I can find someone else," Lorna murmured.

"Well, you'll have to do it without my help. I won't be about much in the next few weeks. I have the Christmas bazaar and then my bunion surgery."

Lorna nodded, and Bridie thought she saw a flicker of relief cross her face.

"Nor will I," Fiona added, sounding concerned. "My appointment schedule is full with students who have just woken up to the fact that they're failing."

"That's all right," Lorna told both of them. "I can see to things here."

They left after Winifred shot Fiona a barely disguised look of disbelief at her statement.

Lorna refused Bridie's help with the dishes, but insisted that she take home some of the leftovers. Samantha was sitting in front of the television in that dreary little sitting room off the kitchen, and Bridie made one last attempt to connect with her while she waited for Lorna to finish packing up her food.

She sat down beside her, debating different approaches. She could always tell the truth. *I saw you in the church,* she could say. *I read your note.* No. Too direct. Any kid would draw back from that like a turtle being poked with a sharp stick.

Maybe she could invite Samantha out for a Coke and get to know her a little at a time. Yes, she decided. That was the best option. Get her away from home. Show some interest and see where the conversation led, and she was just getting ready to do that when Samantha turned toward her.

"So are you a social reject?" Samantha asked, her brown eyes looking amazingly cold.

Bridie laughed in spite of herself, but Samantha didn't even smile. "The reason I ask," she continued, "is that usually the people my aunt invites over are social rejects who don't have any friends."

Bridie felt a stab of pain. Ridiculous, she knew, to let an unhappy teenager get to her. "I suppose I am a social reject," she admitted.

Samantha raised her shoulder in a shrug as if to say she'd expected as much. "By the time somebody ends up here, they're pretty messed up," she said, not taking her eyes off the television. "This is the end of the line."

Bridie stared at her, trying to think of what to say to that. She suddenly felt ridiculous. Stupid, out of place. What had she been thinking to come here today?

"Here you are, Bridie." Lorna came toward her, carrying a sack. "I'm so happy you came," she said, beaming.

Bridie gave her a smile back, the best she could muster. "Good-bye, Samantha," she said. "It was nice meeting you."

"Yeah." Samantha didn't look at her, just pushed the button on the remote.

"Samantha," Lorna murmured, but Bridie took the sack from her and interrupted the awkward moment.

"Thank you for the lovely dinner. I'll look for you next week at the store."

They chatted their way to the door, and finally Bridie was outside where she could breathe again. Funny. She had felt like a prisoner at other times in her life, and the feeling had returned as soon as she'd stepped through the doorway of that depressing house. She almost felt lighthearted to be leaving. She felt a small stirring of guilt, an echo of accusation. *You came to help the child,* it said. *You haven't done that.*

I've done the best I could, she answered herself, though she knew that particular excuse was wearing thin.

Not a sparrow falls, but your father in heaven sees, she remembered. Well then, she smarted back, He was going to have to look after this one himself. She hitched her purse up higher on her shoulder and headed toward the bus stop; then she turned and looked back one more time. She thought she glimpsed a flickering movement in the drapes by the door. Or had she? Yes, there it was again, and for just a second she glimpsed Samantha's white, thin face framed in the window, watching her walk away.

≳ *nine* ≳

ONE MORE TIME AROUND. JONAH paced off the exercise yard for the one thousand six hundred twenty-seventh time since he'd arrived here. It was one of his hobbies, keeping track of things. It kept him from going crazy in this world of concrete block and asphalt. He stepped forward, each foot taking the same measured stride. He paced exactly one hundred fifty feet, then raised his head and looked out past the double-wire, razor-ribbon fence at the license plate factory. A square of gray concrete. Not much of a view, but looking out across the landscape was better than looking down at blacktop and cigarette butts. He turned left and began walking again. One hundred fifty feet. He cast his eyes to the flat hospital building where he had spent twenty days in the psych ward tied to his bed like a trussed hog while the meth left his system, then was twelve-stepped nearly to death for months after that. He turned left and began walking again. Took one hundred fifty more measured steps. Lifted his head, and there was the solitary confinement unit. He turned left again, took another hundred fifty steps. Looked across the landscape in that direction, but there was nothing to see but thirty acres of scrub grass and razor wire. Jonah gazed at it hungrily, sniffing the air like his old hunting hound used to do. If he could keep going in that direction, he would eventually find the hills he longed for, dappled canopies of maple and oak and pine, spongy carpets of leaves and needles.

"Porter." The guard called out Jonah's name in a bored monotone.

Jonah turned.

"Lawyer," he said, jerking his head toward the door.

Jonah nodded and felt a surge of jitters. His lawyer made the trip to see him only when she had to, so she wouldn't have come just to bring him the file he wanted to see. She must have some news for him. Not that he gave lawyers any credit. But even a blind pig found an acorn now and then.

He accompanied the guard through the locked doors and waited while the signal was given. The locks electronically released, the doors slid open and shut again behind him. He counted his steps down the corridor automatically, noticing each stride measured exactly three squares of linoleum. Eighty-seven steps and he was at the visitors' center. He'd only had one visitor. His mama. She'd covered her mouth when she'd seen him, then wept. He'd asked her not to come back.

"You're jumpy today." The guard patted him down, frowning.

Jonah didn't answer. The stuff he got in here was barely enough to take the edge off. The guard finished his search and passed him through. Jonah went into the little room where he met with his attorney. She was in there waiting, a bony little woman. A black woman. Court appointed. Almost worse than no lawyer at all. He sat down in the green plastic chair and scooted it up to the table. The guard locked the door.

"Mr. Porter," she greeted him.

He nodded.

"How are you faring?"

He stared at her for a minute, not answering. "How am I faring?" he finally repeated. She killed him. She just killed him. Probably went to law school on some welfare program, and here she was dressed up in a business suit, with her leather briefcase and cell phone, asking him how he was faring.

"Oh, I'm faring well," he answered her. "They treat me real good here. I'm waited on from morning to night, don't have to do a thing for myself. I get a wake-up call every morning. I have breakfast served to me. The state even gives me a free lunch. I have complete recreational facilities, which I was just enjoying when your visit interrupted me. I'll probably finish up here just in time to be served my supper, then I'll spend a delightful few hours visiting with my companions in the dormitory until the lights are turned out for us at midnight. Oh, I'm faring very well. Thank you for asking."

His attorney stared at him for a moment. She looked as if she might smile. He decided to wipe it off her face.

"I don't want to be your friend. I don't want any colored friends," he said, just to be mean, and sure enough, the smile faded. "Why don't you forget about being friends and just do your job. Did you bring my file like I asked?"

She was silent for a minute, gave him a little stare, then took a folder from her briefcase. She handed it to him. "You can look at it while I'm here. And this, too." She set down another file and smiled, just as if he hadn't insulted her at all. "This is the brief I filed for your appeal."

"How long until they decide?"

She shrugged. "They do things on their own schedule."

He felt a surge of anger. "If they overturn my conviction, how long after that would I be released?"

"If they order a new trial, your case will be remanded back to Nelson County and a date set at that time. It's a lengthy process. Your best hope is that the Commonwealth's attorney might cut you a deal rather than go to trial again. Then it's possible you'd be released immediately with credit for time served."

"That's fine," he said. He ignored the brief and pulled the other file toward him. The search had been bogus. Even a no-account, state-appointed lawyer had been able to see that. He opened the jacket and shuffled through the papers until he found the police report. There it was. He scanned it until he found the part he was looking for.

Officers dispatched following 9-1-1 call from female. Transcript below.

He read the transcript. It was pure Mary B. Sweet, polite, and cutting right to the throat. She'd given them everything. Names, locations, amount of business done, even the directions to the place. His jaw clenched. He shut the folder and passed it back to his lawyer. She took it from him and put it back in her briefcase. Jonah called for the guard and rose to leave.

"Oh, Mr. Porter . . ."

He turned back. His lawyer had a silly little smirk on her face.

"One of the appeals court justices who'll be deciding your fate is African American."

He didn't answer, just turned away. He waited while the guard buzzed open the door, then headed back toward his cell. Let her have her little laugh. Black, white, yellow, green—he didn't care what color the judges were as long as they let him out of here. He didn't waste his anger on stupid things.

He went back to his cell, went to supper, went back to his cell, and waited for things to settle down inside him. They didn't. He felt stirred up, his insides churning and hot. He had been prepared to find out for certain that Mary Bridget had turned him in. He hadn't been prepared for the fact that he would feel something about that.

He lay down on the bed and did something he almost never did. Went someplace he almost never visited anymore. He took a little journey back in time. Back to the past. He could see it, smell it, taste it, hear the voices of folks he hadn't seen in years.

He had known Mary Bridget Washburn all his life. He had been seven when she was born, and he remembered watching her grow up from a towheaded little girl to a beautiful woman.

And he remembered the day that had changed everything. It was after Uncle Joshua had died. He'd headed down the road and knocked on her back door, rain dripping off his head, soaked clear to the bone. His life was bad, and he knew for a fact that hers wasn't much better.

She had thrown open the door, and he could still see her perfectly before him, wearing blue jeans and a white cotton shirt that wasn't tucked in, a pair of tennis shoes without any socks. He smelled something stewing—a chicken, maybe. That and the stench of stale whiskey rolled out at him. She'd been crying. There was a red welt on her cheek, and Jonah felt his hands clench and his collar grow tight as the scene replayed itself.

"Where is he?" he'd growled.

"In jail," she'd said and then burst into full heartbreak. He had gathered her to his chest, and even now he felt if he reached down, his shirt would be damp from her tears, that if he opened his callused hand, he would feel her silky head underneath it.

"They took the children," she'd sobbed. "The welfare people came and took them off."

"You come with me," he had whispered. "We'll get away from here."

She'd said no, that she was going to try to get custody, so he'd trudged on back up the mountain. But it wasn't too long before she'd shown up on his doorstep, that green duffel in her hand.

"They're gone," she had said with a tone he hadn't heard before—hard and angry. They'd left that day, neither one of them looking back. They joined up with some fellows Jonah knew, mostly just to have a place to crash, but it wasn't long before they were cooking a little candy to sell, and after that it seemed like there weren't any more choices. Like the only ones that mattered had been made a long time ago, and not by either of them.

Jonah felt his chest harden up again, and suddenly he was going to scream if he sat still one more minute. His arms itched. His face itched, even his eyeballs itched. He needed something. He got up and paced around the cell some more.

He wondered for the hundredth, the thousandth time, what she had done with the money. He knew she hadn't spent it. Oh, a little maybe, but he had no doubt that most of it was still in that green duffel, and as careful as she was with things, it was hidden somewhere. Knowing her, it would be somewhere close to home. He pictured her old granny's house. She'd probably put it somewhere around there. In that old hollow where she used to play or in one of her grandpa's empty bee stands. Maybe in the old springhouse down by the creek or tucked behind a pile of rocks.

Didn't matter. She'd tell him herself. And soon. He would make sure of that. He smiled at the fact that her betrayal of him would be his ticket to freedom—the fact that they'd based their search on an anonymous tip.

It gave him a hard, bitter satisfaction, and suddenly he felt angry with himself for covering those back roads, going down the trails of memory that took him nowhere, accomplished nothing useful. He reminded himself that he didn't waste time on regrets and he didn't waste time feeling sorry for himself. He didn't waste time feeling sorry for anything. He took a deep breath, and when he released it, he was back to feeling like himself again. Everything solid, firmed up, and where it belonged. He would get out of here soon.

Then he had four things to do, no more, no less, and in specific order. Walk into Boo's Tavern and have a cold beer, a T-bone steak, baked potato, and all the trimmings. Spend a nice evening with Connie, the barmaid. Get high. And find Mary Bridget Washburn. Thinking about her this time gave him no warm memories. In fact, he felt nothing at all.

⁊ ten ⁊

"WHAT DO YOU MEAN YOU can't take them?" Alasdair fought to keep his voice reasonable.

"I mean, they're obviously sick." The day-care attendant crossed her arms and looked annoyed. "I'm surprised you aren't more concerned about their welfare."

Alasdair didn't bother to explain that this was the tail end of their illness. He just gathered them up and put them back in the car. He would have to call and cancel everything when he got home. He would try to work in his telephone calls around naps. His head throbbed, and he snatched off his glasses and tossed them on the seat beside him.

He drove the short distance to his home and parked the car in the garage. By the time he got the children into the house, the telephone was ringing. Of course. Let's see, today was Monday. Monday's calls were the sermon complaints and clarifications. On Wednesday it would be the inevitable last-minute requests to fill in for someone who had a duty at Wednesday service. The same on Friday. Saturday's calls were about the announcements. And always, every day, the calls from those who were just unhappy and needing a listening ear or a scapegoat. Alasdair heaved a huge sigh. He let this particular call go to the machine and listened to the message while he took the twins' jackets off.

"Pastor, it's Ellen Smith."

He was glad he hadn't answered. He knew what the church treasurer wanted.

"Could you hold off from cashing your paycheck for a day? I'm going to have to transfer some money, and I can't get to the bank until this afternoon." He gave his head a shake. Another neck-and-neck race between income and expenditure. It was ridiculous. That's what it was. He didn't believe for a minute that the money wasn't there. But the congregation was unhappy with him, and therein lay the rub. He burned with anger at the fact that the church could be controlled with one small gesture, the collective closing of the wallet.

He put the twins in their playpen and went to make his calls. Fortunately his sermon outline for next week was nearly complete, and his column for *Sound Doctrine* was ready to be mailed. He canceled a counseling appointment and called the producer of his radio program. "I'm ill," he said, admitting the truth.

"I think I can cover it," the producer said. "At least for a while."

He took down his notebook and began scanning the notes for this week's sermon. The telephone rang again. The babies began to fuss. He checked his watch. It was much too soon for naps.

"Yes." The terse greeting was all he could manage.

"Pastor—" He recognized the no-nonsense tones of Margaret Beeson, a longtime member. "I was just going over my notes from Sunday, and I find myself concerned about a quote you used in your sermon. It was from *Mere Christianity*, by C. S. Lewis."

"Mm." Alasdair made a noncommittal noise and wished he hadn't picked up.

"Are you aware Lewis was not a Calvinist? He was distinctly Arminian in theology."

"I'm aware of it. In nonessential doctrines, charity and tolerance of divergent views should be the rule."

"I hardly call the doctrine of salvation nonessential. Was he a pre- or a post-Millennialist?"

"I'm afraid I don't know. Why don't you put your concerns in writing and mail them to me," he suggested, trying to keep his tone mild. "I'll consider them in detail."

He hung up and rubbed his temples. Anyone's opinion about the timing of the return of Christ to earth, whether before or after the thousand-year reign of peace, seemed entirely irrelevant to anything that was happening of real importance in his life. His only thought on the subject was a burning wish that it might be today.

Bonnie wailed, and Cameron joined in. Alasdair's head began to hurt in earnest, and he became aware of an uneasy sensation in the pit of his stomach. He knew he should go to the babies, but instead he went to the couch and sat staring at the wall in front of him.

Perhaps he should resign his church. Take Gerald Whiteman's offer and end the misery.

The thought shocked him, but there it was, demanding to be recognized and considered. Immediately Anna's face appeared before him in imagination. He felt a stab of some strong emotion. It was ironic that he would consider resigning now that she was gone, when he had resisted it so steadfastly while she was alive.

"It's the highest calling in life." It was his father who spoke now, and Alasdair saw him, florid and intense, gesturing and expounding. *"It's your pulpit. Take charge of it, and don't let anyone turn you aside. No one,"* he had repeated often, as if he somehow had overheard the conversations, the whispered pleas that were made behind the closed bedroom door. No. He would not quit. Not after he had sacrificed so much to keep going.

Cameron's voice took on the shrill vibrato that meant he was reaching the end of his rope. And Alasdair's own head was pounding, his pulse skittish and racing. He hacked a cough every few moments, and his stomach had begun to churn and twist in earnest. He was hot and cold, then hot again.

He would feed the children. They were probably getting hungry. He stood in the middle of the kitchen floor and felt his stomach roil and heave, but he finally managed to put together a meal for them. Afterward, he changed their diapers and put them down for their naps, then lay down himself.

The telephone woke him at three-fifteen. Oh no. He was late for picking up Samantha.

Sure enough, it was Lorna, calling from the school. "Alasdair, is Samantha sick, too?" Alasdair frowned and put a hand on the counter to steady himself. His head felt light, and he was dizzy.

"She's feeling fine as far as I know. Why do you ask?" His pulse began to speed even faster.

There was a pause. "She wasn't here today. I assumed she was ill."

"Samantha wasn't at school today?"

"No, she wasn't."

"I left her off this morning." He sighed. "She must be cutting class."

"Wouldn't she have come back by three to be picked up if she were cutting class?" Lorna pointed out.

Alasdair's skin grew cold, and his heart began to race even faster than it had from his fever. "I'll give her another hour," he said. "Then I'm calling the police."

It was busy, then slow, busy, then slow, all afternoon. Bridie had cleaned all around her check-out stand, tidied up the photo and sound display, even got out the Windex and cleaned the doors. She waited on one lone customer, a little lady with four cans of cat food, then looked for something else to do.

Winslow solved her problem for her. "Go on back there and clean up the dairy case," the manager told her. "Somebody spilled a gallon of milk."

Bridie bristled. She thought about telling Winslow that was a job for one of the courtesy clerks, but even as the words formed in her mind, she could hear her grandmother's voice. *"If the Lord of glory left heaven and came to earth, then you can surely pick the beans,"* or clean the toilet, or whatever it was Grandma had in mind for her to do. She smiled, closed her check-out stand, and headed for the dairy case.

It was the worst job of shoplifting Bridie had ever seen. For one thing, the culprit was dressed all wrong. Her outfit was too skimpy, and the bottle of whatever she had was clearly outlined under her shirt, no matter how she tried to shield it with her arms. Plus, she darted around like she was hiding from enemy fire. Right now, for instance, she was hovering behind the end-cap display, peering past the stack of pork and beans like she was waiting for the gunfire to slack off before she made a break for it.

Bridie came up behind her. "Go ahead. I'll cover you," she whispered.

The girl whipped around, dropping the bottle. Dark glass flew across the aisle, and burgundy liquid splashed everywhere. Cabernet Sauvignon, not MD 20/20 or Boone's Farm like most kids took. Bridie looked up from her tennis shoes, now sporting pink polka dots. The stunned face looking back at her was growing increasingly familiar. She stared at the girl for a minute, then gave her head a little shake.

"I keep running into you."

Samantha stared back, eyes huge, tears pooling.

"What's going on here?" It was Winslow, skidding to a stop, nostrils flaring, cheeks a healthy flush. The manager could sniff out a shoplifter faster than a bloodhound and was vicious when he caught them. "I prosecute to the full extent of the law," he was fond of saying, and then would go on and on about how he was really doing the kids a favor. "Well?" He was almost panting, he was so excited.

Bridie put on a smile. "Just a spill."

Winslow wasn't going to be put off that easily. "No, sir. I don't believe so. A young girl like this wouldn't be buying a bottle of wine, and what was she doing with it if she wasn't going to buy it? No, sir. She spilled it because she was stealing it."

Samantha's tears spilled over and started rolling down her cheeks. A child's cheeks, Bridie realized, looking at her. Just a child.

"Who said *she* spilled it?" She turned toward Winslow and looked him full in the face. His already flushed cheeks turned a darker shade of red.

"Are you telling me she didn't?"

Bridie hesitated just a bare second. "That's exactly what I'm telling you. I'm the one who had the wine. She came around the corner too fast, and it went flying."

Samantha's tears stopped flowing. She sniffed and waited to see what would happen. Her eye makeup was slowly following the course of the liquid, making tarry pools under her lower lashes. Bridie had to hold back a smile.

"I don't believe it," Winslow said. His voice was flat, and his eyes bored mean little holes into Bridie's lie.

But instead of feeling ashamed, she felt angry. Why couldn't Winslow, just for once, leave it alone? But no, he always had to push everyone to their very last inch of nerve and then jump up and down on it.

Bridie crossed her arms and glared right back.

"Let's just see," he said.

Bridie frowned; then realization hit her like a cold wind in the face. What had she been thinking? The security cameras would have it all on tape.

"Let's just go push Rewind and see what we've got."

Her gut twisted as if somebody had tightened a noose around it, but she nodded. "Fine," she said. "Let's go see." Bluffing again as she had with Jonah that night long ago when he'd shined the light in her eyes. But Winslow was not strung out on meth. Whatever brain cells he had were clicking along right on track, maybe one well-worn, narrow track, but they were making good time. She glanced at Samantha, who was back to flood stage.

"Let's just go see," he said, ordering more than inviting, and gestured for them to lead the way. Bridie held her head up high and swept through produce, past the line of check-out stands. Her co-workers watched them pass, some curious, some with knowing expressions on their faces. They'd seen this drama play out many times before. Carmen's mouth was open, and before Bridie's eyes, her face transformed from surprised to outraged.

"What's going on here?" she called out.

"I got me some shoplifters, that's what's going on," Winslow shot back.

Carmen's eyes narrowed and her lips tightened. She drew her cell phone from its holster and began firing numbers. Winslow led the march into the office and began fiddling with the security camera. Bridie's thoughts were racing. If he called the police, everything would come unstrung. Her identification would probably not stand a close inspection, and then what would happen? She knew Jonah better than to think he had flipped and given her up. As long as he thought she had his money, he wouldn't be telling any tales on her, but there was no telling what Dwayne had said. If they found her real identity, they might also find a warrant for her arrest. Dread overtook her. The life she'd so carefully constructed turned dark around her and began to close over her head. The opening above her that let in light and air was growing smaller and smaller. She found herself breathing in little gasps as if she really couldn't catch her breath.

Samantha looked at her, obviously worried. Bridie was afraid she might be sick. Winslow was oblivious. He had the tape cued to where he wanted it.

"Let's just see," he said and pushed Play.

There they were in grainy black and white. Bridie could see the tip of her leg in the far right-hand corner of the screen, just finishing up her cleaning of the dairy case. In the foreground was Samantha, teetering on those high heels, looking behind her, guilty face turning this way and that, looking for witnesses before she reached up, took a bottle of wine from the shelf, then thrust it up under her shirt. Bridie watched, hypnotized, as she saw herself straighten up, dust off her hands, turn, and spot Samantha. Now she was coming toward her. Oops. There went the bottle. Now she and Samantha were talking. Here came Winslow. It was surreal. Now the three of them were talking, replaying the moments before. Winslow gestured toward the office, and then one by one they disappeared from view. The last scenes were of the wine and beer aisle, empty now except for the spattered mess of glass and dark liquid. Winslow turned, triumphant.

"I've got the proof," he said. "Right here. The two of y'all on tape. You been in cahoots for a while? What? Bridie looks out and gives you the high sign, and then you come in and rob me blind?"

Bridie said nothing. She was going down. Down. And no one could help her.

"You've got proof I was stealing. And that's true. I was."

Shock opened Bridie's eyes. Samantha spoke, her voice bold and clear. Her cheeks were pale and her eyes still ringed, but she didn't look frightened anymore.

"You've got me on tape, but that's all you've got. She wasn't my lookout. She was busting me."

Bridie blinked. Samantha stared back at her. Winslow narrowed his little beady black marbles and twisted his mouth into a satisfied smile. "Is that why she lied for you when I caught you red-handed?"

There didn't seem to be an answer for that. Bridie heard her grandmother's voice, cautioning her that lying never solved a problem, only took a bad situation and made it worse. She closed her eyes again.

"Is there a problem here?" A new voice entered the mix. Bridie felt light-headed. She reached for the chair and sat down before her knees buckled.

"Carmen called and said you were having some difficulty. I was close by and thought I'd see if I could be of service." Bridie shaded her eyes from Newlee's gaze, but when she peered through her fingers she could see his face was kind, not accusing. Samantha, apparently seeing she might be staying awhile, pulled out a chair as well.

"Why don't we all sit down?" Newlee suggested, smiling. He pulled out a chair, too, and sat down with the creak of leather. Winslow looked as if he might have apoplexy. He remained standing and began punching at the security camera, rewinding the tape. "The problem is this young lady stole from me with the help of my employee," Winslow said. "I was just fixing to call you."

"How old are you, miss?" Newlee addressed the question to Samantha. She blanched. Apparently just being spoken to by an officer of the law was enough to shake her composure.

"Thirteen." Her voice quivered. She looked more like a child than ever, no matter how much makeup she clumped around her eyes.

Newlee nodded and pulled a notebook from his pocket. "What's your name?"

Samantha cleared her throat. "Samantha MacPherson."

Newlee wrote. "Address?"

"Nine-twenty Fairfax Street."

Newlee wrote more.

"Telephone?"

Samantha answered. Newlee wrote.

"Parents home?"

"My dad—" Samantha cleared her throat and her eyes spilled again. The tarry puddles moved south, led by a dark trickle. "My dad's probably home." She made a sound that was halfway between a hiccup and a sob.

Newlee nodded and looked up. Winslow was ready with the tape.

"Right here. You just watch, officer. Here we go." He pushed Play and the tawdry little scene enacted itself again, and suddenly it seemed as if Bridie's entire life was like that. The same scene played out over and over again. Never a break, never a variation. Doing all right for a while, then a fork in the road presented itself, and without fail, without a doubt, without variation, she chose the wrong one. She covered her eyes again.

"I see," Newlee said, voice calm. "Looks like somebody got caught in the act."

"Darned right," Winslow crowed.

Bridie shut her eyes even tighter. Samantha's noises were definitely leaning toward sobs.

"And one of my own employees lied to cover it up," Winslow continued. "I think the two of them's in cahoots."

"We are not." Samantha spoke again, her voice adamant in spite of her distress. "She didn't know anything about it."

Winslow started to argue back, but Newlee held up his hand to stop him. "I think you'd have a hard time making that accusation stick," Newlee said. "From what I see on the tape there's no reason to think your employee was involved in any way. I suggest you let her go back to work. I'll take a report and escort this young lady back home."

Bridie held her breath. Maybe, maybe, maybe things would work out after all.

"No, no, no." Winslow was shaking his head. Samantha's sobs got a little louder. She was probably having visions of herself, prison pale in an orange jumpsuit and leg shackles. "You go on and take *her*,"

Winslow said, nodding toward Samantha. "I was fixing to call you anyway. But I'll deal with Miss Collins here."

Bridie dropped her hand from her eyes and sat up. There was no hiding from reality any longer. "I'll spare you the trouble," she said, rising.

"Oh no you don't." Winslow barred the door with his body. "You're not going to quit before I can fire you."

"Am I under arrest?" Bridie looked toward Newlee for an answer. He shook his head, his eyes looking troubled.

"Then I'll get my things," she said to Winslow. "You can write whatever you want on my paperwork."

"You bet I will. Nobody else will hire you after I finish."

"I'll give you a ride home," Newlee said.

"That's all right," Bridie protested. The last thing she wanted was an intimate conversation with Newlee.

"I insist."

She looked at him. He looked back at her. Samantha's sobs slowed. Her head bobbed between the two of them like she was watching a tennis match.

"Sure," Bridie agreed, making her voice easy. "Let me get the stuff from my locker. I'll be down in a second."

Winslow gave Newlee a malicious look and moved reluctantly away from the door.

"Take your time," Newlee said and creaked back down into his chair.

Lorna arrived just as the police were pulling up in front of the parsonage. She came through the doorway first, her eyes already red from crying.

"Oh, Alasdair." She clung to his arm. "Maybe she's just playing hooky."

"Maybe," he said, gripping her hand. "Calling the police is probably an overreaction." The twins were wailing from their cribs upstairs. He'd been sick once while he was waiting for the police and felt as if he might be again. The room swayed slightly, and when he closed his eyes it spun. A dark little figure huddled in the basement of his psyche, whispering evil. He'd failed his daughter in some elemental way. He'd known that for months, years, perhaps, and now she was alone in the world, long before she was able to negotiate it safely. He had failed her. The realization hit him like a vicious stab through the diaphragm.

The policeman arrived at the door and came into the hallway. As he began asking questions, Alasdair was transported back to another time when he'd answered those same sorts of questions. *"Did she seem upset when she left?" "Do you know where she was going?" "Who saw her last?"*

"Do you have a current picture?" the policeman asked him now.

Alasdair's inner screen was showing its own pictures, too awful to bear. He coughed and began shivering.

"I'll find one," Lorna said through her tears.

The knocker rapped. He and Lorna both bolted for the door, and Alasdair felt if it was someone from the congregation with some niggling complaint, he might knock them to the ground. He flung it open, and his relief was so great it rushed through him like a surge of heat. It was Samantha, with another policeman following close behind her and a woman behind him. He didn't speak a word, just gathered her into his arms and nearly crushed her.

"What were you thinking?" he demanded, pushing her to arm's length so he could look at her, hearing his voice, hoarse and loud.

Samantha began crying. Again. Her makeup was already smeared, her nose red. He wanted to stop shouting, to comfort her, but all the emotion he'd felt as illness and guilt, panic and anxiety, were finding their way out through this tunnel of anger.

"Alasdair," Lorna murmured.

"What were you thinking?" he shouted again, his hands still on her shoulders. "Where were you?"

"At the Bag and Save," she said through her sobs.

"There was a little problem." The new policeman spoke,

nodding to his comrade. They stepped away and began a murmured conversation.

Alasdair let go of Samantha. She took a step back. He shook his head. None of it made any sense. That fact joined the rest of his existence. Every day was beginning to have the same feeling. As though some cosmic mind took joy in dumping a handful of random puzzle pieces onto his head. "Here, see what you can make of these." Blasphemy, he knew, but there it was. The truth of how he felt.

"Why were you at the Bag and Save?" He had visions of Samantha dawdling at the candy counter, looking at comic books, the things children do when they run off from school.

Samantha ducked her head. The second policeman stepped forward. "Your daughter was caught shoplifting—a bottle of wine."

Alasdair's stomach did a flip, and he wondered if he would be sick again right there in the hallway.

Samantha lifted her face to him. It was sad and bleak and perfectly matched his own feelings. "Go to your room," he said. She turned and left, silent the stairs for once.

The babies were screaming. He stood and stared at the wall behind the policemen, who were having another huddle. Lorna went upstairs to see to the children. The woman who'd been standing behind her came into view. She looked very familiar, but he couldn't seem to place her.

"Sir, I think we're finished here." The first policeman spoke. "We won't fill out a report on this unless the store manager insists."

"I'll handle the situation," Alasdair said. "She'll be punished."

"Is that your solution?" the woman asked sharply.

Alasdair turned toward her. "Do I know you?"

The two policemen shifted their weight. Lorna came back down with a child on each hip. The woman who had spoken held out her arms to Cameron. He went to her, shuddering with sobs, and buried his runny nose in her hair. The woman nuzzled his neck and began making soothing circles on his back. Alasdair remembered her now. She'd been a guest for a meal. Thanksgiving dinner.

"Your daughter needs help," she said, her voice lower but her tone still iron hard. "A man of your intelligence ought to be able to see that. Punishing her isn't going to solve anything."

How are you involved in this matter? he wanted to ask her. *Why are you here?* But nausea rose just ahead of the words. He turned and left the room. When he was finished being ill, the policemen were gone and the hallway was empty. He could hear voices from the kitchen. He climbed the stairs, feeling as if each one was a journey in itself, passed Samantha's door without stopping, and lay down on his bed without even turning down the covers.

❧ *eleven* ❧

BRIDIE LAY ON HER BED and stared at the ceiling. There was no particular reason to get up. After all, she had no job. She jabbed her pillow and pulled the covers up so that just her nose was exposed. This was a fine mess she was in. Again. What was that her papa used to say whenever Mama wanted him to help somebody? No good deed will go unpunished? "You were right about that," she said out loud to the empty room.

It had been a mistake to come to Samantha's rescue. Another mistake in a lifetime of mistakes, beginning with Jonah. It had seemed like her only choice at the time, but it had only led to something worse. Then she'd thought that getting away from him would be the answer to all her problems. The one tiny little complication was that she'd decided taking his money would be a good idea, and then she'd been stupid enough to let it get stolen from under her nose. And the real insult to the injury was that for all the time she spent thinking about Jonah and Dwayne and being afraid of them, looking for them behind every bush, she might as well still be there.

The prayer she'd whispered long ago came back to mock her. *"Oh, that I had the wings of a dove! I would fly away and be at rest. I would hurry to my place of shelter, far from the tempest and storm."* She gave a snort from under the covers. No matter how many miles she tried to put between her and her past, she couldn't get away from herself. And she was getting tired of running.

What if? What if she'd never left with Jonah? What if Mama hadn't died? She'd probably be a teacher right now. That's what she'd wanted to be. She imagined herself with a classroom full of shiny-headed children looking up at her with love and affection as she taught them things—good things they would need to know. But that would never happen now. How could she march into the college and say, "Sign me up; I want to be a teacher"? No. She would never be a teacher, or a nurse, or a mother, or have anything but a no-account job and a no-account life.

She might as well go back to dealing.

The thought shocked her chattering mind into silence.

Not that it hadn't occurred to her before. But the suggestion had always been quickly dismissed, usually with a shudder. Now it presented itself as a logical option. She had no job. She had one friend— Carmen. Lorna didn't count. Church people had to be friendly.

And there would be another benefit. If she wandered back to the old haunts, she could hook up with somebody scarier and badder than Jonah was. If she made herself useful enough to him, he might make good what she owed Jonah, or more likely, run him off when he got out of prison. She had enough saved to get back to her old stomping ground. Just barely—after she paid Carmen what she owed.

She lay there another moment and weighed her choices. Go back to dealing, or get up and read the want ads. Stay, or go back to the life she'd run away from. She felt like flipping a coin. She would throw her life up in the air and see where it landed. Why not?

Getting up to find a penny seemed like too much effort. She decided to make a wager instead. With God? With whoever was listening. She sat up in bed and nodded as she reached a decision. If she found a job by the end of today, she would stay here in Alexandria until it was time to put a little more distance between her and Jonah. If she didn't find a job by the end of the day, she would wander back to the hills, make herself indispensable to somebody else's operation, and let them deal with Jonah. By the end of this day, one way or another, her fate would be decided. She stood up and felt a little better, though it was a hard, brittle better. She looked around her room through narrowed eyes.

She didn't bother to make her bed, just went to the bathroom, then padded through the apartment and took the phone off the hook. Thank goodness Carmen's door was closed tight and Newlee's car was gone. Their ride to the reverend's house had been uncomfortable, the conversation one-sided.

"Carmen's concerned about you," he had started out.

She had listened, arms folded, staring out the window, reminding herself of Samantha.

"If you're in trouble, maybe I could help," Newlee had offered, his voice concerned, too.

"Thank you," she'd answered. "I appreciate that. I really do," and for just a moment, looking at Newlee's broad, honest face, she was tempted to tell him everything. To pour it all out and let things fall where they landed. What a relief that would be. The silence had drawn out between them and finally snapped. "This is something you can't help me with," she'd finally said.

Opening the front door now, she leaned out over the landing and retrieved the paper, then closed the door quickly against the morning, which like her mood was cold and dark. She thought of Samantha and wondered how her day was shaping up. Remembering Alasdair MacPherson's stern face, she felt a stab of pity for the girl and wished again that there were something she could do to help her. The words "lost soul" formed themselves in her mind, but oddly, it was Alasdair MacPherson's face that accompanied them, not Samantha's. It ought to be her own, she told herself, and resolved to tend to her own business.

She prepared coffee and went to perform her other morning ritual. Sitting down at Carmen's computer, she booted it up and signed on, using Carmen's Internet server. With a few clicks she was on the Virginia Department of Correction's inmate locator for Jonah Porter. She did not click on the picture, just checked the release date, still comfortably far away.

The coffeemaker gurgled. The coffee was ready. She poured herself a cup and opened the want ads.

"It's true influenza." Fiona's husband, the internist, had diagnosed Alasdair after a house call last night. "Bed rest and chicken soup," he'd prescribed.

Lorna shook her head and wondered how they'd manage this new trial. She had stayed last night in the guest room to see to the babies, who still woke, crying and upset, several times a night. Like their sister and father, they seemed troubled by anxieties they couldn't name. She'd taken last night and today off, to the displeasure of both of her bosses. There was no way she could hold this fort indefinitely.

She put another handful of Cheerios on each twin's tray and checked her watch. It was almost time for Samantha to leave for school, and she hadn't heard her stir since waking her up forty minutes ago. After moving the twins to their playpen, she climbed the stairs and pushed open her door. Samantha was still in bed, an immobile lump of sheet and blanket.

"You're not ready for school." Stating the obvious bought her time to think.

"I'm not going." Samantha's voice was muffled and distant.

"Are you sick?"

Long pause. "Yes."

Lorna sighed. Closed the door. She checked on Alasdair and found him asleep. She went to the kitchen again. The twins were happy, so she let them be, poured herself a cup of coffee, and sat down to think.

She remembered sitting in this very spot weeks ago, praying for poor Alasdair, and as she might have expected, her prayers had seemed to make an already bad situation worse. Alasdair still had his ministry troubles, amplified. Samantha had jumped a notch on the rebellion scale. Now even their friends were being drawn into their web of despair—just look at poor Bridie.

Lorna stood up and went to the sink. A casserole dish from two nights ago was still soaking, the scalloped potatoes clinging in a determined, crusted ring. She plunged her hand in and retrieved the scrubber, her cheeks flushing at her presumption. She'd thought she heard God speak to her. Make promises. She shook her head. In this morning's gray light even she, queen of denial, could see the truth. Alasdair was flat on his back in the dim room upstairs, his ministries left dangerously unattended. Samantha was huddled in a depressed ball in her bed. The twins would drift through another aimless day. No, she realized. None of this could be mistaken for an answer to prayer.

Hard times come, she told herself. Nowhere does God promise to take them away. She reached into the drawer for a spoon and began slashing away at the baked-on potatoes rimming the casserole dish. She felt as if her heart had been split by a huge wedge and someone was pounding on it, determined to cleave it. Of course *her* prayer would be the one to bring down the house, to knock out the last beam that was holding the whole thing up. *Her* prayer, *her* attempts to help.

She scraped and scrubbed and there, in the gray dishwater, without wanting to, she saw the vision again—Alasdair, his face open and smiling, Samantha laughing, the twins loved and cared for. She turned the hot water on full blast as if to wash it away. *This is what I'm going to do*, she thought she'd heard. *And you may help.*

She tossed down the scrubber and braced her hands on the edge of the sink. She was hotly angry. She resisted the impulse to pick something up and break it, to fling that awful casserole dish at the wall and watch the suds and bits of potato slide down to the dingy floor.

Instead, she put away the clean dishes, made up the twins' bottles, and switched on the radio beside the sink as she wiped down the countertops. It was time for Alasdair's program. It would give her something to focus on besides these dark thoughts. The theme played, the announcer pitched the study Bible and latest book and said, "This week's programs will feature the best of MacPherson." A series of sermons he'd given at the Reformed Theological Convention ten years prior. My, they were scraping the bottom. Scraping reminded her of the dirty dish. She went back to it with the spoon. Good grief, there was enough potato to feed another person still sticking to the sides and bottom. She made a face as she dumped the soggy heap into the garbage can. The musical theme, a bagpipe number, faded away, then came the catchphrase, something culled from each day's sermon and used as a teaser. Her brother's voice boomed forth from the tiny AM/FM radio.

"Every time God gives you a promise, or gives me a promise, or whenever He shows us in our mind's eye what He intends to do, we can count on one thing. It will be tested. Almost invariably after God shows us His plan, events will conspire to make us believe it is impossible."

Lorna stood stock-still, her hands still plunged into the lukewarm dish of potatoes and soap. She felt as if a divine hand had just dangled a message in front of her face. "Yoo-hoo. Are you listening, Lorna?" Suddenly she felt ashamed and joyful at the same time. She took her hands out of the dish and dried them on a paper towel, then sat back down at the table. After a moment she bowed her head. Her brother's voice continued on, background to her conversation with God.

"It wasn't my imagination," she whispered. "I know it wasn't. You're working. It's just that Alasdair was right. For every promise of God there comes a test." She closed her eyes and waited patiently for something. For a voice to speak, a hand to move. Some reward for her insight.

Nothing happened. She opened her eyes. Everything was just as it had been. No miracles this time. No visions. She smiled and after a moment went back to the sink. Alasdair continued on with his sermon, and Lorna was transported to the past, to happier days when the passion of Alasdair's faith could still light a fire in a cold heart. She finished washing the dish and put it in the drainer, then cleaned out the sink.

When she'd finished, she sat back down at the table and took another sip of coffee, replaying again the events of the day before in spite of her renewed hope. Poor Bridie. Now she would be looking for a job.

Two facts migrated from their separate niches in her brain and introduced themselves. She went over the idea carefully. It was good. Not the answer to all her prayers, by any means, but it would solve at least two problems. She thought about calling Winifred or Fiona and asking their opinion but realized she couldn't wait to speak to them. And Alasdair was in no shape to be consulted. It was a true emergency. Decisive action was needed. It was up to her. She felt a fluttery little thrill.

She took down the telephone book and leafed through it until she found the right page. The name she sought wasn't there. She thought again, then looked up the number for the Bag and Save. She asked for the manager and introduced herself, then with fingers crossed asked for what she wanted.

"I'm only doing this because you're calling for the minister and all," the manager protested. "I can see why you'd want to have a piece of her hide. Corrupting your niece and whatnot." Lorna didn't bother to contradict him, just made appreciative noises and jotted down the information he gave her. She dialed the telephone number but got only the voice mail, time and time again. It wouldn't do to leave a message. Not for a thing like this. Her request would be too easy to refuse. She looked down at the other item she'd written on the scrap of paper—Bridie's address. She made up her mind, and after checking on Alasdair and Samantha one more time, she loaded the twins in the car and set out.

Bridie scanned the classifieds, marking some listings, but more out of a sense of duty than any real hope she would get the jobs. There were no ads for grocery checkers, and that seemed to be all she was qualified for. A knock came at the door, and involuntarily she stiffened. She went to the peephole, looked out, then stepped back, debating for a minute. The second knock made up her mind. She would rather face the person on the step than have her roommate wake up and have to deal with her questions. She slowly swung open the door.

"Hello, Lorna," she said.

Bridie listened while Lorna explained her offer. She watched the babies making a mess of Carmen's Tupperware drawer, swirled her cold coffee around in the cup, and thought awhile. "Would it involve living in?" she finally asked.

"It might on occasion."

Lorna looked worried, as if that might be the point that broke the deal. But actually, any reason to avoid Carmen and Newlee right now was welcome.

"Alasdair travels quite a bit, and in fact, I'm in a bit of a bind right now. I have a second job I can't afford to quit, and with Alasdair ill, there really should be someone there with the children at night. But as a rule, you could leave at suppertime. You'd be welcome to take all your meals with the family and use their car. You could do whatever you wanted. Act as though it was your home, your family," Lorna added. "I know the salary isn't much, but the church could add you to their medical insurance policy."

Bridie thought. It wasn't a permanent solution, but it would give her some time to think and a place to go away from Newlee and Carmen. She had said if she found a job today, she would stay. And this was a job, she realized with a flood of relief that surprised her.

"I can't make a long-term commitment," she cautioned.

"Any amount of time you can give us would be a blessing," Lorna said simply.

Bridie thought some more. The silence sat between them. "All right," she finally said. "I'll do it for a while. When do I start?"

Lorna's face relaxed into a beautiful smile. "Yesterday," she said.

⋞ twelve ⋟

TWELVE HOURS LATER BRIDIE STOOD in the reverend's kitchen and nodded dutifully at everything Lorna said. Her eyes were pointed straight at Lorna's face, but her mind was busy whirring through all the reasons she should have said no. No, no, no. N–O.

Lorna flitted around her, pointing things out. "Here are the dishes. Canned goods are here. The baby food is in the pantry there. Samantha's lunch money is here. I'll see about giving you money for groceries and household expenses. Here's a little schedule I wrote out—Samantha's school hours, naptimes, things like that." Lorna paused.

Bridie nodded again.

"I'm not overwhelming you, am I?"

"No. Not at all." She wasn't overwhelmed, because she wasn't listening. She was going over what she should have said instead of the yes that had come out of her mouth. But Lorna's eyes had looked so hopeful.

"Now, you're sure you don't mind sleeping in for a few days?" Lorna asked.

"No, I don't mind." That was the first true thing she'd said. Still, there would have been easier ways to avoid Carmen. Checking into a motel, for one. This place was a mess.

Well, not exactly a mess. It was picked up on top but felt dirty underneath. Like having things look just so was real important to somebody, but that it had been years since anybody had turned over the cushions, taken up the carpets, opened the windows, and given things a good going-over. Everything was arranged for how things looked to visitors rather than how they felt to the family.

Take, for example, the living room. It was the biggest room of the house, but did it serve any purpose? It was stuffed full of that awful furniture and pretty to look at, but uncomfortable didn't begin to describe it. She doubted a person could sit on one of those chairs for more than a minute or two without something going numb. And every inch of it was taken up with delicate antiques, every surface covered with things the children shouldn't touch. Things that appeared lovely at first glance, but on second look seemed neglected and sad. The clocks were fine old pieces, but none kept time. The silver pieces were in various stages of tarnish. The framed pictures and samplers, porcelain figurines, vases, and candlesticks were nice, but hadn't been dusted in a month of Sundays. And there was a whole lot of useless stuff, an entire collection of thimbles, for heaven's sake, another of little glass animals just begging to be broken. The dining room and even the hallways were the same way. In fact, she realized, there wasn't a place in the whole house where it was safe to let go of a child's hand.

The only room that actually looked lived in was here in the kitchen, but again, the priorities were evident. There was a tiny space, not much bigger than a good-sized closet, where they'd jammed a small couch and the children's playpen. The china cupboard in the dining room had been packed full of beautiful dishes, but here in the kitchen, where they actually ate, was just a cast-off collection of plates, bowls, and glasses that looked like a shelf at the Goodwill. And not enough of anything to set the table for all four of their little family.

"Well, I guess that's all," Lorna was finishing up. "Are you sure you'll be all right?"

Bridie nodded once more. Inside she smarted back. What could go wrong? *Reverend MacPherson is at death's door upstairs. Samantha's taken to her bed, overcome by disgracing the family. And let's see,* she thought, checking her watch, *if what you told me is true, the twins should be waking up for the first of their nightly tizzy fits in about an hour.* "I'll be fine," she said, keeping her tone warm and fighting back her choke of feelings as she escorted Lorna to the door.

"Here's my work number," Lorna told her, handing her a piece of paper.

Bridie took it and put it in her pocket. Those pieces of paper. That's how the trouble had started.

"I'll check back on you tomorrow," Lorna promised.

Bridie nodded. Lorna gave her a quick hug. The door closed.

She stood for a moment feeling the weight of the huge old house. It pressed down on her, its chill seeping into her bones. She put on her sweater, went into the kitchen, and distracted herself by emptying the dishwasher and straightening up the counters. It didn't help.

The house was full of people, she reassured herself, and then realized that was the problem. She had a feeling she wasn't alone. As if there was a presence, but cloaked to her eyes. It was an odd sensation. She stared at the empty corners, illumined by the dim lights, and saw nothing, no one. But she had the feeling that if she could adjust the fine tuning on her eyes, something would come into focus. She made a note to buy some brighter light bulbs. She checked her watch. It was nearly ten o'clock.

She finished her work in the kitchen, then locked the back door, the one that opened off the little family room adjoining the kitchen. She could see the backyard, at least the part in the arc of the porch light. The grass was stiff and white with frost. The church loomed, a dark shadow in the lot next door. She looked toward the cemetery and wondered if her odd feelings were due to the presence of some restless soul.

It is appointed unto a man once to die and thence cometh the judgment. Ain't no such a thing as ghosts," her grandma had said when she'd asked her about it once. She smiled slightly. Just thinking about her grandmother calmed her skittish nerves.

She clicked off the porch light, then continued her rounds of the house. She visited each room, ostensibly turning off lights, but really, she knew, she was checking. Just checking. Seeing for herself that all the corners were empty. She turned off the Tiffany lamps in the living room, flicked the hall light off the faces of the MacPherson forebears, an angry-looking bunch lined up on the walls, hit the dimmer switch that canceled the dining room chandelier. The front porch light she decided to leave on. She flipped the deadbolt and went upstairs.

The steps creaked under her feet. Of course they would. She peered into the room at the head of the stairs. Its door was ajar. Reverend MacPherson's study, she supposed. She didn't turn the light on or pass through the doorway, but the hall light was enough to see that all four walls were lined with books. There was a huge mahogany desk to one side which was covered with stacks of papers. There were two chairs and a small table opposite the desk and a threadbare Persian rug on the floor.

She went on to Samantha's room. The door was open a crack. She could see her hair on the pillow, the angle of her cheek.

She peeked into the babies' room. They were sleeping but huddled into tight little balls as if they were cold. The room was barely furnished. A changing table, the two cribs, and one dresser. Few toys. No decorations. As if no one had taken the time to welcome their arrival. She crept in as quietly as she could. The little boy was breathing through his mouth and she could see where he'd wiped his nose across his cheek and it had dried. Poor little thing. Poor little things. Her eyes and heart stung. She covered them up with heavy blankets and slipped back out again. Reverend MacPherson's bedroom door was tightly shut. She didn't open it.

The guest room was at the other end of the hall. It was small, but that suited her fine. The furnishings were few: a hard four-poster double bed, a mahogany dresser, a small bookshelf half filled with leaning volumes. A wardrobe whose doors didn't stay latched. The floor was scarred oak. There was no rug. Bridie unzipped her backpack and took out her pajamas, glad she'd brought flannel. She put them on and went to hang her clothes in the wardrobe. She paused, sniffing gingerly for mildew, then smiled and took a deep breath. It smelled nice—a mixture of cedar and old paper—and she was transported back to Grandma's. It was the first nice thing that had happened to her here. She hung up her clothes and took an extra blanket from the shelf. She was glad the doors didn't shut. The scent would take her home. She put the blanket on the foot of her bed, then brushed her teeth, washed her face, and searched the bookshelves for something to read, finally settling for an old copy of *Girl of the Limberlost*. She read until she felt sleepy, then turned off the light and drifted off, reassuring herself that the old house's creaks and groans were settling wood and bricks, not the cries of restless, wounded spirits. Finally she coasted into an uneasy sleep.

Something was after her, crying out and chasing her. She sat up in the bed, her heart thudding furiously, her mouth dry, her body shaking. For a moment she didn't know where she was. She stared at the open door of the wardrobe and within seconds she'd oriented herself. She was in Alexandria at the parsonage. She'd had a nightmare; that was all. She stayed still for a minute, slowed her breathing, and swallowed down her fear by telling herself it was just a dream.

She got up, still shaky, and turned on the bedroom light. The room looked odd and offbeat. Scary and creepy. She went back to the bed and sat down, forcing herself to look carefully at the things around her. There was her backpack, her clothes hanging in the wardrobe. Her shoes by the bed. The book she'd been reading. The dream began to fade, but she still felt afraid.

She looked around at the bed, the room, but the ordinary still looked shifted, and she realized it had seemed that way from the moment she'd stepped through the door of this house. As if things were tilted off their foundations just a fraction of an inch. Crooked. Half a bubble off plumb. After you'd lived here awhile, it would seem normal. Your eye would get used to it, or you would tilt your head without thinking. People wanted things to line up.

She turned on the bedside lamp, adding its light to the overhead. That helped a little, but the shadows the ordinary objects threw seemed cold and disturbing. She'd been afraid many times since childhood, of course, but of real things. Not afraid of shadows, of the dark, of dreams, and not with this creeping sense of dread.

She recited the Twenty-third Psalm a few times, stopping to repeat, "I will fear no evil, for thou art with me." After saying just those lines to herself five or six times, she felt her breathing slow to normal.

She heard a cry and startled, her heart lurching as if a heavy foot had floored it. It was only the babies, she realized, and felt a surge of relief. That's probably what had prompted the nightmare to begin with. Not some creeping spookiness, just the babies crying and the sound working itself into her dreams. She got up and made her way to their room, turning on lights as she went.

It was the little boy who was crying. Cameron. She went to him, picked him up, and he buried his runny nose in her shoulder, happy to let a stranger comfort him. She nuzzled his neck, rubbed his back. His diaper was heavy and soggy. A big boy like this ought to be potty trained. And why wasn't he talking?

She laid him on the changing table and put on a fresh diaper, replacing his damp pajama bottoms, too. She wiped the nasty-colored discharge from his nose, gave her shoulder a swipe with the same tissue, and took down the bottle of baby Tylenol from the high shelf. She gave him a dropperful. Tomorrow she would call the doctor. This child was sick. Probably had an ear or sinus infection.

Lorna had said to give him a bottle and he'd go back to sleep. Bridie looked at him. He was sitting on the changing table now, his dark hair standing straight up, eyes at half-mast, his face miserable. His little hand batted at the side of his head.

Bonnie was awake now and standing in her crib, swaying slightly. Her hair was a fuzzy blond halo. Her pacifier moved rhythmically as she watched with huge blue eyes.

These children didn't need a bottle. They needed a person.

She scooped up Cameron and settled him on her hip, then lowered the crib rail and loaded Bonnie, flicking off the light with her chin as she went out the door. She made her way back to her room, closed the door with her foot, and set both babies down on her bed. She turned off the overhead, then crawled in between them. Bonnie sat up and looked at her for a moment, still working the pacifier in a hypnotic rhythm. Bridie let her alone and settled Cameron on her shoulder. After a minute Bonnie cuddled down, too. She took the silky edge of the blanket and rubbed it between her thumb and forefinger.

Bridie lay there staring at the ceiling and wondering what sad world she had stepped into. There was a grief here, a timelessness of misery. But the babies beside her were soft and sweet. Warm bundles on each side of her heart, their breathing regular and deep. She burrowed down into the covers, not sure who was comforting whom.

❧ *thirteen* ❧

THERE WAS A FINGER IN her eye and a wet spot on her pajamas by Cameron's padded bottom. Bridie opened the eye that wasn't occupied.

"Good morning," she said to Bonnie, the owner of the finger.

Bonnie smiled, and the pacifier dropped out. Bridie remembered a game she'd played with her sister when she was a baby. She retrieved the pacifier and replaced it in Bonnie's mouth, upside down. Bonnie flipped it over without using anything but her tongue. Bridie laughed, perhaps the first truly genuine mirth she'd experienced in months. Years.

Cameron sat up and scrambled around until he could see the two of them. His nose was messy again.

"You're a mess," Bridie told him. "A big mess."

"Uh?" He made a questioning sound.

"You," she confirmed, then lifted up his pajama top and made a loud noise by blowing on his stomach.

He smiled and rubbed his stomach with a chubby hand.

"You want another tummy tuba?" She blew again. He chuckled this time.

"What's going on?" It was Samantha. She pushed open the door and peered in, trying her best to mask the interest on her face with a frown of irritation.

"We're playing. That's what's going on."

"No, I mean what are you doing here?"

Bridie quit tickling Cameron and sat up. "Didn't anybody tell you?"

"Nobody tells me anything." The dark look returned.

Bridie didn't bite. Someone should have told Samantha, but there had been things going on, and at least part of the drama had been of Samantha's own making. "I'm working here now. I'm your new"—she searched for the word with just the right connotations—"housekeeper." No, that wasn't right. "Nanny." She tried again and was rewarded with a dark frown.

"Uh?" Cameron questioned, saving her. Bridie grinned and blew on his stomach again.

"You are a mess," she repeated, then stood and picked up the soggy baby. "Let's go clean up," she said. Bonnie slid down and came, too.

"I don't need a nanny." Samantha followed behind them.

"They do."

Samantha couldn't argue with that. Bridie stripped off Cameron's wet pajamas and outfitted him with a dry diaper, zipped him up in a clean blanket sleeper, then repeated the process for Bonnie.

"Watch them while I throw on my sweats." She left the room before Samantha could complain and was back in less than a minute.

The four of them went downstairs, and once in the kitchen Bridie folded up the playpen and upended the toy bin onto the floor. Those children were not spending another minute penned up as long as she had breath. They got interested in the toys right away, and she started breakfast. Samantha still stood, watching her out of narrowed eyes.

"I'll put on some oatmeal. You go shower or you'll be late for school."

"I'm not going to school."

Bridie didn't stop her work. She filled the pot with water, sprinkled in some salt, turned the burner on high, and took down the box of rolled oats. "Then you'd better get back to bed. You're going to be one of two places today. In school or up there in your room." She didn't look up. Just measured out the oats and watched the pot.

Tiny bubbles began to form here and there, coalescing into larger ones. One broke, rose to the top. Then another. When they were rolling merrily she stirred in the oats, then put four slices of bread in the toaster, cut up a banana, and filled three glasses with milk. She started a pot of coffee for herself. Samantha still stood and watched.

"I hate that school."

"More than you'd hate any other school?"

"Yes." *You moron,* her tone added.

"Why?" Bridie stirred the oatmeal and kept an eye on the twins, still playing happily.

Samantha's face darkened, and Bridie saw true pain replace the pout of a moment before. "I don't know."

The silence cooked along with the oats. When they were finished, Bridie scooped four bowlfuls, buttered the toast, and set the plate of bananas on the table. She brought Cam and Bonnie to their high chairs, put a little brown sugar in their oatmeal, and cut their toast into fourths. "Let's pray," she said to Samantha, years of habit dying hard. She reached across and took Samantha's hand.

"Bless this food to our bodies, Lord, and make us grateful for our many blessings. In Jesus' precious name," she said. "Amen." She felt like a hypocrite, addressing God as if she were actually on speaking terms with Him.

When she raised her head, Samantha's face wore the churlish expression again. Bridie didn't let it bother her, just started in on her oatmeal. It was good. She would take some to the reverend in a while.

"Here's my problem, Samantha," she said, and the declaration seemed to startle the girl. "I'm a visitor here. An employee, so to speak. I might think you have perfectly good reasons to hate school, but unless I know what they are, I can't very well let you lay out. What would I tell your father? You see what I'm saying?"

Samantha gave a grudging nod, and probably hearing the possibility of getting her way, she dribbled out a little information. "The kids there treat me like crap."

"More details," Bridie said in between bites.

Samantha glared but eked out a little more. "They say I'm deranged. None of the girls will sit with me. They say I'm going to, like, get a gun and shoot everybody."

Bridie paused, the oatmeal suddenly seeming like a foreign presence in her mouth. She recovered, swallowed it down, and stood up to pour herself a cup of coffee. She carefully kept her face neutral. "Why do they say that?"

Samantha shrugged. "I don't know."

Bridie thought hard. Samantha could be laying it on, going for sympathy. Or she could be telling the truth. It would take some investigation to find out. Investigation she didn't have time for today. She made a decision. "I'll tell you what. I need help today, just getting things settled and all. I need to take Cameron to the doctor, somebody needs to take care of your father, and there are some things to be done around here. I'll give you a choice."

Samantha nodded, and there was a new brightness in her eyes.

"You can stay here and be my helper, or you can go get dressed, and I'll run you to school."

"I'll help you," Samantha promised, and the hint of desperation in her voice caught on Bridie's heart. She smiled at Samantha and, taking a chance, smoothed her hair. The girl didn't flinch or pull away, just stiffened slightly.

"All right," Bridie said. "Let's get busy."

The reverend was sleeping when Bridie crept in to check on him. The room was dark, shades pulled against what little light there was. There was a musty odor of dust and stale sheets and sickness. The bed was a wrestled mess of covers. She set down the tray she'd brought and went close to the bed. He was lying on his side. His cheeks were red. Bridie touched his forehead gently. It was hot. His eyes opened and gazed at her, glazed. She took the glass of juice from the tray and held it to his lips. He took a sip and some dribbled down his chin. She blotted it with a napkin. He lay back down and closed his eyes, as if the effort had exhausted him.

She went to the bathroom and came back with two aspirins, holding the glass again while he took them. She didn't speak except to urge him to drink, and waited, giving one sip at a time, until half the juice was gone. Then he shook his head, rolled over, and closed his eyes. She left the tray and went out, closing the door softly behind her. She stood there and considered, biting her lip. He looked really sick. She wondered if she should call the doctor or take him to the hospital.

After she and Samantha had bathed the children and she'd made a doctor's appointment for Cameron, she went back to Reverend MacPherson's room. The aspirins must have helped. He was cooler and sleeping. It would probably be all right to leave him long enough to take Cam to the doctor. When she returned, she would decide what to do about him. With any luck, Lorna would have called by then. She thought about leaving Samantha at home to watch over him, but glancing toward her, Bridie rejected the thought. Samantha had had too much on her shoulders. It was time for her to learn to be a child.

*

"Is he talking?" the young doctor asked while examining Cameron.

"Not much, but I don't really know. I just took this job," Bridie said, reminding herself that's what it was. She looked toward Samantha for an answer.

"He doesn't say anything," Samantha said, giving Bonnie's block tower a shove with her foot.

The doctor raised an eyebrow but nodded and went on with his tests.

"Uh-oh," Bonnie said, just to emphasize the point. She had a pretty fair vocabulary. *Up, down, mine, have that. Please* and *thank you.* But Bridie hadn't heard Cameron speak at all except for that little questioning sound he made. His eyes were wide open and he didn't miss a trick, though.

"Do they talk to him?" the doctor asked when he'd finished his examination and was writing out the prescription for Cameron's sinus infection.

Samantha's head rose.

"Why, of course they talk to him," Bridie answered, half offended, but even as the words formed, she remembered that pathetic room, bare and dim like the rest of the house. She tried to imagine their mother. Perhaps she'd felt too poorly to prepare for their coming. And it seemed that since her passing, the family had been strained just to keep the children's bodies and souls together.

"Nobody talks to anybody at our house," Samantha contributed. "Why should Cam be any different?"

"Suppose they did need a little more conversation?" Bridie asked, careful to remain neutral. "What would you recommend?"

"No speech therapy at this point. Just lots of interaction. Play with him, read to him. It's not rocket science." His smile softened the words. "Just talk to the kid."

Bridie nodded. She could do that.

By the time Lorna arrived at suppertime, Bridie and Samantha had covered a lot of ground. They'd made the doctor visit, bought groceries, filled Cameron's prescription, and given him his first two doses of antibiotic. Bridie had run four loads of laundry, changed the beds, and become concerned enough about Reverend MacPherson's condition that she'd called the doctor brother-in-law again, who was seeing to him now. Lorna had come straight from work, and the two of them were folding laundry, waiting for word.

"I feel so blessed to have you here," Lorna said, her eyes filling with grateful tears.

"I'm enjoying myself," Bridie admitted and realized she wasn't lying. Something about the way she'd spent the last twenty-four hours seemed to wash a little of the grime of her past away. How many hours would it take before she became clean? she wondered with a twist of bitterness. She thought of kids—like Samantha, troubled and alone—who had probably used the product she'd helped manufacture, and her happiness dimmed. There weren't enough hours in eternity to wash that guilt away.

"What is it?" Lorna asked. Her eyes were trained on Bridie's, and her face showed concern.

"Nothing," Bridie assured her, putting on a bright smile. Dr. Calvin came down just then and spared her further explanation.

"He's not well," he admitted, in what Bridie thought was the understatement of the century. Every time she'd checked on the reverend today he had been glassy eyed and out of it. Reminding her of Jonah when he was high, except for the paranoia, which was mercifully absent. "His fever is high," Calvin went on. "I'm hearing some congestion in his lungs. However, he is taking fluids. I've given him an injection as well as the oral antibiotics." He sighed deeply, seeming to weigh his options. He gave a little nod when he reached his conclusion. "I'll give him tonight, but if he's not better tomorrow, I'm going to admit him."

Lorna looked worried. Bridie nodded. "Is there anything I should do?"

"Force fluids. He should drink half a cup at least every hour."

Lorna murmured. "You'll be up all night."

"Would you rather I admitted him now?" Calvin asked.

One more trauma for Samantha, and in her state of mind she'd probably blame herself. Bridie shook her head. "No," she answered. "I'll take care of him."

"I can come tomorrow straight after work," Lorna promised. Bridie nodded again. Calvin left.

She and Lorna bedded down the twins and then made themselves a cup of tea. Samantha was engrossed in the movie of the week.

"Shall we take it in the living room?" Lorna asked, cocking her head toward the blaring TV.

"Sure," Bridie answered, and followed Lorna down the hall.

That living room. She looked around her at the moldering opulence. In her mind there were two choices. Clean everything out—beat the carpets, vacuum the drapes, polish the silver and brass, wind the clocks—or haul the whole mess upstairs to the attic.

She began talking, filling Lorna in on her conversation with Samantha about school, the doctor's evaluation of Cameron's speech problems. Lorna listened intently, her kind face drawn with concern.

"And about things around here," Bridie said, "I have a few ideas I wanted to run by you."

Lorna nodded.

She told her.

Lorna's eyes widened as she spoke. When Bridie had finished, Lorna nodded resolutely and took a sip of her tea. When she'd replaced the china cup on the saucer, she looked up and met Bridie's gaze squarely.

"I think those are very good suggestions," she said, and Bridie heard only a hint of what this stand would cost her. Years of battling those overbearing sisters flashed through her imagination. "As I said before," Lorna continued, "you're in charge. Act as if this is your home, as if these are your children. Do as you see fit."

"Are you sure?" Bridie asked, giving her one more chance to back out.

Lorna nodded and gulped down the rest of her tea. "I'll explain things to Winifred and Fiona," she said, replacing the cup in the saucer. Bridie could see the artery on her neck pulse. She could only imagine that conversation.

"We'll have a few weeks before they show up again," Lorna said, mostly to herself. She nodded and seemed a little comforted. "Well, I guess I'd better go," she said, sounding regretful. "I work at the photo factory tonight. Thank you again," Lorna said, her eyes intent on Bridie's. "You can't know how much this means."

Bridie smiled and patted Lorna's shoulder, then took her teacup and saw her to the door. She wondered what kind of train wreck had left her holding down two jobs at a time when she should be reaping the rewards of her life, but it was not her place to ask. She hugged Lorna good-night, got Samantha off to bed, then went into the kitchen and debated what kind of liquid to take to the reverend. The reverend. She couldn't very well go on calling him that, though Alasdair seemed too intimate. It didn't much matter what she called him, the state he was in. She selected a Pepsi from the refrigerator. It had sugar, which couldn't hurt, since he hadn't eaten in at least a day, and it would settle his stomach. She poured it into a glass and, using a fork, whipped out some of the carbonation in case his throat was sore. She took it to him. He roused enough to drink it down but barely opened his eyes, and as soon as he finished, he was out again.

She closed his door quietly and decided she would set her alarm for every hour and doze in between. But first she went through the house performing the same ritual as the night before. She locked the doors, doused the lights, pausing to look out the front window to Fairfax Street. A light snow was falling. She could see the thin, whispery flakes in the light of the streetlamp.

She stood still for a moment, listening for the old house's groans and creaks. It did not disappoint. With everyone gone, the feeling of shadowed secrets returned, but not with as much force as the night before. She wondered if she'd simply grown used to the atmosphere, as they all seemed to have. She climbed the stairs, still feeling like a character in a gothic romance.

The bedroom doors were closed, the hallway dim. Her imagination, always overactive, conjured up a wraithlike figure. It was so real, Bridie could almost swear she saw rather than imagined it. The ghost was slim and graceful, with Samantha's face. She hovered outside the children's rooms, her hands pressed against their doors, powerless to enter in and help them.

❧ *fourteen* ❧

BRIDIE OPENED HER EYES AND shut off the radio alarm. It was one o'clock and time to check on Reverend MacPherson. She got up, pulled on her robe, and went to his room. She pushed open the door and walked softly to his bedside. His face was red and hot again. So hot it frightened her, but she managed to get two aspirins down him. Then, after filling a basin with water, she sponged his face and hair, trying to cool him off. She threw the blankets off the bed and pulled the sheet down to his waist, gently wrestled him out of the T-shirt he wore, then dampened his chest. She was rinsing the washrag in the pan of cool water when he cried out.

"Oh!" His voice was loud and fervent, his gaze fixed on her with hot intensity. "Oh!" he cried again.

She dropped the cloth and leaned over him, jumbled thoughts of heart attacks and exploding arteries competing for her attention.

"What is it, Alasdair?" She used his name without intending to. "Alasdair, what's wrong?"

His expression became radiant. His eyes were dark polished sapphires, shining with fever and whatever hallucination was bringing him such joy. "You've come back," he said in an awed whisper.

"I'm here," she soothed and took his outstretched hand.

"You've come back." He murmured the words this time, but with such intensity and passion that Bridie felt embarrassed. He kissed her open palm, then pressed it against his heart. She felt the mat of hair on his chest, the heat of his skin, could even feel the thumping of his racing pulse. She felt a rush of strong emotion, confused with the knowledge that she was playacting, standing in for some character from his dreams or his past. He reached the other hand toward her and caught a handful of her hair. "You'll give me another chance, won't you?"

Another chance. Someone else wanted another chance and wanted it so desperately she could feel his breathless pain pierce her own heart. Her eyes filled. She nodded, only part of her remembering she was nothing more than a substitute, a figure in a poignant dream.

His face darkened and filled with pain. "Can you ever forgive me?" He sat up and reached the other arm toward her.

"Yes, I forgive you. Of course," she soothed, taking both his arms and lowering him back onto the bed. "Lie down, now."

"You won't leave?"

"No. I won't leave. Now you lie down." She gently lowered his arms to his sides. "Here, drink." She held the glass to his mouth and wiped away the dribbles when he was finished. He allowed it, and that particular dream must have passed, for the next time he opened his eyes, they were without the profound joy. He was going on about budgets now. Later it was mowing the lawn. He had accidentally mown down Mother's daisies, and on and on it went, all night long. She sat beside him in the chair, dozing in between offering him sips of water or soda and sponging him off.

In the darkest part of the night, between three and four, she was awakened by the sound of crying. He was weeping. Deep, racking, dry sobs. His fever had robbed him of tears.

Bridie tried to soothe him. "Alasdair, come on now," she said. "It's all right. Everything's all right." She patted his face, held his hands, but now it was as if he was oblivious to her presence. She sat back down beside him, helpless, and in desperation she thought about calling the paramedics. He was a very big man and strong. What if he became violent? What would she do then? She felt like crying herself. Why had she come here to this terrible, sad place?

If she believed that God would answer her, she would have prayed over him. Perhaps that would have comforted him. That's what Grandma would have done. And Mama. She thought of nights when she'd been sick or frightened and her mother had sat beside her and calmed her. And she remembered how she had done it.

"Have mercy on me, O God, have mercy on me," she quoted from that long-ago Sunday school project, raising her voice so it could be heard above his crying. "For in you my soul takes refuge. I will take refuge in the shadow of your wings until the disaster has passed."

It might have been wishful thinking, but it seemed as if his sobs lessened in intensity. She wiped his face with the damp cloth and quoted another psalm before he could start in again.

"I call to God and the Lord saves me. Evening, morning and noon I cry out in distress, and he hears my voice. He ransoms me unharmed from the battle waged against me."

He turned his gleaming eyes on her, and they calmed a little; their burning light drew down. When he tried to moisten his cracked lips, she offered a drink and another verse.

"Cast your cares on the Lord, and he will sustain you; he will never let the righteous fall." Her voice was soft and soothing now.

Alasdair lay still. She went on.

"He who dwells in the shelter of the Most High will rest in the shadow of the Almighty. I will say of the Lord, 'He is my refuge and my fortress, my God, in whom I trust.' "

He closed his eyes. She sat back down in her chair.

"The Lord is compassionate and gracious," she recited, the words coming from someplace deep inside her now, "slow to anger, abounding in love. He will not always accuse, nor will he harbor his anger forever; he does not treat us as our sins deserve or repay us according to our iniquities."

His face relaxed.

"For as high as the heavens are above the earth, so great is his love for those who fear him; as far as the east is from the west, so far has he removed our transgressions from us."

Alasdair's breathing became deep and regular. He was asleep, but she went on just the same. On and on throughout the rest of the night, she recited the hundred verses. Every time Alasdair stirred in his sleep, he seemed to hear her voice affirming the ancient promises, and he would rest again, comforted.

It must be true that God didn't give you more than you could bear, because the babies slept through until seven o'clock. She must have dozed off herself, for she was startled awake by their cries. She sat up in the chair she'd pulled close to the bed and carefully disentangled her hand from Alasdair MacPherson's. He was pale but cool, and sleeping peacefully. She looked at him for a moment, wondering if he would remember this night, then pulled the blanket over his bare shoulders and crept out to see to his children.

❧ *fifteen* ❧

BRIDIE SWUNG OPEN THE HEAVY front door of the parsonage and couldn't help smiling. Carmen, hair apouf and dressed in a black leather miniskirt and jacket, was leaning back against the porch railing, taking one last, long drag on her cigarette. She ground out the butt in the potted Norfolk pine.

"Well, if it isn't Mary Poppins," she said.

Bridie's smile spread even wider, and impulsively she opened her arms for a hug. Carmen grinned back and walked into them. Bridie's nose tickled from the feather of sprayed hair that brushed it.

"The old Bag and Save's been pretty dull without you," Carmen said, giving her a squeeze and releasing her. "And so has home."

Bridie felt a moment of uneasiness. She hadn't been back to the apartment since she'd taken the job over a week ago. "I have the money for this month's rent in the kitchen," she said quickly.

"Save it." Carmen waved her away, then looked a little awkward herself. "Newlee's been staying over since you've been gone. He's helping out."

Bridie nodded. She'd been replaced. She supposed she should have seen it coming, but still. Carmen seemed to read her mind.

"Your room's still yours as long as you want it," she assured her.

Bridie nodded. She tried not to think any farther ahead than her nose these days. "Thank you. I'll be here at the parsonage more often than not until the reverend gets on his feet, though. And after that he's off to Boston for a week. He's speaking at a *theological conference*," she said, giving the words the emphasis they deserved.

"Woo-hoo-hoo." Carmen raised an eyebrow. "Look who's hanging out with the hoity-toity."

Bridie grinned. "It's good to see you," she said and was surprised to find how deeply she meant it. "Thanks for helping me out with the children."

"Are you kidding? I wouldn't miss this for the world." Carmen stepped all the way into the foyer, draped her jacket over the stair railing, and slung her purse into the corner. "This setup reminds me of that movie where the governess comes and this guy's got his crazy wife locked up in the attic."

"*Jane Eyre*?" Bridie supplied.

Carmen snapped her fingers and pointed at Bridie. "That's the one." She craned her neck up the stairs as if she were listening for insane laughter, then headed toward the sitting room, gawking every step of the way. Bridie, shaking her head, followed after.

"This place is a real piece of work. Who's that? The first wife?" Carmen pointed to the oil portrait of Alasdair and Lorna's stern-faced mother hanging in the hallway.

Bridie gave her a look calculated to squelch.

Carmen only grinned again. "I'm playing with you," she said and walked around the dining room, hands behind her back, ogling everything. "Don't worry. I'll behave once I get this out of my system. It's just that I've never been in a real-life blueblood's house before. This is a new experience."

"For me, too." Bridie made a little face.

Carmen's eyes lit with sympathy. "You look tired."

"It's been a long week." She felt a stab of guilt that it had taken her and Lorna so long to get around to dealing with Samantha's school situation, but even though there had been no bad nights like a week ago, the reverend had just begun perking up yesterday. Samantha had taken a cold as well, and Lorna had decided to keep her out until they could talk to the principal. Bridie had been hoping that the reverend would be well enough to see to things himself, but even though he was mending, he was still too weak to do much.

"Mrs. Tronsett will see us tomorrow," Lorna had said yesterday, and just as Bridie had been about to beg off tagging along, she'd glanced at Lorna's face. It had looked so grim and defeated that Bridie hadn't had the heart. Besides, from what Lorna had been telling her, the reverend would have his hands full when he recovered. His church was trying to run him off.

"I'd better go," Bridie said, glancing at her watch. "Our meeting's at ten. Come into the kitchen and I'll show you what's what." Carmen followed, looking only too happy to have a new area in which to nose around.

"I been thinking about the kid. Why don't you just let her hang out?" Carmen suggested. "It's almost Christmas vacation anyhow. By January her pop will be up and around, and he can deal with things himself."

Bridie nodded. The thought had occurred to her, too. It would make one less thing for her to worry about. "It's up to them," she said. "I'm along for moral support."

It only took Bridie a few minutes to orient Carmen. Her friend was quick and apparently had taken care of lots of younger brothers and sisters. She took to the twins right away.

"*You* are *such* a *doll*," Carmen said to Cameron and was rewarded with one of his brilliant smiles. He looked like his father, Bridie could see, now that the little face had grown familiar. His hair was the same dark brown, his eyes the same smoky blue. His medicine was working, too. No more runny nose.

"And *you* look like a little princess," Carmen cooed to Bonnie, who charmed her by lifting tiny arms. Carmen picked her up and nuzzled the downy hair. She turned to Bridie. "I can see why you're in love."

Bridie felt embarrassed for no good reason. "Samantha's reading in her room," she supplied quickly. "Cameron's medicine is in the refrigerator. He needs another dose at lunchtime. I meant to make sandwiches, but I ran out of time."

"I'll take care of it," Carmen promised. "What about his holiness? Will he need anything?"

Bridie rolled her eyes at Carmen's nickname for the reverend. "Take him a tray. Soup, crackers, juice. I'll be back before naptime."

Carmen nodded and gave her a knowing smile. "Naptime, huh? You're starting to talk like a mama."

Lorna maneuvered the reverend's huge station wagon out of the garage onto Alexandria's narrow, icy streets. They were crowded with Christmas shoppers and looked cheerful and bright in spite of the sleet and rain. White lights twined around the antique streetlamps, and swags and wreaths of evergreen and holly adorned each shop window and door. Bridie felt a moment of excitement that time and circumstance had failed to dampen. It was almost Christmas.

"I should fill you in on a little family history," Lorna said, not sounding as if it was something she relished.

"All right," Bridie said, equally unsure she wanted to hear it. Every fact she knew, every event she took part in, became a thread that tied her to this ragtag little group. What would happen when she was bound tight? She had no idea what the future held for her. But whatever her fate, it would not include these people that she was coming to care about. This was a temporary arrangement, she reminded herself, hardening her heart once again. In fact, come the new year she would see about extricating herself from this web. She would help them find a new nanny, someone permanent. Then she would be free. But somehow that fact didn't give her the happy feeling it should have.

"Samantha's mother, Anna, passed away a little over two years ago," Lorna said, glancing at Bridie as she steered the car onto the arterial.

Bridie nodded. She knew that much.

"Samantha was at school, and Alasdair at the radio studio taping his program. I'd taken the twins to my house for a few hours so Anna could get some rest. They were ten days old."

Bridie felt a stirring of dread.

"Apparently Anna decided to run errands and go to the grocery. She wanted to get some chocolate chips so she and Samantha could make cookies. That's what her note said. But she must have become disoriented. She skidded into the river. Several people saw the car go in. One man dove in after her, but he couldn't get her door open.

Finally the divers came, but by the time they got her out, it was too late."

Bridie blinked. She'd had no idea what the circumstances of Mrs. MacPherson's death had been. And now that she knew, she had no idea what to say. It was an awful, awful story.

"Things were terrible," Lorna said. Her voice was ragged, her cheeks wet. "So dark. My husband and I were still together, and I wasn't working. I stayed over most nights and took care of the twins."

Bridie said nothing, just continued to listen. The sleety snow had turned to freezing rain. It pelted the car windows. The windshield wipers thumped a comforting rhythm against it, and the warm air from the heater felt good against her legs.

"At first Samantha was distraught, as you might imagine. Very angry, almost wild. Then she settled down, and I thought—" Her voice broke, and Bridie reached across to comfort her. "I'm sorry," Lorna said, taking the tissue Bridie handed her from the packet in her purse. "You'd think after all this time I'd be able to talk about it, but it's so hard." She pressed the tissue against her nose for a moment, then cleared her throat and went on. "I thought she was recovering. I can see now that things were too perfect. I suppose it was her way of trying to make things right again. Her grades were perfect. Her room was perfect. Her clothing was perfect. Her manners were perfect. She must have needed things. Things she couldn't ask for. But Alasdair was trying to keep the church afloat. I was busy with the twins. I guess we all just forgot about Samantha. . . ."

"When did she start acting different?" Bridie asked after a moment.

"About six months ago. Right around the time she turned thirteen. It was as if someone flipped a switch. Instead of our sweet, compliant child, she became angry, defiant, hostile. Her grades started slipping, then crashed. She began sneaking out to meet boys, but her friendships with the other girls ended, and badly. They talked about her. You know how girls that age will gossip."

Bridie remembered what Samantha had said. Being labeled homicidal wasn't exactly what she'd call typical teenage backbiting.

"Anyway," Lorna finished, sounding sad, almost despairing. "I've prayed so long and often, and yet things just seem to be getting worse. Until you came," she added, her voice lifting in hope, and Bridie felt a warm thrust of happiness at bringing something good to this sad little group.

"How has Alasdair done with it all?" Bridie asked boldly, feeling her cheeks heat.

Lorna answered without looking up from the road. "Sometimes," she said, her voice quiet, "I'm not sure he even knows Anna's gone."

Mrs. Tronsett was around sixty years old, and an old, not a young sixty. She wore a no-nonsense navy polyester suit and low-heeled pumps, a Timex watch with one of the little black string bands that probably hadn't been sold since 1965. She reminded Bridie of any number of tight-permed, blue-haired little ladies from her past, but the moment Mrs. Tronsett opened her mouth, the resemblance was gone. She was a combination of intelligence and plain talk, and Bridie liked her at once.

"This child is circling the drain, and we've got to move quickly," she said. "The seriousness of her acting out is escalating." She turned forthright gray eyes on Bridie and Lorna. "I've suggested she see a counselor, but her father seems reluctant. Frankly, considering what they've been through, I think the whole family could use some help."

"Alasdair might be open to that now," Lorna said, and Bridie read between the lines. Now that everything in his life was headed down the drain, too. There was something about complete failure that left a person open to suggestions.

"Good." Mrs. Tronsett bobbed her brillo head. "I've made a list of psychologists who speak Presbyterian." Her mouth hinted at a smile. Lorna looked a little shocked to hear the principal of the church school cracking jokes.

"I've called Samantha in on several occasions, but our conversations never seem to get past go." Mrs. Tronsett was all business again. She leaned over and brought a file from the drawer. "Her English teacher gave me this. It was the subject of one of those conversations. I asked her why she'd chosen this topic, hoping to get her to open up. She simply said she was interested in her mother's new home."

Mrs. Tronsett handed over three wide-ruled pages, stapled in the corner. Lorna held out her hand for them, then scooted near Bridie so they could read together. The handwriting was the same neat, penciled cursive Bridie remembered from the note on the church bulletin board. "Hell," the title read, and Bridie got a chill deep in her gut.

"Take a look at this." Bridie looked around to make sure Samantha was nowhere near, then handed Carmen the paper.

Carmen took it from her, gave her a quizzical look, and began to read: "The Westminster Larger Catechism asks, 'What are the punishments of sin in the world to come? Answer: The punishments of sin in the world to come are everlasting separation from the comfortable presence of God, and most grievous torments in soul and body, without intermission, in hell fire forever.' Whoa!" Carmen murmured.

"Go on reading," Bridie said grimly.

"What, exactly, is hell like?" Carmen read. "Is it a lake of fire, a place where worms eat your body day and night? Do you see reruns of all your mistakes and sins over and over? Or is it nothing? Just empty and black? No one knows for sure, because once you get there, you can never leave." Carmen gave her head a shake. "This is pretty tortured stuff for a thirteen-year-old. Next thing you know she'll be like one of those Goths with the black lipstick and hair and the nails through the lip."

Bridie snatched the paper from her hand and gave her an irritated look. "Carmen, that's not exactly helpful right now," she snapped.

"Sorry." Carmen had the grace to look ashamed.

Bridie slumped down in the kitchen chair and looked at that awful essay one more time. She practically knew it by heart.

"What are you guys gonna do for the kid?"

"I don't know," she said, her voice flat. When she looked up Carmen was biting her lip, looking at her sympathetically.

"You really care about her, don't you?"

Did she? She rubbed her neck, which felt kinked and knotted. She had absolutely no idea what to do, but the truth was, that fact bothered her deeply. "I guess I do."

Carmen held out her hand for the paper. "Please?" she asked. "I'll be nice this time."

Bridie handed it over.

Carmen reread the essay, her face intent, then looked up. "She said this is where her ma was?"

Bridie nodded. "Said she wanted to learn about her mother's new home."

"Now, why would she think that?" Carmen asked, as usual coming straight to the point. "Her ma must have been religious to end up married to his holiness. So why would Samantha think she'd go to hell when she died?"

❧ sixteen ❧

ALASDAIR LAY IN THE BED and stared up at the water-stained ceiling. His covers were soft and fragrant, not the scratchy, balled-up mess he'd begun with. She'd changed them, the first time early in his illness. He'd gotten up to use the bathroom. He'd come back and the bed had been fresh. A quilt he vaguely remembered from his childhood had replaced the wool blanket. The sheets had been changed, the corner turned down invitingly. A clean pajama bottom and a pair of underwear had been draped at the foot of the bed. The tray on the bedside table held a fresh pitcher of water with ice and lemon and a clean glass. The wastebasket had been emptied of the used tissues.

It was true what was said of illness, that it made the world end at the foot of your bed. For ten days now, by his calculation, his world had consisted of heat and thirst, swirling illness, ravaging coughs, dry, wasting, lip-cracking fevers, and Her. Their connection felt primal and intimate. Hers had been the hands that held the pan when he was sick, taken it away when he was finished, and cleaned him up. Her cool palm had pressed his forehead, held his hand. Her steady blue eyes brought him back from the jumbled jungle of fever dreams. Her calm voice was like a strong rope tying him fast when he had no strength left to hold on.

During that time the realities of his life had loosened their hold. He had children. They visited his dreams, but he didn't see them in the flesh. The things he did in the world that had seemed so important became far points on a distant horizon that receded even farther each day. Even the church no longer had the power to lift him up or cast him down. He was cast down already. His spirit, along with his body, felt wracked and broken. He'd been cut back like a pruned vine. Back to the ground. Back to the root.

"When I said, 'My foot is slipping,' your love, O Lord, supported me. When anxiety was great within me, your consolation brought joy to my soul."

He said it aloud, his voice sounding ragged and out of use. It had been one of the verses she'd recited. Promise after promise she had poured from her heart to his. He didn't think she'd been reading, though he couldn't be sure. In fact, he couldn't be sure it had actually happened. The whole memory might have been one of his overheated dreams. But he didn't think so. The scene was too real, too clear to have been a dream. He remembered weeping as the sheer weight of his sins and omissions had crashed upon him. He remembered her leaning over him, reminding him, reciting the words that kept despair at bay. No. It had not been his imagination. It had happened. Of that much he was sure. If she had not been the one who had defended him against the darkness, then it must have been one of God's own messengers, sent to fight for him when he had no strength of his own.

He sat up. The light-headedness was almost gone. Calvin, his brother-in-law, had examined him again yesterday. "You've had influenza and pneumonia," he pronounced after listening to Alasdair's lungs. "It's clearing."

She had checked on him again after Calvin left, moving around the room silently. Since the fever had broken she spoke to him only if he spoke first, and he hadn't often had the energy.

She'd brought him a tray and an extra blanket.

"Thank you," he said.

She nodded. "Are you feeling better?"

"Yes. Thank you."

She gave him a slight smile. "You look like you'd have to get better to die."

He had managed a smile of his own, leaned across to sip the glass of clear liquid she held toward him, straw considerately bent.

"Seven-Up," she had explained. "I beat the fizz out with a fork so it wouldn't hurt your throat," and he was touched again. Such a small thing, but so kind.

He sat up higher on his pillow now and took a deep breath. He smelled something wonderful. It was the unmistakable aroma of bread baking. He closed his eyes and was back in Edinburgh at the house on Whipple Street, watching their housekeeper—what was her name?—pull the golden loaves from the oven. He could see her just as if she stood before him. Tall and lean with a square, honest face. She wore a cotton shirtwaist dress and black lace-up shoes and the ever-present sweater. Her hands were thick and knotted. He could almost see her slice the bread into thick slabs, spread them with a swipe of butter, which quickly became a dripping puddle dotted with great islands of bumpy blackberry jam. His stomach twisted, but not with illness this time. He was hungry, he realized as it growled.

He rose, pulled on his pants and shirt and slippers, and emerged from his room. He blinked. Things seemed different somehow, and the impression was even stronger as he reached the landing. Things looked different. He felt curiosity instead of his usual flatness. Proceeding down the stairs, he could hear voices coming from the kitchen and he began to notice the changes.

The windows were uncovered, for one thing. The heavy drapes that usually hung over most of them were pulled back and tied, even the sheer panels drawn aside. The glass had been washed. He descended the stairs and at the bottom had to step over one of those plastic baby gates he'd been meaning to buy. He blinked again as he passed through the hall and on impulse went to the living room. Things were different there, as well as in the dining room. Things were missing. The knick-knacks and bric-a-brac that had been there for three generations were gone. Every table was bare.

When he got to the kitchen, he saw why. Instead of being penned up in their play area, the twins were running free. Cameron was sitting on the floor, banging a plastic bowl with a wooden spoon. His hair had been trimmed. His nose wasn't running. Bonnie was leaning over the bottom drawer, tossing plastic freezer containers and lids behind her without even looking to see where they landed. She was wearing clothes he hadn't seen, and her hair was combed prettily and held back with a barrette. The kitchen was warm and filled with the scent of fresh bread, and now that he was closer he identified the perfume of cinnamon and ginger as well. Bridie was bent over the counter, doing something to a mound of dark brown dough.

"Good morning," he said.

She stopped her work and looked up. Her eyes were disconcertingly blue and clear. Something about her, or perhaps their situation, put him off balance.

"Good morning." She smiled but quickly ducked her head back down over her task. Perhaps she felt it, too. "I see you're feeling better."

"Much better, thank you."

"What will you have for breakfast?" She tossed him a quick look. "I'll make you scrambled eggs, hot cereal, anything you want."

"Cold cereal will be fine."

She leaned over, reached past Bonnie, and retrieved a pot and lid. "Oatmeal will go down easy and stick with you."

Alasdair pictured the steaming bowl. He hadn't had a proper bowl of oatmeal in years.

"Thank you," he said, then, not seeing what more was required of him, he sat down at the table. The woman—Bridie—Miss Collins— he coached himself, busied herself with the oatmeal, then turned up the heat on the kettle. In a moment she placed before him a cup, warmed, and a teapot. He lifted the lid. Loose tea leaves floated on top of steaming water. She set the strainer beside his cup along with a pitcher of cream, a saucer of lemon slices, and the sugar bowl, then went back to her work. He looked around for a moment. Both babies were jabbering and playing. He poured out a cup of the tea, added a little cream and sugar, took a hesitant sip. His taste buds felt traumatized and his stomach tentative. He rolled the liquid around on his tongue. The tea tasted good at first but quickly became too strong and acidic. He set the cup aside.

After a while Bridie served his oatmeal. It was thick and creamy.

He sprinkled it with brown sugar, poured a little cream onto it, and ate it slowly, taking small bites.

The bread came out of the oven before he was finished, and it was as if she had read his mind. She sliced off a large hunk, put it onto his plate, handed him a pot of jam and the butter dish. He broke off a small piece, not risking the butter and jam. It was good just as it was, but after a few bites he was full.

"It's delicious, but I'm not up to par yet."

"You'll know you're really well when your appetite comes back." She smiled at him and didn't seem offended at his half-finished breakfast.

Cameron was pulling on her leg. Bridie leaned over and smiled at him, held out her hands. "What do you say?" she asked.

"Up," Cameron answered, clear as a bell.

She picked him up and set him on her hip.

Alasdair watched as they played and talked. The two of them had obviously forged a relationship in the time he'd been out of the picture. He smiled and felt a moment of contentment.

The telephone rang. The moment went away.

Bridie answered the telephone. "Just a moment, please," she said.

Alasdair felt a familiar weariness, nodded, and reached for the receiver. He noticed the stack of phone messages on the counter beside it. His oatmeal began to churn uncomfortably.

He listened with half his attention to the Sunday school super-intendent's concerns about the fourth-grade curriculum, then hung up the phone and carried his plate to the sink.

"Are you going to be fit to go to Boston by Friday?" Bridie asked him, her face concerned.

More weariness piled on. He hoped the arrangements Lorna had made weren't about to come unraveled. He nodded. "Yes. I'm sure I'll be completely recovered by then. Will it still be convenient for you to stay with the children?"

"Oh, sure. I was just thinking of you."

Someone was thinking of him. He gave his head a small shake.

"Thank you," he said, putting the plate down and turning to face her. "Thank you for everything. For nursing me through my illness. For taking care of me and my family. You can't know how much it has meant."

She was silent again. She set Cameron back onto the floor, and her shiny hair slid from her shoulder. She stood up, an unreadable look in the forget-me-not eyes. "You're very welcome," she said.

He nodded, and not seeming to find any further reason to stay, he dragged himself heavily up the stairs. His reprieve was over.

✎ *seventeen* ✎

BOB HENRY SAT ON THE hard motel mattress and gazed at the water stain on the ceiling. It was his second week at the Capitol City Motor Inn. Here he was, just a few miles away from the Hilton and the Sheraton, but they were in a different world. Even a Motel 6 would have been an improvement over this.

He'd been schmoozing and buying people coffee and doughnuts for a week and a half. The locals seemed only too happy to gripe about their pastor. He had made numerous visits to the county courthouse to check records, and his laptop was so overheated from the hours he'd spent online, he'd probably scorched the bedspread. His preliminary inquiries hadn't exactly come up dry, but neither had he found the pot of gold.

Two of the sisters were completely clean. Not even any rumors, and he'd certainly beat the bushes to cover that angle. Too bad being a battle-axe wasn't a crime, or he'd have Winifred against the wall. He'd nosed around the university to see if there was an academic skeleton in Fiona's closet—plagiarism, hanky-panky with a student, but nada. Zilch. And the youngest, Lorna, had divorced a year ago. There was a declaration of bankruptcy on file, but no police reports for domestic abuse, no restraining orders. Nothing good.

He was still waiting for the police report from Anna's accident. That should come in any day now. The daughter was a strong contender for black sheep. He'd been asking around, and the scuttlebutt seemed to be that she was "troubled," which was slightly encouraging. Still, he didn't really have anything he could take to the bank.

Which was problematic. He leaned back onto the pillow and

locked his hands behind his neck. He would have to regroup and come at this from another angle.

He went through all the categories of ecclesiastical hanky-panky in his head. The big one, the brass ring, would be a woman, of course. An improper relationship, usually with a distressed counselee, was the number one reason a minister got taken out. He'd asked around, but not even MacPherson's enemies knew of any women.

What else? Money, of course. He glanced over at the stack of papers on the corner of his bed. He'd had central accounting send him a copy of the church's balance sheets for the last year, but he'd hoped to avoid going though them. Nothing bored him more than numbers. His mind ran through other categories of moral failure: drugs, perversions, addictions. None of those seemed promising. He couldn't picture Alasdair a closet addict, and perversion was a stretch even for his imagination.

Bob flipped on the television with the remote, watched a few minutes of the news, then sat up and rubbed his face. He was going back to Richmond tomorrow. Gerry had summoned him, but he hated to leave without what he'd come for. He sighed and picked up the first of the spreadsheets. He might as well order a pizza. It was going to be a long night.

❧ *eighteen* ❧

Bridie turned sideways to get the last box through the narrow attic doorway. She smiled, thinking what a mess of nonsense Carmen would be carrying on about crazy wives living up here. Bridie, however, was quite certain there were no wives here, crazy or otherwise. This attic had become very familiar in the last few days. She wished she had a nickel for every trip she'd made up those narrow stairs, a penny for every piece of bric-a-brac she'd stashed away—carefully packed, of course. Layers of tissue kept Mama MacPherson's treasures safe for the next generation.

She'd even brought a little order to the cluttered mess, though she hadn't intended to reorganize the MacPhersons' attic.

"Do you have any Christmas decorations?" she'd asked Lorna a few days before. The spirit of the season was coming upon her whether she liked it or not.

"They'd be in the attic," Lorna had answered. She'd checked her watch, and Bridie knew she would probably make herself late for work at the photo processing plant if she came back inside.

"That's all right. Forget it."

"No," Lorna had protested. "I think it would be nice for the children. Would you mind taking a look?"

She'd shrugged and said she guessed not. Now she understood Lorna's apologetic expression. The place had been a rat's nest—packed from corner to corner with castoffs of the rich and snooty who hadn't thrown anything away in centuries. She'd looked through ten or more boxes and found lots of hats and clothes that smelled of camphor, but so far no Christmas decorations. It hadn't been a complete waste of time, though. She'd discovered a few useful things—an entire set of good, sturdy pottery dishes, which she'd immediately brought down to the kitchen, as well as a wool plaid tablecloth, two afghans, spare bedding, including a few beautiful old quilts, and a large overstuffed chair that had been buried under a mound of faded draperies. She'd found three ginger-jar lamps that would nicely light the living room.

Now if only she could find what she'd come up here for. It was time, she realized with a familiar thrill of anticipation. There was something about the holidays that brought out the child in her.

She set down the box she carried and wiped the moisture from her forehead. She was hot from her labors but would cool off soon enough. It got nippy up here. She marked the box with a felt-tipped pen in big black letters. Extra white damask tablecloths. She shook her head. How many white damask tablecloths could a person use? They'd make a pretty set of spring curtains. She smiled, imagining Winifred's face. Anyway, she told herself, replacing the cap on the marker with a firm snap, she wasn't going to be here in the spring.

She pulled one of the unexplored boxes toward her, opened the flaps, and frowned as she looked inside. What in the world? It was a small backpack, pink. Attached to the Pooh Bear zipper was a laminated class photo. *Miss Wilson's Kindergarten,* it said. *Knox Presbyterian School.* Bridie smiled and found Samantha in the picture. She was in the back row, wearing a pretty pink dress, her hair in braids, a sweet smile lighting her little face. Bridie unzipped the pack. It was filled with worksheets, wide-lined papers, artwork featuring people with huge heads, big stomachs, stick-thin arms and legs, spidery fingers and toes. She smiled. Someone had filed away nearly everything Samantha had done that year. She put everything back, zipped it up again, and looked back into the box. It was full of backpacks. Seven in all—each school year from kindergarten through sixth grade. Someone had loved doing this. Had obviously enjoyed and cherished every little thing Samantha had produced. She closed the box back up and set it against the wall, labeled it with the black marker.

A mess of baby clothes spilled over the edge of the next box. She smiled and picked up one of the garments off the attic floor. So tiny. She wished for a moment she could have seen Cam and Bonnie when they were babies. She would have to ask about pictures. She picked out another outfit, this one pink, and held it up. She frowned as she saw what lay underneath—a package of tiny undershirts, still wrapped in plastic. She rummaged further. A set of receiving blankets, also unopened, was underneath them. She shook her head as she continued removing unused baby items from the box. Someone must have just sealed everything up after Anna's accident.

She was beginning to feel uneasy about going through these things, but she kept on, not sure if curiosity or something else was driving her. Things got even stranger the closer she came to the bottom of the box. These last items were still gift wrapped, unopened. One package was decorated with sleeping babies. The bow was squashed flat, but the card was attached. *Congratulations, Alasdair, Anna, and Samantha. Hope your blessings arrive safely and on time! Best wishes, Bill and Sarah Andrews.* She put the card back and gazed hard at the flattened stack of boxes, trying to understand what she was seeing.

If the baby things had gotten packed away in the days after Anna's accident, she could certainly understand that. But these gifts seemed to have been given before that. Why hadn't Anna opened them? Why hadn't she unfolded the tiny garments, washed them fragrant and soft, ready to meet tender skin? Could this be the same woman who had so painstakingly preserved every remnant of Samantha's childhood?

She picked her way toward the remaining boxes. At least half of her was yapping that she should stop. That she was nosing around in what was none of her business. She flipped open the lid of the closest one. It held an assortment of leather-bound scrapbooks. Bridie took out one of the books and opened it. The handwriting was neat and small. The entry was dated fifteen years before.

> *Alasdair says I should keep a record of our life together so not one moment will be lost. I think he's right, for once a moment is lived, it is gone, and our time together is too precious to meet that fate. I will write it all down, and when I am old and gray and my children are grown, I will read it back to them so they can know us as we are today.*

We found our apartment. Alasdair felt badly that it was small and dark. I say it is a beautiful place. I shall make it our home. I'll set a beautiful table tonight to celebrate and have supper ready when he returns from the library.

Bridie stopped reading, forcing her eyes away from the page. She replaced the book. Her hand hesitated before selecting the last one. She flipped open toward the back, to an entry dated two years prior.

Sometimes I feel as though the empty pages of this book are my only friends. As if some evil power has cut me off from every other human soul. Alasdair says I should counteract these thoughts with Scripture, and I know he is right. But when they come upon me, I can't seem to muster the strength to resist them.

Last week when I was feeling well, I took Samantha shopping and out to lunch. We picked out new dresses. Seeing her little face light with joy, I felt almost overwhelmed with sadness and regret for all the lost time. When we came home, I took out my Bible and wrote down some verses. I'll try to remember to read them when the darkness comes back.

Bridie turned her eyes away from the diary. This was private. This was none of her business. She closed the book, then sat silently, wondering what had happened to change Anna from the hopeful young girl to the woman who talked of darkness as if it were a person, evil and familiar.

"What are you doing?"

Bridie startled and turned toward the voice. Samantha's head bobbed up from the stairwell.

"Those are my mother's, aren't they?" She thumped up the stairs, crossed the attic, and took the journal from Bridie's hand. She looked inside, long enough to read a few lines, then turned pale. "These are none of your business," she said.

"I know it."

"Give them here."

Bridie rocked back on her heels and didn't try to prevent Samantha from taking the box. Samantha gave her another malevolent look and clutched the box against her chest as she disappeared back down the stairs. Bridie shook her head and massaged her temples. Just what she needed. Another situation. She got up, turned out the light, and firmly closed the attic door behind her. She would buy whatever Christmas decorations she needed at Wal-Mart. She wasn't looking in any more boxes.

Lorna felt a warm satisfaction. The last dish was dried and put away, the last baby changed and bedded. Alasdair had finished his first full day of pastoral duties in two weeks and retired gratefully to bed. Samantha's future was decided, at least for the present. Alasdair had agreed that she would remain at home through the New Year, which bought at least a temporary reprieve. She seemed greatly relieved, the proof being that she was in her room reading instead of sulking at one of her disaffected friends' homes.

"Tea?" she offered Bridie.

Bridie nodded gratefully as she flipped on the dishwasher. She looked tired, Lorna realized. And no wonder. For the last two weeks she'd been tending to Alasdair all night and the children all day. Lorna breathed another prayer of gratitude that Bridie's path had crossed theirs. She longed to be able to care for the children herself, but the important thing was that their needs were being met. She was thankful. "You sit," she encouraged. "Let me serve you."

For once Bridie didn't argue, just flopped into the chair.

"The house looks wonderful," Lorna said. "I can't tell you how I appreciate what you've done." She put the thought of Winifred, almost recovered from her bunion surgery, out of mind. She took out the tea, then sat down to wait for the kettle to sing. "And I'm so grateful you can stay with the children while Alasdair attends his conference."

"No problem," Bridie said. "I'm going to potty train the babies while he's gone and get them to sleep through the night," she vowed. "It's time."

Lorna smiled.

"I found some things in the attic today," Bridie said after a moment. Lorna looked up quickly. Bridie's eyes were troubled. "They looked like diaries, scrapbooks."

Lorna nodded and felt a cold chill stir her insides. So that's where they had gone to. "Anna's journals," she supplied.

Bridie nodded.

Lorna got up and began fiddling with the dishrag, wiped the already clean counter, then rinsed and refolded the rag, hanging it up where it had been moments before. "Anna was a great record keeper," she said. "Journals, photo albums, every piece of paper generated by this family. I didn't know what happened to them. Alasdair must have put them up there." She thought of her brother's icy competence in the weeks following Anna's death, and somehow it didn't surprise her at all that he'd boxed up her sister-in-law and locked her in the attic.

"Samantha came up and saw me looking at one. She took them," Bridie blurted out, her expression a cross between guilt and defensiveness. "I'm sorry. I just didn't feel it was my place to tell her she couldn't have them."

Lorna took in a deep updraft of air.

"I didn't know who to tell, so I'm telling you."

"I see." The kettle whistled and Lorna turned, grateful to have a task. She put the tea in the pot, then poured in the boiling water, and had time to think while she gathered the cups and took the carton of milk from the refrigerator. By the time the tea had steeped and she'd poured them each a cup, she'd reached a decision.

"That's all right," she said, stirring in a teaspoon of sugar and watching the tiny shreds of tea swirl into a miniature maelstrom. "Let her keep them."

The silence was thick for a moment. "Aren't you afraid she'll find out more than she needs to know?" Bridie finally asked.

Lorna had considered this, of course, but a conviction was taking hold with the stubbornness of a barnacle. "I'm beginning to think part of the problem with this household is that no one talks about anything. There are too many secrets. Let her keep them," she repeated, even more firmly. "You know what the Bible says about knowing the truth. . . ."

Bridie's eyes still pointed toward her, but they had glazed over at the word "secrets." She was probably wondering what they might be. Lorna kept silent, and after a moment Bridie shifted back her gaze.

"It's supposed to set you free," Lorna finished her sentence.

Bridie looked confused.

"The truth," Lorna clarified. " 'You will know the truth and the truth will set you free.' "

"Oh," Bridie said, her head nodding but her face saying something else. "Right. That's what they say."

Samantha made sure her door was shut. Just for safety's sake she shoved her chair up against it and piled a few books onto the seat for added weight. She took the box and set it in the middle of the bed, then sat herself down. Her feet were cold, but she didn't want to take the time to find a pair of socks. She crossed her legs and looked at the cardboard square before her. Her mom was in there. All that was left of her. Finally she leaned forward and flipped open the lid.

She heard someone coming. She stashed the box on the far side of her bed. It was Dad. She could tell by the footsteps. They stopped outside her door. He knocked.

"What!"

"May I come in? I'm leaving early in the morning, and I'd like to say good-bye."

The chair was in the way, and if she moved it, he'd go ballistic and want to know why she'd had it there, and if he found out about the diaries, she would totally be in trouble.

"I'm busy."

She waited.

"Good night, then. And good-bye. I'll see you in a week."

Samantha felt bad. He sounded so sad. "Hang *on*," she said, but he must not have heard because his bedroom door opened and closed. She blew out a mouthful of air and just sat there for a minute. She could go to him. And do what? Ask him to give her a hug bye-bye? That would be, like, totally lame. She sat thinking for a few minutes.

She got out of bed, moved the chair, and went into the hall. The light was already out in his room. Great. If she knocked now, it would be like a huge big deal. He'd have to get all dressed again, and it would look like she was this totally desperate little kid. And he might decide they needed to have one of their *talks*. Translation—he would totally yell at her for all the ways she was messing up. She shook her head, went back into her room, and replaced the chair.

After a while she got the box from beside the bed and opened it up again. She stared at the books, like, forever. Finally she picked one from the middle of the stack and opened it up.

Samantha spoke today. She said cupcake. That is Alasdair's name for her and it's fitting. She is sweet and tiny and delicious.

Samantha closed the book. Her hands were shaking as she set it back in the box, replaced the lid, and shoved it in the closet. She turned out the lights and burrowed down under her covers. She put on her headphones and turned up the music as loud as she could stand it. She cried for a while, smashing her face down into the pillow so no one would hear. She wondered if someone would come. Aunt Lorna or maybe Bridie. They were both totally pains in the butt. She waited and finally she started getting sleepy.

She remembered the chair. She got up and put it back where it belonged, then opened her door and looked out into the hall. She could hear voices downstairs. She left the door open, then went back and got into bed and put her headphones on again. No one came. That was fine, she told herself, wiping her eyes on the sheet. She didn't want to talk to anybody anyway.

❦ nineteen ❦

SAMANTHA ROLLED OVER AND OPENED her eyes. She looked at her clock, and then she remembered, and it was like something hard hit her. Dad was gone, and for just a minute she felt really sad, like she used to feel when she was a little girl and didn't get a chance to say good-bye to him before he left for work. She had that same feeling now. Sort of empty and wishing she'd gotten to say stuff, and sort of scared that she might never get a chance to say it again. She blinked for a minute, then got a grip. You're being totally lame, she told herself. She wasn't five, she was thirteen, and Dad would be back in a week. Besides, he was totally a pain, and there wasn't anything she wanted to say to him at all.

She rolled over and her eyes landed on the poster of *The Misfits* she'd bought at the record store. She should dye her hair black. Maybe she would. With Dad gone there'd be nobody to yell at her, at least not right away. She sat up and frowned. Somebody was singing. She could hear the voice, all chirpylike, coming up the heat vent from the kitchen. She clicked her tongue in irritation. Why couldn't she live in a normal house instead of one where you could hear every single thing a person said?

She got up and went downstairs, purposely dragging her feet, liking the sound of her slippers flopping behind her. It drove Aunt Winifred nuts when she dragged her feet. Or slumped her shoulders. Or let her hair hang down into her eyes. But Aunt Winifred wasn't here. Just Bridie, the hillbilly from Hooterville, and it was *her* singing, of course, some lame Christmas carol nobody'd ever heard of.

Samantha leaned against the kitchen doorway and listened to the words. They were totally moronic. Something about birds singing and the house full of friends and family and logs popping in the fireplace and carols sung off key. Well, that part was right at least.

Bridie looked up and stopped her singing. Cam and Bonnie were clueless as usual, playing with some toy over in the corner.

"What's the matter?" Bridie smiled at her, which was even more irritating. "Don't you like Christmas?"

"Sure," Samantha said. "I like Christmas. I just don't like Christmas on Walton's Mountain."

Bridie didn't answer, just started humming and went back to whatever she was doing at the sink, which really annoyed Samantha for some reason. She narrowed her eyes.

"Do you see many friends and family gathered around the old Christmas tree?" she bit out. "Is there a birdie outside the window pecking out a happy song? Let's just look and see if there's a snowman in the yard."

She went to the back door and peered out the window. It *had* snowed last night. Big deal, she told herself. She wasn't some little kid who would go crazy making snow angels. "Nope," she said. She leaned against the counter, arms crossed, and glared. It was so irritating how Bridie smiled all the time. Suddenly she had the urge to make Bridie as unhappy as she felt herself this minute. "I don't need any phony Christmas cheer from somebody who's totally clueless about the way things really are. If you're looking for happy stories, you should just go home to Mayberry. If you had a clue, you'd know that real life isn't like that, at least not around here."

Bridie stopped smiling. Samantha drew in her breath and felt a little scared. She hadn't really meant to be mean. Bridie stood still, just looking at her. Now Bridie would quit like the other baby-sitters, and everybody would be ticked at her. Again. As usual. She thought about trying to take back what she'd said, but it was too late. Bridie's face had gotten really serious. All of a sudden she bent over at the waist and twisted her hair into a knot, and Samantha couldn't figure out what she was doing. Then she stood back up and bared her neck. There was a jagged white scar running from her ear to the collar of her sweats.

"See that?" Bridie asked.

Samantha leaned forward and took a good look. The cut had been deep. Even now it made a gouge in Bridie's neck. Big deal. So she had a scar. "So?"

"My daddy did that to me," Bridie said, not changing her tone or the nice expression on her face. "With a whiskey bottle."

Samantha stared. Bridie stared back.

"Now." Bridie let go of her hair. It slid back down and covered up the scar. "It's just going to be you and me and the children for the next week, and I've got some ideas. If you're finished with your hissy fit, maybe we could have a little fun around here."

Samantha picked at her cuticle. It bled. She stuck the finger in her mouth and chewed on the fingernail. She shrugged. "Whatever."

"Go get dressed," Bridie said. Her smile came back, and Samantha felt a little rush of relief. "We've got places to go and things to do."

"*Fine,*" she retorted.

"Hurry," Bridie called after her.

Samantha took the steps two at a time. She wondered where they were going and what they were going to do. Not that she cared, though.

♃ *twenty* ♃

ALASDAIR LOOKED AROUND HIS HOTEL room, restless. He had attended services, met with the conference organizers to finalize his speaking schedule. His notes were complete and so familiar they were almost committed to memory. He was thoroughly prepared and had nothing to do until tomorrow morning when the conference began. He had no desire to stand around the Welcome Room sipping stale coffee and exchanging pastoral war stories with the attendees. This would be the perfect time to make his annual call on Professor Cuthbert. But perhaps he shouldn't go this year, he thought, knowing the probing conversation that would ensue.

He shook his head with impatience. He was beginning to live his entire life like a man walking through a minefield. Picking up the thick Boston telephone book, he looked up his old mentor's number before any more anxieties could waylay him.

"I'm sorry to give you such short notice," Alasdair apologized.

"Nonsense," Professor Cuthbert replied, his voice warm. "You know how I enjoy seeing you." He refreshed Alasdair's memory as to which train to take and where to transfer, and a half hour later Alasdair had arrived at the professor's brown-brick row house.

Bridie looked at the fruits of yesterday's shopping trip now spread over the kitchen counters.

"Well, how do you like this place?" she had asked Samantha when they'd stepped inside the store. Its aisles were festooned with red and green garlands and garish decorations, the air heavy with the sweet fragrance of caramel corn. You could probably go to a Wal-Mart in Kowloon and still smell caramel corn. Not exactly an upscale sort of place, and Bridie wondered what was going on behind Samantha's guarded eyes.

Samantha raised a shoulder in a half shrug. "I've never been to a Wal-Mart. Aunt Winifred takes me to Lord and Taylor twice a year. I get to pick out stuff from the bargain rack."

Yes, Bridie considered, that fit with her view of this family. The view she was coming to have. They might not have much, but it would be from the right store, on the off chance somebody might look inside their collar at the tag. Keep everything looking good on the outside; that was their motto.

Not that she didn't have a few faults of her own, she thought, looking at the stuff she'd bought. All right. Maybe she'd gotten a little carried away, but really, she couldn't see what she could do without. She had to have the supplies for her decorating projects. That was all there was to it. And she needed a few strands of Christmas lights to even out what she'd finally found in the corner of the garage—not the attic after all. The red and green pillar candles had been on sale, two for a dollar fifty, so they hardly counted. The big velvet bow would dress up the greens the man had given her for free when she'd bought the Christmas tree. She was going to make a door swag from the pieces of the balsam fir, and just think how much one of those would cost ready made! She had actually *saved* money there. The decorations for the tree were hardly anything, though she supposed she could have lived without the CD of Christmas music or the Christmas video for the children. But they absolutely needed the boots so they could play in the snow, and the toy airport and doll had been on sale, and the big-boy and big-girl underpants were a big part of her plans for the week, too. That left a few miscellaneous things: cookie decorations, including the little silver balls she liked, the makings for spice tea mix, the welcome mat, and red and green dish towels. She probably should take those back.

No, something argued back, and the passion she felt surprised her. *I'm tired of living without. It's Christmas, and I'm going to celebrate.*

Where did that come from? she wondered. She hadn't heard from that part of herself in a long time. She didn't know exactly what it was, but she thought it might be responsible, as well, for the last item she'd stashed in her cart. She picked up the box now and held it in her hand, looked at the corn-silk blond hair dye and wondered why she was doing this. She was only setting herself up. This could only end badly. That fierce part of her that was rising up and demanding things should go back to sleep, she warned herself severely. She put the hair dye back in the sack and shoved it in the corner behind the toaster.

"I need some help here," Samantha complained. Bridie glanced toward the table where Samantha was pinning and basting. The idea of having her make a dress had seemed inspired. Samantha had unbent a little as they picked out the material, and it had given them something to talk about.

"Oh, I see your problem," Bridie said, walking toward her. "You've got the sleeve in backward."

"It won't go the other way. It's too weird."

"I know it seems like it won't," Bridie said, adjusting the sleeve and repinning it. "But that's the way it works. Baste it, and when we turn it right side out you'll see."

Samantha frowned and leaned over the pieces of the dress.

"Setting sleeves is the hardest part of this dress," Bridie encouraged. "After this you'll be able to make almost anything."

Samantha didn't answer, just continued to work in silent absorption. Bridie sat down and watched in case more help was needed. Samantha glanced up, then quickly shifted her eyes back to the fabric. "How'd you learn to do all this?" she asked.

"My grandmother and mother taught me how to sew. My grandma had an old treadle sewing machine, and she used to let me make doll quilts. My mother had an electric Singer. She helped me make quite a few of my clothes."

"My mother never taught me anything." Samantha's voice was cold, flat. She didn't look up from her pinning. Bridie remembered Anna's longing and guilt when she wrote about her daughter.

"I'm sure it wasn't because she didn't love you," she said.

Samantha looked up sharply, eyes wide, then ducked her head down again. She didn't speak.

"When shall we decorate the tree?" Bridie asked after a minute or two.

Samantha raised the shoulder up again. "I don't even remember the last time we had a Christmas tree. We always decorate the one at the church."

Bridie gave her head a tiny shake. What had happened to these people?

"Well, you're going to have one this year," she promised. If she'd been hoping for much, she was disappointed. Samantha kept on pinning, head down, her brown hair in her face so that Bridie couldn't see her expression.

"Let's do it tonight," she suggested.

"It's Sunday."

"So?"

"Church." Samantha said slowly, sarcastically, just in case she didn't understand.

"I'm not preaching," Bridie shot back. "Are you? I think Cam and Bonnie have the night off, too."

That got her attention. Samantha raised her head and gave her an incredulous look. "Are you saying we don't have to go?"

Bridie edged her way out. "I'm saying everybody's entitled to a little family time. And I paid fifty dollars for a tree that's drying out on the porch."

"Whatever," Samantha said, but her eyes looked bright, and when she went back to her work she was humming.

Alasdair looked around him at the cotton-batting sky as he climbed the steps. The air felt thick. Even the sound of his feet was muffled. It would snow before long. He rang the bell.

After a few minutes the professor came to the door, and Alasdair experienced his usual moment of surprise. Somehow Professor Cuthbert was perpetually middle-aged in Alasdair's mind, frozen at the point in time at which they'd met. Every year he was unprepared for the reality of the marching years. Since last year's visit his friend had lost his rounded look, though he was still far from frail. The hair that encircled his shining pate had lost the last bit of its ginger color, and it could have been Alasdair's imagination, but his once snapping blue eyes seemed a little faded. Cuthbert drew Alasdair into a strong embrace, though, and clapped him on the back, his pleasure evident on his face. "Come in," he urged and opened the door wide.

Alasdair smiled, followed him into the narrow hallway to the room he indicated, and a flood of memories washed over him. How many hours had he spent in this house, in this very study, reading and arguing, praying and discussing? He looked around the warm little niche, at the collection of bulging bookcases, the huge desk covered with sliding piles of paper and tippling stacks of books. Light spilled from two antique Tiffany lamps, forming golden puddles on the faded red carpet. The drapes were heavy old brocade and pulled shut, enclosing them in a cozy cocoon. A low, steady flame burned in the small fireplace over a bed of glowing red coals.

"Please sit down," Cuthbert invited. "I've made us a snack."

Alasdair took the chair indicated and settled back into its worn leather arms. He rubbed them and could feel the tiny cracks of age. The coffee table before him held the refreshments. A ceramic teapot was draped with a terrycloth towel doing duty as a cozy. Two chipped china plates held thick sandwiches. A bowl of store-bought chocolate sandwich cookies sat beside two heavy pottery mugs. The food looked good to him.

"I see you're staying busy," Alasdair observed, gesturing toward the overflowing desk.

Cuthbert nodded. "As always."

"Are you working on a journal article? A text?"

The professor shook his head. "No. A devotional."

"Really?"

"Surprised?"

"A little. Only because you seemed to favor theology rather than—"

"Faith?"

Alasdair gave him a sharp look. Cuthbert was smiling. "Certainly not," he protested. "Your faith has always been evident in everything you write. In all your life."

"That's very kind of you." Cuthbert pulled the cloth from the teapot and picked it up. It jiggled slightly, and a little tea sloshed onto one of the sandwiches. He seemed not to notice. "But I'll be the first to acknowledge that my faith has been somewhat top-heavy. North of the neck, shall we say?"

Alasdair wasn't sure how to respond. The professor filled the mugs and managed to set the teapot down, then replaced the makeshift cozy.

"How are your sisters?" he asked, handing Alasdair a mug. Alasdair took it and added sugar and milk.

"Well as always, sir."

"Fine. And your children?" The professor leaned over and began doctoring his own tea, giving Alasdair a moment to think. Had he come for help? And if so, could his old mentor give it to him? Or would he simply be burdening his friend with problems he could do nothing about?

"Your silence answers for you." Cuthbert sat back in his chair and sipped his tea. Alasdair took another long swallow of his own. It was hot and burned his tongue. He set down the mug on the floor beside his chair.

He met Cuthbert's gaze, which was unflinching. "There have been a few problems," he evaded. "I hope we're coming out of our rough patch."

"No one is ill, I hope."

"No."

Cuthbert nodded, prompting more. "So? Tell me."

Alasdair took off his glasses and rubbed his eyes. "I wouldn't know where to begin," he said, putting them back on.

"Anywhere. We can always circle back."

Alasdair smiled, but still he didn't answer.

"I've heard of your troubles at the church."

Alasdair sighed but didn't even lift a brow. The denomination was like a small town. There were no secrets.

"I had my own pulpit at one time, you know."

Alasdair nodded politely.

"Yes, I captained the ship, so to speak." Cuthbert gave a dry chuckle, and the mug he was resting on his chest jiggled dangerously.

"No one tells you about the pirates," Alasdair murmured darkly.

The professor's eyes lit with amusement and he gave a nod. "That's an apt analogy." He set down his mug and readjusted himself in the chair, leaning forward. "Did I ever tell you about my battle with Clive Newby over who would take over the pulpit back in 1967?"

Alasdair shook his head, feeling a little surge of relief that they wouldn't be discussing his problems.

Cuthbert didn't seem to notice. He licked his lips with relish at recounting his tale. "I was pastor, Clive the associate. Congregation up to two thousand. Three services every Sunday. Offerings up. Sanctuary paid for and the building campaign for a new one well begun. I'd built that place from the ground up. When I'd first come, we met in the music room of the high school. Thirty-five of us. Now we were one of the biggest and most vital churches in the city. When Clive decided to make a play for the pulpit, I got wind, of course. Maudie was a great one for keeping her ear to the ground."

Alasdair nodded. The professor's wife, rest her soul, had put him in mind of Winifred on a bad day.

"Clive was stirring things up, moving toward a vote to have me ousted. But I mounted a preemptive strike. Called together the ruling elders I knew were behind me, and we went house to house mustering support. Numbering the troops, so to speak. We thought we had him beaten, but we'd underestimated his persuasiveness. At the congregational meeting we were nearly equally split. Stalemated. Neither of us had the majority necessary to win. Neither side was willing to concede. Well, the fight raged, as you might imagine." The professor paused to take a sip of tea, and Alasdair realized he was tense, waiting to hear how the story ended. But instead of finishing, Cuthbert rose stiffly, rearranged the logs with a poker, sending up a shower of sparks. He apparently decided another log was called for. By the time he'd extricated it from the box, added it to the fire, closed the screen, and replaced the poker, Alasdair was ready to scream.

"Well?" he prompted. "What happened?"

Cuthbert sat down and took another sip of tea before he answered. When he did his eyes were filled with what looked like fresh pain. "I won," he said. "I kept the pulpit. But it was a hollow victory, I can tell you."

"In what way?" Alasdair asked, not sure he wanted to hear the answer.

"Ichabod."

Alasdair's eyes widened. Ichabod. Hebrew for "the glory of the Lord has departed." After a moment Cuthbert carried on but with sadness rather than animation.

"The building was mine. The congregation was mine. Newby left. Took some members with him, but we were basically unscathed. The only problem was, the hand of the Lord seemed to have stopped moving among us. He'd set us aside. And I knew why. I'd forgotten what I was about, why I was left here on earth. I'd gotten my calling confused with my job." He gazed at Alasdair's face, but Alasdair knew he was seeing the past. "I kept on preaching, but it was no good. After a year or so I took the job at the seminary. The church carried on with someone else. You see," he finished, a bittersweet smile on his lips, "I'd forgotten who really was captain of the ship. The church wasn't mine, but His."

"So what then?" Alasdair responded, his surge of anger coming out through his voice. "I'm supposed to just let someone come in and wrest it away from me?" The pirate analogy was a stupid comparison, and he wished he'd never made it.

"No, but have you asked God whether or not He wants you to have it?"

"What would He do?" Alasdair shot back. "Tape a note to the refrigerator?" His voice was sharp.

Neither one of them said anything for a long while. Alasdair broke the silence first. "I'm sorry."

Cuthbert smiled. "You're forgiven."

They sat together, the only sound the hiss and crack of the log on the fire. The glory of the Lord had departed. Alasdair tried to remember the last time he'd sensed God's presence or heard His voice. He couldn't recall just now.

He began speaking without making a conscious decision to do so. "A darkness seems to have settled over my home," he said. "Samantha is troubled. I don't care for her friends, but I don't forbid them because she has so few. She hates me. I can feel it. It almost radiates from her when I enter the room. I don't give Cameron and Bonnie the attention they need. I feel a heaviness I can't seem to shake. Sometimes the darkness seems literal. I keep turning on lights, but nothing helps."

"I'm sorry." Cuthbert's eyes shone with kindness and concern. "I thought you might be struggling, but I didn't know absolutely."

"The worst of it is that I feel like what you just described. The glory of the Lord has departed. I preach, and there's no movement of the Spirit. I pray and sense no answers. I read the Scriptures, but they are only words. They don't seem to touch me. Not like they used to." He didn't quite know what he expected Professor Cuthbert to say, but he was surprised at his response.

"You know, Alasdair, the older I get, the more I realize only one thing matters."

"What is that?"

"To know Him. To walk with Him. Just as Adam did in the garden in the cool of the day. There's nothing else."

Alasdair felt a hollow ache, a coldness in his chest. "Well, He doesn't seem to be returning my calls these days."

"He seems to have left you to your own devices," Cuthbert said after a pause.

"I suppose He has."

"I wonder why," the professor mused, his head tipped slightly, as if he were pondering a particularly intriguing puzzle.

Alasdair would have smiled if he hadn't felt such empty misery. "I don't know," he said. Quickly. Flatly.

Cuthbert's eyebrow raised a millimeter.

Alasdair tensed.

"Perhaps, as in my case, the Lord's work has led you away from the Lord," the professor speculated, his voice soft.

Alasdair relaxed and felt a momentary relief. This was on the target but not dead center. The probe had landed just short of the abscess. Still, there was truth here, unpleasant truth. He felt bitter amusement at the irony. He hadn't even had the momentary pleasure of sin, the oblivion of an alcoholic binge, the surge of euphoria from a drug-induced high, the sensual release of illicit sex, the wanton satiation of greed. His had been a cold, gray sin, but it had led him to the exact same spot of desolation. The most insidious of the enemy's tactics had been unleashed on him. Success. And success that was unassailable. Success in the work of the Lord.

"Well, there's nothing I can do about that now." It was too late for a career change. Much too late for many things.

Cuthbert lifted a brow and took another small sip of his tea. "I disagree," he said.

Alasdair frowned and waited for him to explain.

"You could stop doing it."

Alasdair frowned at the ridiculousness of the suggestion. "How would I make a living? What would I do?"

"Or more to the point, who would you be?"

Alasdair felt a strike of irritation and didn't bother to hide it. "I can't see the point of abandoning the good along with the bad. Even if I have misaligned my priorities"—a point that remained to be established, he added to himself—"I hardly think resignation is the cure for the ill."

Cuthbert didn't answer. He didn't react at all. Taking a cigar from his pocket, he unwrapped it, then put it in his mouth and gave an imaginary puff or two, a habit that had always seemed ridiculous to Alasdair and now irritated him almost beyond endurance. "You don't need to be salaried to do the work of the Lord," Cuthbert said around the mouthful of tobacco.

"Paul was a tentmaker. You could shine shoes and do the work of the Lord. He doesn't need your speaking engagements and radio programs. The work of the Lord is nurturing souls. For that you don't need a commission to preach."

"You're suggesting I should walk away from everything I've worked so hard to attain, given up so much to achieve."

Cuthbert shrugged. "I'm not telling you what to do. I'm simply pointing out alternatives. One always has a choice."

Alasdair shook his head slightly. His emotions roiled, though they hadn't yet settled between anger and despair.

Cuthbert spoke again, this time taking out the cigar. "I imagine it would be like picking a loose thread on a sweater," he observed dispassionately. "Admitting you'd made a mistake."

Alasdair frowned. *What in the world are you babbling about?* he wanted to shout.

Cuthbert turned the oddly penetrating eyes on him once again. "What I mean is, where would it end?"

Alasdair set down his mug. He wanted nothing more than to leave. He didn't though, and after a moment the professor gracefully picked up the conversation like a lost thread, wound it around to books and articles, their old familiar ground. Finally Alasdair felt he could depart graciously. "I suppose I should go," he said when the conversation paused.

"You haven't eaten your sandwich."

Alasdair looked at the untouched plate. He'd lost his appetite. He stood up, and the professor followed him to the door and out onto the stoop; then the two of them paused, awkward at this last good-bye. It was snowing, and when Alasdair looked across the darkened street, he could see a small circle of light around the streetlamp. The flakes came from nowhere, floated across it, soft and yet relentless, then disappeared into its glowing penumbra, that region where light met dark and neither reigned.

"Alasdair—"

He turned. The top of the professor's head shone in the light from the streetlamp.

"Forgive me if I spoke out of turn. Please don't hold an old man's bluntness against him."

"I never would," Alasdair promised him, and after one last hand-clasp, he stepped out into the cold night and walked over snow-carpeted sidewalks to the train. He would not hold his words against him. But neither would he forget that one last question. *"Where would it end?"* It would end in the churchyard, in the corner in the back, at a small square of earth marked *Anna Williams MacPherson*. That particular journey, were he to take it, would undoubtedly end there.

✎ twenty-one ✎

"How in the world did you do that?" Lorna asked as she stood by the front door, preparing to leave for her night job. Bridie smiled. Lorna sounded as amazed as if Cam and Bonnie had learned to fly instead of just peepee in the toilet and sleep through the night.

"Well, the potty training was helped along with M&M's," Bridie answered. "Besides, they were ready. And as far as their sleeping goes, I Ferberized them."

"I beg your pardon?"

"Dr. Ferber. He's a pediatrician who wrote a book. I checked it out of the library. Basically, you love them up all day and then ignore them when they cry at night."

Lorna smiled. "Well, they look more cared for than they have in ages," she said, and her pretty brown eyes filled with tears. "Cameron's saying words. Even Samantha seems happier. You are a treasure, Bridie."

Bridie felt a flush of pleasure.

"Just look at all this," Lorna went on, gesturing around her at the house. "Everything looks wonderful. I just can't get over it."

Bridie nodded. She was pleased herself. Somehow painting and scrubbing and fixing things up had rearranged her insides as well. Taking care of a home and children had brought back memories of being mother to her brother and sisters. She'd often seen their faces in her mind's eye this past week as she painted and cuddled and cooked. It hurt, but it was a sweet pain, and she wouldn't wish it gone.

Samantha thumped down the stairs just then and twirled around. "Ta-dumm," she sang, holding out her arms.

"Oh, it looks beautiful!" Bridie exclaimed.

"Samantha, is this the dress you've been working on?" Lorna's voice was filled with amazement.

Samantha nodded with pride.

"Why, it's lovely."

"The collar's a little crooked," Samantha apologized.

"Where?" Bridie protested.

"I'm not sure I got the hem exactly even."

Bridie shook her head. "It looks good to me. Besides, it'll never be noticed on a galloping horse. That's what my grandmother used to say."

Lorna stood, eyes tearing again, looking back and forth at the two of them as if they'd just graduated or gotten married. Bridie hoped all the emotion didn't spook Samantha. She needn't have worried. Samantha was preening in front of the mirror on the coatrack. "It *is* pretty, isn't it?" she asked.

Bridie looked past the puckered side seams and the off-center collar. "It's beautiful. And you did it yourself. You should be proud."

Samantha turned and looked at her, met her eyes for just a minute. "Thanks," she said shortly. She darted for the stairs before Bridie could answer.

"My pleasure," she said softly to Samantha's retreating back.

Samantha carefully hung her dress on the padded hanger Bridie had scrounged from the attic. It *was* pretty. She held it up again. She wanted to look at it, not put it in the closet. She looked around for someplace to hang it and settled for the back of the closet door. Her *Misfits* poster was covered up, but oh well. She put on her pajamas, then turned down her bed and got under the covers. They were soft, not scratchy, and they smelled like roses instead of Clorox since Bridie had been doing the laundry.

After a minute she went and got the box and pulled it close to her bed. Maybe she would do it tonight.

She stared at it. Her heart started beating hard and her mouth got dry.

All she had to do was reach down and pick up a journal. Just pick it up and start to read.

Samantha wanted to know her mother. She really did. She had pulled that box by her bed every night. She looked at the scrapbooks inside. She'd picked up each one and checked the dates in the front and put them in order. Every night she took the first one out and held it on her lap. She just couldn't manage to get any farther than that. She sighed and stared at the box. Dad would be back tomorrow. Then Bridie wouldn't be here at night anymore. She liked having Bridie here at night. The house felt full when she was here. It annoyed her that she liked it.

She picked a book from the middle of the box. She flipped it open.

> *I keep watching Samantha play with her blocks. She patiently builds a house, bit by bit, then when she is finished, she knocks it down. She stares at the mess for a moment, then begins building again. I think I know how it would feel to be a tiny person in that house of blocks. To build your world, piece by laborious piece, only to have a mysterious hand reach down from time to time and sweep it to bits.*

Samantha closed the book hard. She threw it back into the box, then sat and stared at it, blinking. She heard feet on the steps. Her door was open, and if she didn't want company, she should close it. Bridie came closer, then poked her head into the room.

"Hey. I thought you'd be asleep by now."

She almost said obviously not, but decided not to. "Not yet." She glanced toward the box by the side of the bed. Bridie looked where she was looking. Her face didn't change at all.

"Can I come in?" she asked, all casual-like.

Samantha shrugged. Her heart started thumping again. "I guess so."

Bridie strolled over to the dress again. "This sure is pretty," she said, smiling. "We'll have to look for some nice earrings to go with it."

"There's a bead shop on Duke Street," Samantha said. "We could make some."

"What a good idea!" Bridie gave her a huge smile like she'd just invented peanut butter or something.

"It's no big deal," Samantha said, feeling grouchy and then mad at herself because she hadn't really meant to act that way.

"Well, good night," Bridie said. She walked toward the door and put her hand on the doorknob. Samantha felt like she had once when she'd been messing around in the car and had played with the gearshift, and it had started rolling.

"Light on or off?" Bridie asked.

"What?" Her voice came out funny, all strangled sounding.

Bridie paused and her face got serious. "What's wrong?" she asked, taking a step closer to the bed.

There was no answer. Samantha just blinked again, and her face froze into that hard look that could shatter with the wrong word.

Ah. This Samantha was back again. Not the tough girl who stole wine and skipped school. This was the child from the church, the little girl with the sagging shoulders who'd penned the note.

Samantha pointed her glazed eyes toward the floor again. Bridie followed her gaze. She felt a stirring of some odd emotion—dread or fear—when she saw Anna's journals there.

She sat down on the bed, thinking. Why should she be afraid of what was in those books? It wasn't as if the contents were going to affect her in any way. And she had nothing to do with this family or this child, either, part of her brain reminded her. Cut and run, it advised flatly. Bridie rubbed her forehead. Her mind was a piece of window glass, and thoughts pelted and rolled off, none staying put long enough to examine.

Samantha's trauma increased. She buried her head into the pillow.

Bridie reached out and rubbed the shuddering back, wishing someone else were here, someone who knew how to help. Who wanted to help.

God, please send someone to help me, Samantha had prayed.

Well. Here she was. Not exactly what Samantha had prayed for, but apparently she was the answer.

"I can't read them," Samantha was saying into the pillow.

Bridie felt a surge of a very familiar emotion. She hated watching things unravel and not being able to help.

But you can help. You just won't.

Well, fine. Now she was hearing voices. She thought back to what she'd read about the long-term effects of drug abuse.

You know who I am.

Oh. Better yet. She wasn't having flashbacks; she was hearing the voice of God. That was quite an improvement.

Read the books, the voice suggested quietly.

Bridie shook her head.

Read them.

"Oh, for crying out loud," she muttered.

Samantha raised a startled face.

"Oh no, I wasn't talking to you," Bridie soothed, rubbing her arm.

Samantha stared at her. Well, at least she'd stopped crying.

Bridie decided to throw all her chips onto the table. "Are you afraid to read them?"

Head back into the pillow. More sobs, and suddenly Bridie couldn't tighten her heart any longer. Her own eyes flooded, and it seemed she could almost see the sparrow plummeting toward the hard ground.

"Come here," she invited, and Samantha turned and buried her face in Bridie's shoulder and hair. Bridie wrapped herself around the bony little body, kissing the curly head. "Shh. Hush, now. It's all right."

When the sobs tapered off, Bridie plunged in, landing right in that spot where the angels tiptoed.

"Listen," she said, brushing the hair back from Samantha's wet face. "I think you need to know what's in those books, but I can guess how hard it is for you to read them."

Samantha looked at her wide-eyed, waiting.

"Would you like for me to read them with you?"

The tension drained from Samantha's pinched little face. She nodded. The water level in her eyes rose again but didn't overflow this time.

So. She had caught this sparrow before she hit ground. A close save, but a save all the same. The thought flew by that the reverend wouldn't exactly be happy to know the hired help was perusing his personal history. She had no right to pry into Alasdair and Anna MacPherson's private lives. None whatsoever. Everyone would have a hissy fit if they knew.

She smiled, the humor unavoidable. If they knew the truth about her, reading Anna's journals would definitely be small potatoes.

You came to help the child, her invisible friend reminded her.

"That's right, I did," Bridie said, and suddenly the decision didn't seem so hard to make. She wasn't here to make friends with the father or the aunt. She wasn't here to play house or mama to the babies, though those things had all been fun. She had come here to help the child, and this was how the child was asking to be helped. Besides, the worst that could happen would be she'd get caught, booted out, and then she could leave with a clear conscience.

She could almost hear her mama, though, horrified, rebuking her for nosing around in other people's private things. She hadn't even let Bridie explore Grandma's trinket drawer without asking permission.

Well, she had done quite a few things Mama wouldn't approve of. And on that thin comfort, she took the first journal from the box and climbed onto the bed.

"You can sit up here," Samantha invited in a rare show of warmth.

Bridie scooted up beside her. Both of them leaned back against the pillows, and Bridie positioned the book on their laps.

It was big and fancy, with a brown leather cover. Anna had written a word on the front with metallic gold paint. *Ephemera.*

"What's that mean?" Samantha traced the letters.

"Let's just see." Bridie opened the book and pointed to the word, written again in beautiful script. *"Ephemera,"* she read, *"The transient documents of everyday life."*

"What's transient?"

"Here today, gone tomorrow," she said softly.

Samantha was silent.

"This is the journal of Anna Ruth Williams," Bridie read, and beneath the inscription was Anna's picture. She was beautiful. The photo looked as if it had been snapped at a party. She was standing in a doorway, leaning against the wall. Her hands were behind her back, and she was smiling as if she had a secret. Her hair was long, curling loosely around her shoulders. She wore pearl teardrop earrings and a black dress.

The next page had two pieces of heavy rag-rich paper attached meticulously to the scrapbook page. There were no glue bumps or Scotch tape. Again Anna had written in calligraphic script.

> *I should be studying, but instead I am reading my favorite book,* The Lion, the Witch, and the Wardrobe. *Again.*
>
> *"What do you like about it that you read it over and over?" Father asked me once. I said I didn't know, but now that I've thought about it, I think I like the way the White Witch's power begins to crumble once the king is back in the land. I feel that way now. It's as if spring is here, even though it's October. Father says I'm giddy at being let loose at the university and I should keep my mind on my studies. I'm sure he's right, but I believe I am happier than I have ever been. It feels so good to be away from home. I feel guilty as I say this. He is so kind to me and worries so, but sometimes I fear I'll suffocate. Here I can breathe. I go to my classes, return to my room. My roommate is seldom here, and I savor being alone. I brew myself a cup of strong tea and just sit on the desk and gaze out the window at the leaves turning all shades of rust and russet and brown and gold. It's raining today, and the wind tears them off and splats them onto the ground in wet clumps. It's warm and delicious inside. The steam pipes clang and tap. I take another sip of tea and turn the page of my book.*

Bridie turned the page. There was a class schedule from the University of Edinburgh attached. Anna had been no slouch academically. Creative Writing, Ancient History, Physical Science, and Introduction to Classical Literature.

"Go on," Samantha urged.

"Hold your horses." Bridie shifted her eyes toward the photographs of Anna with her friends that were arranged artistically on the next page. Anna and two other girls were sitting at a table in a restaurant, mouths full, obviously enjoying their food. The menu was taped beside it—Brody's Pub—with a circle around what Anna had ordered.

The next picture was of Anna and a pleasant-looking young man. Not Alasdair MacPherson. Anna was wearing a silly-looking hat, and the man was carrying a huge bag. Bridie read the caption.

Hugh and I take in the High Street Jumble Sale. Treasures galore—this lovely chapeau as well as a donkey lamp and pink che-nille bedspread. This may call for a new decorating scheme. I think the peacock on black velvet would make a perfect focal point. Will give some thought to it.

"She would have liked Wal-Mart," Samantha said.

"And I like her for that," Bridie said, smiling.

Bridie turned the page. There was another picture—Anna at her desk, reading.

"My roommate snapped this," Anna wrote, and beside the word *roommate* was a picture of another girl. She was big and happy look-ing with red curly hair.

Her name is Ruby, and she is a nursing student. I said perhaps I'd become a nurse, but Ruby said no, I was too sensitive. "Stick to your writing," she advised. I suppose she is right. Still, I like the idea of taking care of someone. Making the world right for them. Ruby laughed at that. "As if that's what nurses do," she said. Here's Ruby's solution:

An arrow pointed downward to another photo. It was Anna at her desk again, wearing a paper nurse's cap.

She made this for me and says I can play nurse as I study litera-ture. The best of all worlds.

Samantha scooted a little closer and rested her head lightly against Bridie's shoulder. Bridie turned the page. There was another class schedule. Winter quarter Anna would take writing again and another literature class and sociology and art. Beside it was fall quarter's grade report. Bridie gave a little whistle. "Look at that." She pointed at the grade point average: 3.96.

There were more pictures of her and her friends. There was a train schedule taped onto the page and underneath Anna had written:

> *I feel myself tense as I think of returning home for the holidays. Father will want to talk about Mother again, and I don't want to talk about Mother. I want to be happy. I suppose I am borrowing trouble. I will go home. This time. After all, he's bought me the ticket. But if things turn out as I expect, I'll spend future holidays at college.*

Bridie turned the page, interested. She wondered what kind of problems Anna had had with her father.

> *I am back at school, and not a moment too soon. I awoke this morning seeing through the dark glasses. As always, the mood came out of the blue. I went to bed last night happy as a lark, glad to be back, and awoke this morning as gray and droopy as the dripping bare branches outside my window. I didn't get out of bed. Ruby came in at lunchtime and asked what was wrong, was I ill, and I said yes. She brought me soup from the dining hall, then sat at the edge of my bed, giving me knowing looks. "You should talk to someone," she said. Go away, I wanted to shout at her. Just go away and leave me alone. Perhaps, I answered instead. Finally she left, and I pulled the covers over my head and went back to sleep.*

There were no pictures on the page. Just her train ticket from Christmas break, and not glued neatly but stuck to the page with a piece of masking tape. Bridie glanced at Samantha. Her face was tense again. Bridie turned the page and kept blundering on.

The sun pours through the windows. The last week seems like a dark dream. I don't know why I let these little ups and downs throw me into such a spin. It's over, that's the main thing, and I'm ever grateful. I think I'll see about getting a job. My classes are going well, though I have a little catching up to do from my spell last week. But on the whole, I think it might be good for me to have a schedule, someplace I must go each day and see people. I have made a promise to myself. Whether I find a job or not, every day I will make my bed, shower, and eat.

Bridie frowned. Those were pretty low expectations. Having to promise yourself to eat was not a good thing. But then again, she was probably taking one statement out of context. After all, judging from the papers and assignments pasted in the scrapbook, Anna's grades were still very good.

There were lots of pages of mementos after that. Flyers for plays she'd been to, movie ticket stubs, more photos of Anna and her friends. Lots of entries about her writing projects, the plots of her short stories, which sounded awfully depressing, but what did she know? Apparently winter quarter passed without another spell of the dark glasses. Spring quarter's class assignments were glued onto the next page. Bridie flipped past it, and there, staring back at her, was Alasdair MacPherson. It was a small picture with printing underneath, probably clipped from the campus phone book or yearbook. *Alasdair MacPherson, Teaching Assistant, Divinity Department.* Bridie smiled.

I have met a new friend. His name is Alasdair MacPherson, and he teaches my Biblical Literature class. Doesn't teach it, exactly. He is a graduate student—a teaching assistant. He doesn't ask me out, of course. That wouldn't be appropriate, but he did call me up to his desk after class to discuss the thesis for my paper and we got on to other subjects, and before I knew it an hour and a half had passed. That happened twice last week. He volunteered to lead a study group, and of course, I signed up immediately. Shameless, I know.

I am so glad Renaissance Literature was closed. Otherwise I'd never have met him. I am carrying on too much, but really, he is a very attractive person, and I mean that in more ways than physical, although there's nothing to complain about in that department.

A few pages followed of inconsequential things, but then it got interesting again.

Alasdair's teaching assistantship will end in June. This message was delivered with a meaningful look. I smiled, knowing that he is telling me that when he is no longer my teacher, we can meet with no excuse whatsoever except that we want to be together.

"That's very interesting," I said, not admitting to a thing. He looked a tiny bit flustered and said he would be in Scotland until August. That took me aback. I suppose I hadn't thought about his leaving the country, but of course, he would be. He looked positively pleased at my reaction. Unkind brute. I must get to work. My grades won't be what they were earlier in the year, I'm afraid, except for one class. I seem to show a distinct appreciation for Biblical Literature.

"I can't believe she was that goofy about Dad," Samantha grumbled. Bridie stared into space and thought about Alasdair MacPherson's smoky blue eyes and handsome features. She remembered the feeling of his hot lips on her palm, the warmth of his strong chest under her hand. She could believe it.

"Read," Samantha demanded.

Bridie snapped to and turned the page. More pictures, these featuring Alasdair and Anna together. The first one featured the two of them standing in the middle of a narrow, curved street, smiling. This time Alasdair was the one carrying the sack. Anna must have been back to the jumble sale. She felt a funny sensation looking at the two of them, and she didn't care to analyze it. She shook off the melancholy and read on.

"Show me Scotland," Alasdair said to me the day school let out for the term, and I have obliged. Every day this week we've taken another tour. I now understand the term "whirlwind romance."

Monday we took the train to the highlands and went hiking.

We stayed overnight at a hostel. Separately, of course. He touched me for the first time. When we were up on the hilltop looking at the landscape, he pulled me close, brushed away the hair blowing in my face, leaned in, and kissed me. He was gentle, yet so intense. I have never felt this way before.

"TMI—too much information," Samantha said.

Bridie turned the page. More pictures. Anna and Alasdair standing in front of a castle. Candy wrappers, a couple of pressed flowers, postcards. More pictures. A train schedule. A calendar with Alasdair's name written in every square. Wednesday they'd gone to the observatory, Thursday they'd had dinner at the Caledonian Hotel. Friday Anna had given Alasdair a choice between going to hear *The Siege of Troy* by Berlioz sung in French, a talk on postmodern dance, or *Cosi Fan Tutti* in Italian. Bridie smiled at the next entry.

He chose a concert by the Scottish Chamber Orchestra at Queen's Hall. It was lovely. Afterward he bought us big cups of creamy chocolate at a café. We drank it, walking through the cemetery downtown, reading the epitaphs. Some were quite sad.

"I want a big gaudy headstone when I die," I said lightly, wishing we'd walked somewhere else.

"I hope that won't be for a long, long time," he answered back, and suddenly I realized that I am alive, not dead yet. There's no need for mourning.

He reminds me of a chivalrous knight. I half expect him to wear armor and carry a sword, but it's probably just reading too much Chaucer that's affecting my perceptions. Still, he has such a gentle strength about him. It does me good, and the proof is that there have been no dark times at all since he came into my life. I know it's fanciful, but it's as if his soul is the other half of mine. I don't know what I will do when he leaves. I won't think about that now. Instead, I will thank God for hearing the longing of my heart.

Bridie turned the last page. It was empty. She closed the book. Samantha blinked. "That's it?" she asked.

Bridie nodded toward the clock. It was nearly one. "It's time for bed now, but we can read the others, too, if you like."

Samantha nodded.

Bridie placed the journal in the box with the others. "Good night."

"Good night."

"Light on or off?" Bridie asked, her hand on the door.

"On, please," Samantha said instead of her usual "whatever."

Bridie's heart was heavy as she undressed and prepared for bed. It was as if Anna had become flesh and blood to her and she could see that this new friend, instantly dear, was headed for trouble. Anna's hope and vulnerability fairly cried out from the pages of her journal. She had trusted so much in what Alasdair MacPherson's love could heal.

"The arm of flesh will fail you," Bridie's grandmother had been fond of reminding her, especially after she'd started dating, bringing home this one and that one, going on and on about them. *"Love with all your heart, Mary, but don't look to anybody but the Lord to fill up your empty spots. There's never been a man born of woman who can do that, and I don't care if he's the finest thing since store-bought pickles."*

Grandma was right, Bridie thought, climbing into the bed. Apprehension suddenly gripped her. What was she doing? Reading Anna's journals might have seemed like a good idea, a healing thing to do, but what if she was wrong? What if lancing the boil only spread the infection?

She didn't pray. That would have been presumptuous, considering. But she whispered her doubts and questions into the darkness for quite a long while, wishing with all her heart that someone was listening. She finished and then lay there, thinking. She had no idea what this family needed to be healed from and even less idea as to how to do it. She supposed she would just take things one step at a time. She supposed that the first chance she got, she would go back to Samantha's room and begin reading journal number two.

❧ *twenty-two* ❧

ALASDAIR APPROACHED HIS HOUSE. HE blinked. It was his house, was it not? Or had it been sold and new owners moved in during the eight days he'd been gone? He pulled to the curb, bumping over the ridges of frozen slush left by the snowplow, then turned off the ignition and the lights and just sat for a moment, staring.

Someone had shoveled the walk, but not with the neat, orderly strokes of the maintenance men from the church. This job looked as though it had been performed by drunken elves. The cleared path zagged through the piled-up snow, darting a foot or two to the left, correcting, then aiming toward the right, cutting a crazy course to the porch. Small footprints dotted the snow beside it and converged out in the middle of the lawn. He smiled. A family of snowpersons congregated under the snow-covered oak branches. They were a sagging, leaning, tipsy-looking bunch, but regally adorned. He squinted and recognized Father's good derby and Mother's old fox stole, its head and feet perched jauntily on snowmother's ample bosom. Oh my. Winifred should not see this.

He got out of the car, so fascinated he didn't bother to bring his suitcase, and followed the maze toward the porch. The house was lit up, from the outside as well as the megawatts spilling from the windows. Someone had retrieved the Christmas lights from the garage, and it looked as if they'd taken every set purchased over the years of his childhood. There were big colored bulbs running along the roofline, glowing in Jell-O tints, sagging in places where the cord had slipped from its fasteners. Apparently unfazed by running out of lights before the roofline, the artist had simply taken up with the newer sets—smaller twinkle lights. They outlined a third of the roof and the windows and the colors blinked on and off in furious rhythm. Three of the windows, that is. The fourth shone with all white lights, as did the door. He felt his face breaking into the unfamiliar shape of a grin as he made his way to the porch. It had been similarly cleared, and the workers' identities were given away by four sets of boots lined up by the doormat, one adult sized, one slightly smaller, two tiny sets—one pink plastic, one red, the price tags still attached. The doormat, also, was new. Santa waved from his sleigh, a wreath of words encircling his head. *Ho. Ho. Ho. Merry Christmas.*

Unaccountably, Alasdair's throat closed. His eyes filled. He breathed in and out—a spicy, fragrant breath from the massive concoction of evergreen boughs and red ribbon that hung from the door knocker. He took hold of the knob, turned it, and stepped inside.

He felt a moment of confusion, not sure which of his senses he should attend to first. Smell won. Someone had been making cinnamon rolls, and recently. The aroma lay over the scent of fried chicken, and both of these competed with the sharp, fresh tang of new paint and the resinous spritz of evergreen.

Sight sprang to life simultaneously. This entry hall was the origin of at least part of the paint smell. The wallpaper was gone. And good riddance, he thought with a burst of relief. The walls were now a warm cream color, and strung from one corner to the next were dripping, dipping ropes of thick red yarn from which dangled Christmas cards of every shape, size, and color, interspersed with homemade snowflakes cut from lined notebook paper.

He debated which sound to follow. Christmas music wafted from the direction of the kitchen, complete with organ and bells, but the other music had a greater appeal. The sound of children's laughter mingling with the boinging background and silly voices of cartoons drew him like a piper's call. He passed through what he vaguely remembered as a dim, shadowed hallway, briefly noted that the MacPherson family gallery had been removed to make way for the new paint, and glanced into the bare-looking dining room, obviously a work in progress. The table was covered with a sheet, the walls half stripped of their paper.

He rounded the corner into the living room. No one noticed him for a moment, so he had a chance to take in the scene.

Everything familiar was gone. Mother's antique Chippendale furniture had disappeared. All of it. Now the place of honor was held by the old brown couch that had been in the kitchen sitting room. It was covered with toys: some kind of plastic parking garage peopled by tiny figures that resembled corks from wine bottles, two naked dolls, and a stuffed panda bear. Several picture books splayed open across the pillows. The walls had been painted a butter yellow. All of Mother's framed prints, china plates, knick-knacks, and collections were gone. The mahogany piecrust tables were gone, but on second look he wondered if they were under the red plaid skirts on each end of the sofa. The only things on the tabletops besides a few small metal cars were two inexpensive lamps on ceramic pot bases that glowed warmly through buttercup yellow shades.

The television was where the curio cabinet had been. The children seemed to be watching a rendition of *A Christmas Carol*. Alasdair recognized a few of Dickens's famous lines being spoken by Mickey Mouse. His children, all three of them, were plopped in front of it on beanbag chairs in jelly bean colors. Samantha, hair braided, wearing a red-and-white flannel nightgown and thick athletic socks, was watching along with Cameron and Bonnie. If it *was* Cameron and Bonnie.

His son sat cross-legged on his own brilliant blue beanbag, alternating between taking bites of his supper—a chicken leg, macaroni and cheese, and carrot sticks—and pointing and exclaiming at the television. He was drinking something from a covered cup, which tipped over each time he set it down. Milk. A trickling puddle of white spilled out and disappeared into the carpet.

Bonnie had lost interest in the television. She was moving huge beads along wires on something that looked like an abacus. Behind them, in the corner, was a Christmas tree. Actually, on closer look, Alasdair could see that it didn't reside in the corner. This huge tree, a fir from the looks of it, took up nearly a quarter of the room. It almost pulsed from the number of lights strung on its branches. It was covered with construction-paper chains, more of the homemade snowflakes, a string of popcorn and cranberries that ended halfway across, and some of Mother's collection of ornaments, but oddly, they covered only the top half of the tree. The bottom half was decorated with iced cookies hanging from what looked like strings of licorice. The whole arrangement was topped by a cellophane angel whose bulb seemed to have burned out. A pile of colorfully wrapped presents sprawled over the knitted afghan that seemed to be doing duty as a tree skirt.

Samantha was the first to notice him. She smiled at something on the television, then turned her head toward the doorway. She wasn't exactly bubbly, but at least she didn't look tortured, as she had when he'd left. "Hi, Dad," she said.

"Hi," he answered back, afraid to say more, afraid of breaking the spell, afraid that all of this would disappear.

"Hi, Dad," Bonnie mimicked, looking up from her toy and giving him a brilliant smile.

"Hi," he said again, his own feelings too deep to fit into a smile. He felt something break open inside him. He was flooded with tenderness for these children and with shame that he was seeing them for the first time.

Cameron stood up, knocking over his plastic cup again. He stepped on the remains of his chicken and macaroni, sending his carrot sticks flying as the plate went over. He ran toward Alasdair and hugged his legs. Alasdair lifted him up. He'd been freshly bathed. His hair was still slightly wet around his neckline. He was wearing new red zip-up pajamas, still fuzzy. "Hi," Cameron said. Alasdair hid his face in the boy's shoulder. He could feel the warm skin, smell the soap. He squeezed his eyes shut until the tears had abated.

"Well, look who's home," Bridie said, her voice warm and welcoming. He turned to greet her and was struck almost physically by the change in her appearance. Later he would realize it was only the color of her hair that had changed, from the light brown to a shimmering white-blond. But as he turned his head that first moment, it seemed to him that more than that had shifted.

"I was going to have them wait to eat until you got here," she apologized, "but I wasn't sure when you'd get in."

"Oh no, that's quite all right. Really. That's fine." He was blathering like an idiot.

Cameron squirmed to get down. A buzzer sounded.

"That's my pie," Bridie said. "Excuse me." She turned and left. Alasdair set Cameron down and followed her into the kitchen.

She was leaning down to check on her pie, hair cascading over her shoulder in a shiny waterfall. She flicked him a glance and flushed. Or perhaps it was only the heat from the oven. She closed the oven door, stood up, and turned toward him. The small artery on her neck beat out a pulse. Just behind it he thought he glimpsed a pearly white rope of scar. He forced himself to look away, down at his shoes.

"The children seem very happy. And the house looks wonderful." He looked up and as he watched, the artery took on a hummingbird's pulse. "I can't begin to thank you."

"I've enjoyed every minute of it," she said, and there was that look again, the sad cloaking of the eyes, a haunt of sadness breathing cold breath upon what should have been a happy scene. What was it about him that had that effect on people? He shook his head, took a deep breath.

Bridie, apparently deciding some fullness of time had been accomplished, opened the oven door again and took out the pie. It was a work of art. The golden filling bubbled through the slits, an eruption of cinnamon and sugar and apples, and the smell was heavenly. It dragged him away from his dismal ruminations.

She pointed toward the table. "Your supper is ready. There's salad in the fridge, chicken and vegetables there." She pointed toward covered pots on the stove.

Your supper, she had said. "Aren't you eating with me?" The words were out before he thought.

She flushed again. "I was going to give you your privacy. I can eat at home."

"Nonsense."

She gave him a sharp glance, and he berated himself. Why did he always speak like his father? He tried again. "What I mean is, I'd be delighted if you would stay and eat the dinner you prepared. Won't you, please?"

Her flush deepened. The thought occurred to him that perhaps he'd violated some employer-employee etiquette. Perhaps she wanted to maintain firm boundaries between work and personal life. "It's all right, though, if you'd rather not," he said quickly.

"No." She shook her head. "That'll be fine."

"Good." He smiled. "I'll go wash."

She nodded and turned her pink face to the cupboard as she took down another plate.

Alasdair had demolished his chicken and salad, mashed potatoes and green beans, and now he was making inroads on his pie. The ice cream was real vanilla and pooling in delicious puddles around the tender apples. It tasted better than any he'd had before.

They sat over coffee. For just a moment Alasdair savored it—a moment of normalcy that he hadn't had in years, a quiet conversation at the end of the day over dessert and coffee. He relaxed and leaned forward, resting his elbows on the table. "This is quite good," he said, taking the last bite, enjoying the last crumbling, melting mouthful.

"It has a secret ingredient," Bridie said with a smile. She had a beautiful smile. White, even teeth and deep, merry dimples. The cornflower blue eyes completed the picture of innocence and light. Just looking at someone so obviously untouched by the disappointments of life gave him a moment of pleasure.

He smiled back. "It's delicious, whatever it is."

"Where I'm from it's apple country," she said. "I don't suppose there's a way to cook an apple that I haven't tried. Fried, baked, cobblers, pies, cakes, turnovers, popovers, doughnuts, candied, frozen, canned, dried—you name it."

"Is that right?" he asked, more to keep her talking than for any other reason. He loved the animated look she took on when she talked about her home. Bright and cheerful.

"Yes, sir. Every hill, valley, and mountainside has an orchard tucked away. Red Delicious, Golden Delicious, Stayman, Winesap, Rome, York, Empire, Granny Smith. We grow them all. I wish I had a penny for every apple I've picked. I'd be a rich woman."

"The land is especially suited to apples?" he continued, picking a leading question at random.

She nodded. "Full of lime. Good for fruit trees."

"How interesting."

Bridie quirked her head, acknowledging the fact. "My grand-mother said she thinks the Lord put her house down right in the middle of the Garden of Eden." Bridie smiled. "Sometimes I think she's right." Her eyes softened and focused on some point far away. "It's beautiful there. The morning fog will lift, and all of a sudden there's the river spilling over big old boulders that look like somebody put them there, just right. Then it tumbles through the valley, rippling and singing over those flat slabs in the riverbed. There's an old dead tree that fell across the shallows, and I used to sit there for hours when I was a kid. I especially loved it in the wintertime when all the balsam firs and spruces were covered with snow."

"It sounds beautiful," he prodded. "Are there many lakes?" he asked, thinking of Scotland.

She shook her head. "Not too many lakes, but lots of rivers and creeks. And trees, more trees than you can shake a stick at. Beech, hickory, oak, hemlock, white pine. My great-uncle used to cut down a hickory and make mountain dulcimers. He sold them to big music stores, and people would pay hundreds of dollars for one of his instru-ments. He's famous around those parts. Was. He's passed on now." Her face sobered, then lit again as she remembered something else. "My great-grandma used to be the granny. The midwife. She knew every herb and what it would do for you and to you. She planted bloodroot and hepaticas under her dogwoods, and she'd go out into the woods and pick things to make her remedies. She said nothing would beat a bloodroot for getting rid of warts, and she swore that the roots of the hepatica would bring down a fever quicker than aspirin. Of course, aspirin comes from white willow bark," Bridie said with a blinding smile. "Isn't that right?"

"I suppose so," he murmured. She was fascinating, and for the first time he could hear the full range of her accent. Talking about her home had brought it out.

"Even the dirt is pretty where I'm from," she said with a smile. "You'll be walking along and there will be little shiny bits of isinglass, glittering in the sun. Shiny little mirrors under your feet."

Alasdair had a vision of heaven, where precious gems would be building materials. He smiled. "It sounds absolutely beautiful."

Her smile faded. "Parts of it are. I guess it's like everything else. There's bad with the good."

"I suppose."

She seemed to grow restive, fidgeting with her coffee cup, swirling the dregs around. "What about you?"

"Hmm? Oh. I grew up right here." He smiled and his eyes seemed more topaz now than blue. She leaned forward to get a closer look. They were hazel. Sort of. Dark, vivid blue with flecks of golden brown. No. Aqua now. Ah, gray. He tipped his head, and they changed again. They were a different color every time the light shifted.

"Except for when you lived in Scotland," she contributed to get her mind off his coloring.

"Right." He made a little face. "My sisters filled you in on that, I'm sure."

Bridie felt a surge of embarrassment. She knew things she shouldn't know. Things he didn't know she knew. She'd better watch her step. "It's where you spent your formative years," she quoted Winifred, and Alasdair's smile grew wider.

"Exactly." He chuckled. "I was nine or ten when we moved to Scotland. We lived there for four years—close to five. When we returned here Father came right back to this church. They hadn't even replaced him—used an interim pastor for four years. Can you imagine?" he asked.

Bridie gave her head a polite little shake. She hadn't ever really thought about it, but if that was unusual, she could only imagine how hard it must be on Alasdair that the same folks were angling to oust him now. His thoughts must have followed hers. He was staring off, his face a picture of gloom.

"Then what?" she asked, prodding him out of it. He glanced at her and smiled briefly.

"Then I finished high school here in Alexandria, went to college and seminary in Boston. I did a year in Scotland midway."

He was staring at the wall, seeing the past playing on it like a movie, and Bridie could see it, too. She saw Anna with her bright eyes and beautiful mane of hair. Anna, serene on the surface, churning and frothing underneath.

"My wife was from Scotland," he said, telling her what she already knew. "I met her then. Her father was not happy when I took her away." Then he went again. Off to that lonely, private place where he spent so much time. She followed him there, tried to fill in the blanks, and felt a stirring guilt that soon she would know things about his wife that even he might not know unless he, too, had read her journals.

"We returned to Boston, where I finished my last year of seminary. My father retired the year after I finished. This church called me to the pastorate, and I've been here ever since."

She met his eyes, making sure her smooth face was on, but underneath it her thoughts were in a tumble.

The front door opened and closed.

"Hello!" Lorna's voice rang down the hall. Relief and regret surged up together. The awkwardness was over, but so was the conversation.

"I've enjoyed the visit," the reverend said, resting his hand on the table, inches from hers. It was a nice hand, wide and strong looking for someone who spent his time reading and writing. Blue ink stained the writing callus of his middle finger. She remembered holding that hand during the long, long night of his illness. He had held on to her like a drowning man clings to wrecked pieces of the ship. Anything to keep his head above water.

"I've enjoyed it, too," she said.

Alasdair gave her a slight nod, another hesitant smile. "Perhaps you'd like to stay and eat with us every night."

Bridie's eyes widened, and she didn't answer for a moment.

He noticed her hesitation and shook his head. "I'm imposing. I'm sorry."

"No," she said quickly. "I could stay."

He smiled, and she noticed again how it changed his whole face, softened the hard lines and gave it warmth. "Fine," he said, then rose to greet Lorna.

Bridie began putting the plates into the dishwasher, glad to have a place to hide her flushing face. Lorna came in and spared her from any more thinking. After they chatted a minute Bridie excused herself, put on her coat, said good night to Samantha, and went home to Carmen's. All the way there she scolded herself. Their home is not your home. They are not your family. He is not your—whatever. Don't get attached to him, she scolded herself, but all the time a part of her was wondering if it was too late.

⁊ twenty-three ⁊

THE TALKS WITH ALASDAIR CONTINUED, no matter how many lectures Bridie gave herself. In fact, their time together became a nightly ritual. Between the twins' bedtime and the hour or so she and Samantha spent poring over Anna's books, Alasdair would come down to the kitchen. She felt crazy. She felt deceitful. She felt torn. She thought about stopping one or the other—the snooping into his life, or the sharing of it over dessert. She couldn't bring herself to do either one. So she continued to sit across from him each night, sipping coffee or tea, taking sweet bites of whatever she had made, and talking.

And, oh, the things they talked about. She knew his favorite things: butterscotch and caramel, a good bread pudding, mountains, and small towns. His favorite holiday: Christmas. His favorite color: blue. His favorite book: *Mere Christianity*, by C. S. Lewis. His favorite vacation: the year his family had rented a cottage in the mountains of Pennsylvania. There he swam in the lake before breakfast every morning and slept outside on the screened porch.

They spoke of what he was like as a boy. His dreams, his thoughts, his interests. He had never intended to be a pastor. He'd intended to teach. He had been crazy about knights and castles, read every book written about King Arthur and the Knights of the Round Table. He had collected insects, probably just to bother his sisters. He had loved to read. Anything. He had loved running and throwing the discus. Why had he stopped doing it?

"It took too much time away from what the Lord wanted me to be doing."

"Are you sure He didn't want you doing that?" she'd pursued. "It seems like the whole thing was His idea. After all, He's the one who made you good at it."

He had paused, eyes taking on that faraway look, imagining what lay down that road not taken. "You might be right," he'd said quietly.

"What about you?" he had asked, and she had told him about that girl she had been. She had liked swimming, too, and fishing, and walking through the woods. She had swept out a little clearing by her grandma's and made a playhouse. A tree stump for a table, logs dragged from the woodpile were chairs. She'd prepared dinners of acorns on oak-leaf plates. She would sit there and play by herself, think and read, and talk to Jesus as if He were stretched out beside her on the bed of pine needles, hands pillowing His head, listening.

She told him about her grandmother, the way she prayed. And told him other things about herself and her life. Silly little things that no one else would care about, like how Grandma never opened any presents, that you could look in her drawer and find unopened packages—jewelry and underwear, hand towels and slips—all being saved for some special occasion that never came. She told him a little about her mother, a little less about her father, brother, and sisters. Nothing at all about the life she'd lived before coming here. But she wanted to. More and more she was having to shout down the voice inside that urged her to tell him everything.

Perhaps if she told him he would understand, she thought again, checking her cookies to see if they were done. Perhaps he would gaze at her, eyes warm and steady, would reach his hand across the table and clasp her hand, close his warmly over hers. "Those are things you've done," he might say. "Not who you are."

Or perhaps he would not.

Don't fall into that trap, she warned herself. *He's just a man. He can't forgive sins. Only God can do that.*

She sighed. The timer pinged. She took out the sheet of cookies, and the teakettle began to whistle just as she did. She listened for his feet in the hallway, knowing that when she heard them, in spite of everything, her heart would lift.

Alasdair adjusted the desk lamp so that the light pooled onto the sermon notes he was making. He had been working hard, giving no occasion for criticism. He'd visited homes, listened to complaints, soothed the malcontents. And oh, how tired he was of it all.

He hated the whole underground, backstabbing, tittle-tattling business of church politics. It was the main reason he had never desired to enter the clergy to begin with. If all the job entailed was serving the Lord, teaching His Word, encouraging the saints, what a joy that would be. But reality was different.

If his leadership came to a vote, the decision would be close, he realized, and suddenly the professor's little story came back to him. It was possible to win and lose at the same time. Perhaps he should put a stop to it all and allow the church to find the person they wanted to lead them.

Or become that person again yourself, the still voice suggested.

Easier said than done, he dismissed, not wanting to enter that familiar morass of guilt and self-recrimination just now. He put his mind back on Bridie and checked his watch again.

She was a lovely young woman. Physically, of course, but inside as well. She confided she had never been to college, yet she was obviously intelligent. She was bright and funny, had deep insight, almost uncanny perception, and a huge endowment of common sense.

His family had been socially conscious. Too much so, he remembered, his mouth tasting sour at the memory of the tolerant condescension they had offered to others less appropriately connected. Bridie was refreshingly free of that, and even though she was a simple person and said she was from simple stock, her manners were impeccable. Love trumped etiquette, he realized, and love was something she had in abundance, even for the unlovely. He remembered how she unfailingly treated Winifred with kindness. She would have even been kind to his mother.

He thought of her warmth, her tenderness, her generosity, her quiet strength, her faith, her silky hair, the way it tumbled down onto her shoulders, slipping and cascading in a shining platinum waterfall. The blue of her eyes, piercing and vivid, yet warm and engaging. Her heart exposed for all to see.

When he sat and talked with her, their voices twining together in murmured conversation, something in his chest, something that up until now had felt tight and held in, began to loosen and expand. He could almost feel it as a physical sensation of warmth and relief. "Aaah," he wanted to say. "That's better."

Take care, his better sense counseled, and under the flat warning his greatest fear yawned—a sharp, bottomless crevasse of self-condemnation. He did not have what was necessary. When her soul opened to him in the most intimate of relationships, he would be lacking in some fundamental way. He would fail her.

He struggled against that dark current for some time before he came to himself again. He was not opening his heart and soul, he reproved himself with bracing firmness. He was having dessert and coffee. He checked his watch again. Ah. It was time. He set down his pen and headed down the stairs.

⚱

"I love butterscotch-chip cookies."

Bridie smiled and watched him bite into his third one and take a sip of the tea. She'd made it hot, steaming, with a teaspoon of sugar and a tiny splash of cream. Just the way he liked it. She leaned her elbows on the red plaid tablecloth and watched the flame from the fat candle burn bright and steady.

"So," he said. "I've been doing most of the talking again."

"That's all right," she said quickly. "I like hearing about your life."

He nodded. "But don't I deserve the same privilege? I'd like to hear about yours."

"Mine's not very interesting."

"I'll be the judge of that."

She forced a smile.

"Here," he suggested, "I'll help you begin. Let's see, we'll start out simple. What's your favorite color?"

She thought for a minute. "White."

He tipped his head. "I'd have pegged you for a blue person. To match your eyes. Why white?"

She thought for a moment. "It's pure and clean."

"Yes," he nodded. "It is. Favorite music?"

She thought about the music she listened to on the radio, but the answer came from someplace deeper. "Old hymns."

"Really?"

"You think that's odd?"

"No. Not at all. Just unusual for someone your age. Why do you like them?"

"The memories they carry."

"Which one is your favorite?"

She didn't just remember it. She could hear it again, in Grandma's warbly soprano. " 'Rescue the Perishing,' " she said. "I don't think it's in your hymnal."

"I think I've heard of it," he said, but he was probably only being polite. "Refresh my memory."

"I only remember part of it."

"That's all right."

She sang it softly.

> "Down in the human heart, crushed by the tempter,
> Feelings lie buried that grace can restore;
> Touched by a loving heart, wakened by kindness,
> Chords that were broken will vibrate once more."

"That's beautiful," he said quietly.

"My grandmother used to sing that song." Bridie blinked several times and was silent. She was there again, feeling that secure and steady way she'd always felt at Grandma's, even after things had begun to go to pieces. Sometimes when Papa went on one of his benders, she would take her brother and sisters there. Grandma would feed the younger children, and when they'd eaten and were outside playing, she would have Bridie lie down. She would rest, listening to Grandma's soft singing and the sound of her snapping beans. *Snap, snap, snap,* then *thunk* as they landed in the enamel bowl. *Snap, snap, snap, thunk. Snap, snap, snap, thunk.* In the background would be the whir of the fan, the far-off cawing of crows, the baying of a dog, the *shhhh-te-te-te, shhhh-te-te-te* of the pressure cooker. She could almost smell the dry, slightly musty fragrance of Grandma's bedroom, the pungent cedar of her closet, the sweet sunny perfume of the sheet she would pull over Bridie's bare legs, the aroma of apples and woodsmoke. She remembered her relief that, at least for a while, she didn't have to worry. Someone was taking care of *her.* She gradually became aware of Alasdair's eyes on her, watching silently.

"Where have you been?" he asked softly.

"Home," she answered, her throat tightening.

He said nothing, just nodded slightly. "You never talk about your home. Not really."

So he had noticed.

Alasdair said nothing. He put down his cup and waited for her to continue.

"I'm the black sheep of the family," she finally said.

He kept his face impassive and resisted the urge to contradict her. He suspected she was being overly dramatic, but then again, who really knew another, no matter how many cozy conversations you shared? "And for that reason you feel alienated from them? You don't feel free to return home?"

"I'm *not* free to return home," she said with a wry smile. Something about what he'd said seemed to give her a certain ironic amusement.

"They're not a forgiving people?"

"It has nothing to do with them," she said. "I know I'm talking riddles. I'm sorry."

He gave his head a small shake.

After a moment she spoke again. "I used to have faith," she said abruptly. "Now I'm not so sure."

Alasdair looked at her for a moment, and the longing was evident on her face. "Is it that you're not sure of the promises any longer or just not sure they belong to you?"

He'd hit the mark. Her eyes filled with tears, just briefly, before she blinked them away.

"You're not the only one who has disappointed God." He remembered his torn confession to Professor Cuthbert after Anna's death, of his failures, his deep, deep regret.

"What would you tell a person like me?" she asked, sniffing back her emotions.

"A person who's left the fold, so to speak?"

She nodded, and again he caught the yearning look in her eyes.

"I would tell them that where sin abounds there does grace much more abound." And it was odd, but as soon as he spoke them, the words beckoned him as well, like a lifeboat with room for them both. "The greater the loss and failure, the greater God's redemption and grace."

"Not for me. I've lost all that." Her voice was flat, but behind it he heard fear and longing. They called out to him, and he answered them.

"You can't lose it," he said simply. "It's impossible." Where were these things coming from? He didn't know he believed them himself, and again it seemed that everything he said was a message to both of them. " 'Where can I go from your Spirit?' " he quoted. " 'Where can I flee from your presence? If I make my bed in the depths of hell, you are there.' "

She was silent for a moment, and the eyes she finally turned toward him were hollow and haunted. "What if you've made your hell?"

He didn't even pause but answered without hesitation. "Especially then."

"You don't know what I've done," she said, barely breathing.

"I don't need to."

She was silent so long he spoke again. "But I'm not afraid to hear it."

She was quiet for a long time, and he waited, patient, to see what she would decide.

"Maybe next time," she said, rising to refill his teacup.

∾

Bridie was completely drained by the time she arrived in Samantha's room to read.

Samantha pounced. "What took you so long?" She had apparently been ready and waiting, pillow propped at the head of the bed, Bridie's spot empty. She frowned, seeming to notice Bridie's red-rimmed eyes.

"Allergies," Bridie said, waving a hand and heading her off. "Let's read."

Samantha continued frowning.

"Unless you want to skip tonight?" Bridie asked hopefully. "My feelings won't be hurt."

"No, I want to read." Samantha gave her one last curious look. "Close the door," she ordered.

Bridie gave her a look, but she did it.

They'd been through several more scrapbooks, though it had taken them a while. More pictures and poems, clippings and lists, ticket stubs and lots and lots of pages in Anna's beautiful script detailing everything that was praiseworthy about Alasdair MacPherson.

Bridie climbed onto the bed.

"Hurry up," Samantha urged.

"Don't get your knickers knotted," Bridie answered back, taking her time arranging herself. "All right," she finally said. "You may begin."

Samantha moved the book so that it rested on both of their legs and opened the leather cover. No pictures greeted them this time, just several handwritten pages stapled onto the scrapbook.

We visited Father last weekend. He doesn't care for Alasdair. I
am disappointed, though I shouldn't have expected anything else. Of

course, he doesn't admit it. He says his hesitation hasn't anything to do with Alasdair but from his belief that I'm not ready for a serious relationship—blah, blah, blah.

We had barely returned from the visit before I received a long letter from him, full of cautions and pleading. He confided he is going to a new counselor, and this one has the key to all knowledge and insight. Of course, he wants me to see the man, too. He cited my ups and downs, which I felt was unfair of him. All women have these spells. I see no need to try to meddle with nature by going on expeditions into the past. No good will come from sifting through the dustbin of old memories. I'm happy now, and life moves on. Perhaps I'll ask Alasdair what he thinks, but I'm sure he would agree.

The thought of Alasdair brings up many conflicting feelings.

Bridie paused in her reading. She knew that feeling, too.

I am so aware that our time together draws to a close. I try not to think about that, just to enjoy each day.

Maybe that's what she should do. Give herself fully, enjoy the situation for as long as it lasted. A beam of hope sliced into her heart on that thought.

"Go on," Samantha urged. Bridie turned her attention back to Anna's journal.

Alasdair and I attended services together today, and the message was about leaving behind the past and pressing on to what lies ahead. Really, what are the chances? I took it as a confirmation of my decision to tell Father gently, but firmly, that I support his decision to go to yet another counselor but see no need for it myself. He's troubled. I am not. I am happy now. More happy than I've ever been in my life.

This afternoon I toasted a muffin, spread it thick with butter and honey and just savored a bite. I let it lie on my tongue, rolled it around in my mouth. That is what my life is like now. Sweet and satisfying.

I read Ecclesiastes this evening. I love the verse that says God has made all things beautiful in His time. This is my time.

There were more ticket stubs and concert programs. Lots and lots of pictures of Alasdair and Anna on outings. More flowers.

"Boring." Samantha flipped through the pages.

"Slow down," Bridie said, turning the page back.

Samantha sighed. "She just goes on and on about the same stuff all the time. It's like she thought everything Dad did was perfect."

"Hush," Bridie said and continued reading.

He has that fierce, single-minded devotion to God that I've longed for all my life. None of my own wavering. No, he is solid and dependable.

Samantha snorted. "My point exactly."

"Mind your manners," Bridie said without looking up. Samantha sighed.

I wonder if being around him will do me good? Perhaps some of his consistency will rub off onto me. I smile as I write this. Wouldn't the world be a better place if people could be thrown into a pot and mixed together?

There were a few more pages of pictures.

As it turns out, I won't have to think about his leaving. Ever. Alasdair has asked me to marry him! I am the happiest woman on earth. I called Father to tell him, and of course, he had to spoil it by asking me all sorts of questions, objecting that things have happened too suddenly. Why can't he just be happy for me? Why must he ruin everything? I put him out of my mind and relish my joy. I am so grateful to God. It is true that He gives us just what we need.

"Oh, gag me with a spoon."

We will marry here. Alasdair says it will be better that way. Something about his sisters. I do hope they like me. He says not to fret. That there is absolutely nothing I can do about that particular circumstance. I'm not sure what he means, but it doesn't sound very good.

"She got that right," Samantha said.

I will put all that out of my mind. Today I am engaged. I am marrying my prince, the one for whom I was made and who was made for me.

Samantha poked her finger down her throat. Bridie ignored her and turned the page.

The Marriage of Anna Ruth Williams and Alasdair Robert MacPherson, the heading said, again in the beautiful script and gold ink. Anna had illuminated the *M.* All kinds of beautiful flowers spilled from it and flowed down the page in different colors of ink. A professional wedding photograph was mounted under the heading.

She was beautiful. Her dress was ivory satin, off the shoulder. Her hair was piled onto her head, tendrils escaping. The train spilled down the steps of the church. Alasdair wore a black suit and blue vest, and Bridie could see the chain of a pocket watch. He was smiling and happy. Anna held on to his arm. He pressed her hand, as if he were afraid of losing her in a crowd.

Our wedding was small but beautiful. Just a few friends and family and Reverend Twisp, of course. But my roommates covered the altar with roses, and my dress was beautiful. Father came and didn't make too much of a fuss, though it was clear he wasn't happy about any of it. Least of all Alasdair's taking his only child to America. I put it out of my mind. We will stay tonight in London. We leave tomorrow for Boston, where Alasdair will finish his schooling at the university there. After that he said he might take a teaching position. But who knows what the future holds? Joy. That much I know as I see him here beside me.

Bridie sighed. Samantha reached across her and turned the page.

Boston is big and bustling and frightening. Our room is dingy and in a bad part of town. Alasdair promised that we could look through the apartment listings tonight when he is finished with his evening class. I hate that he must leave me alone here at night. He said if I lock the door and bolt it, I'll be safe. I did, but I'm still afraid. It's hot, but I'm too frightened to open the windows.

I had another bad spell yesterday.

"Anna," he said, "you must learn to fight. You mustn't lie down and let your moods run you over."

"You're right," I agreed. "Please pray for me. It's so hard when it's upon me."

He put his hands on my shoulders and prayed. "These shoulders are so tired. Give her strength, Lord." I wept, but afterward I felt much better. He put on water and made me a cup of tea. He had to leave then, but just the memory of him makes me feel stronger. I know it's fanciful, but it's as if his strength pours into me.

I remembered his advice and read my Bible and prayed. I did feel a little better. This will make me stronger.

Bridie glanced at Samantha to gauge her reaction. Her little face looked sad. Bridie tried to think of something to say.

No, that little voice said again. *It's the truth. Tell it.*

We have found our apartment, and I feel joyful today.

Good. Bridie felt the tension in her shoulders ease, and Samantha's face had relaxed a little. The next few pages had paint chips and little pieces of material glued to the pages. Anna had filled more pages with sketches of her decorating ideas—slipcovers she was making, furniture she was painting, arrangements of plants and pictures and rugs. There were pictures of the apartment, room by room, and it was beautiful. Anna had a flair for decorating. It was done in white and light green and pink, and there were lots of baskets and green plants, wicker and chintz, and scrubbed white tables. The paintings looked like oils in soft, muted pastels. Everything roses.

Donkey lamp, Anna had written, with an arrow toward the table. Samantha smiled.

> *I've discovered the American equivalent of the jumble sale. They call them flea markets. Why, I have no idea, since there is no such thing as a flea about. At any rate, I went last week and will go again, as my treasures are almost too numerous to mention. I found a beautiful rug, only slightly threadbare, a wrought-iron chandelier that will look quite spectacular painted white with small pink candles. Chintz pillows, an entire set of china in quite good condition, and find of finds—another pink chenille bedspread that will look quite lovely covering the old brown davenport. It's ordained I should have it. Alasdair says he shall have to take another job to pay for it all, but I think he is pleased. He seemed even more delighted when I told him that wouldn't be necessary. That I've decided to take a job.*
>
> *"What about continuing your schooling?" he asked.*
>
> *"I'm going to look into that next," I announced and could fairly feel the happiness radiating from him. We had a wonderful night. The best we've had in ages.*

Samantha rolled her eyes. "Whatever. Keep reading," she said. The next entry was dated a week later.

> *Alasdair hurt me today. For the first time I felt that sharp prick of emptiness. I went to him for prayer when he was studying. I think it was all the more hurtful that he was so calm. If he'd been angry, I could have chalked it up to words spoken in haste, but really, he was cool and collected. "I'm just a man, Anna. Not a priest," he said. "Go to God yourself. There's no need to have me pray for you. No more magic than you praying for me."*
>
> *I tried to explain to him how God uses him to center me and give me peace. Isn't that a husband's job? "Isn't that what two being one means?" I asked.*
>
> *"No," he answered back. "I'm not sure what it means, but I don't think it's that. The arithmetic of it isn't half a person and half a*

person equaling a whole, but whole and whole coming together to create something new entirely." I said I thought he was talking rubbish and I began to cry. He stared at me quite peculiarly, as if I was some frightening mutation of a person. I left the room.

He came to me after a while. He was very gentle and tender and said he was sorry he'd upset me. He looked so sad, and I felt my own spirits sink even further, as if they were tied to his and both to a stone cast into the lake. He left after that to go to the library to prepare for class. He usually prepares here. I have driven him away.

Alasdair returned late and brought me a university catalog. He said I should take some literature and writing classes at the university here. Even though the quarter has begun, I could enter late and audit. I said perhaps, but I know he's just trying to find ways to keep me busy. Occupied, so he'll be free to pursue his own affairs. His family is coming to meet me next week, and I'm afraid they won't like me.

"Uh-oh," Samantha said. Bridie began reading the next entry without comment.

The sun is pouring through the windows of our apartment this morning. It is a beautiful day with a hint of autumn in the air, and I'm cheered immensely. And I've identified my trouble. Who wouldn't be depressed, thousands of miles from home, alone in a new country? I feel much better now. I even made a cake for Alasdair's family.

"I've got a bad feeling about this," Bridie said, agreeing with Samantha. A glance at the next lines confirmed it.

The visit from his family was horrible. His one sister Winifred is beastly, and I'm afraid to say his mother is just like her.

"You'll have to come to Alexandria for a proper ceremony and reception," she said. I said nothing, just smiled, but wanted to say that I was properly married and what more was there to it? I was a little vexed that Alasdair didn't say more. He just watched, and sometimes I thought he was amused.

His father was brusque and preoccupied, always dragging Alasdair off for whispered consultations, of which I overheard only a word or two—elders and budgets and meetings. Church things. Only one member of the family was kind to me—Alasdair's sister Lorna. I can tell she knows what it's like to be the underdog.

My new mother-in-law offered to take me shopping and help me decorate the apartment. "It is decorated," I answered, and there was a deadly silence before Fiona began chattering. It was horrible the entire day. After they'd taken us to dinner, I served the cake, and it wasn't done in the middle. They all sat there, spooning soupy bites of chocolate into their mouths. Oh, I wanted to die. Lorna tried to help, saying she'd heard pudding cakes were quite popular and wasn't I clever to make one, but it didn't fool anyone. In fact, Winifred argued with her. "This is no pudding cake," she said. Then Fiona began asking me about what classes I would be taking, but she set her cake aside without touching it. Winifred wouldn't let it alone. "I know pudding when I taste it," she said, "and this isn't pudding." Then Mother MacPherson said, "Winifred, that's quite enough. Regardless of Anna's problems with the cake, your behavior is quite inexcusable." And the most unbelievable part of the entire day was that when I repeated the conversation to Alasdair, he laughed!! "That's each of them in a nutshell," he said. "They each just gave you a little character sketch of themselves."

I tried to explain to him how I had felt—stupid and worthless. I hoped he would hold me and tell me that I wasn't any of those things—at least not to him. But all he did was say they were the ones who had the problem, and I should try to take them all with a grain of salt, or I would go mad, and then he left to do some work on campus.

"Read Psalm 146," he said in parting. I am furious at his high-handed ways and even more furious that I did as he asked.

"Do not put your trust in princes, in mortal men, who cannot save. When their spirit departs, they return to the ground; on that very day their plans come to nothing. Blessed is he whose help is the God of Jacob, whose hope is in the Lord his God, the Maker of heaven and earth, the sea, and everything in them—the Lord, who remains faithful forever."

I don't know whether to be angry or grieved. I am going to bed.

Bridie stopped and looked at Samantha.

"Keep going," Samantha said, sounding irritated.

Bridie read on.

> *I have decided to take life by the horns. I have signed up for my classes, gotten myself a job. At a retirement home. I will lead them in activities—crafts and such—three times a week in the afternoon. And my first time there, while knotting beads, I made a friend. Her name is Elizabeth Bacon, and she is quite an interesting person. A former jeweler, and I was quite embarrassed at my clumsy craft project.*
>
> *"Stringing beads must be child's play to you," I apologized.*
>
> *"Not at all," she said. "It gives me something to do."*
>
> *We chatted quite a bit. She admired my wedding ring and said the diamond was first-rate. She is forthright and cheerful. Just the kind of friend I need.*

There were a lot of entries after this about Boston. Things Anna was doing. It seemed in the next weeks she had succeeded in crafting a life for herself. She attended her classes, even made a friend in the apartment building, or at least an acquaintance who enjoyed going with her to the flea markets and secondhand stores. There were more poignant entries, almost desperate sounding, of the depth of her love for Alasdair.

"TMI," Samantha said, waving her hand. "Skip those." Bridie flipped quickly through, not sure if she was motivated by respect for Anna's privacy or something else.

> *Alasdair is quite cheered by my new approach to life and apologized if he had seemed to thrust me away. I told him that I don't believe he realizes what a healing effect he has on me, on everyone. I believe the Lord uses people to meet our needs. One day I'll try to explain it to him better. I must go and do my assignments. I am behind in my literature class and have a paper due tomorrow for creative writing that I can't face. I don't feel exceptionally well.*

Bridie closed the book.

"I hate that."

"What? What's the matter with you?" Bridie asked.

"I just hate the way she quits right in the middle of things."

"Patience. We'll get back to her tomorrow. And after that we'd better get busy on Christmas things."

Bridie said good night, kissed Samantha on the forehead, and turned out her light. The house was quiet. A light burned under the door of Alasdair's study, but the door was closed. What would he say if he knew what they were doing just on the other side of that wall? She let herself out and stepped into the cold night, locking the door behind her to keep them safe.

❧ twenty-four ❧

BOB HENRY THREW DOWN THE last of Knox Presbyterian's spread-sheets in disgust. It would be Christmas in a few days, and here he was. Still grinding away and getting nowhere. His girlfriend had gone to the Bahamas. Without him. And here he sat in his windowless office still looking through balance sheets. Perfectly legitimate balance sheets.

Nothing was missing from petty cash. There were no slush funds. Nothing unaccounted for. He'd been looking over this mess for weeks now. Had even brought in one of his accounting buddies to take a closer look. Nada. Zilch. And he was running out of time. Gerry had been asking for his input for weeks, wanting to get back to the Knox elders. Just yesterday he'd brought it up again.

"Edgar Willis called again, Bob. I must have your report soon."

"There are just a few more facts I need to document, sir," Bob had hedged. But he couldn't hold things off much longer, and not just because of Gerry's impatience. Bob's own timeline was tight. The General Assembly Council members had to make their recommendation for president four months before the annual meeting. That meant decisions were being made right now. If Bob was going to pull something out of the hat to make the Knox elders swoon with delight, now was the time. He sighed, rubbed his stiff neck, and went back to the paperwork spread all over his desk.

He started in again with the current month. Offering was down, but that was to be expected around the holidays. Besides, the first thing that happened when congregations weren't happy was that they shut their wallets. He shook his head and flipped through the pages. One more time. The second to the last paper, a yellow carbonized form, caught his eye. He frowned. Someone had been added to the church health insurance policy. Bridget Collins. Her birth date was listed along with social security number. Who was she?

He flipped open the phone book and dialed the extension for Human Resources. No, the woman assured him. There had been no new hires at the Alexandria church. The only open position was the associate pastor, but it hadn't been officially posted yet.

Bob hung up and scratched his chin, mildly interested. He looked up another number—Knox's office. The secretary answered. He remembered her—a young brittle type with suspicious eyes that he'd tried to chat up when he was there. She hadn't liked him. She'd almost accused him of stirring up trouble and completely clammed up when he tried to ask a few innocent questions.

"This is Henry Fallon from Human Resources," he lied, picking the first name that came into his head—his maternal grandfather's. "I've got an add-on for the health insurance, and I'm confused."

"Yes," she answered, not committing herself to help.

"Um. This Bridget Collins. What's her capacity? I need to have something to put down. We can't just add people to the policy."

"She's the nanny, and before you start arguing, let me just say that I told Lorna I thought there might be a problem. I'll give you her number if you have a question."

"Whose nanny?"

"Reverend MacPherson's. He hired her to watch his kids."

"Does she live in? Because if she doesn't live in, she's not considered a full-time employee and wouldn't be eligible for benefits." Brilliant. And he had hardly been trying.

"I don't know. Call Lorna—Reverend MacPherson's sister. Here's her number." She reeled off digits Bob didn't bother to copy. He signed off and sat there for another few minutes, thinking.

He checked the birth date and did a little math. Bridget Collins was twenty-six years old. He wondered what she looked like. His job would be easier if she was a babe. He copied down the social security number, feeling uninspired. The odds of Alasdair having an affair were slim to none, but, he reminded himself, he didn't have to prove anything. He just had to get enough to convince MacPherson that it was in his own and his family's best interest to resign.

He would go back to Alexandria and see what he could find out. Slightly cheered, he picked up the telephone one more time and put in a call to one of the denomination hacks whose son was a lawyer for the Commonwealth Attorney General. He'd lean on him to get the goods on this nanny, though he could probably find out all he wanted himself from the Internet if he looked in the right places. There was almost nothing you couldn't find out about a person if you had their name and social security number.

~ twenty-five ~

"Do you think Aunt Lorna will like this?" Samantha asked, holding up the necklace she'd been working on.

"I think she'll love it," Bridie said. The visit to the bead shop had been a big success. Everyone would be getting something strung for Christmas. "Don't forget to tell her what the woman said."

"That moonstones give a woman an allure of mystery," Samantha quoted and bent back over her project. "I'm writing it on the card."

Bridie watched her a moment longer, then climbed onto the bed and opened the book Samantha had left on the pillow. Anna's face looked back at her from the first page and Bridie was startled at how close she felt to this woman. How real she had become. Her face was familiar, like a dear friend's. Ah! She'd cut her hair. It suited her, softly framing her face and curling behind her ears. Her face was so pretty, her features so fine and exquisite. She was smiling in this picture, and her eyes were shining. Alasdair stood beside her, a younger, more vivid version of himself. His face had grown even more familiar. Bridie resisted the impulse to trace its lines with her finger. She strained her eyes but couldn't make out whether there was a stain of ink on his finger even then. She took a deep breath, then began to read.

"Show me Boston," I told Alasdair. "Turnabout's fair play." And to my great surprise, he did.

"Wake up," he said to me this morning, handing me a steaming cup of tea and a fresh croissant on a tray. He even put a doily on it—stolen from the end table. "Today you're mine," he said. I loved the sound of that.

I ate my breakfast, then dressed. He was tapping his foot, waiting.

The morning was spent touring bookshops. He bought me a beautiful edition of Blake, and I bought him a volume of Calvin's Commentaries he's been wanting. The city is beautiful. All the leaves are turning, and the air is crisp and cool. We ate lunch at a little café near the French Cultural Center and the library. We had onion soup with thick cheesy crust and shared a chocolate crepe for dessert. In the afternoon we saw Old North Church and the site of the Boston Tea Party. We finished at the observatory just as the stars were coming out. It was lovely. A completely lovely day.

"Are you sure she's talking about Dad?" Samantha asked, stringing another bead. Bridie gave her a look. The next entry was dated November.

Winter has descended on us in earnest. Our little apartment is snug and warm while the freezing rain beats hard little taps on the window. I suppose it's not all that difficult to heat two rooms and a loo. Ah, well. What it lacks in space, it makes up for in charm.

I have a secret. I've told no one yet, but I think I'm pregnant. I can feel the changes in my body, even though I'm just a few days late. I feel very heavy, sort of overripe and queasy. We shall see. Next week should be soon enough to test. I wonder what he will say. I think he will be pleased, but one never knows. We've only been married a few months, after all. Perhaps he would rather have waited. I'm afraid to tell him. Why is it the woman always feels as if it's her situation, and the man merely a spectator rather than a participant?

Another thought dawned. Father. My heart sinks. If I am pregnant, the news will send him raving. Perhaps I won't tell him until I'm well along or maybe even delivered. Spare myself the continued exhortations to talk to someone. Well, at any rate, I won't let worries about him spoil my joy. Just because something happened to Mother doesn't mean it will happen to me. I'm thinking Devon if it's a boy and Clarice if a girl. Or perhaps Ellen and William. We shall see.

"Clarice." Samantha made a face. "She must not have seen Hannibal."

"It's a perfectly fine name," Bridie said.

"I like your name," Samantha said. "Mary Bridget."

Bridie turned toward her sharply. Samantha's head was bent again over the beads. "How'd you know that?" she asked, keeping her voice calm.

"Your Bible. It was in the guest room, and I saw it when I dusted. How come it says Washburn on the front when your name is Collins?" she asked, still not looking up from her beading.

Bridie's heart thumped, and she answered recklessly. "I have a secret life."

"No. Really." Samantha looked up, interested, innocent, not at all suspicious.

"It was my mama's." Bridie felt a jolt inside as the lie left her lips. She had the sudden urge to take it back. To tell the whole truth.

And get thrown into jail just in time for Christmas. Now that would be a fine how-do-you-do.

"It's a pretty name," Samantha said, head bent back over the beads. The moment was gone. Bridie focused her attention back on Anna's book and tried to quiet her guilt.

A lab slip from Brigham and Women's Hospital decorated the page. An order for a pregnancy test with the word *Yes!!!* written across in red ink and the date. Anna had attached an antique baby cap beside the paper. It was covered with lace and satin ribbons that trailed to the bottom of the page.

I told Alasdair, and he was wonderful. He was surprised at first, but then the happiness spread over his face. I asked if it was too soon for a baby. He shook his head and kissed me. He said it wasn't our plans that mattered, but God's—that he had thought we would wait, but obviously we'd been overruled. I feel a great relief and now am even more joyful. I called my father at Alasdair's insistence, and even he was pleasant about it. He did chat with Alasdair for quite a time afterward, though. I asked what they talked about, and Alasdair was vague. "He just wants me to take good care of you," he said, kissing my cheek, but I think his eyes were a little troubled. Trust Father to suck the joy out of an occasion from clear across the ocean.

I won't allow it. If he wants to color his life with gloom, that is his choice, but I will not. This very day I went out and began shopping. I was looking for a crib in secondhand shops but instead found this little cap. I do feel rather ill, and looking at it reminds me of the joy at the end of the road.

I have to go to work this afternoon. Sometimes I regret having taken the job, but I do enjoy visiting with the old people, especially Elizabeth. She was quite overjoyed when I told her the news. She and I have become fast friends. I told her about Alasdair's family's visit, and she laughed and laughed. "Oh, honey, don't take them seriously," she advised. "They obviously have no class."

I smiled at that all day. At how positively outraged Mother MacPherson would be to be told her clan has no class. Lorna excepted, of course. She is a dear. Here is the note she sent me after the pudding cake fiasco.

A small piece of white stationery was pasted beside a Victorian-era Valentine, erupting with hearts and lace in shades of pink, green, and white.

I saw this card in an antique shop and thought of you, Anna. Even though it's not Valentine's Day, I had to buy it. I enjoyed meeting you so very much. Your home is lovely. I hope you don't mind that I copied one of your ideas. I found an old wrought-iron chandelier in Mother's attic. I painted it white, and it now hangs in my dining room with tiny pink candles. I think of you each time I see it and thank God for giving my brother such a wonderful wife and me such a delightful sister-in-law.

Love, Lorna
PS: I'm looking forward to seeing you at Christmas.

"Uh-oh," Samantha said, "I smell trouble brewing."
Sure enough.

Alasdair says we must go to Alexandria for Christmas holiday. I went in the bedroom and cried but dried my tears before I reemerged.

I know I am being silly and immature. I told Elizabeth, and she just said I should show them what class looks like. I suppose.

Alasdair says his father has a matter to discuss with him. I hope it's not that there is some ghastly family name that must be passed down. Suppose instead of Devon or Clarice they insist on Imogene or Orbit? Borrowing trouble. I have dropped my writing class. I have no energy to spare once I go to work.

Bridie looked over. Samantha was smiling. She'd stopped her beadwork and was listening intently. Pages and pages followed of baby matters. A summary of her doctor visit. Different lists of names. More paint chips for a corner of the bedroom she intended to make over into a nursery. More names. Descriptions of sewing projects she had planned: blankets and little outfits. Bridie couldn't help but contrast that to the box of unopened baby gifts in the attic. There was probably a perfectly good explanation for that. She flipped the page, and it was Christmas then, as well as now.

It's a bit of a letdown spending the holiday here. We arrived this afternoon, Christmas Eve. There is no tree. Few decorations. The parsonage is big and cold. They don't seem to understand the principles of central heating. And they say Europeans are bad.

The main event of the day seems to be the Christmas Eve service, which was nice, though too long for my taste. I was fighting to stay awake. The family decided not to exchange gifts this year, my father-in-law informed me. "Each member of the family will donate to the mission fund on Christmas Eve in honor of the others," he explained. I just nodded, and Alasdair produced our envelope. Already prepared and not a word to me about it. I brought gifts in my valise, but I think I'll keep quiet. Except I will give Lorna hers. She is a dear person. I hope she likes the antique combs. They'll look quite pretty in her hair, I think.

The next entry was dated December 25.

It wasn't as bad as I feared.
It was worse.

The dinner was all right except for their constant carping about who would sit where and nagging poor Lorna because she made sweet potato soufflé instead of some carrot dish that Winifred had to throw together at the last minute without the right type of currants. It seems that the menu has been carved in stone since before the Battle of Hastings. Roast lamb, scrubbed new potatoes, the above mentioned carrot casserole that was really quite inedible, and for dessert plum trifle, which Mother MacPherson says is a recipe that has been passed down in their family for seven generations. It tasted dry enough to have been baked seven generations ago.

Shame on me.

Samantha giggled. "Some things never change."

"Is that really what you eat at Christmas?" Bridie asked.

Samantha nodded. "Every year."

Bridie felt her stubborn streak emerge. "It sounds like it's time for a change."

Samantha's eyes lit. "Cool. What'll we have?"

"We could do a turkey."

"Steak," Samantha countered.

"Steak's too expensive."

"How about fried chicken?"

Bridie nodded. "Sure. Chicken's cheap. Everybody likes it. Even Cam and Bonnie. All right. Fried chicken it is. What else?"

"Mashed potatoes and gravy."

"I'll make homemade rolls."

"Jell-O. Red and green."

Bridie smiled. There would be some knickers in a twist, that was certain. Red and green Jell-O instead of carrot currant casserole.

Samantha seemed to read her mind. "Aunt Winifred's going to go ballistic."

"Oh, well," Bridie said, then they both burst into laughter.

"What shall we have for dessert?" Samantha asked. "That's the most important part."

"What do you like?"

"Anything but that gross plum stuff."

"Pumpkin pie?"

Samantha shook her head. "Something chocolate."

"My grandma has a recipe for chocolate fudge layer cake that's so good it'll make you cry."

"Can you call her and get the recipe?"

Bridie's heart thumped. "I know it by heart," she said, and quickly, before Samantha could say anything else, she began to read again.

> *I am horrified. Alasdair, without consulting me at all, has consented to take his father's church. "How could you?" I asked, feeling as if I might faint or explode by turns. He said I was overreacting, that his father must retire for health reasons, and it has been decided. "For how long?" I demanded. "Why wasn't I informed it had been decided? Why did you never say anything when I spoke of taking a teaching post in some small town?"*
>
> *He appeared uncomfortable. "Well, perhaps I thought I might do it," he said. "But really, Anna. Do you realize what an opportunity this is? It's a prestigious church. This could be a wonderful career move for me. Besides, we'll have a child to support."*
>
> *"How could you, without even asking me? Or at least telling me?"*
>
> *"I should have consulted you," he apologized. "I'll call and tell Father I need more time."*
>
> *I said nothing. We didn't speak again that night. I don't know if he called his father or not. I was asleep when he came to bed, and he was gone before I awoke this morning. I will go, I suppose, without making a fuss. But somehow it feels like a death of my dreams of the life we could have together. Going there, amidst his family, shall be the end of those.*
>
> *I told Elizabeth when I arrived at work. She said I should make the best of it. That you don't just marry a man, you marry his family, too. I don't know if I would have married this particular man had I met Winifred and Mother MacPherson first. I feel ashamed just writing that. I do love him, and I know I am overreacting as he says. Perhaps it's my pregnancy that's making me feel so upset.*
>
> *Alasdair brought me flowers today when he returned home from his night class. I told him I would go to Alexandria, and that I wouldn't*

make a fuss. He stared at me quietly for a long time without saying anything. I don't know what he is thinking. He did not volunteer to refuse the position, though, which tells me I was hoping he would. I feel deeply hurt. As if he has failed some test I never told him he was taking. I'm going to bed now.

Bridie flipped ahead. That was the end.

"Bummer," Samantha said, but not really looking too troubled. Apparently the ins and outs of marital intimacy weren't high on her list of concerns.

"I'm sure she got used to the idea."

Samantha nodded. She held up Lorna's necklace. "It's done."

"Lovely, my dear." Bridie stood up and replaced the journal in the box. Any further reading would have to wait until after Christmas.

"You need to leave now," Samantha said, giving mysterious looks toward the sack from the bead shop.

"Ah," Bridie said, "Santa stuff."

Samantha nodded. Bridie left, trying her hardest not to think about the fact that she'd lied to Samantha.

❧ twenty-six ❧

"I THINK IT WILL BE fun, both of us staying the night on Christmas Eve," Lorna said.

Bridie gave her a smile. There was something about Lorna that was impossible not to love. A sweetness and innocence. She felt a pang of sorrow. That's what people used to say about her. "I'm looking forward to it, too," she said, slicing apart a chicken breast.

The telephone rang. Lorna picked it up, and immediately the air filled with tension.

"Yes." Lorna nodded, telephone clasped under her chin. "Uh-huh. Yes." Long pause. "All right." She hung up.

Bridie was guessing Winifred. Usually Fiona at least let Lorna have a few words of her own. But the absence of anything but agreement and Lorna's heightened tension was a tip-off that it was the older, unhappier sister she was talking to.

Lorna gave her an apologetic smile, as if she'd done something to feel sorry for. "Winifred's upset because Audrey Murchison insists on having the coffee hour after services tonight in spite of the fact that it's Christmas Eve. Winifred, however, insists that no one will come. She's coming over to speak to Alasdair about it."

Bridie crooked an eyebrow. Going to the pastor about a little thing like that seemed like overkill, but what did she know? Maybe it was an insurmountable temptation when the pastor was your little brother. "Why does Winifred care? If she doesn't want to go, why doesn't she just stay home?"

"You obviously don't know Winifred," Lorna said, giving her a weary smile. "Just knowing they were there would be enough to make her come unstrung." She put away the last of the groceries and turned to face Bridie. "I wanted to tell her to drop the whole thing."

"Why didn't you, then?"

Lorna gave her an amazed look that said wasn't it obvious?

Bridie just stared back. "What's she going to do? Put you in jail?" She hadn't meant to say that. It had just popped out.

Lorna looked as if she'd been given a new piece of information. Bridie finished her work, put the chicken away, washed her hands, and scrubbed the sink and countertop.

The doorbell rang, and Lorna nearly jumped out of her skin. "That's her," she said, and there was no doubt in either of their minds who she meant.

Bridie dried her hands and followed her out. If Winifred was coming over here in a snit, she would leave in an even bigger one. And Winifred's impending fury was her fault. She wouldn't leave Lorna to twist in the wind.

Winifred hobbled in, one foot still bandaged from her surgery. It took her a moment to negotiate the entry, for she was using a cane. Her face was paler than usual and a little drawn. Bridie felt a moment of sympathy. You didn't appreciate the humble parts of your body until something went wrong with them. She, for one, would be in vast amounts of trouble without fast-moving feet, she realized with a twist of irony.

Lorna closed the door behind her sister and wiped her palms on her apron. Winifred lifted her head and looked around with a slight frown. Bridie saw awareness come over her in stages, the full impact not hitting just yet. Then, as she took inventory, her usually tightened mouth went slack and drooped down slightly at the edges. Her cheeks pinked up next, the mouth flattened into a thin line and disappeared. When she spoke, her voice was quiet, almost conversational. "What have you done?"

Bridie had her mouth open to answer, but Winifred had addressed the question to Lorna and was looking at her, waiting for her to respond.

"We've done a little redecorating." Lorna's voice was bright.

Winifred didn't respond. She pushed past and limped slowly down the hallway. Bridie saw her scan the walls, finding no MacPherson portraits. She looked into the dining room and must have noticed that the walls were no longer crowded with shelves of china and crystal that threatened to topple. She came to the living room and paused in the doorway. Bridie took in the scene, imagining how it must look like through her eyes: the gaudy beanbags, the old worn couch, the silly tree. Uh-oh. Cam and Bonnie were busy eating cookies off the bottom limbs, and the floor around their feet was covered with crumbs. Cameron had apparently used the bathroom and unfortunately had forgotten to put his underwear back on. His little bottom was buck naked. He didn't seem concerned.

"Hi," he said, shoving another piece of cookie into his mouth.

"Hi back at you," Bridie answered.

Winifred wasn't amused. "Where is Mother's furniture? Where are all her things?" Her face was white. "Where are the sofa, loveseat, and parlor chairs?"

"In the attic," Lorna answered, her voice a little less chipper.

Winifred launched a cold silence their way, turned, and made her painful way to the stairs. Bridie took the opportunity to find Cam's pants and help him put them on.

"I have that?" he asked, holding up the cookie he'd already begun eating.

"Sure, you can have that." Bridie gave him a quick smooch on the cheek and brushed the crumbs into the carpet with her foot. Winifred reappeared after a few minutes. This time she turned her attention to Bridie.

"You've done all this," she said, her voice flat.

Bridie opened her mouth to take responsibility.

"Why would you assume that?" Lorna interjected sharply. Her cheeks were red with anger.

"I assumed it because you would know better."

"Know better than to cross you?"

"Don't be ridiculous."

"Am I being ridiculous? Or is that the way it really is? Is this your house, Winifred? Is your name on the deed?"

"This house belongs to all of us, as you well know."

"But it's Alasdair and the children who live here. And if these changes make life more comfortable for them, why would you object? Perhaps simply because the idea didn't originate with you?"

"This is the parsonage, Lorna." Winifred's eyes were cold with fury. "And it's not only Alasdair's residence, it's the repository of our family history. All of Mother's things are upstairs packed away. How do you think that feels?" Her voice trembled, and Bridie felt a little sorry for her. It must be hard to let things change when you had such a heavy history. But that kind of past could be a crushing burden, keeping you stuck in place, burying you by inches.

"Mother's glass figurines have been displayed since I was a girl," Winifred went on. "I remember looking at them for hours."

Bridie looked at Lorna, and she had a strange expression on her face. It was as if she were seeing her sister for the first time. As something other than a force. Her eyes lit with a combination of pity and understanding. "Why don't you take them home with you, Winifred?"

The sympathy in Lorna's voice seemed to snap Winifred out of her nostalgia. Her back straightened and that chin jutted out again. "That's not the point, and you know it. I turn my back for a moment, and you have the entire parsonage in an uproar."

"I hardly call it an uproar."

"Well, what do you call it, then? She's painted the entryway that mewling white. In the dining room she's replaced Mama's lovely wallpaper with a gaudy print."

It was Waverly and had cost her a bundle. "They're Victorian cabbage roses," Bridie put in.

"And I think they're beautiful," Lorna defended staunchly.

"I see she has papered the kitchen with coffee cups and teapots."

"It's whimsical," Lorna said.

"The children's toys have taken over the house."

"It's their house, too. Besides, the pediatrician said they needed more interaction," Lorna recited.

"Pediatrician! What's wrong with Calvin?"

"Nothing's wrong with Calvin," Lorna said, and Bridie could have been mistaken, but she thought she saw the beginnings of a smile on Lorna's face.

"I just happened to peek into Samantha's room," Winifred raged on. "It looks positively diabolical. Full of images of sorcery."

"I hardly call a blue bedspread with sprays of stars images of sorcery. The Lord made the heavens to reflect His glory. Besides, if that offends you, you must not have seen *The Misfits*."

"Just wait until Fiona hears about this." Winifred slapped down her trump card.

"Actually, she already knows." Lorna took the trick and had the grace not even to smile. "She stopped by last night to ask what to bring tomorrow and said it was quite an improvement. She said she should have suggested some of the changes herself."

"Oh, of all the ridiculous things to say. What do you mean she asked what she should bring? It's her year to make the trifle."

"We're not having trifle," Lorna put in almost nonchalantly. "We're having fried chicken, mashed potatoes, chocolate cake." She savored the last words, dropping them out slowly like morsels. "And . . . red . . . and . . . green . . . *Jell-O*."

Winifred said nothing. She stood perfectly still. The front door opened. Alasdair walked in and looked from one face to another, his expression wary.

Winifred turned toward him, then pointed at Bridie. "She has completely ruined this home," Winifred said, her voice shaking as well as her hand. "She has taken away all Mother's lovely things and replaced them with this garbage."

Alasdair did nothing for a moment. He looked at Winifred, then at Lorna, and finally at Bridie, who was having a crisis of her own. She'd overstepped. Her cheeks were hot with shame. Who did she think she was, coming in here and changing everything around? She couldn't help but remember Alasdair's response when Anna had stood up in the family boat. He'd pulled her back down. And she certainly didn't have the status of Anna. She was the hired help.

He stood motionless, staring at the wall beyond her head, perhaps seeing Anna and the pudding cake, Anna and the Christmas dinner, Anna and virtually any encounter with his family. His face was unreadable. After a moment his eyes focused back on the present, on her own face actually. She darted her eyes toward the floor and kept them there. After a minute she saw the black wing tips turn and walk away. So. History would repeat itself. Her heart plummeted down toward her tennis shoes.

"Winifred, I have to admit, I never really cared for Mother's furniture."

Bridie's head rose up just in time to see Alasdair plump one of the beanbag chairs with his foot and sink down onto it. "I much prefer this," he said, and Bridie felt something break open in her chest. Alasdair was way too long for the chair, and he looked ridiculous with his head hanging off one end and his legs off the other. He crossed his arms under his head and assumed a posture of total relaxation. She had to stifle the urge to break into laughter, so great was her relief.

She glanced at Winifred. Alasdair's siding with the enemy had sent her into full fury.

"No!" she shouted. She pounded her cane on the floor. "You cannot do it. It is wrong. It is ridiculous. It's vulgar and inappropriate. Mother would hate it. Father would hate it. I hate it. You cannot do this. No! No! No!" She blew out little drops of spittle along with the words, and her whole body trembled.

Bridie stared. Lorna was shaking her head. Now Alasdair looked as if he were seeing his sister for the first time. There was silence for at least a minute, and when Alasdair spoke his tone was flat and unequivocal.

"Not only can we do it, we have. It's done, and this is the way it will stay. Your only choice is whether you will accept it or not. I would hope our relationship wouldn't be damaged by a fuss over furniture, but I can't allow you to come into my home and treat Bridie and Lorna like this. It's inexcusable, and I won't tolerate it."

Winifred stared. Her face crumpled. No one moved for several minutes, and the only sound was Winifred's muted sobs. Bridie finally broke the silence.

"Here," she said, moving toward Winifred, touching her arm. "Come on, now. Everything's going to be all right." She found her a tissue, and Winifred allowed herself to be led to the couch.

Alasdair rose from the beanbag. "Show me what you'd like to take home, and I'll carry it down for you." His tone was kind but unapologetic. "That is, if Lorna doesn't mind, and of course, I expect you to consult with her and Fiona about who should have what."

Winifred nodded and sniffed. "Do you?" she asked Lorna.

"Do I what?" Lorna looked as if she were trying to solve complicated math problems in her head.

"Do you mind if I take some of Mother's things?" Winifred repeated with a surprising lack of impatience.

"No. Of course not."

Winifred nodded and dabbed at her eyes and nose. "I'll take the glass figurines and the tea service today," she said, sounding so subdued Bridie felt sorry for her. It must be very difficult to realize you're only human, after all, after so many years of running your world like a powerful little deity.

"Here, let's put that foot up," Bridie suggested. She helped Winifred get settled and found a pillow for her foot. "How about I bring you a cup of tea?" she offered.

Winifred nodded without speaking, but her eyes filled again. Bridie gave her a smile and patted her arm.

"I'll be right back," she promised and went to make the tea.

Lorna followed her out. When they reached the kitchen and Bridie had the kettle on, Lorna turned toward Bridie, her face still wearing an expression of amazement.

"All these years," she said, "and this is all it would have taken."

≈

Alasdair refused to cancel the coffee hour after the Christmas Eve candlelight service. It was not well attended, though, and Winifred seemed to have recovered enough to enjoy this small triumph. She manned the silver coffeepot and emphasized her victory by filling far too many Styrofoam cups than this tiny crowd could drink. They lined the table in front of her, rows of them, silent witnesses to the fact that she had been right and Audrey Murchison had been wrong. Bridie sat sipping her cider. She turned to look for Lorna, and came face-to-face with Alasdair, leaning inches from her.

"What are you pondering?" he asked with a smile.

She tried to ignore the rush of adrenaline that shot through her. She was surprised to see him. That was all. "How did you know something was on my mind?" she came back, keeping her voice calm, even though her poor heart was still galloping like a runaway horse. "You shouldn't sneak up on people like that."

"Sorry." He smiled, put his foot on the folding metal chair, and rested his arms on his bent knee. "I can tell you're preoccupied, because it's all over your face. I've lived with you for some time now. Give me a little credit."

Such innocent-sounding words. *I've lived with you.* Bridie took a sip of her cider and wished it were iced instead of hot. "I wear my heart on my sleeve, I guess. My grandma always used to tell me that."

"Some people are incapable of pretense." He smiled. Someone called him. He turned away, held up a hand in greeting to a man who beckoned to him. "I'd better talk to him."

"I should go, too," Bridie said, taking the last sip of her drink. "I've got stockings to fill." She rose from the table, aware of several sets of curious eyes on her.

"I'll be home soon," he said, stabbing her heart again. *Home. Our home.* She nodded but was all stirred up as she went out the squeaking double doors. She heard them click and clatter shut behind her as she stepped onto the frosted lawn. It crackled under her feet, and the air was sharply cold. It felt good to her fevered face. Her fevered brain. She had the feeling she was flying down a mountain road in a car with bad brakes, foot flat against the pedal, headed full-bore for trouble. She needed to stop. At least slow down. The trouble was, she didn't want to.

⁊

It was after midnight. Officially Christmas now, and the house was finally silent. Everyone was tucked away, dreaming of sugar-plums or some such. All except him. He was alone with a familiar companion.

Alasdair leaned close to the bedroom window, his breath fogging it. He could see the faint outlines of the gravestones, the ghostly tables where no feasting would occur, and for the first time in his practical life, he understood how people could believe in hauntings.

It was odd, but it did seem as if some, when they breathed their last, passed gently and quietly from one life to the next like a child falling asleep on the sofa and waking up in their own bed. Others, though, seemed to leave this life but not move on.

Like Anna.

It seemed she still clung to him every day. She was the silent listener to every conversation. She observed him each night as he lay on his bed. She watched as he sipped tea with Bridie, as he played with his children. She listened when he preached.

In those months after her death he had begged and pleaded with her. Don't leave me, Anna. Please don't leave me. Little had he known that those words, along with her presence, would come back to haunt him.

He stood back from the window, irritated at his irrational hyper-bole, then climbed back into the bed. He lay there, eyes pressed tightly shut, willing sleep to come.

⁊

Bridie waited until the house was silent before she crept out of her bed. She and Lorna were sharing the guest room on this special night. Lorna was asleep beside her, breathing slow and deep. Bridie crept downstairs, expertly avoiding the two steps that creaked. She pulled aside the curtains and peeked out the hall window. No snow.

Oh well, you couldn't have everything. The night was still pretty in a sparkly, luminous way. The little particles of frost were suspended in the air, making haloes around the street and porch lights. She dropped the curtain and padded toward the living room. She didn't turn on the table lamps, but she plugged in the lights on the tree.

She grinned. It was a mess. All the cookies were gone, so the bottom was bare except for the tropical fruit refrigerator magnets Samantha had hung on with paper clips. The children's presents were piled underneath, their stockings tipping up against the boxes, candy canes and tangerines and chocolate kisses spilling out. Bridie turned on the CD of Christmas music, softly, so no one would be disturbed. She sat down on the beanbag, laid her head back, and let the music wash over her. *O come, O come, Emmanuel, And ransom captive Israel, That mourns in lonely exile here.* . . .

Something stirred in her, something deep and eternal, and it was rocking and shaking the deep crevasses of her heart like an underground earthquake.

So many secrets. Hers and Anna's and Alasdair's. So closely guarded. So much energy required to keep the confession from spilling out of the lips. Walking through life was nearly impossible, for the feet were always cautious. Always testing the ground before letting the weight shift, then quickly doing the same again with the next step. Nothing could be trusted. Never could the guard relax. The earth itself was unsteady, unstable. Perhaps thick enough to be trusted, but more likely concealing underground caverns, whole rooms and tunnels, passageways, vaults. Sepulchers and tombs. The secrets, like Lazarus, lay still and cold inside them, bound tightly with gravecloth, somewhere between dead and alive. Waiting for someone to call them into the light of day, to loose them and let them go.

What was it that Lorna had said when they'd discussed reading the journals? About the truth setting you free? She smiled, bitter at the irony. Her truth, were she to tell it, would do the opposite. If she told the truth, she would go to jail. But just now she hardly cared. Wasn't she in jail already? Wasn't she?

What could be worse than this yawning emptiness inside her that had once been filled with the presence of the Lord? Now there was a gaping hole where He had been. Wouldn't jail be better than this if her heart could be clean again?

Ah, but that was the problem, wasn't it? Could it be clean again? Really? She knew what her grandmother would say, her mother, Alasdair. But something inside her couldn't believe them. She was afraid this stain went too deep, perhaps clear through to who she was instead of just tainting what she'd done.

"Oh, how my heart yearns for thee," she whispered, the words coming from an unguarded place. "Oh, how my heart yearns for thee. More than the watchman waits for the morning."

Oh yes. She felt she could endure a lifetime in prison easier than another day away from Him. For she had known Him, no matter what that accusing voice said to her in the tiny hours of the morning. It had been more than filling out a card at the end of a service, or raising a hand during a prayer, or even going forward during an invitation. She smiled, remembering how she'd tried to explain it to her grandmother. "It's like having an invisible friend," she'd said. An invisible friend who also happens to be the God of the universe. An invisible friend who gave His very life for you.

Her breath came softly in and out, in and out, a continual gift from the one who held everything together, who waited patiently, who would wait until the rocks grew old, wait and wait until she grew tired of running. She blotted her eyes with the sleeve of her pajamas. She was tired and would stop now if only she knew how.

twenty-seven

"I ALWAYS WANTED TO BE a woman of mystery." Aunt Lorna put on the moonstone necklace, pulled her pajama top down so one shoulder showed, and sort of squinted up her eyes.

"You look dumb," Samantha said.

"Thanks." Aunt Lorna smiled, put her pajamas back, reached across, and kissed Samantha on the cheek. "I love it even if I don't quite live up to the label."

"You will," Bridie promised. "I just know that one of these days romance and mystery will be your calling card."

Aunt Lorna laughed really hard at that.

"Open yours," Samantha urged, turning toward Bridie. Samantha shoved Cam's tape recorder out from under her leg. He was clueless as usual, hanging on Dad, playing with the fire engine Samantha had given him, and not even opening the rest of his presents. She smiled. Bonnie liked her talking doll, too. She'd already taken its clothes off.

Bridie looked at the little pile of presents in front of her. Samantha had made sure she had the same amount as everybody else. She had even gone to the drugstore last night and bought some more stuff just in case there wasn't enough. But actually it was okay. Dad had gotten something for Bridie, and Aunt Lorna had wrapped up some stuff from Cam and Bonnie.

"There." Samantha pointed out the paper she'd picked—with the birds on it because it had reminded her of that dumb song Bridie had sung. "Those are from me."

Bridie took one. Samantha tried to remember what was in it. Oh. That was the hair spray.

"Well, for goodness' sake, how did you know I needed one of these for my purse?"

"She's thoughtful, that's how," Aunt Lorna said, and suddenly, for no good reason, Samantha was glad she was in this family. She brushed her hair back, leaned against Dad's legs, and watched Bridie open the tiny little comb and brush and the fold-up mirror.

"Well, I'm all set," Bridie said, her face all smiling and happylike.

"You haven't even opened the best one. There. Do that one."

Bridie picked up the box with the earrings. Samantha forgot the name of the stones, but they were the same bright blue as Bridie's eyes and were set in real silver. She almost held her breath as Bridie opened the box.

"Oh!" Bridie held them up. "They're beautiful!" Bridie was, like, crying and all. "Oh, Samantha, I'll treasure them forever."

Samantha smiled. "They'll look better with clothes than they do with your sweats."

"You had to ruin the moment, didn't you?"

Samantha smiled again. Her dad bumped her with his knees. "Go get us some coffee, Samantha. It's probably ready now."

"Check the cinnamon rolls, please," Bridie said.

"Don't open anything until I get back."

They promised they wouldn't. She put the cups and coffee and sugar and cream on the tray as fast as she could and went back to the living room. Dad had put on the MacPherson plaid vest Bridie had made for him, and it looked dumb over his sweatshirt.

"The cinnamon rolls will be done in five minutes," Samantha announced, plopping down again. "Now, whose turn is it?"

"Why, I believe it's yours," Dad said, and he handed her a package, a tiny box. She opened it, and there, resting on a bed of black velvet, was a necklace, a heart with a tiny diamond in the center. Dad took it out of the box and hooked it around her neck. "There," he said, patting her shoulder. "Now all the boys will know who you belong to. You're mine until I give you away." Samantha still didn't say anything. She leaned up against his knees and watched Bridie and Aunt Lorna open the rest of their presents, and every now and then she picked up the little heart and adjusted the chain.

❧ *twenty-eight* ❧

JANUARY BLEW IN WITH A foot of snow that stayed on the ground for weeks, another inch or two being added as soon as one melted away. Samantha's school was closed for three days, and Bridie played outside with the children until their faces were numb, then brought them in for cocoa and baths. She made snapping fires and hearty soups and loaves of bread. She knew everyone's favorite foods and favorite clothes now and how they liked their eggs and whether they wanted the crust on or off their sandwiches. It was easier and easier to pretend that they were hers. All of them.

Her talks with Alasdair continued over pots of tea and cakes and puddings and cookies. Sometimes they would just sit there in silence, the sticky plates between them, the sweetness lingering. She knew him. And he knew her. Not facts, perhaps, but you could know a person's heart without knowing their history. Couldn't you?

Something troubled her greatly, though. Bridie cleared up the last of the supper dishes now and realized what it was. It was as if she were two distinct people. One who played with the children, had helped them make Santas from cotton balls and tempera paint, reindeer from corks and pipe cleaners. She was the one who bought their big-boy and big-girl beds and taught them to stay in them after she turned off all but the night-lights. That woman lay awake at night, searching for her own way back from the other person she'd become in that life she didn't like to think about. So far she had not found it.

And the continued deception of Alasdair was an ache on her conscience. Her only comfort was that they were very nearly done with Anna's journals. They should have been finished by now, but they didn't read every night anymore. It was as if neither of them was anxious to probe this part of Anna's life, only continuing on because they'd already begun.

They were different, these scrapbooks. From Samantha's birth onward, Anna seemed to spend most of her energy documenting her daughter's life rather than her own. There were some personal entries, of course. Accounts of a couple of violent quarrels over what she saw as Alasdair's overinvolvement in ministry to the neglect of his family. Followed by a sense of resignation. Resignation to everything—to the unromantic partnership her marriage had become, to the unhappy relationship she had with her in-laws, to the way she couldn't seem to make anything happen in her own life. Without Alasdair encouraging her, without the hope that had sprung from her fantasies of his perfect love, she seemed to have settled into a flattened-out, dimly lit life, brightened only by her daughter.

Bridie watched Samantha's reaction carefully as they covered these years, but it was hard to tell what she was thinking. Listening to the story of her mother's life didn't inspire the smart-alecky "TMI" anymore, but she didn't seem like the falling, desperate sparrow, either. She seemed to be coming to a realization of her own. Her parents were human. Real people with feelings, conflicts, attractions, and failures that had nothing to do with her.

Samantha had perked up considerably when Bridie suggested they explore the seven backpacks. They'd pored over every piece of paper Samantha had generated in her grade-school years.

And they'd almost gotten caught.

"What do you girls do in there?" Alasdair had asked one night, gesturing toward Samantha's bedroom as she came out.

Bridie had frozen. There was no way she could lie to him. Not now. Not anymore. "We tell secrets," she had said. Not understanding, he had smiled.

Well, she consoled herself. Soon there would be no more need to lie. Anna's journals would have served their purpose. She would pack them back into the attic. There was only one left.

❧ twenty-nine ❧

SONDRA SAT IN THE NELSON County Commonwealth attorneys' conference room and waited for him to arrive. They would settle the matter of Jonah Porter's fate today, and she had little doubt how things would turn out. The Court of Appeals had found in her client's favor and overturned his conviction. She was also fairly certain that Thomas Dinwiddie would decline to pursue a second trial. Why, then, this feeling of dread? She thought of her client—his chilling silences, his flat, empty eyes—and her question answered itself.

Jonah Porter was convicted on improperly obtained evidence, she reminded herself.

He's guilty, she answered back, *and you know it.*

She opened the cover of the case file and pulled out the brief she'd submitted to the Court of Appeals. She read it again, hoping that this time she would feel better about the outcome. She scanned the facts. Officer Hinkley of the Charlottesville Police Department had been called to investigate the abandoned truck at 5:09 P.M. He arrived at the Piggly Wiggly parking lot at 5:22 P.M. The Hazardous Materials team was dispatched at 5:35 P.M., after which Officer Hinkley called in, suggesting there was probable cause for a warrant to be issued to search Mr. Porter's residence. However, at that time he was told that the Nelson County Sheriff's Department had already been dispatched to the residence based on information given in an anonymous tip. She flipped to the Charlottesville police's transcript of the 9-1-1 call, hoping she'd overlooked something. There was no mistake. There, highlighted in yellow, was the entry: *At 4:09 P.M. an unidentified female gave information concerning possible methamphetamine lab location. Referred to Nelson County sheriff.*

She turned to the last page, the nail in the coffin, so to speak. Another dispatch log, this time from the Nelson County sheriff. Officers were sent to the location of the possible methamphetamine lab at 4:45 P.M.

Sondra set down the file. There was no getting around it. The search was illegitimate. Anonymous tips required corroboration, and theirs—the drug paraphernalia found in the truck—had come after the fact. Twenty-four minutes too late.

She turned to the last page, the judgment the Virginia Court of Appeals had handed down. They'd granted Jonah Porter a new trial, remanded the matter back to the Nelson County Circuit Court. She should feel triumphant. Why so much anguish over a victory? she wondered again.

She heard footsteps, and Thomas Dinwiddie sailed into the room, derailing her thoughts. It was just as well. She greeted him. They shook hands, and he set his briefcase on the table and popped it open. He glanced at the judgment she'd been reading, and she felt slightly embarrassed, as if she'd been caught gloating. He didn't seem offended, though. In fact, he gave her an ironic smile.

"Democracy in action. Gives you a warm, happy feeling, doesn't it?"

She glanced at him sharply. His face was benign, apparently used to the yawning gap between justice and verdict. She shrugged, too ambivalent about what she'd done to defend it. "That's the system," she said. "Everyone deserves representation."

"Yeah. God bless America."

Sondra was thinking what to say next. He spared her the trouble, looked quickly through the folder in his hand, then turned clear blue eyes back to hers. "I don't see the point of going to trial again on the original charges. I'll deal down to possession instead of distribution. With credit for time served he can be back in Butcher Holler as soon as he pleads."

"I'm surprised you're caving in so completely," she protested, aware she was arguing against her own client.

The prosecutor shrugged. "You won this round."

Sondra nodded, shook hands again, and left. She had little doubt Jonah Porter would take the plea. And be out in a matter of days. She walked to her car and felt very weary, in her spirit as well as her body. She had only one desire—to be done with this matter, never to have to lay eyes on Jonah Porter again. Or anyone like him, she realized.

ҙ thirty ҙ

JONAH WATCHED THE BARE-LIMBED VIRGINIA winter flash by the window of the Department of Corrections bus as it jounced and bumped its way from the prison to the Nelson County jail. The woods were stark, the underbrush tangled and matted with dead leaves. He could see someone's deer stand. They passed an apple orchard that would be covered in blossoms before long.

He thought about his great-uncle Joshua. He had roamed and ranged over every blessed inch of Nelson County and could tell you where every beaver dam, turtle egg, and rabbit hole was. He had known everything there was to know about planting and growing and harvesting. He had kept bees and made honey—sweet and clear and pure. He had even raised peafowl for a while. Jonah closed his eyes, and there were his uncle's hands, thick and callused. He wondered what his uncle would say if he could see him now. He opened his eyes and and gazed out the window again, not really wanting an answer to that question.

The ride was over too soon. He stood, ducking his six-foot-four frame to meet the ceiling of the van, hobbling along as fast as his leg shackles would allow. He followed the guard into the jail and made his mind a blank while they processed him and took him to his cell. Only when he was alone inside it did he come back into focus, and even then he wished he sould stay in that other place. He felt like something was drumming and working itself up inside him. He tried to ignore it. He looked around him.

Prison and jail cells were all the same. Didn't make any difference if you were in North Carolina or Virginia. Those were the only two states whose hospitality he'd sampled, but he imagined a jail cell in

Seattle, Washington, would look about the same as this one: concrete floor, stainless steel toilet, cot, no pillow.

It had started raining outside. A storm had come up while they were doing their paperwork. He couldn't hear it through the double-paned, reinforced windows, but if he positioned his face just right and stood on tiptoe, he could see it through the thin slits of Plexiglas. He used to like the rain, but now it only made him nervous. Itchy and uncomfortable in his skin.

He stopped watching and began to pace around the cell. The first day he and Mary Bridget had run off, it had been raining. Hard, gully-washing rain. He had driven through the white sheets that pounded the windshield of his old truck, and she'd slept, her head in the crook between his shoulder and neck. His arm had gone to sleep, but he'd never even thought about waking her up.

He stopped pacing abruptly and lay down on the cot, stared at the same sort of white pockmarked insulated ceiling he'd seen a hundred thousand times. He felt a surge of anger. Now that freedom was in sight, it couldn't come soon enough. He couldn't wait any longer. A day was too long. An hour was too long. He needed things right now.

Here in the county jail he couldn't get anything. None of the little tidbits the old fellows smuggled out of the infirmary. Nothing at all to take the edge off.

He clenched his jaw and told himself to take ahold. There wasn't any other way. To get out he had to plead guilty in court tomorrow, and to do that he had to be transferred here. He would just have to stand it until he could get out and get what he needed. He made himself think about something else. He went over the things he was going to do when he got out, who he would call on, and in what order. How he would track her down. He lay there and stared at the ceiling of his cell until lights out, counting the ceiling tiles and the hours till his release.

❧

Sondra turned toward the door of the holding area. Here came her client, looking like a hardscrabble farmer in the Salvation Army suit and shirt she'd bought with her own money. He hadn't thanked her. Not that she'd expected him to. She wondered again why she bothered with him and all the others like him. It was a rhetorical question. The answer had everything to do with who she was and nothing to do with them. The guard led him to the counsel table, and Jonah Porter sat down beside her, silent and stoic. His dark hair was too long but combed back neatly. His high forehead bespoke intelligence, and she had to admit he was bright. One conversation with him had revealed that. There might be a few fried spots from his steady diet of meth, but so far she hadn't seen them. Still, something about him gave her the creeps. His eyes were dark empty caverns. You could peer inside, and instead of seeing his soul, there were only miles and miles of nothing. He was completely without natural affections, as far as she could see. Without emotion of any kind. His affect was paper flat, as if everything had stopped mattering to him a long time ago. As if he would—literally—just as soon kill you as look at you. She suppressed a chill. And this was the man whose release she'd obtained.

The judge entered. They rose. She wondered if it was too late to rescind their plea agreement. Even bringing up the matter would be outrageously unethical, she reproved herself. The judge called the court to order before she could pursue her thoughts any further. Mr. Porter stood when his name was called, pleaded guilty to the charges they'd agreed on. She said her bit, Dinwiddie said his, and then it was over.

Porter gave her another look from those eyes and walked away without a word to her. She watched his receding back and resisted the urge to cross herself.

Dinwiddie tapped on her table, a cheery little salute.

"I'll get him next time," he said, reading her mind, or perhaps just her guilt-twisted face. "And trust me, there will be a next time." He smiled. No hard feelings.

"I know." She felt the weariness again, and along with it a sense of shame.

Thomas Dinwiddie gave her a snappy nod, then sauntered off, whistling softly.

"Wait," she called after him, feeling as if he were the last lifeboat pushing off from the sinking *Titanic*.

He turned, eyebrow raised. She shoved the handful of papers into her briefcase, snapped it shut, and then trotted to catch up to him.

"I was just wondering . . ."

He waited, politely expectant.

"Are there any openings in your office?"

Jonah walked from the jail into downtown Lovingston. He could try to thumb a ride out to Woodbine, but nobody would pick him up. He probably had prison written all over him. Besides, there wasn't any point in it. There was nobody for him there, nothing he cared about, and going home wasn't on his list of things to do. He walked along the highway, turning back toward the mountains every so often. There they were, the misty blue hills, their tops covered with a low-hanging bank of clouds today. He walked, then turned and looked, then walked some more.

He passed the school, the Baptist church, the grocery store, the furniture store, the farm supply, then cut across the parking lot of that old gas station Ted Willis sold heating oil out of and went behind the building to the back entrance of the bowling alley. Just like he'd thought. The same bunch was there. More or less. There were a few new faces, and some of the old ones gone, probably enjoying a little of the state's hospitality, same as he'd been. But he recognized a few, one by name, and he jerked his head in greeting.

"I thought you was gone," Bobby Lee Wilcox said, returning the nod and flicking an ash off his cigarette with his thumb. "I heard you and Heslop was doing some time."

"My time's done," Jonah answered, without going into the details.

Bobby Lee nodded and took another draw of his Colt 45.

Jonah passed him by and went inside. He blinked a time or two until his eyes adjusted to the dark. There was no one he knew in here. He went to the bar, bought a pack of cigarettes, and ordered himself a beer. Another. Drank quickly, listening to the music thumping and the clatter of the balls and pins. When he'd finished, he went into the tiny bathroom, latched the door, and counted what was left of his release money. Eighteen dollars and some change. Not enough to buy anything. He needed to get some clothes. He needed to find Mary Bridget and get his money back. But first he needed to take the edge off. He went back to the bar and ordered a third beer. By the time it was on its way down, he was feeling a little better. He took it back outside. Bobby Lee was still holding up the wall.

"I need some ice," he said. Bobby Wilcox wasn't his first choice, but there didn't seem to be many others.

Bobby rubbed a hand over his pocked face and shook his head. "Ain't got none."

Jonah waited. There was more coming.

"It's hard to come by nowadays. They been cracking down."

"Yeah. I heard."

Bobby Lee didn't get the joke. "Once upon a time I'd of sent people to you," he said. "Why don't you just cook you up some?"

Jonah didn't bother to answer. He had no equipment, no makings, and no money to buy what he needed. Thanks to her.

"Try Tim McPhee," Bobby suggested. "He had some a while back."

Jonah tossed his bottle onto the pavement. It broke with a satisfying pop. He'd decided what he'd do. There were still another few hours before the shift was over at the furniture factory. Time enough to pop a stereo or two. That would get him enough to buy his equipment, and then he'd be back in business. He cut through the woods and headed toward the factory parking lot.

❧ thirty-one ❧

SONDRA RUBBED HER TEMPLES AND resisted the urge to lay her head on the table and weep.

"How come it is Jonah gets out and I don't?" her client repeated, his eyebrows puckered, his lip poked out in a massive pout.

God had a sense of humor. Just as soon as she'd dispatched the case of Jonah Porter, one of the other attorneys on the rotation for assigned counsel had had a heart attack, and his caseload had been divided up among the rest of them. She'd been assigned that of Porter's partner in crime, one Dwayne Junius Heslop. Compared to Mr. Heslop, Porter had been Stephen Hawking. She took a deep breath and began again.

"Mr. Porter was awarded a new trial because he was arrested as a result of an illegal search. The prosecutor didn't think he had enough evidence to convict in a second trial and released him with credit for time served. You, however, were not arrested during the raid that ensued from the anonymous tip. You were picked up in downtown Charlottesville with methamphetamine on your person, which you were attempting to sell to an undercover police officer. Just because the two events happened on the same day doesn't mean your situation is the same as his."

Sondra watched Dwayne Heslop strain to put two with two and arrive at four and wondered if it was too late to go to nursing school.

"It ain't fair, him getting out and I don't." Dwayne Heslop's massive face collapsed into a sullen pile. "We was all in it together. Now he gets out, and I'm still in, and them others ain't got in no trouble at all. It just ain't fair."

"Well, sometimes life isn't fair, Mr. Heslop." Sondra gathered up her things. She felt a stab of guilt. She was supposed to represent her clients aggressively, and not just the ones whose IQ was larger than their shoe size. She had a thought, a dim possibility, but she felt obligated to mention it. "Who are these others?"

Heslop raised his huge shaggy head. "They was a couple of fellas who sold the stuff for us, and Jonah's gal bought the makings for the candy. It just ain't fair all of them and Jonah getting clean away and me still sitting here for another six months."

Sondra sighed and turned back to her client. "If you'd give names and details, I could go to the commonwealth attorney and see if he'd be willing to cut you a deal."

Heslop's dull eyes glinted with a sly light as he considered. "I ain't no squealer," he said, as if she'd accused him. "But it just ain't fair they get off and me still sitting here."

She waited, hoping he would talk, and feeling a slight twinge of guilt at her motive. She'd been looking for an excuse to call Tom Dinwiddie to see if he'd decided whether or not to hire an assistant.

"Yeah, all right," he said. "I'll tell you."

She sat back down and took out her pad, uncapped her pen.

"The two fellas was Eldon Hightower and Smartie Henderson. Now, Smartie's already doing time in North Carolina for a job over in Wautauga County. But Eldon's around somewhere. I could probably find him."

Lord, give me patience, Sondra prayed silently. "And the woman?"

"Her name's Mary."

Sondra lifted her eyes and pen, waiting for him to finish. "Her last name?" she prompted.

"Hold on. I'm thinking." His face crumpled in concentration, the massive head shook. "Started with a W. Winston? Worthington?" He slumped. Sondra put the cap back on the pen.

"Washburn!" He almost shouted in triumph. "Gal's name is Mary Bridget Washburn."

Sondra nodded and made a few notes as he filled in the details.

This Mary Bridget Washburn had apparently made a break for it the day Mr. Porter had been arrested. According to Mr. Heslop, she'd run off with the money. That made sense. And she'd been the anonymous informant, no doubt.

Sondra frowned, remembering that she'd shown Mr. Porter a copy of the 9-1-1 transcript. Suddenly the set of his jaw and the glint of his eye when he'd read it took on an ominous meaning.

"I'll get back to you," she said. She stood, took her leave of Mr. Heslop, and headed straight back to her office and placed a call to Tom Dinwiddie. She didn't even ask about the job, just told him about Mary Bridget Washburn and her concerns. She finally calmed down when he promised her he'd take care of it.

The sooner they issued a warrant for the arrest of Ms. Washburn, the better she'd feel. Not because Sondra had any burning desire to bring her to justice. It was just that she would rest easier when this young woman was safely locked in jail. She recalled Jonah Porter's dead eyes, and suddenly the discovery of Mary Bridget Washburn lying in a ditch somewhere with her throat cut didn't seem like much of a stretch for the imagination.

Jonah went back to the apartment and knocked, taking care not to burn his knuckles on the numbers, for they were white hot, just like the mat on the concrete step in front of him.

Somebody was home this time. He could hear the television. Nobody'd been home when he'd come before, so he'd gone and gotten himself fixed up again. But now he was back, and pretty soon he'd know what he'd come to find out. He rubbed a hand across his jaw and thought again about what she'd done. She'd run off and left him. Stolen things from him. She didn't care a thing about him, and as it all came back, it was like something sharp plunging into his soft parts.

He hated her.

He let the hate take hold inside him and fill up the hurt place. It was a hard, cold, gunmetal gray hate, and it felt good to him. It helped him. It felt like armor, like one of those concrete and steel bunkers inside his chest. Yes, that's exactly what it was like. It was just exactly like one of those inside him.

He knocked on the door again. A woman opened it. She was scrawny, skinny, with earrings and tattoos. She was carrying a baby. She stared at him, and Jonah tried to remember the name of the fellow he'd come to see.

"You want Eric?"

He nodded. That was it.

"Just a minute." She shut the door on him.

Jonah lit a cigarette while he waited. A kid came out of the apartment next door. He bounced one of those big red rubber balls. Probably stole it from school. He cast a glance toward Jonah, then stopped bouncing and went back inside. Who was he? Who was he going to call? Jonah thought about going after him, but before he could decide, the door opened again. It was the redheaded fellow. Jonah had forgotten his name again, but he remembered what he wanted.

"You made an ID for somebody, and I need to find her."

The redheaded fellow shook his head. The door started to close.

Jonah's cousin had been redheaded. They'd hounded her. *Better be dead than red on the head. Better be dead than red on the head.* Jonah stuck his boot in the door and reached for the gun he'd stuck in the waistband of his jeans. *Better be dead than red on the head.*

"Whoa," the fellow said. "You don't need that."

That's right. He didn't. He'd forgotten the plan for a minute or two. He put the gun back and reached into his pocket. Pulled out the money he'd gotten from a week's worth of selling. "I could pay you something," he said.

The fellow rubbed his forehead, but Jonah was cold and tired of waiting. Besides, there was that boy next door who might come back any minute. He stepped forward, shoving the door open with his knee, and the fellow sort of stumbled back. They stood there inside the apartment. There was a kid, a girl, watching television. Why, it was Mary B, right there, gone back to being a child. "There you are,"

Jonah said, feeling the rage bubble up. "Why'd you take it? What'd
you do with it?"

Mary B was scared, he could tell. Well, she ought to be. She got
up and went to the tattooed lady, left her cartoons playing.

"Look," the redheaded fellow said. "Let's find what you want and
get you on your way."

"Come on, Brittany," the tattooed lady said to the girl. "Come
with me."

The girl turned her eyes toward Jonah on her way out of the room.
Big brown eyes. Not blue. So. She'd just been pretending to be Mary
B. He narrowed his own eyes and turned them on the fellow.

"You better quit messing with me and tell me where she went."

"Tell me who we're looking for," the fellow said, and he was over
at his computer, punching buttons and clicking the mouse.

"Mary Bridget Washburn."

The fellow clicked again for a minute or two, then shook his head.
"Nobody by that name."

Jonah shook his own head. "Look again. I know she'd come here.
Wouldn't know to go anywhere else."

"What's she look like?"

"Blond hair. Blue eyes. Pretty."

The man shook his head again.

Jonah started to feel the anger rise, but then he remembered
something. He laughed. The redheaded man's eyes got big.

"She was probably toting around a big green duffel bag. Full of
my money."

The fellow stared at Jonah for a minute as if he was trying to decide
what to do. The baby squalled from the back of the apartment, and
that seemed to help him make up his mind. He went back to messing with his computer, clicked some more, then after a minute the
printer made some noise, and he handed Jonah two sheets of paper.
"Here's a copy of her new driver's license and social."

Jonah took the sheets and looked hard at them, trying to understand what this meant. After a minute it was clear to him. She'd gone

and turned into her mama. That's all right. Didn't make any difference to him. "I need to know where to find her," he said.

The fellow shook his head, and Jonah felt something hot work its way up from his belly. His chest got full of it, and he felt like he just had to scream. Like he was going to come apart or tear somebody else apart. "You better quit messing with me," he shouted at the redheaded man.

"All right, all right!" Redhead looked scared again. "If she's working, I might be able to find out where, but it'll take a while. Come back in an hour."

The heat started going back down. "I'll wait," Jonah said. He didn't sit down, though. The furniture had bugs on it, he could tell.

He watched the cartoons the little girl had left on, and he didn't know how long it was, but after a while the fellow was tapping him on the shoulder.

"Here." He handed Jonah another paper. Jonah tried to read it, but it wasn't any use. The words were changing places too quick for him to follow.

"What's it say?"

"Bag and Save grocery," the man said. "In Alexandria."

"Alexandria," Jonah repeated.

The man nodded.

"Why, that's not in California."

The man stared at him. "No. It's in Virginia. Take highway 64 to 81, then cut over to 66. You can be there in three or four hours."

Jonah nodded. That was good. He didn't know how he would have gotten to California. He pulled the money from his pocket and sorted out two fifties. The fellow didn't even ask for more, just hustled him out the door. He was barely outside when it shut behind him and the deadbolt clicked.

๛ *thirty-two* ๛

BRIDIE WORKED ON THE BREAKFAST dishes and wished she could reach him. He was the other Alasdair today. The one who was absorbed in his own world, and she'd figured out what made him transform. It was all this church business. When he got taken up with it, he turned into another person. One who was driven, who didn't talk about the things of the Spirit and forgiveness and nothing being able to separate you from the love of God. No, this Alasdair looked as if he'd never heard the word *grace*.

Not that he was receiving much himself. He had been killing himself trying to do a good job for these people, working on his sermons until all hours, calling on his parishioners and listening to their complaints, turning down speaking engagements that would take him out of town. But in spite of all his hard work, they wanted him out. Just last night they had come to the house again, led by that frail old Edgar Willis fellow. Alasdair hadn't said much afterward, but Lorna had filled her in. They were going to call a congregational meeting to vote Alasdair out unless he came with them to Richmond for a powwow with the big chief this Saturday.

"They're hoping he'll take the job the president is offering," Lorna had said.

"Do you think he will?" Bridie asked.

Lorna had given her head a half shake. "I don't know. If he fights, it will split the church. There are no good choices."

Bridie glanced at him now, her heart heavy with concern. He was here and not here, and she wished she knew how to call him back. He'd been sitting at the table behind her for fifteen minutes, not reading the paper, not talking, just staring into space. He'd probably be happier pumping gas, but of course, she couldn't say that to him. She tried to think of what she could say, and again came up with nothing.

Samantha thumped down just then. She clattered around getting her cereal and milk.

"Are you sure I can't get you something to eat?" Bridie asked Alasdair. He stood up, pushed in his chair, and started toward her. He looked so sad. She had the sudden urge to reach out and touch his hand. In spite of all their talking, they never touched, except for those nights of his illness.

"No. Thank you." He shook his head and reached around her to put his cup in the sink. "About this weekend," he said, "are you sure you don't mind staying with the children while I go to Richmond?"

"No, of course not. Will you need me to stay Saturday night as well as Friday?"

"Probably not. I'll drive down tomorrow afternoon and stay in a hotel. The meeting's early Saturday, and I'll drive back as soon as it's over."

Bridie nodded. He met her eyes then for the first time today, and oh, where had she gotten such an imagination? And why did it torment her so? But it seemed as if he was begging her to stop him. *Do something,* he seemed to plead. *Don't let me keep going farther away from myself. Don't let me stay this man I've become.*

But what can I do? she sent back. *How can I help you when I can't even help myself?*

Samantha wormed between them and set her bowl and spoon in the sink. A few circles of cereal bobbed in an inch of milk. "Who's driving me?" she asked, breaking the current.

"I am," Bridie said, her face flushing for no reason. "Let me get Cam and Bonnie, and we'll go."

She turned away from Alasdair and forced herself not to look up when the back door opened and closed.

"Could you hurry it along?" Bob asked. The government computer system must be powered by a mule train.

Gerry'd been leaving messages like crazy, but Bob wasn't going to return them until he had good news. He was only too aware that the sands of time were moving at a pretty good clip through the hourglass of life. Today was Thursday. Gerry had left word that the Knox Presbyterian elders had run out of patience. They were coming to Richmond for a Saturday meeting to settle this thing one way or another. Bob knew it was time to make something happen. His future was at stake. If he had to go with what he had, he would make do, but at this point every little bit helped.

"Look, I'm not even supposed to be doing this," Jim Wigby complained. "The only reason I'm helping you is because my father asked me to, and most of this stuff is a matter of public record, anyway."

Bob ignored him.

Jim scrolled up the list, and there was the name and social security number of Bridget Collins. But it didn't add up. Literally. Bob frowned and tried to make sense of what he was seeing. According to the Commonwealth of Virginia, Bridget Collins was dead and way too old to be this woman.

Suddenly he remembered his own, oh, what should he say, experimentation with the facts when he'd pumped the church secretary for information. He had used his grandfather's name. It had come quickly and easily to his tongue when he was pressed. Maybe MacPherson's nanny had done the same. Which meant maybe she had something to hide. His pulse speeded up.

"Run her for marriage and birth certificates," he said.

Jim grunted but obeyed.

It took a few minutes and detours, but eventually Bob had a list—four certificates of live birth had been issued to Bridget Collins Washburn, and he had the dates and socials for each kid.

"Look up this one," he said, pointing to the listing for the oldest child. "It checks out for sex and approximate age. Her social's there. Getting her name shouldn't be a problem."

"It'll take a while."

"I'll wait."

With an impatient sigh, Bob rested his foot on his knee and tapped a rhythm on his shoe. He would have prayed if he'd been a praying kind of person.

"I got her. Name's Mary Bridget Washburn." Jim jotted down the information and handed it to Bob.

"Run her for wants and warrants. And I'll need a picture."

"I'm not supposed to do this."

Bob sat up, no longer in the mood for playing around. "I beg to differ," he said. "If this woman is using an alias and caring for children, it's obvious there's something nasty in this soup. I'd hate for it to come out that you knew and didn't pursue it."

"You really are a piece of work," Jim said, but he typed in the Internet address for the National Criminal Information Center Web site.

"It'll take some time." This delivered through clenched teeth.

"I'll wait," Bob repeated.

Jim gave him a nasty look. "I've got twenty more minutes to give you. If you need more than that you should hire an investigator." Bob ignored him. He went into the hall, bought a sandwich, poured himself another cup of the sludge that passed for coffee around here. He was onto something. He could feel it.

He ate the sandwich, tossed back his coffee, and headed back to Jim's dismal little office. Then the long night ended. Jim was beaming when Bob entered the room.

"Take a look at this," he said, pointing to the computer screen.

Bob hurried in and peered over his shoulder. Hello! Pay dirt. Mary Bridget Washburn was wanted for the manufacturing and distribution of a controlled substance.

"If this is the nanny, she's got a few secrets," Jim said.

"I'd say so," Bob agreed, his pulse pounding.

"Shall we call the police and have them pick her up?"

"No," Bob answered quickly. "I'll handle this myself." Timing was critical. He printed out the dirt on Mary Washburn and went back to his office. He needed to think.

$\mathcal{L}$

Bridie almost drove past the Bag and Save to the Safeway but decided she was being ridiculous. She had to face them sooner or later. She unloaded Cam and Bonnie and went inside. She greeted a few people she knew as she wheeled past the check-out stands. Jeremy the courtesy clerk, Florence in Pharmacy. She didn't see Winslow, for which she was grateful. Carmen was at the lead check-out stand, grinning and talking and snapping her gum. Bridie gathered up her groceries quickly, then got in Carmen's line.

"How's it going?" Carmen asked, beaming. She reached under the counter and gave a handful of stickers to Cam and Bonnie. Bridie made a note to check their clothes for them when she did the laundry. Once a sticker went through the dryer nothing could get it off.

"Pretty good," Bridie said. "How about you?"

"We've set a date, and I got my ring," Carmen announced, flashing her hand. It was a pretty big diamond, and Bridie oohed and aahed appropriately over it.

"I want you to be in the wedding," Carmen said, serious.

Bridie stared into those kind, warm eyes of Carmen's, and suddenly her situation seemed unbearable. She was locked into some kind of limbo. It was worse than prison. At least in prison you could do your time and get out. She would never be free from this. She would never be able to say where she would be in a year, a month, a week, even a day. Her whole life could be rearranged by a series of numbers on a computer screen. She felt a shrill little shock. She hadn't checked the prison Web site in weeks. Carmen was looking at her, hurt swirling in the lively eyes.

"Nothing would make me happier than to be in your wedding," Bridie said truthfully. She leaned across the check-out stand and gave Carmen a squeeze. When she let her go, she could see Carmen was back to her normal happy expression.

"If you're worried about money—don't. We can work that out."

"Thank you," Bridie said, taking the excuse Carmen offered.

Carmen chattered on about the wedding, about the date, about the location, the reception, her dress. Bridie listened and smiled, kept Cam and Bonnie out of the candy bars and breath mints, and finally peeled off two twenties and paid for her groceries.

Carmen gave her the change, then held up a finger. "Hold on," she said. "There's a phone message for you in the office. I guess she called twice, and the only reason I know is that Jeremy took the last call. Winslow's such a baby." She made a face, and Bridie tried to imagine who would be calling her here, especially with such persistence. Who would be calling her anywhere?

Carmen handed her the paper. *Did not leave her name. Call her,* Jeremy had written. She shook her head. It was probably a mistake. Still, it was odd, and her stomach gave a little twist and rumble. "Did she say what it was about?" Bridie asked.

Carmen shook her head. "Not to Jeremy, and if she told Winslow, he'll take it with him to his grave—unless it makes you look bad. Then he'll put it in the *Post.*"

Bridie felt another twist of dread. Guilty consciences didn't make for having much of a sense of humor. She crumpled the note into her pocket. She would call when she got home.

"I'm giving up the apartment, Bridie," Carmen said, expression apologetic. "We're buying a house out in Herndon."

Bridie nodded. She'd been expecting that. It was just a matter of when. "Let me know the dates, and I'll get my things out."

"No rush," Carmen said. Bridie pushed her cart out and waved good-bye. There was someone else behind her in line.

"I'll be home tonight, but after that I'll be staying at the parsonage for a few days. Alasdair's taking a trip."

"Alasdair," Carmen repeated, smiling as she scanned a bag of flour.

Bridie didn't smile back. She said good-bye. It seemed as if things were drawing to a natural ending point. Carmen was getting married. Alasdair was back on his feet and would most likely be moving the family to Richmond. She and Samantha were almost finished with the journals. It was time to move on. She didn't feel anything but a cold heaviness at that thought. She loaded her groceries and children into the car and drove back to the parsonage, being careful not to call it home, even in the quietness of her own mind.

ℒ

Jonah flipped on the motel bathroom's exhaust fan and turned the flame on the Coleman stove a little higher, shoving back the coffee filters and almost tipping over a Mason jar full of lye, his hands were shaking so bad. He clenched his teeth. Three days of scratching and scrounging to keep himself high, lifting car stereos and cell phones. He wanted his money. Then he could hire somebody to round up makings for him, set himself up in business again. He was getting close, he soothed himself. It wouldn't be much longer.

He'd found the grocery store today. Gone inside to buy his cold medicine and shot the breeze with one of the bag boys who was smoking out back.

"You know Bridie Collins?" he'd asked.

The kid had nodded. "She doesn't work here anymore, but I think she still lives with Carmen."

"Carmen?"

"Head checker. She'll be in later."

Well, it was later now, Jonah realized, steadying his hands as he went through the whole routine, burning his fingers twice as he cooked and shot a spoonful. By the time he reached the motel bed and pushed aside the sackful of cold pills, the meth hit his head in a rush. It was like his whole body was roaring. Like ocean waves crashing inside and every one carrying away bad things with it and leaving a trail of glittery, sweet, sandy golden dust. He saw himself bending over, picking up the shining sand and eating it. Oh. It tasted like rock candy, like sugar straight from the sack. It melted on his tongue. He licked his lips. They were dry, but they sure tasted sweet. The waves crashed again and again and again. Little bits of him started washing away with each one, though. He got up and started walking. If he kept moving he could keep ahead of them.

He locked the door of the motel room behind him and crossed the four-lane highway. He'd taken to keeping the Fury parked in the restaurant parking lot across the highway. He'd rather walk a ways than get picked up again.

Jonah had given the bag boy a twenty to keep his mouth shut. The boy had said come back this evening. Carmen would be there then, and he'd point her out for another twenty. Then Jonah would follow this Carmen home, and she would lead him straight to Mary. He got into the car, started up, and drove, careful and slow, back to the Bag and Save.

Bridie called the number as soon as she got back to the parsonage, her hands shaking as it rang; then the hollow voice said the cellular phone she'd called was not in use at the moment. She clicked off and calmed herself, tried to think of who it might be. She finally remembered the lady who gave Tupperware parties. She'd said something about calling Bridie someday. That must be it, she thought, trying to believe it. She was paranoid, that was all.

Still. This phone message—another innocent-looking piece of paper—seemed like an omen. Whatever magic had been on her life seemed to be wearing off.

Alasdair barely touched his dinner and begged off dessert because he didn't feel well. He said he would be in his study. She dumped his nearly full bowl of stew into the garbage. She'd been living in a fantasy world, she realized. One where the story would have a happy ending without the pain of telling the truth, of seeing the stunned disgust on the faces of the people she'd come to love as she told them about her past. Her self.

She finished the dishes quickly and went upstairs to read the last journal with Samantha.

While Samantha made herself comfortable, Bridie flipped open the book, feeling a murmur of apprehension. Anna's first books had a sense of completion, of her personality shining through the pages, a coherence and integration. In the last journals they'd been hit and miss. The entries Anna had made were full of the familiar person, but there weren't as many of them. In those books Anna let the letters and photos tell much of the story of her life. As if she had been growing tired of filling in the gaps.

This one, even from the little Bridie could tell from a quick flip-through, was even less coherent. There was no careful gluing, no paint chips, no essays, and not many entries in her hand. This journal seemed to be a testament to the persistence of habits. Once a record keeper, always a record keeper, even as life came unglued around you.

There were a few written entries, but not on rag paper neatly affixed to the page. These were spiky slashes covering the page itself, outpourings of the heart in thick black marker. The transient documents of Anna's life were there as well, but not glued neatly to the pages with comments and captions. No, these parts of paper, these pieces of life, were stuck in randomly. A bill here, a card from a parishioner there, appointment cards from doctors and dentists nestled against grocery lists and Samantha's graded assignments and drawings. Everything was heaped together without organization. Her life was in pieces, jammed helter-skelter between the heavy pages. In her journal, and Bridie wondered if in Anna's life as well, events became random and accelerated, coming too quickly to be interpreted and filed away. Just dumped in to be sorted through later.

Samantha, maybe feeling the same sense of dread, drew a little closer and rested her head against Bridie's shoulder as they began the final leg of their journey. This was the last piece of highway, the winding mile of road that had taken Anna from being the woman who had scrupulously photographed and documented every year of Samantha's life to the mother who hadn't even unwrapped gifts for her newborn children. They would trace the trip, but if Bridie had ever thought it would be a healing journey, she doubted it now. More and more, their destination was becoming clear.

She opened the book.

A professionally finished portrait stared back at them, several of them, Bridie noticed, lifting the first one slightly. There they were: Alasdair, Anna, and Samantha, posed on a set. Alasdair stood behind. He rested one hand on Anna's back, the other on Samantha's shoulder. He looked tight, strained, as if he were holding his family together with an effort. Samantha must have been about ten years old. She looked gangly, like a girl just ready to step over the threshold into womanhood. Her eyes weren't dark and tortured as they'd looked when Bridie had first met her. But they were a little too wide—anxious and watchful. But it was Anna upon whom Bridie's eyes finally rested.

Oh no. I'm so sorry, she wanted to say. She murmured, but wanted to groan instead.

"What?" Samantha asked, her voice sounding as tense as her face in the picture.

Bridie shook her head instead of answering. Anna's face was still beautiful, but she looked so tired. So worn and weary. She was thinner than before. The bones of her face were clear beneath her delicate skin. It was paper white, and it looked as if an artist's brush had shaded half-moons under her eyes.

The next photo was of the entire family. Mother MacPherson and the clan. Mother sat regal on the wing chair this time. Alasdair stood central behind her. Winifred and Fiona flanked him. Lorna and the out-laws clumped around the edges. There was Anna, hiding in the back, her white face sandwiched between Fiona's and Winifred's husbands and the grown children. Where was Alasdair's father?

Samantha looked at the portraits without comment, then set them aside. Beneath them was a folded-up paper like a church bulletin. On the front was a cross banked with lilies.

"I am the resurrection and the life. He that believeth in me, though he die, yet shall he live."

Samantha opened it up. *In Memoriam. Douglas Rutherford MacPherson.* So Papa MacPherson had died.

"What did he die from?" Bridie asked.

Samantha shrugged. "I don't remember. He was in the hospital for a long time, and Grandma died right after he did."

Sure enough, there just behind it, dated just a few months later, was another piece of folded paper. New picture, new verse, same thing. *Eileen Marie Rushford MacPherson.* "*Well done, thou good and faithful servant.*"

A page of thick permanent marker followed.

> *We buried them both in the space of a few months. Odd, I always thought they were the trouble with us. I never wished them dead, of course, but somehow I thought if they could be magically transported away, I would be free. Gloriously free, with no one watching over my shoulder to tell me I'm doing it wrong. First Father MacPherson went, and now Mother, and instead of a huge sense of release, I feel sad. So many things come to me now that I wish I had done or said. So much of their lives was worthy of praise, but I painted them with the same dark brush. Instead of being gloriously free, I feel lonely. The house seems empty without Mother sitting on the loveseat, reading and sipping her tea. I don't like to go in there anymore.*

There were newspaper clippings after this. About Alasdair. One showed him in his robes behind the pulpit. He looked determined, fierce. The caption underneath said he'd been given some kind of award for excellence in broadcasting. The next one was a column by the religion editor, the one Lorna had told her about. Where they said he was the greatest apologist since C. S. Lewis. Bridie skimmed it. Pretty heady stuff. Hard to keep your wits about you when you were being compared to Samuel Rutherford and John Knox.

"I wonder what Anna did with her days," Bridie mused. "Do you remember?"

Samantha shook her head. She frowned a little. "I remember she was always waiting for me when I got home. She wanted me to talk to her."

The heaviness of the burden came out even in the words. "That must have been a hassle sometimes," Bridie said. Samantha looked shocked.

"No." Flat, no discussion allowed.

Bridie shrugged. "I loved my mama, but I wouldn't have wanted to be her everything. That's a pretty heavy load to carry."

"Turn the page."

Bridie did. A few snapshots spilled out. A birthday party. Good. Bridie felt a surge of relief. What could be sad about a birthday party? She peered closer. There was an unfamiliar face among the others grouped around the table. There was the usual crew, Alasdair, Samantha, the sisters, but a man—lean, with salt-and-pepper hair— sat beside Anna, who had the center seat at the head of the table, a cake full of candles in front of her.

"That's my mom's dad," Samantha said, pointing to the new face. "He's dead now, too."

"Mmm," Bridie murmured again. So many gone.

Papa came for my birthday. All the way from Scotland. And I know why. I am thirty-one, the same age Mother was. I am worn out trying to argue with him, and even if he is right, what's to be done? What will happen will happen, regardless.

"How did *your* mother die?" Samantha asked Bridie, her voice sounding hollow.

"She died of cancer. She wasn't quite forty. She was sick for a year, and I missed a lot of school taking care of her. But I was glad to do it." Bridie stared into the past, felt that same tense fear that used to fall over her as she came up the path from the school bus, then the same flood of relief when she entered the house to see Mama still with them, propped up in the hospital bed they'd moved into the living room, Grandma fussing around her when she was well enough herself. Just thinking about it made her feel as if she were there again. Her heart thumped so hard, she feared it shook her body. It must have been her imagination.

Samantha didn't comment, just said, "Turn the page," again with that grim tone.

Father must have talked to Calvin. He visited me last weekend when Alasdair was at his office preparing the sermon. "Let me prescribe an antidepressant. Anniversaries can be very significant," he said and asked if I would see a counselor. I simply nodded. What is it about counseling that inspires such confidence? They must be our modern-day alchemists, the ones we hope will take the lead of our lives and turn it into gold. What folly. They're just blind and stumbling people trying to lead others in a journey that must be taken alone. I've learned at least one thing. There is no mate for the falling soul, no other half that will fill in the gaps. I didn't argue, though, just thanked him and took the prescription and the name of the counselor.

And apparently had made an appointment and taken the pills. The next few entries, dated a few months after this one, had a little of the life of the earlier books. They'd taken a trip together, Anna and Alasdair and Samantha. To New York. Bridie took out the envelope of snapshots, and Samantha spread them out on the bed. There were the three of them in Times Square, at the Statue of Liberty, Ellis Island. Just a happy little family enjoying the sights.

"Was that a fun trip?" Bridie asked Samantha.

She nodded and pointed to a photo of the three of them sitting around a red-checkered table, a candle burning in the middle. "That was in Little Italy. We had dinner at this Italian restaurant, only there wasn't anybody Italian in it. The waiter was Chinese or something, and the cook was this Indian guy, and the hostess was African. We were laughing about it. The food was good, though." Bridie examined the picture. Anna looked better. The dark circles were gone.

She flipped through the rest of the pictures. Turned the page.

Alasdair and I have been getting on well lately. Actually talking again. We took a trip to Rehoboth Beach for the weekend, and Lorna came and stayed with Samantha. We had a wonderful time. It was like our first days together. We walked and talked and sat beside the fire in our condominium for hours. It feels like a great relief. Like a load I've carried has been lifted off.

"What shall I do?" he asked, "if the dark times come again? How can I help you when you're feeling that way?"

I didn't know what to tell him. "They won't come back," I said, wishing more than promising.

There were a few pages after that of the old Anna. Journal entries neatly written and pasted on the page. Photographs of Samantha's school play, Samantha's birthday party, Alasdair's sermon notes, an appointment card for Dr. Albert Chenowith, OB-Gyn.

As I suspected, I am pregnant. Bridie looked at the date and did the arithmetic. Cam and Bonnie.

I knew even before I took the test. I stopped taking my antidepressants as soon as I suspected. The counselor says there might be another one I could take, but I don't want to do anything to hurt the baby.

I am a little stunned at history repeating itself. I never intended to become pregnant again at all, much less this year. The same age Mother was when she conceived me. Just thinking about that brings up a mix of feelings, none of them good. I begin to wonder if I am in some sort of cosmic time loop. Some sort of predestination. It does seem that the harder I try to not become like my mother, the more magnetic the pull toward her fate becomes.

I won't think like that. It's unhelpful. I went to counseling again today, the first time in many months. Father would be happy. I only wish he were here to tell. If I have a son, I would like to name him after my father and my husband. Cameron Alasdair MacPherson. The two men in my life.

"She got a bonus," Bridie quipped.

Samantha just nodded. It seemed the closer they came to present day, the more tightly strung she became.

The next section was mostly about Samantha. School stuff. Plays, music recitals. A few more church programs.

There were lots of blank pages following this clump. Toward the end was another mass of papers stuck between the pages.

An invitation to a shower the ladies of the church were throwing in Anna's honor. A photograph. Anna, hugely pregnant, surrounded by presents, her face oddly devoid of expression. Not sad. Not happy. Just there.

A list, one of those made at every shower that listed the present and the giver so thank-you notes could be sent. And there were the notes. A few begun, the rest still pristine, their envelopes banded beside them.

More photos. Of Alasdair smiling, holding two tiny bundles. Of Samantha and the babies, Lorna and the babies. Fiona and Winifred and the babies. Of Anna, wan and pale, propped on pillows, a twin on each arm. Bridie peered closer at her face and again was struck by the blank expression. Checked out. Nobody was home.

Nothing more until the very last page. She tensed. Samantha felt coiled beside her like a tightly twisted spring. Would there be any ending here, or would they leave with more questions than they'd come with? Suddenly Bridie had a sharp twist of regret. Maybe they shouldn't have taken this trip at all. Still, they were here at the end. Quickly, before Samantha could bark at her to turn the page, she did so.

> *Calvin came to the house today and talked to me about post-partum depression. He suggested I check into the hospital for a while until I can be started on a new medication and it has time to take effect. "Lorna will care for the twins and Samantha," he said. "You don't need to worry." And suddenly I realized he was right. Lorna would care for them.*
>
> *She is so kind and gentle-hearted. Consistent. Always there whenever she's needed. She would be the perfect mother, and suddenly it is clear to me why she has no children of her own.*
>
> *I told Calvin that I would consider it and tell him the answer on Monday. I spent the weekend making my decision, and today I am sure. Alasdair said he will go to the radio station today to record his broadcasts, and that he arranged for Lorna to come and take care of the children.*

Samantha was trembling. Bridie put down the book and took her in a strong grip. "Do you want to stop?"

Samantha shook her head, and this time it was she who picked
up the album. The last entry. Just one paragraph.

*I picked up each of the babies before Lorna came to take them.
It was as if I was seeing them for the first time. Up until now looking
at them made me feel too tired and overwhelmed, but today I didn't
feel that way. They are precious. So tiny and perfect. I kissed them,
blessed them. Lorna came. We had a cup of tea and a muffin. "You
look better," she said. "I feel better," I told her, and it is the truth. I feel
a great weight has been lifted away. As if I've struggled and struggled,
and now I can stop struggling. I kissed the babies again, and she took
them, promising to return in time to meet Samantha's bus. I wrote a
little note to Samantha. I am so proud of her. She must know that.*

And then it ended. Just like that. No more. The last words. Samantha was crying silently, the tears coursing down her cheeks. She rose
and went to her dresser, came back with a worn envelope. She handed
it to Bridie, and Bridie recognized the writing. The beautiful, careful
script was back, not the spiky slashes of the depressed months.

Dearest Samantha,
    *You must know how you fill my heart with joy. I desire only the
best for you. I want you to have happiness and joy and no darkness
at all. I know that is impossible, and yet I think that a clean sorrow is
better than a lifetime of shadowy dread. In a perfect world you would
have neither one. Only happiness and warm sunshine on your face.
No storms or deep waters.*
    *I read the Bible, and there I see God stilling the storm, parting
the sea, holding back the mighty waters. He is ruler over even the
most powerful and inexorable of forces. I wish I had lived in those
days when He could reach out His hand, and the waves would be
firm beneath my feet.*
    *I love you, forever and always. May your life be full of joy and
blessing.*

                            Mother

Bridie blotted her eyes on her sleeve. Samantha wept quietly in her arms. After a minute or two the shoulders stopped shaking. She took a tissue from the drawer beside her bed and blew her nose. The silence was calm and seemed emptied of all energy, good or evil.

"She killed herself," Samantha said, and Bridie saw the dam crack and the first trickle of water begin to flow out. Samantha had known it all along. Now she was finally putting words to what she'd carried all alone.

"Yes," she agreed quietly. "I think she did."

"Why?" Anguish loaded the word, and the tears returned. Bridie took her hand and stroked it, let her cry again. Possible answers flicked through her mind like a tape played on too fast a speed. Anna had struggled with depression all her life. Hints about Anna's own mother's death suddenly took on new meaning. But those weren't answers. Not really.

"I don't know," Bridie said, taking a deep breath, "but here's what I do know."

Samantha lifted her face.

"There wasn't anything you could have done to stop it."

Samantha shook her head. "What if I'd been home? I could have talked to her, and maybe she would have listened."

Bridie shook her head, wondering how well-worn those questions were, how many times they had been asked in the silence of Samantha's mind. "You read that last entry. She'd gotten to the place where she took things out of context. Whatever happened, she took it as a sign that what she'd decided was the right thing. She'd convinced herself that Lorna would be a better mother to you and the babies than she was. Nothing you said would have mattered. Look how many people tried to help her. Her father, your uncle Calvin, Lorna, you. Your father tried his best."

Bull's-eye. The head dropped again. The tears flowed. "I thought it was his fault."

"I know you did, but it wasn't."

"Do you think he'll forgive me?"

"I know he will." Whether he would forgive himself or not was another matter entirely.

Samantha was quiet, but Bridie wasn't thinking they were even close to being finished. After a minute Samantha edged around to the greatest of her fears. Bridie had seen it coming a long way off, since that day in the principal's office. *Lord, give me the words,* she prayed. *I'm an unclean vessel, but use me anyway.*

"Do you think she went to hell?" The words landed with the impact of an explosive, but Bridie was ready for them. Her head was shaking before they were even out.

"I most certainly, absolutely, without a doubt do *not* believe she went to hell." And the Lord must have answered her prayer because there, just like a pretty little jewel dropping into her open hand, came one of the hundred verses. " 'My sheep hear my voice, and I know them, and they follow me. And I give them eternal life, and they shall *never perish*, neither shall any man pluck them out of my hand.' "

Samantha took that in, and her face lost that tight, pinched look. She cried a little more.

"What if I get sad like she did?"

Lord—again? Bridie pleaded, holding her hand open as if the answer might literally fall into it. It did.

"Your mama's sadness was her undoing," she said, "because she ran from it. First she ran to college to get away from it. Then she ran away by putting all her attention on your daddy; then she ran away by coming here to America, thinking if she left the sad place she could leave the sadness. Then she ran away from it by putting her mind on you. But you can't run away from things," Bridie said, and she saw herself in the old rusty truck, coasting down the dirt road, the bag of money on the seat beside her. "They just keep after you if you try to do that. You finally have to stop, turn around, and face whatever's on your heels. Otherwise it hounds you right into the grave."

Samantha heaved a huge sigh. Bridie took a close look at her face. It was sad but calm.

"If you feel sad, tell your daddy. Tell Aunt Lorna. Turn around and look the sadness in the eye, and it won't get the best of you. Everybody feels sad," Bridie finished. "There's nothing there to be afraid of. It's running from things that gives them strength."

Samantha nodded. She threw her arms around Bridie's neck, and Bridie rocked her for a long time. She stroked Samantha's hair and wiped her own eyes on her sleeve again and again.

Alasdair looked down at the half-finished pile of sermon notes on the desk before him. He should put them away and prepare for his trip to Richmond.

Why? another part of him asked. Why was he going to Richmond in one last attempt to save his career? Why was he doing any of this? He imagined himself standing in the pulpit, the sea of faces before him. Hungry people, waiting for him to turn the five loaves and two fishes into food for a multitude. All holding pens poised over blank pages. Pages he should fill with words of wisdom. He felt unbearably weary.

What did he have to tell them? Where would he point them to? When was the last time he'd heard the voice of the Lord? Felt that swelling in his heart at the movement of the Spirit? When had the Scriptures last come to life before his eyes? How long had it been? Was it any wonder the people he led were dull and hard of hearing?

His own desire for the Lord had become deadened along with the rest of him. He had his own stone rolled firmly against the mouth of his tomb, blocking any resurrection. It remained there, regardless of his straining and pushing, his despairing prayers. And there didn't seem to be any angels nearby.

He knew when it had sealed him up. He recalled the very day. He had come home from the radio studio after a long day of recording. The police car had been waiting in front of the house. No sirens blaring, no flashing lights. It had been pulled to the curb, idling, waiting. And he had known. Immediately he had known. The only question had been how, and that had been answered in short order.

He had tried to take care of things after that. Tried to clear away the debris as quickly as possibly, to keep it from hurting anyone else.

To put out the fires and bury the dead. He had done the best he could, but obviously it was not enough. It was never enough, was it? It never had been.

He dropped his pen and rubbed his neck. Why had he become a pastor? Why was he enduring so much misery to hold on to something he'd never wanted in the first place? He thought and thought, and to save himself, he couldn't remember. His father had told him to do it, and ever the good son, he'd obeyed.

He sighed, tried to gather the pieces of himself together. He could hear Bridie's and Samantha's voices twining together from the next room. None of this was Bridie's fault. He had seen the hurt on her face when he'd left after dinner, barely speaking to her. It wasn't too late to approach her. He stood up. He would ask her to come downstairs and talk to him. Not out of any sense of obligation. He wanted to, he realized as he walked toward the door. He needed to.

✒ thirty-three ✑

SAMANTHA WATCHED BRIDIE PUT THE last journal back into the box and looked again at the picture she'd kept out—of Mom in the party dress. She wondered what her dad would say if she hung it on her wall. The door opened.

Oh, my gosh. This was so not good.

Dad came in all smiling and everything, and then he saw the picture in her hand. He looked over at Bridie and then down by her feet at the box of journals, and his face went completely white. Like the refrigerator or something. He looked straight at Bridie then. It was like she wasn't even there.

"What have you done?"

"It was my idea," Samantha said, trying to explain.

"What is all this?" he asked, still talking to Bridie. "Where did you get these?"

"Don't get mad at her."

"You stay out of this, Samantha."

"They were in the attic," Bridie said. "I never meant to deceive you, Alasdair."

Dad got totally stone-faced then. "There are things in there she shouldn't know." His voice was sounding funny.

"I already knew," Samantha said. "I knew she did it on purpose."

Dad looked at her, then turned around and looked at Bridie again, and for the first time Samantha got a little scared. He didn't say anything for a huge long time, and Bridie's face got white. Samantha thought maybe she was going to cry.

Then Dad said, really quiet, "This is what you've been doing in here."

Bridie nodded, and then Dad said, "I need to talk to you."

Bridie went with him and Samantha followed them out. Dad led the way downstairs. It was so not fair that Bridie was getting blamed for this.

"Go to your room, Samantha," he hollered back at her.

"Fine," she said and went straight to the heat vent. She lay flat on the carpet and put her ear against the grate. After a minute she heard them. Perfectly. They were both talking really loud.

"I did it for Samantha," Bridie said.

"For Samantha."

She knew that tone. He used it when he was just trying to get it straight exactly how you'd messed up.

"Yes," Bridie answered. "She's why I came here to begin with. I saw her in the church. She pinned a note to that board—the one with the falling sparrow—that's why I came, and this is what she needed."

Samantha blinked. She hadn't thought that prayer had been answered. Huh.

"She needed for somebody to tell her the truth," Bridie said. "She already knew it, but since nobody would say it, it was eating away at her."

"You have no idea what the truth is."

Dad sounded mean.

"I know Anna killed herself. It's obvious if you have eyes to see. She got more and more depressed, and nobody could help her no matter how hard they tried. Finally she just got tired of fighting and drove into the river."

There was this huge long silence. Samantha could feel her heart thumping. She wondered if she should go downstairs.

"Did Anna write about *her* mother?" Dad asked, a little quieter, but in this dead sort of voice. Samantha pressed her ear down so hard it hurt. "How she took an overdose of sleeping pills when Anna was six weeks old? Did she write about how her father talked of it time and time again, trying to get Anna to open up? Did she document the parade of counselors that marched through her life and how powerless they were to keep history from repeating itself? Enlighten me. What should I have done? If silence doesn't work and talking doesn't work, what would?"

"I don't know," Bridie said, and now *she* sounded mad. "But maybe there's something in between those two extremes of pretending nothing ever happened or being so sure she's a ticking bomb that she finally explodes just to end the tension."

Uh-oh.

"How dare you accuse me of pretending Anna's death never happened? Her death has colored every moment of my life, every movement of this household since the day she died."

"Then maybe it was time she was laid to rest."

"And how should I do that?"

"I don't know," Bridie said. "But this is a start. Raise your voice. Cry out to God. It's those who mourn who'll be comforted."

They were both quiet then. Samantha waited for a really long time, and still nobody said anything.

"Do you want me to come back tomorrow?" Bridie finally asked.

"I suppose so," he said, and he sounded really mad. "It's too late to make other plans now."

Then Samantha heard the door open and shut, and she got up and ran into the guest room so she could look out the window to the street. There went Bridie. She didn't even bring her coat. Just her purse. That made Samantha feel better. Bridie would be back.

Samantha dropped the curtain and went back into her room. A couple of months ago she would have gotten mad at Dad, like maybe even hated him and all. But now she felt sort of bad for him. But he was just going to have to get used to the idea that she knew stuff.

❧

Jonah had been waiting out in front of the Bag and Save forever. He idled the engine and felt like he was going to explode if he didn't get out of the car. He needed to move around. They were working their way out again, those little glass splinters. He picked at one place on his arm, then another. He scratched until his hand came away sticky with blood. He chewed his lip and lit another cigarette. His hands were shaking. He put in another CD and turned it up so he couldn't hear that chopping anymore. He wished they'd stop, but he knew it wasn't any use.

The automatic doors opened again and he flicked the cigarette out the window. It was an old woman, and that kid who'd pointed out Carmen to him was carrying the woman's groceries. He leaned back in his seat and beat the rhythm of the music onto the steering wheel. He needed gas. That little dark-headed fellow staying in the room next to his at the motel had been sucking it out at night while he slept. He'd seen him over there with his lips pressed against the gas tank.

The kid went back inside with the empty cart. The doors opened again. A woman came out. She was fat and had a little fat girl trailing after her, and her fat husband came along after the both of them pushing the cart.

Fat. Fat. Fat. At. Fat. Cat. Sat. Hat. Fat. The doors opened again. There she was, the woman who knew where Mary was. Carmen. She looked at him, and he wondered what she had in that sack. Could it be Mary in that sack? Maybe that was the chopping he'd heard. No. Mary was somewhere else. And Carmen was looking at him, and that wasn't good.

He leaned over like he was reaching for something on the floor. He stayed hunkered down for a minute or so, and when he lifted his head up, a police car had pulled to the corner. Jonah froze. That's what the demons rode in. That meant they were back. Oh no. And Carmen was in cahoots with them, because the demon car pulled to the curb, and just like that she leaned in and gave him a kiss. Judas kissed. Judas was a woman. Who knew about that? And now Jonah knew what was in the sack. It was the thirty pieces of silver. He wondered if he would find her hanging, swinging, when he went to find Mary and get the pieces of his brain back. And his money. His money. He hung on to that thought as the Judas girl got into the demon's car.

His hands shook as he started up his engine. His only chance was to follow them to wherever they were going, then wait until the demon left, then go inside and find Mary.

He crept along behind them all the way to the little apartment house, but instead of leaving, the demon parked his car and got out with the girl. That's when Jonah decided he couldn't stand it any longer. He would have to come back later. He wrote down the address on a piece of paper and put it in his pocket. That way, if they cut out that part of his brain tonight, he would be able to find this place again tomorrow.

ও *thirty-four* ও

FRIDAY MORNING BOB COMBED HIS hair, gargled with mouthwash, put on his tie and jacket. He inspected himself in the small mirror of the hotel bathroom. His eyes were red, but he looked pretty good, considering. After he'd left Jim Wigby, hands clutching the still-warm dirt on Mary Bridget Washburn, he had thought hard. It hadn't taken long to work things out. It would do him no good whatsoever if Gerry and MacPherson and the Knox elders resolved this situation tomorrow afternoon over tea and crumpets. The only way he was going to benefit from the months of hard work he'd been putting in was if he personally delivered MacPherson's head on the silver platter before that meeting took place.

He'd burned the highway, arriving in Alexandria around four yesterday afternoon. He'd managed to finagle a meeting with the religion editor of the *Washington Post,* which had gone even better than he'd hoped, then swung by the Bag and Save. He'd shown Mary Washburn's last driver's license photo to the manager, and he'd verified the ID. Then Bob had checked in here and stayed up all night, writing. The article he'd produced—a work of art if he said so himself—was neatly printed and in the envelope in his briefcase, along with the documentation he'd been collecting. Either way today's events went, he didn't see how he could lose. Risky? Yes. But then again, he'd never been afraid of rolling the dice.

He packed away his shaving kit, zipped his suitcase shut, turned off his laptop, then checked his watch. It was seven-fifteen. A little early to come calling, but he didn't want to take a chance on missing MacPherson. He nodded in satisfaction, gathered up his things, flicked off the light, and went to turn in his key.

Jonah pulled out the paper he'd written the address on. The numbers were jumping around, and he couldn't read them, and he couldn't remember the way he'd taken yesterday to find the place. Yesterday? Yeah, he was pretty sure. He slowed down and cruised down the alley, turned onto a street that looked a little familiar, a U-shaped red-brick building with a courtyard in the middle. That was it. And there was the demon's car, still parked in the front. He rubbed his jaw and took another drink of the malt liquor.

He had planned on going to the door, but he thought maybe he'd best wait for someone to come out. He checked the address one more time, but the numbers were gone now, jumped clean off the paper.

Alasdair sat at the kitchen table and drank another cup of coffee. He hadn't slept. Well, a little perhaps, here and there. Mostly he'd looked through the journals, determined to take the same journey his daughter and Bridie had taken. How could they talk about it unless he did? He had found his wife again in the pages of her books. He'd smiled, and wept, and anguished. This is it, he'd realized, turning the heavy pages. This is what you've fought so hard to hide. Or whom.

The doorbell rang. He glanced at the clock. Too early for Bridie, and he was glad, for he still didn't know what he would say to her. He wasn't angry anymore but wounded. Hurt by her duplicity. Yet what would he have said if she'd come to him? He could almost hear himself declaring there was nothing to discuss, all the while looking for a safer hiding place for Anna. A safe deposit box. A vault that no one could open but him. Somewhere she wouldn't get out this time. He went to the door and opened it without looking.

"Bob." The name came without thought, automatically, though now that he had a chance to think, the man who stood before him looked quite different than the seminarian of fifteen years before. Heavier, a little less hair, a little darker, perhaps, or it could just be the light.

"I was wondering if I could have a few minutes of your time."

"I have a meeting to prepare for."

"This doesn't have to take long."

Alasdair stepped back from the door automatically, years of training taking effect. "Please, come in."

"Thank you."

He shut the door. He almost pointed toward the living room but remembered it was no longer the parlor. Besides, Cam and Bonnie were already playing in there. "Why don't we go up to my study?" he suggested, and Bob Henry followed him up the stairs. He tapped on Samantha's door and asked her to go downstairs and watch the children, then led Bob into his study and invited him to sit down.

They settled themselves, Alasdair pulling the desk chair out so he could face Bob. They exchanged inconsequentials. Bob's eyes still darted around when he was being spoken to, Alasdair noted. As if he were trying to keep track of all the possible directions the conversation might take and be prepared for any one of them. A disconcerting habit.

"You're wondering why I'm here," Bob finally said, giving him an unexpectedly direct gaze.

Alasdair gave a slight shrug. "I assume it has something to do with the other matter." The other matter. How delicate, how euphemistic. There he went again, tucking something unpleasant away in the dark. How much energy he expended just finding names for things. Ways to talk about things without really talking about them. "The fact that my congregation wants me replaced," he corrected. "The matter of Gerald Whiteman's job offer."

Bob nodded. "Exactly." He popped open his briefcase, and Alasdair had an uncomfortable flashback to the meeting with the Big Three. Nothing good had ever come out of a briefcase in his experience. He doubted if this would be the exception.

Bob set a piece of paper onto the small coffee table as if he were playing a hand of cards. Declaration of Bankruptcy, the first one said.

"What is this?" He felt a jolt of anger seeing Lorna's name under the heading.

"This, my friend, is your life."

Not my life, my sister's, he started to say, but before he could get the words out a second piece of paper joined the first. It was a police report. Alasdair picked it up. *November 30. Juvenile shoplift. Bag and Save Grocery.*

"Where did you get this?"

"The manager made me a copy of his report. He was happy to do it."

"What are you doing? Who do you think you are?"

"I'm a man with a job to do," Bob said, his face untroubled. "Shall I stop? Or shall I go on?"

Alasdair clenched his fist and wanted it to make contact with Bob's sharp nose.

"Because if you'd like me to stop, all you have to do is sign this." Another flourish. A piece of heavy cream stationery. Alasdair read the first sentence. His resignation, complete with the date and a signature line at the bottom.

"I'll do no such thing."

Bob held up a hand. "Don't ever say never." He laid down another sheet. Anna's accident report.

Alasdair picked it up. He had that strange sensation again, as if he were an observer to the scene instead of a participant. He read it—for the first time. The details were all there. The ones he knew but never talked about. Single motor vehicle accident. Location: George Washington Memorial Parkway. Time: 1:32 P.M. Road condition: Wet. The responding officer wrote that after divers recovered the victim, CPR was performed by paramedics, but the victim was pronounced dead on arrival at Mt. Vernon Hospital. Estimated speed on impact: 65 miles per hour. No skid marks noted. Witnesses said the vehicle accelerated prior to leaving the roadway and entering the water.

He laid the paper on his knee. "You are despicable."

"I'm thinking the *Post* might want to run a feature. Especially when you throw in this." He slapped the last batch of papers down.

Alasdair picked it up. It was an arrest warrant for someone named Mary Bridget Washburn. For manufacture and distribution of a controlled substance. Drug dealing, he translated.

"I have no idea who this person is." But even as he said it, he thought, with a lurch of his heart, that perhaps he did.

"You poor, naïve fellow," Bob said. He slapped down a color copy of an expired Virginia driver's license.

Alasdair took a ragged breath in and out. So. That was her secret.

There had been hints. Yes. He looked back and saw the things he'd been determined not to see. The vagueness about her family and home, how she always took the bus, paid in cash, but mostly the sadness and the guilt. He had known there was something buried. He just hadn't known what, and he hadn't known where. And he'd been quite satisfied to leave it that way, he realized.

"I'm seeing the headlines now," Bob went on. " 'Prominent Minister Harbors Felon.' Maybe a few hints of a relationship. The rest of the article will fill in the details of your life. Your history. Your sordid little family secrets. Maybe they're not quite as juicy as Jim Bakker's and Jimmy Swaggart's, but they'll do on a slow news day. You know, it even occurred to me that you knew about this. Maybe she was supplying you. You've been awfully calm during all this trouble. Have you had a little help? And I'll bet anything she was supplying Samantha, even back when she was working at the Bag and Save. The store manager thinks so. He thinks they've been—what did he say?—*in cahoots* for a while. He made the statement for the record. How about this headline: 'Pastor Hires Daughter's Pusher.' The ultimate in convenience. She can get her fix without ever leaving the house."

Alasdair set the arrest warrant back on the table. "What do you want?" he asked.

"I want your resignation in my hand," Bob Henry answered without hesitation. "I'll fax it to Whiteman, and he'll fax back an offer of employment with the denomination. We've come up with a plum job for you."

"And if I refuse?"

Bob Henry shrugged. "Whatever you decide, I'll go from here to the *Post*. The religion editor's quite a great guy. We had a talk yesterday, and he's saving room in tomorrow's edition for a feature on you. Written by me." Bob leaned back in his chair, and a little smile played on his lips. "Did you know it's always been my dream to be a reporter, Alasdair? I took journalism, you know, after I left the seminary. The problem is," he continued, "to get any kind of real job, you have to show you've got that reporter's instinct—that intuition that sniffs out the story and the fortitude to follow it wherever it leads. You take someone with writing experience—like me—and combine it with a dynamite story, then, who knows, the doors might just open. Anyway," Bob said, "I've got two pieces written, and I don't much care which one I turn in. I can see advantages either way. If you sign the resignation, I'll give the *Post* the one about your new job at denomination headquarters and the sidebar about the pressures of ministry, then go back to Richmond with Gerry singing my praises. If you don't sign, I'll turn in the *other* story. You won't like it as well. It's up to you, though," Bob Henry said, looking as if he couldn't care less what Alasdair chose.

He could take the job, Alasdair realized. He could make all of this go away. A heavy weariness came with the realization. There would be more secrets then. More secrets and more people knowing them. More strings hooked onto him that could be yanked at a moment's notice. More reason to lie awake at night wondering who might guess the truth.

"Sign it, Alasdair. Otherwise," Bob said, giving his head a little jerky shake, "I'll have to strip you bare and parade you through the streets."

Stripped bare. That's exactly what had happened. Bob Henry had ripped aside the curtain, and he would follow through with his threats. Alasdair had no doubt of that. Everyone would see the great and powerful wizard was nothing more than a man. Once he lost his reputation, he would have nothing left to lose.

That would be almost peaceful, he realized. Yes. You would have almost perfect peace when there was nothing left to protect. What more could they do to you then?

There would be others caught in the fallout, he reminded himself. Lorna, and Samantha, and yet even as he recognized that fact, he knew what they would tell him to do.

"I'm not signing anything," he said.

"I'll tell," Bob threatened, and Alasdair actually smiled. It reminded him of a child's taunt.

"You do whatever you want," he said, and as the words left his mouth, he felt the first rush of freedom.

The heavy feeling hit Bridie before she even opened her eyes. She pulled the covers up, wanting nothing more than to go back to sleep and not wake up again. In this morning's gray light her fantasies of happy endings seemed hopelessly childish. She gave a bitter little smile as she thought of the times she had almost poured out the truth to Alasdair over coffee and dessert. A fine mess that would have been. If he was ready to cut her loose because of Anna's diaries, what would he do if he knew the truth? What had she been thinking?

She rolled over and looked at the clock. It was time to get up if she was to perform her last duties for him and the children. She would go to the parsonage, get Samantha off to school, and spend these last two days with the children. And after that she would be unemployed again. She remembered that day, not so long ago, when she had made a wager with God. A job by the end of the day or she would go back to dealing.

She didn't bother to make a wager this time. She felt somehow that her fate had been decided long ago, maybe before she even existed. So this is how it happens, she realized as she showered and dressed, as she gathered up the few things she wanted to take with her and shoved them into her backpack. This is how a person ends up a loser. A bad break here, a poor choice there. Pile up a few months of those, a few years, and there you were. Out of luck, out of ideas, ready to do whatever it took to get by.

She counted out what was left of her money and put most of it into an envelope with a note for Carmen and left it on her dresser.

She walked quietly into the living room and peeked out the window. Newlee's patrol car was parked out front, but they weren't up yet. She looked around the little apartment one more time and the words she'd written to Carmen didn't seem enough now. She reached her hand into the pocket of her jacket to get the key to the apartment and came out with a slip of paper as well. The mysterious telephone number. After last night's drama she'd forgotten all about it. She went to the phone. One more time she dialed the number.

"Hello."

"This is Bridie Collins." Her pulse was loud in her ears. She swallowed, and her tongue stuck to the roof of her mouth. "You've been trying to get ahold of me."

"Just a minute," the woman said. There was a rustling sound, and Bridie thought she heard a baby whimper. A door closed. "Yeah," the woman said. "I live with Eric. In Charlottesville."

Her stomach clenched. "Why are you calling me?"

"Somebody came looking for you, and Eric gave you up."

"Who was it?" Bridie asked, her voice calm, her insides a twisting mess.

"Tall, thin dude. Weird, whacked out on speed. He kept chewing his lip and picking at himself."

"What did Eric give him?"

"Everything he had. If I found you, he will, too."

"Thank you," Bridie said.

"We're even now," the woman answered and then hung up.

Bridie's hands shook as she replaced the telephone and turned on the computer. She almost screamed with impatience as she waited for it to boot up, then clicked on the heart for her favorite place and was immediately routed to the Virginia Department of Corrections Inmate Locator. She punched in the familiar name one last time: Porter, Jonah.

When the screen appeared, she stared, too frightened to move. Her breath came in shallow little gasps. Porter, Jonah. Status: Released.

She leaned forward, reading it over and over, trying to think of what she should do. She clicked on the picture. There he was. The same angular face, the same raw features. His striking eyes were blank, vacant, like the soul inside had been gradually eaten away. He was out. And he knew where she was.

She had to leave. That much was clear now. She shouldn't even go to Alasdair's. She could be leading Jonah to them, and that could only be trouble. She paused, chewing her lip.

"Hey."

She jumped.

Carmen was standing in the doorway staring at her, giving her a strange look. "What's going on?"

Bridie didn't answer. She went back to the computer and turned it off. When she turned toward Carmen, her roommate was still staring at her. "What's up?" Carmen asked again, her voice a little more pointed.

"Nothing." She answered too quickly.

"What's with that?"

"What?"

"That." Carmen gestured toward Bridie's backpack and gave her another intent stare. "And what's up with you? You're acting like you did that night we ate the espresso beans."

"Nothing's up with me," Bridie lied, trying to make her voice sound as natural as possible. "The backpack's because I'm spending the night at the parsonage. Alasdair's going on a trip."

Carmen stared at her, not smiling or nodding. "You sure you don't want to tell me?"

This wasn't good old live-and-let-live Carmen.

"Nothing to tell. I've got to go."

Carmen nodded, but she didn't pad off to the kitchen to make coffee as she usually did.

Bridie opened the apartment door, determined to get away before Newlee came out and started asking questions. She peered into the gray morning, but she couldn't do too much reconnaissance, or Carmen would get suspicious and wake up Newlee, and then she might as well just raise her hands and give herself up without a fuss. No one was around that she could see. She stepped out and closed the door behind her, but instead of going out the front she looped around the back of the building. It was raining, a light foggy mist. She cut through the alley and took the long way around the block, running to catch the bus one stop north of her usual.

She climbed on board and slid down in the seat, nothing moving but her eyes as she scanned Alexandria's sidewalks, slick but already full of people. He wasn't there. She didn't see him, at least.

Her breathing finally slowed, though her heart was still galloping. The bus passed the parsonage and the church. She stayed on, but halfway to the next stop her heart got the better of her good sense. She had to say good-bye. Otherwise Samantha would think she'd just up and left. She pulled the cord and got off, looking around to make sure no one was following before she doubled back.

Jonah rose up just in time to see Mary come out of the bushes by the apartment house. It took him a second to start the car, which was just as well, since he didn't want to spook her. He followed a good ways back, and when she got on the bus, a big SUV got in front of him and blocked his view for a while. He was frantic trying to stay far enough back so she wouldn't spot him if she was looking, but close enough for him to spot her.

He made do as best he could, and finally she got off. He pulled over and turned around, then cruised back as slow as he could, and it was his lucky day, because just when he thought he'd lost her, there she was, stepping through a black wrought-iron gate.

He went on around the block and pulled into the alley behind the church parking lot where nobody would pay him any mind, got out of the car, and walked through the graveyard. He could see all the spirits. They were holding hands, playing frog in the meadow. He could hear them chanting, see them holding hands and moving around in a circle. *Frog in the meadow, can't get him out, take a little stick, and stir him about.* "We'll help you find her," they sang out. "We'll help you get back what she took from you."

He nodded, sat down on the marble bench, and waited until they told him what to do.

↣ thirty-five ↢

BRIDIE LET HERSELF IN THE back door of the house, then stood with her back against it, trying to catch her breath.

Gradually the sounds of normalcy dampened her panic, at least a little. Water was running. A pair of tennis shoes, probably Samantha's, were thumping against the sides of the dryer in irregular rhythm. She smelled coffee scorching on the burner and the citrus-soapy smell of dishwashing detergent. She stepped out of the kitchen into the hallway. From here she could hear Cam and Bonnie jabbering from the living room and the background noise of the television. They were watching the Christmas video again. Would probably still be watching it on the Fourth of July. Her pulse slowed. She set down her backpack and purse and took off her jacket.

She went to the front window and peered around the curtain. No one was out there. No one at all.

"You're here." Samantha's voice startled her.

She nodded but decided to get the truth out right away. "I can't stay."

Samantha's face sobered.

"Where's your father?"

"He's upstairs with some guy."

Bridie nodded, her emotions bobbing between grief and relief.

"Why do you have to leave? Dad'll get over it. I'm sure he will."

Bridie shook her head. "It's not that."

"What is it, then?"

She took a breath. Let it out. "I've done some bad things."

"What kind of things?"

Bridie agonized. "I'd rather not say. I don't have time to explain, and it would take some explaining."

Samantha considered that, then gave her head a little shake. "So you're leaving."

Bridie shrugged. "Sort of. I mean, it's complicated."

"It doesn't sound that complicated to me," Samantha said, folding her arms. "It sounds to me like you're doing what you said last night I wasn't supposed to do."

Bridie stared.

"Running away." You moron, her tone said. Bridie couldn't help but smile.

"Sometimes it's not that simple, Samantha."

Samantha shrugged, obviously not buying it. "Whatever."

Bridie shook her head. There was nothing she could say. Any details she shared would just increase Samantha's disappointment. "Are Cam and Bonnie in the living room?"

Samantha nodded without answering. Bridie went around her and into the living room.

"Hi," they greeted her.

She couldn't even answer them. She gave them each a hug and a kiss, then found Samantha in the kitchen.

"I've got to go," Bridie repeated. Her throat tightened and hurt.

At first she thought Samantha would stay just like that, arms crossed, face glowering, but at the last minute she flung herself at Bridie and hugged her. "Come back if you can," she pleaded, and Bridie couldn't even bear to look at her as she opened the back door and left.

Carmen couldn't get the face out of her mind. She walked around the little apartment and smoked and tried to think of what to do, but nothing would stick to her brain except that dead-looking face and those cold, creepy eyes. For the hundredth time she thought about waking up Newlee, but like always, something stopped her. Once Newlee got into it, there would be no hiding anything anymore, and she was pretty sure this was about things Bridie would just as soon keep to herself. You could go to the grave with your secrets, she reminded herself, and that thought rattled her so much she didn't even notice Newlee appear in the doorway.

"What's wrong, baby?" he asked, and she could almost see cop alertness replace drowsiness in his eyes.

There was no way she could keep this to herself. She took a deep breath and let the truth out with it. "I don't know what's going on, Newlee, but something's not right. I've got a bad feeling."

"About what?" He tensed up, as if anything that could get her this rattled gave him a bad feeling, too.

She hesitated one last time, then decided there was no other way. "Now, you know I respect people's privacy, and I'd be the last one in the world to throw the first stone."

"What happened?" he pressed.

She might as well spill it. "I came in just as Bridie was getting off the computer. She seemed so freaked out, I snooped. She uses my Internet account, so I clicked on the history to see where she'd been. This is what I saw."

She went to the computer and wiggled the mouse around. The screen appeared again, and Newlee leaned over her to take a look. He frowned, and his face hardened. He could probably tell it was a convict face even without reading the words underneath. They gave Carmen another chill, just like they had the first time. Jonah Porter. White male, thirty-three years old. Status: released. Offense description: manufacture and distribution of a controlled substance.

Newlee's jaw muscle clenched. He straightened up, and suddenly he was all cop.

"I've seen him, Newlee," she babbled. "Yesterday after work he was in front of the store. He looked high. That's why I noticed him."

"Where is Bridie now?" He asked the question on the way to the bedroom as he was yanking off his sweats and pulling on his clothes.

"She said she was going to the parsonage." Carmen stubbed out her cigarette and started throwing on clothes, too. She finished as

Newlee was pulling on his boots. "I'm going over there," she said, grabbing her keys and purse.

"Wait." His voice was sharp. It was a command and not a suggestion.

She waited. She wasn't even tempted to argue, just watched, wide-eyed, as he strapped on his gun.

There she is. Go after her, the spirits had said, and Jonah had taken off. Gotten into the Fury and followed Mary. He wondered if that was his money she had in that backpack she'd slung over her shoulder. She got on the city bus, and Jonah followed, running through a red light and two yellows so he wouldn't lose her. She rode the bus clear out onto the highway. They passed his motel, and then the bus pulled into the Greyhound station, and Mary got off and went inside.

Bob stared at Alasdair. MacPherson didn't blink.

Well, this was just great. What did this guy have in his veins that none of this fazed him? Bob couldn't think of anything else to do, any other threats to make.

MacPherson leaned forward, and Bob took heart. Good. Maybe he was catching the far-off scent of the coffee. He gave Bob a squint-eyed look, as if he was looking at a bug under a microscope. "Why do you do this, Bob?" he asked.

Bob stared back, surprised into silence.

"Something must motivate this drivenness of yours," MacPherson went on. "This desire to win at all costs. You have a good job. Why isn't just doing it well enough for you?" He kept staring, not even blinking.

Why wasn't it enough? Bob wondered, and suddenly it seemed like a question that deserved an answer, even if he had no intention of sharing it with Alasdair MacPherson. It *was* odd, now that he really thought about it. The whole time he'd been talking to MacPherson, it was like he was an actor delivering his lines. And it had always been that way. He never just lived events. He scripted and acted them, then judged his performance afterward through the eyes of an unseen audience. Would it impress? Was it dramatic? How had he looked? Was he a hit? Or a flop? What would the reviewers say? Every conversation, every interaction, every friendship, every date, every job was actually a scene he played. Now he peered into the dark theater, looking for the mystery audience. There was his dad front and center with a bag of popcorn. And Bob was still waiting for the applause.

He wasn't an unkind person. Just, oh, preoccupied. Always busy, eyes scanning the horizon for the next assignment. Looking for the next person in need, not even noticing the kid that bumped around his ankles. *"Watch this, Dad,"* Bob would say. *"Look at me."* Then would come the dart of the eyes, the obligatory smile, the distant gaze, the quick disengagement. Back to important things.

He didn't even have the comfort of higher-achieving siblings to blame. His brother and sister had been relegated to that same assignment in oblivion. Each had their own methods of protest. Dennis had gone the negative attention route, and Sherry, the tortured soul, was forever in therapy. Bob had tried achievements of his own. He gave a bitter smile as the picture of himself—full-grown Bob—appeared, still clamoring around his dad's ankles. Still hollering, "Watch me."

He gave his head a little shake to clear it, then focused back on Alasdair MacPherson. He didn't answer his question, just gathered up the papers and stood. "I'll give you an hour," he said. "Call by then or read about it in the *Post*."

MacPherson watched him, not saying a word.

Bob wrote his cell phone number on a business card and held it out. Alasdair wouldn't take it, just kept looking at Bob with an expression on his face that made Bob angry. Bob tossed the card onto the desk, said a terse good-bye, and left. Whatever hesitation he might have had was being washed away by his rising bitterness. MacPherson should save his pity for himself. He was the one who was going to need it. Bob started up his car and headed for the offices of the *Washington Post*. He would wait in the lobby for MacPherson's call and put the finishing touches on his story.

⤞ *thirty-six* ⤝

THE DOORBELL RANG BEFORE ALASDAIR had even gotten all the way down the stairs. He went into the hallway and looked out the peephole. It was a man and a woman, both of whom looked vaguely familiar. He swung open the door.

"Where's Bridie?" the woman asked before he could even get a word out.

He heard the back door open and close. He left them standing in the hallway and almost ran to the kitchen. He came through the doorway, eyes hungry.

"Samantha called me," Lorna greeted him. "Something about needing a ride to school." An expression of concern replaced her usual smile. It deepened as she took in his expression. "Where's Bridie?" she asked, gripping the back of the chair. "What's going on?"

He didn't answer her and went back to the hallway. Lorna followed on his heels.

"Carmen, what are you doing here?" Lorna asked.

"Carmen?" Alasdair repeated dumbly.

"I'm Bridie's roommate," Carmen explained. "This is my fiancé, Newlee Blackstone. We're worried about Bridie. Is she here?"

"She *was* here," Samantha contributed from the stair landing. "She left."

"How long ago?" the fiancé asked.

"About fifteen minutes ago."

"What's going on?" Alasdair asked. Newlee and Carmen looked at each other.

"Where was she headed?" Newlee asked.

"I don't know," Samantha said. "She didn't say. She just said she had to leave."

"Samantha, go to your room. I'll have Lorna take you to school in a moment."

"No way."

"Go," Alasdair ordered. "I mean it."

Samantha, go to your room. Samantha, go to your room. Every time something interesting happened, she got sent to her room. She stared at the floor for a minute, then, sighing, went over to the heat vent. This was getting sort of boring, but how else was she supposed to find out what was going on?

She leaned down and stayed there for quite a while. She could hear everything. Carmen from the Bag and Save said some guy was after Bridie, and Dad was saying how she'd sold drugs and all.

No way.

Samantha listened a few more minutes. They were all trying to decide what to do. The lady's policeman-boyfriend said he was going to call it in.

Samantha straightened up, stepped out into the hall, and went into the guest room, making sure nobody saw her. As if. She went in and sat on the bed. Some of Bridie's clothes were still in the wardrobe. Her Bible was on the bedside table beside the book she'd been reading. Samantha unzipped the white leather cover and opened to the first page.

To Mary,
> *Only one life, how soon it will pass. Only what's done for Christ will last.*

> *Love,*
> *Grandma*

So Mary Bridget Washburn was probably Bridie's name, not her mom's like she'd said. Bridie had lied to her. She flipped past that page. On the next was Bridie's name and address, written in blue ink:

> Mary Bridget Washburn
> Route 4, Box 252
> Woodbine, Virginia 22908

She riffled through the pages to see if there were any other clues to Bridie's past. Two pieces of paper fell out. A clipping from a newspaper and something printed off the Internet. She picked up the clipping and unfolded it. A black-and-white picture of a police car parked in front of a shack. An article about drug dealers getting arrested. She unfolded the printout. It was from the Virginia Department of Corrections Web site. It was somebody's record or something. Jonah Porter. Samantha frowned. This was *so* not good. This meant it was true what they were saying. Bridie was a drug dealer, and she'd been lying to them all along.

Samantha put down the papers. She probably ought to feel mad or something, but she didn't. She sat down on the bed, and it was weird, but it was like somebody started showing her a video in her head. First she saw Bridie coming to dinner and trying to be nice to her and all, and herself blowing Bridie off. Then she saw herself in the Bag and Save trying to steal the wine and Bridie lying to cover up for her and losing her job because of it. The clips started coming faster, one right after the other: Christmas shopping, decorating the house, making cookies, reading Mom's diary, talking, crying. By the time the show was over, Samantha wiped her eyes and folded her arms.

So what? Big deal. She didn't care what Bridie had done or who she'd been before. Bridie. Mary. Whatever. What difference did it make? It's like, a person ought to have a second chance, shouldn't they?

Samantha looked down at the Bible. She didn't know where to go or what to do.

"God, I could use some help. Please," she added. She opened her eyes, then shut them again. No more videos. She shoved the clipping and the printout back into the Bible, went to put it back on the table, then stuck it under the band of her jeans instead. She had a feeling it might come in handy. She went into the hallway. They were still going ballistic downstairs. Samantha darted back into her room and got out the envelope of money she'd gotten for Christmas. Aunt Winifred and Fiona always gave her twenty dollars each. She shoved the bills into her pocket and crept to the top of the stairs.

They were still talking. She walked down past them, all calm and everything, and of course nobody even noticed her. She slipped out the back door, cut across the lawn, then stopped. Where exactly was she going? She bit her lip and decided to take things one step at a time.

If she were Bridie, what would she do?

Get out of town.

How? It's not like she had a car.

The bus.

Exactly. Yeah. Bridie said she'd taken the bus to Alexandria. So she'd probably take it away from Alexandria, too. Well, Samantha knew how to ride the buses. All those days of skipping school were paying off.

⚓

"Coach 223 departing for Fairfax, Gainesville, Haymarket, Strasburg, Harrisonburg, Staunton, and Charlottesville now leaving at gate number two."

Bridie heard the announcement and peered out the bathroom door. She didn't see Jonah. She made a beeline for the departure area but halted halfway there. That girl over by the door looked like Samantha. She frowned. That girl over by the door *was* Samantha. She waved furiously, and Bridie waited as she ran over.

"Samantha, what are you doing here?"

"I came to tell you it's okay."

"What do you mean, it's okay?"

"I mean it's okay that you did drugs and sold drugs. I mean, like, everybody makes mistakes."

Bridie's mouth dropped open. She shook her head.

"I mean, you're not like that anymore. I know you're not."

Bridie gathered her into a hug. Samantha hugged her back.

"Come on back. Dad's already sorry. He's, like, all defending you and everything."

"He is?" Bridie's heart softened, then she shook her head, remembering her situation. "He shouldn't be." She began walking toward the departure area again.

"Just wait a minute," Samantha pleaded. Her eyes filled, and her voice sounded desperate.

"I can't wait, Samantha," Bridie said, slowing. "I'm sorry. I've got to go."

"Just wait. Please." Samantha turned and ran toward the pay phones. She turned away just long enough to put in the change and dial. Bridie looked between her and the bus, already starting its engine out in the loading area. The air smelled like diesel, and she could hear its door close in a whoosh of air. Why was she waiting? If she went back with Samantha, she would just get arrested here and never get to finish this last errand. She wrenched her eyes away from Samantha and made tracks for the turnstile.

A hand grabbed her arm, and the thoughts that flew through her head went too fast to make much sense. At the first touch she'd hoped for Alasdair. But before she could even turn her head, the cues were telling her she was wrong. This hand didn't belong to Alasdair. It wasn't gentle, but gripped her hard. It was bruising, full of hatred and anger and craziness. When she saw who it was, she wasn't even surprised. Her heart had recognized Jonah even before her eyes.

"Don't make me kill any of these people," he said, flipping open his jacket to show her the butt of a gun.

She didn't make a sound, just let him pull her toward the door. She didn't look at Samantha. Didn't want Jonah to notice Samantha in any way. He shoved her toward an old Plymouth, then opened the driver's-side door and made her slide across.

He grabbed her backpack and rifled through it, tossing clothes and toiletries all over the seat. "Where is it?" he asked when he'd finished.

His money, of course. And the minute she told him it was gone, she would be, too. Besides, she could tell from just a glance that he was tweaked out. At the craziest, most paranoid of his high. She'd seen him like this lots of times before. He'd shoot up and use more and more and more, upping the high each time he started to come down. This was the worst, the most violent, the most dangerous time. Next would come a few minutes of sanity followed by a crash. Sleeping, comatose, no danger to anyone. She needed some time. She needed to get him away from Samantha, who was coming back toward her right now.

He took the ticket out of her hand, and too late, she wished she'd dropped it.

He read her destination, gave her a wise look, as if he'd suspected as much, then started up the engine and roared out of the parking lot. Bridie risked a last look at Samantha, but instead of being hysterical as she'd expected, Samantha was staring hard at the car, as if she was memorizing every detail, then she turned and ran back into the bus station.

~

"Slow down, Samantha, and tell me where you are." Alasdair plugged up his free ear, glad he had taken the call in the kitchen. Lorna watched him, her face pale.

"I'm at the bus station, and some guy just made Bridie get in a car, and they took off."

"Stay where you are." He hung up the telephone, grabbed his jacket off the coatrack. He stepped into the hall and motioned for Newlee to join him in the kitchen, then told him in two sentences what had happened.

"Let's go out the back," Newlee said. "If we go out the front, Carmen will be a problem."

"I'll stay with the children," Lorna promised.

"Could you give Carmen a ride home?"

"Of course."

"Let's take my car," Newlee said to Alasdair. "We can radio."

Alasdair nodded, and suddenly nothing mattered—not his career, not his home, not his future, not the secrets he might read in the paper tomorrow. He had one burning desire—to find Bridie and bring her home. He didn't care what she had done. He only knew he couldn't bear to lose her.

Samantha was waiting in front of the bus station, not inside as he'd told her. She jumped into the backseat as soon as the car slowed. "Here's the license number," she said, sticking out her hand. She'd written the series of numbers and letters in blue ballpoint. His heart swelled with pride. She was a scrapper.

"Are you all right?"

"I'm fine. She was getting on a bus that was headed for—here, I wrote it on this hand after I called—Fairfax, Gainesville, Haymarket, Strasburg, Harrisonburg, Staunton, and Charlottesville."

Newlee got on the radio and called in the plates. The car was stolen. No surprise there.

"Here's where I think she's going," Samantha said. She thrust a Bible at him this time, opened to a name and address—Bridie's real name—Mary Bridget Washburn.

"Woodbine is south of Charlottesville in Nelson County," Newlee said. "That makes sense. That's where the warrant's from." He had a few more exchanges on the radio. "I guess we'll head for Charlottesville and hope the police spot the car before we get there."

"Let's take my daughter home," Alasdair said.

"No! I promise I'll stay out of the way. Don't make me go home."

"Time is something we might not have a lot of," Newlee said. "Besides, I won't be picking him up. The state patrol or Nelson County sheriff will do that."

Alasdair nodded. They drove, lights flashing but no sirens, everything silent except for the crackling of the radio.

೪ *thirty-seven* ೪

THEY MADE A STOP IN D.C. so Jonah could rip off somebody's stereo from a car park. Then they had to find some fellow he knew who would give him fifty dollars for it and wait for him to come home. It was after eleven when they pulled into downtown Charlottesville. Jonah had shot up and had been talking nonstop for the last hour. Crazy stuff about spirits and demons and going to hell, and how he had thought it was his brain she had stolen, but actually it had been his heart. He had to be running out of gas pretty soon. He just had to.

"I need something," Jonah said. He pulled into the parking lot of a little grocery. It was closed, and he started yelling and saying he was going to drive the car through the plate-glass door.

"The Piggly Wiggly by the bus station is open," Bridie said quickly. "Want me to drive?"

He glared at her but turned the car in the right direction, and thank goodness, she was right about its being open. But nothing was easy with Jonah. First he wanted her to go inside. Then both of them. Then just her again. Then him. It reminded Bridie of those riddles about a fox and a chicken and a sack of corn and you can only fit two things on the boat and make three trips across. He didn't want to leave her in the car because he knew she'd drive away, and he didn't want to let her go inside because he was afraid she'd run out the back door. Finally he told her to go inside but not to do anything smart.

"If you're not out in five minutes I'm going to shoot somebody," he said and pulled out his gun just to make sure she knew he meant it. "Her," he said, pointing to the woman in the next car, who he said was Annie Oakley, "or him," he said, and added that the man gathering up grocery carts in the parking lot was the doctor who'd run off with his tractor.

"I'll be right back," she promised. "Just don't do anything crazy."

She bought his malt liquor and two boxes of diet pills. She didn't dare pile on the cold medicine for fear they'd get suspicious. She carried her purchases to the register and realized her bitter threat had come true. She'd said she might as well go back to dealing. Well, here she was. How did it feel? she asked herself. Did it feel right? Like she'd landed where she belonged? She couldn't tell. She didn't know how she felt other than tired and hungry and run-down and coldly bitter. She had no idea who she was bitter at. Herself? God, for making it so hard to get a break?

The man who checked her out was a bandy-legged little fellow with thin hair that he had twirled all around trying to cover up his bald spot. He gave her a suspicious look. She paid for the stuff and left as quickly as she could. She looked back once and saw him standing in the window, watching her as she got back into the car.

Jonah drove up the road a ways, pulled off into a dive motel, had her go inside and rent a room. He had his equipment in the trunk, and he made her carry it in—Mason jars, Pyrex dishes, tubing, a bottle of lye. Good. The sooner he cooked himself up some more candy and took it, the sooner he'd peak, and the sooner he'd crash. You couldn't rev your engine forever.

"You set it up," he said once they were inside the room, taking a pull on his beer, still flinging the gun from side to side.

"I don't know how." It was the truth.

He told her how. She did the best she could, washing her hands well when she was finished. He got up and started doing his thing. She rested on the bed, taking care not to turn down the covers for fear of lice or bedbugs, not even taking off her jacket. He seemed to have forgotten about the money, which was good, since she had no idea what she would do when he asked for it.

She must have slept. The next thing she knew he was leaning close, shaking her awake. "Let's go," he said. He made her carry his equipment out to the car, then they got in. Jonah drove. Bridie shaded her face from him as they merged onto the highway.

She must have dozed. When she woke she saw the familiar land-marks, but instead of joy, shame hit her with the force of a blow.

"No. Not here. Not like this. Please."

"I want my money," Jonah said, "and I know you've hid it here."

Alasdair poured himself another cup of the Charlottesville Police Department's stale coffee and found a packet of cocoa for Samantha. He took them back to the reception area's vinyl couch and checked his watch. All night long and still no word since the hope-raising call from the grocery store manager. Odd, to have your heart encouraged by news of a loved one's impending arrest.

Newlee finished talking to the desk sergeant. He rejoined them, pulling up the metal chair, shaking his head. "There's no point in stay-ing here," he said gently. "We'll hear if they find him. *When* they find him, I should say. These types always screw up sooner or later."

The problem was the damage he might do before that happened. Alasdair shook his head. "We're staying," he announced flatly. "You go back if you need to," he told Newlee. "We'll find our way home."

Samantha grabbed his hand and gave him a blinding smile.

Newlee shook his head. "I'm good if you are," he said, then went to pour himself another cup of coffee.

Alasdair settled back onto the couch and tried to relax his tense muscles. There was nothing he could do, he realized. Nothing at all except wait and pray that this story would have a happy ending.

❧ thirty-eight ❧

HATTIE HAD PRAYED AWAY MOST of the morning. She'd had another one of her dreams last night and been laboring over it. Martha had come in a little while ago and joined her in prayer. Finally their spirits had cleared.

"It's all right now," Hattie had said. "The battle's done been won. All that's left is to gather up the spoils."

"Um-hum. *Yes*, Lord," Martha had agreed.

Since then Hattie had been waiting patiently, maybe dozing off a little now and then, reading and listening to Martha's iron shush steam as she smoothed a path across the landscape of wrinkles. She'd press once, twice, three, four times, then flip the pillowcase over and do the same on the other side. The cotton was white beneath her dark fingers. She folded it in half, pressed, then quartered, then pressed again. The pleasant smell of steam and starch mixed with the roast she was cooking.

Hattie must have dozed, lulled asleep by Martha's rhythm. She startled awake to the crunch of gravel.

Martha set down the iron, went to the window, and pulled back the curtain. Her eyes widened, and she put her hand over her heart. "Lord, have mercy," she said. "You were right, Miss Hattie." She dropped the curtain and headed for the door.

There it was. Home, or the closest thing Bridie had to it on earth—this old white clapboard house with a sloping tin roof and wide front porch. The glossy boxwoods and huge azaleas still nestled up against its foundation. Farther out on the wide green lawn, just as she remembered, were the two big oaks—dogwood and redbud underneath, just beginning to pink. Off to the side was the stand of white pines. Behind it, just as they'd appeared in her dreams, were the misty blue mountains. But this wasn't how she'd wanted to come home. Not like this. Never.

Jonah pulled the Fury to a stop halfway down the long driveway. "Where'd you hide it?" he asked. "In the bee stands?"

She shook her head.

"Where, then? Down by the spring? In the woods somewhere? Off by that clearing where you used to play house?"

She shook her head. "Jonah, the money's gone."

He blinked at her, his face blank.

"Somebody stole it the first day. On the bus."

"You're lying."

"I'm not. That's why I turned you in. So you couldn't come after it."

He looked at her intently for a minute. "I think my legs have popped off," he said.

She closed her eyes and rubbed the bridge of her nose.

He shifted the car into park and turned off the ignition. "We're going inside."

"No." That could not happen.

She felt the gun against her temple. She opened her eyes.

"Get out."

She opened the door and climbed out, the crunch of gravel on her feet the only reminder that this was not a bad dream. Jonah followed. The gun wasn't at her head anymore, but it wasn't very far away, either.

The screen door screeched open and closed, and Bridie looked up toward the porch, forgetting about Jonah, the gun, the money. She stopped walking, shocked and frozen in place at what she saw.

The woman who had come out wasn't Grandma. It was a black woman. She stood, one hand on her hip as she inspected the approaching visitors. It was all Bridie could do not to crumple to the ground, so sharp was her grief.

She'd waited too late, stayed away too long. Grandma was gone.

She stood still, only her eyes moving. There was the swing she'd played on as a child. There was the hollow where she'd made a play-house. Back there were Grandpa's bee stands and the apple orchards. Grandma's clothesline peeked from behind the house. Everything familiar about this place now seemed to taunt and mock her. None of it was hers anymore. Now it belonged to someone else, and the one she loved best in all the world, her dearest on earth, was gone. Pain ripped and tore through her chest with every breath and thump of her heart. She had waited too late to come home.

The black woman stood waiting. Bridie's feet began moving, almost on their own. She climbed the steps slowly. The woman cast a doubt-ful eye on Jonah, but she didn't seem frightened. She turned to speak to someone in the house.

"She's here, Miss Hattie," she said.

At that name Bridie's heart leaped into her throat. The woman opened the screen door, Bridie stepped through the doorway, and there was Grandma sitting in a wheelchair, just as though she'd been waiting for them. She was a little more frail than Bridie remembered, more crippled up with the arthritis, but her eyes were still bright and she wore the same sweet smile. She was dressed in a navy blue polka-dot dress, wearing her Hush Puppies, her large-print Bible open on her lap. Bridie went to her, fell to her knees beside the chair, and her grandmother gathered her into her arms. She felt the tears start to flow. Not for long, though. Jonah jerked her away roughly and shoved her farther into the house.

"Shut the door," Jonah ordered the black woman, who gave him a haughty look and didn't budge.

"Go ahead, Martha," Grandma said. "Though I think you should keep a civil tongue in your head, Jonah Porter."

Jonah looked surprised, then mumbled he was sorry.

Bridie wiped her eyes and gave him an incredulous look. She shouldn't be surprised, though. Nothing evil or destructive ever had managed to stay that way in Grandma's presence. Or maybe Jonah was just getting ready to crash and losing his hold on things. He seemed to weave a little bit as he walked around the room. But he was still pacing, counting out loud as he stepped over the squares of linoleum.

Grandma shook her head and gave a little click of her tongue. "They're awful things, them drugs."

You could say that again. Bridie pulled a chair out, sat down beside Grandma, and took her hand.

Jonah stopped pacing and seemed to remember why he was here. "Where'd she put it?" he asked Grandma.

"Put what?"

"My money."

That set Grandma off. "I'm not studying any money, Jonah Porter. And you shouldn't be, either. You should be tending to your soul."

He rubbed his hand over his face and waved the gun toward Bridie. "Get up," he said.

She got up, giving Grandma's hand a final pat.

Jonah went to the wall and jerked out the telephone. He grabbed one of Grandma's carving knives from the counter and cut the cord in two, then shoved the gun against Martha's head and bored his eyes into Bridie's. "If any police come here, I'm shooting both of them."

"Lord, have mercy," Martha said. "Put that thing down."

"Don't do that, Jonah. Please," Bridie begged. How had they ended up here? She had to get him away before somebody got hurt. Where would they go, though? Everywhere there was somebody who might get hurt, whether by Jonah firing a gun at somebody who looked like Annie Oakley or just by selling them meth. And that's when she decided what she had to do.

She went ahead and did what he told her to do for the next four hours. Emptied out every blessed drawer, cupboard, closet in the house and shoved the broom under every stick of furniture. Even went outside and poked around a few hiding places there. "It's not here," she finally said again, as exasperated as she'd ever been in her life. "I'm telling you the truth. It got stolen."

He blinked again and didn't seem to understand what she'd said. She shook her head and went back into the kitchen, leaving him staring stupidly after her. Right about now she didn't much care if he shot her or not. Martha was calmly serving up the pot roast and taking a pan of biscuits from the oven when she walked into the room. He followed after her, blinking, trying to take things in.

"Let's all have some dinner," Grandma said. Bridie smiled. This was unreal. But it was real. There was the table, covered with a red-and-white checkered cloth and those old flowered dishes. Martha put out a Mason jar full of damson jelly.

"Reach that extra chair over there, if you please," she said to Jonah. He did as he was told, and Bridie half expected him to say "yes, ma'am."

They all sat down, Grandma said grace, and Bridie fell to her food in spite of the seriousness of the situation. She was starving. She tried to remember the last time she'd eaten and couldn't.

"Jonah Porter, do you know who you're named after?"

He came out of his stupor long enough to look at Grandma as if she were crazy. "It was my granddaddy's name," he said. His speech was slurred. His eyes at half-mast. He was losing it, and Bridie wanted to shout with joy. She helped herself to another biscuit instead and spread it with butter and plum jelly.

"I'm talking about Jonah in the Bible," Grandma said, and Bridie recognized the Sunday-school teacher voice. She shook her head and grinned. Only Grandma could take a hostage situation and turn it into an evangelistic opportunity.

Grandma peered severely at Jonah and went on with her lecture. "The Lord said go right, and he went left, and you're just exactly like him. Ever since you was a little chap, you was contrary," she pronounced. "Throw you in the river, and you'd float upstream."

Jonah blinked.

"The Lord called Jonah, but instead of obeying, he run off from the presence of the Lord. Just like you're doing."

"Yes, ma'am."

"I know for a fact the Lord's put a call on you, Jonah Porter. Don't you remember that Vacation Bible School when you come forward? And now this is how you go and do."

Jonah's head drooped.

"Don't you fall asleep while I'm talking to you."

He jerked it back up again. "No, ma'am." He blinked.

"Now, the Lord didn't let the prophet Jonah get by with flying in His face, and He's not going to let you get by with it, neither. He sent a great fish to swallow him. And I'd say you're about as near inside the belly of a whale yourself as anybody I've ever seen."

Jonah stared and blinked, eyes drooping again.

Bridie took a sip of iced tea and watched Grandma move in for the close.

"Now you've got a choice to make. You can go on and do like you've *been* doing, or you can do like Jonah in the Bible did. He prayed unto the Lord his God to get him out of the belly of the whale. You can, too. Just because you've done bad don't mean you have to stay that way. Besides, what are you thinking you're going to do here? Kill us all? Don't make no difference to me, nor Martha neither. We're going on to glory. But is that really what you want?"

Jonah rubbed his hand over his face. "Mary B, you've got to tell me what you did with that money," he said, almost pleading.

"Jonah, I swear to you *on my grandma's Bible*, that I don't have it. I'm telling you the truth. Somebody stole it from me, I hope to die." A bad choice of words.

Jonah shook his head. Then he gave her a look that was almost completely lucid, and for just a minute she glimpsed the old Jonah in this brief window between the high and the crash. He gave her a crooked half smile. "You're killing me, Mary. You really are."

"Call on the Lord, Jonah," Grandma urged. "It's not too late."

Jonah stood, almost knocking over his chair. "Yes, it is, Miss Hattie."

"Never." Grandma shook her head, her lips pressed together.

"Um-um," Martha agreed. "No, sir. It's never too late."

"Y'all are driving me crazy," he said, and just as if he were stepping out to take a smoke, he walked out the door.

They stared after him. Bridie bobbed up and went to the window. He got into the Plymouth, started it up, and backed out the long driveway in a cloud of dust.

"Well," Grandma said.

"Um-um." Martha shook her head and took a sip of her iced tea.

Bridie went and sat back down. This was an unforeseen turn of events.

Grandma turned toward Bridie next. "Well, missy," she said, "I guess it's up to you now. What are *you* going to do?"

It didn't take her long to decide. She got up and went out the front door and cut through the woods. She hiked about a quarter of a mile, then went up to the door of the Cassidys, who still lived here, she was happy to see.

"Yes?" Mrs. Cassidy asked, big eyed, not unlatching the screen. Apparently Bridie's reputation had preceded her.

"I was wondering if I might use your phone," Bridie said.

"Who you calling?" Mrs. Cassidy asked. "I'll dial it for you."

She told her, then went back to Grandma's to wait.

"I knew you'd be back," Martha said. She had the dishes nearly done.

Grandma gave her a sweet smile. She'd been by the window, watching. "So did I," she said. "I just prayed you there and back to make sure."

Bridie went to her and knelt beside her again. "I'm so sorry," she said and felt the repentance she'd pressed back for so long start to push its way out. "I know I should have come to you when they took the children, but I was angry at God. I didn't want to hear anything about Him. I hated Him, and I didn't want to be around anybody who felt different. But I know I was wrong. If I could go back and do it over, I would. I wish I could undo it all."

"I know that." Grandma reached over and put a twisted hand on hers. " 'Though your sins be as scarlet, they shall be as white as snow.' Isaiah one eighteen."

"I've done terrible things."

"Don't make no difference. You can't out-sin the cross."

She looked at her grandmother, and suddenly she couldn't think of any reason not to believe her. *You can't out-sin the cross.* That was the same thing Alasdair had said. *"Where sin abounded, there did grace much more abound."* Her heart was struck with a tender awe.

"It's just like the Lord says," Grandma continued. "The one who's forgiven much will love much."

Well, she supposed she would love more than she'd ever thought possible if that was the truth, and right then she laid her head down on Grandma's shoulder and cried out her sorrow to God. She cried and cried, and every time she thought she might be finished, she'd cry some more. And it felt to her as if those tears were washing away time. Day after dreary day dropped off, year after tedious and tasteless year. When she'd finally cried herself out, she felt tired but cleaned out and comforted. She felt His love enclose her, like warm, strong arms. She rested her head on Grandma's chest, just as she remembered doing as a child, and blotted her nose and eyes with the hankie Grandma's friend pressed into her hand.

"Thank you, Jesus," Grandma whispered. "Thank you, dear Lord, for bringing her home."

"Once His child, always His child," Martha murmured. "Nobody can snatch you out of His hand."

※

They didn't send just one police car but two. One from Nelson County and one from Alexandria. Bridie stepped out onto the porch. The night air was sharp but sweetly scented. She took a deep breath and wished she could be here to see the apples blossom.

The Nelson County sheriff's deputy opened the door of the car and climbed out.

She stepped off the porch to meet him.

"Ma'am, are you the one who called to turn yourself in?"

Bridie nodded. "Should I put my hands up or something?"

"No, ma'am," he said. "You're all right." Then he read her her rights, just like on television.

Martha came up behind her and put an arm around her. It was beginning to dawn on Bridie now just what she was in for. She had a sudden vision of her grandmother keeling over, holding her heart, as they led her away in handcuffs.

"This is going to kill her," Bridie murmured to Martha.

"She's been through an awful lot, and it hasn't killed her yet," Martha observed.

The driver stepped out of the Alexandria police car. It was Newlee. Bridie wanted to die for shame. He had a word with the Nelson County sheriff, then gave a nod back toward someone in the passenger seat of his car. Another man got out, and she recognized him at once, even in the dim light of the moon.

"Oh no," she said to Martha. But Martha had gone back inside.

Alasdair walked toward her, straight-backed, holding his head up. He didn't act as though he even saw the sheriff. He paused at the foot of the steps and looked up at her.

"You're supposed to be in Richmond," she said.

"I wasn't in the mood."

"Is Samantha all right?"

"She's at the police station. They gave her a teddy bear. She's furious."

"You know what I mean."

"She's fine. You did the right thing to tell her the truth."

She lowered her head in shame. She couldn't bear to look him in the eye one minute longer. She saw his shoes climb the steps. He stood before her, raised the ink-stained hand, and lifted her chin with his finger. "This isn't who you are," he said, his voice soft but sure. "Don't you believe that for a minute."

The policeman came onto the porch. Alasdair's hand dropped back to his side.

"We'd better go, ma'am," the deputy said.

"Can I just say good-bye to my grandmother?" she asked, fighting not to lose it.

He nodded.

Bridie went inside. Grandma was parked by the open window, listening to everything.

"Grandma," she said, "I can't stay."

"No," Grandma agreed, her sharp eyes fixing on Alasdair. "You need to see to a few things."

"No, Grandma." Bridie felt her heart rip. "I'm going to jail."

"Oh, that won't be for long."

"I'm going to do time, Grandma."

"Ain't no such a thing."

Was she senile? Did she not understand?

Grandma pulled herself as upright as her arthritis would allow and gave Bridie that look that had straightened her out many a time. "The angel came and let Peter loose, didn't he?"

"Yes, ma'am."

"And didn't he send the earthquake to free Paul from the Philippian jail?"

"Yes, ma'am, he did."

"Well," she said as if she'd made her point, "you'll go to the jail for a while, but you won't stay there," Grandma pronounced. "The Lord give it to me."

Martha shrugged from her place behind Grandma's wheelchair. "If she says the Lord give it to her, usually she's right. Last night she dreamed you were coming up those steps."

Bridie smiled in spite of herself. She leaned toward Grandma and pressed her face against the soft cheek.

"Good-bye."

"You'll be back," Grandma promised.

❧ thirty-nine ❧

GERALD WHITEMAN'S WIFE LET BOB in and took him to Gerry's study. "He's on the phone," she said. "He'll be right down."

Bob took the seat she offered and turned down tea and coffee, anxious for her to leave. As soon as she did, he took the *Washington Post* from his briefcase. He still wasn't tired of looking at the article, of reading the line beneath it: *by Robert Henry*.

It was a beautiful spread. MacPherson's dysfunctional family was featured prominently in the local section instead of buried on the religion page. When they'd seen the actual story, the editors had decided it merited some ink. A quarter page with a photo, and he'd managed to hit just the right tone. Instead of being a rag sheet exposé, the piece read like an insightful analysis. A peek behind the façade of perfection into MacPherson's troubled soul, a thoughtful look at the pressures of ministry. The editor had been impressed, and just as Bob had hoped, he'd promised more assignments. After a few months, assuming he kept on delivering, they would give him a desk, a computer, a full-time job. It would be a lateral move, but Bob hardly cared. He had a sudden vision of himself in the busy city room, phone crunched on his shoulder, making notes on a steno pad. The doorbell rang, bringing him back to the present. He heard feet in the hallway, and his stomach fluttered.

The upcoming scene could play out in one of two ways. The Knox elders and Gerry might be grateful to him for dispatching MacPherson efficiently. There should be little or no fallout to the congregation or denomination since the article made it obvious they'd been unaware of the extent of his problems. And there was no way MacPherson could fight resignation after this kind of press. All that remained was the paperwork. However, Bob was a realist. There was also a possibility the Knox elders would become squeamish and take out their guilt on him, even though he'd only made their wishes come true. He tossed the *Post* back into his briefcase. No sense coming across as smug.

The footsteps came closer. He rose as they filed in: Gerry, trailed by Sutton, Sedgewick, and Smith. Fusty little Edgar Willis wasn't here. Neither was MacPherson, not that Bob had really expected him to show.

They sat down. No one was smiling. Gerry's face was gray, and he looked as though he might cry. The visitors were grim. Even angry. Bob felt his gut tighten. All right. So be it.

Before anyone spoke, Sutton flipped open his briefcase and slapped a copy of the *Post* onto the marble-topped coffee table. He turned and glared at Bob. Bob shoved his own copy of the paper all the way into his briefcase and closed the lid with his foot.

"You are responsible for this," Sutton declared, nostrils flaring, a tiny network of broken blood vessels standing out sharply against his pale cheeks. "Edgar Willis was so upset by this article that he's been taken to the hospital with chest pains."

Gerry turned his grieved eyes toward Bob.

Bob attempted to reason with them. "This will all be forgotten once MacPherson is gone," he soothed. "As soon as the next big story comes along. And I'm sure he'll resign now that this has all come out." He smiled encouragingly. "The denomination and the church are completely out of the loop," he assured them. "It's clear you were in the dark about everything criminal. You come out unscathed."

Sutton turned to Whiteman. "We never asked you to do anything other than talk to Reverend MacPherson. We were concerned about him, and you are his spiritual leader."

"I understood that perfectly," Whiteman said vehemently. "Believe me, I knew nothing about this," and then they all turned angry eyes back on Bob.

His heart thumped again, with anger this time instead of fear. This is the way it always was. People wanted things done; they just didn't want the guilt of knowing how they got done. "You wanted

MacPherson out, and you knew whatever you did toward that end would hurt him. What you're upset about now is that you've been embarrassed. You're not upset about MacPherson. You're worried about how you look."

"That is absolutely not true," Sutton lashed back.

"You wanted him out, and you wanted strings pulled; otherwise, you'd have gone through regular channels."

"We didn't want a formal complaint to stain his record," Smith contributed, his face the picture of sincerity. "We thought perhaps if Reverend Whiteman could find him a position at headquarters, he would follow the carrot. An official vote would hurt his career. His father, you know, was one of my best friends. I couldn't do that to his son." His face hardened again. "We might have wanted you to speak bluntly, but there was never any mention of forcing him to do anything, and certainly not some kind of under-the-table blackmail. This is the church, not the Mafia."

"We never would have condoned this," Sutton said flatly, looking at the newspaper article with disgust.

"Certainly not," Whiteman agreed.

"This is the way the world works," Bob shot back. "That's what you don't seem to understand."

They all looked at him, faces grave. Only Gerry spoke. "Oh, but I think we do," he said. "I think we understand all too well."

Bob recognized an exit cue when he heard one. He snapped shut his briefcase and rose, pausing at the door to the hallway for one last look back.

Gerry was leaning forward, head in his hands. "Well," he asked the others, "what do we do now?"

≳ *forty* ≲

THE FIRST NIGHT BACK, AFTER Alasdair had posted bond and brought her home, after Lorna had hugged her and kissed her cheek and patted her hand, after she'd spent a half hour talking with Samantha, who seemed to be energized rather than traumatized, after she had crept in and peeked at Cam and Bonnie, Bridie went to the kitchen to find that Alasdair had prepared dessert for her. Apple pie. Store-bought, but he'd heated it and served it with a scoop of good vanilla ice cream on top. The tea was steeped and ready, and there was a fat candle in the center of the table—a new one—vanilla. Its scent mingled with the aroma of the cinnamon and apples.

"I didn't see the apple trees at your home," Alasdair said, pouring her a cup of tea and putting in a teaspoon of sugar, the way she liked it. "We'll have to go back soon. We'll bring the children, and you can give us a proper tour."

Bridie blinked.

"Eat your pie," he suggested, "before the ice cream melts."

She picked up her fork and took a bite. She forced herself to swallow it. She wasn't very hungry. "I can't pretend nothing happened," she said bluntly.

Alasdair put another spoonful of pie into his mouth, watching her intently as he swallowed and chased it with a sip of tea. "I would never suggest you should. On the contrary. I think when someone moves close to another, all the while guarding secrets and pretending to be someone they're not, they not only owe an explanation, but an apology." He set down his cup. "I'm sorry," he said simply. "You haven't been the only one with a secret."

"It's hardly the same." She looked away from his eyes. She felt so ashamed, coming back like this with her disgrace laid out for all to see. So humiliated. She suddenly thought of the newspaper article and looked at Alasdair's calm expression in a different light. She wasn't the only one who'd been exposed, and she could almost hear her grandmother telling both of them it was a good opportunity to humble down and let God lift them up. Her eyes smarted. She picked up the paper napkin and dabbed at them.

"Not so different. No one died from your neglect," he said quietly.

"That I know of."

He lifted his shoulders in a slight shrug. "So how long do we punish ourselves? I suppose that's the question. No torture can ever pay the price, can recapture what we've lost or undo what we've done."

He watched her face. "What is it?"

She gave her head a shake and traced a pattern on the tablecloth with the tine of the fork. "I was just remembering one of those hundred verses."

"Which one?"

"'If we say that we have no sin, we deceive ourselves, and the truth is not in us. If we confess our sins, he is faithful and just to forgive us our sins and to cleanse us from all unrighteousness.'"

Alasdair looked past her for a moment, then back. He smiled the barest beginning of a smile. "Well, then," he said. "I think our answer is perfectly clear."

"There you go again, thinking you know everything." She took another little bite of the pie. It wasn't so bad.

He smiled, full face.

"I never intended things to turn out this way," she said.

"How did it happen?" His face was open, kind. His eyes were full of compassion.

She hesitated just a moment, then set down her fork, and beginning this time where she'd always trailed off before, she told him.

Samantha didn't listen too long, just until she was sure they were on the right track. Bridie would be okay now, she thought, finally flipping shut the heat vent. Now that she was talking about it and all. She climbed into her bed and pulled the covers up. The quilt was heavy and soft against her face, and it felt like someone's arm around her shoulders. She rolled over and closed her eyes. Maybe they would all be okay.

❧ *forty-one* ❧

SONDRA WAS FINALLY GETTING NEAR the bottom of the stack of cases she had to dispose of. She opened Mary Bridget Washburn's file and tapped it with a nicely manicured finger. "How about this? She agrees to testify against Porter, pleads to simple possession, suspended sentence."

Tom Dinwiddie gave her a skeptical glance. "You think I'm going soft?"

Sondra smiled. "I think you don't want to put this girl in jail any more than I do. She's changed her ways. Besides, we both know who the real players were."

Dinwiddie gave her a wry smile in return. "Call me a sentimental fool," he said and signed his name to Mary Bridget Washburn's plea agreement in an undecipherable flourish. "Tell her I said to go and sin no more."

"I'll pass that message along. She's back in Alexandria. The minister posted bail the day she was arrested."

Dinwiddie nodded and pressed on to their next item of business. "Now. About Mr. Porter."

Sondra reached for his file and scanned it. He wouldn't be so lucky. Somehow he'd ended up waving his gun at a Nelson County sheriff's deputy who'd been trying to arrest him. When Jonah Porter got out of the hospital, he'd be looking at years, not months, in prison.

"He's going down for this," Dinwiddie said flatly.

Oh well, Sondra wanted to say. She didn't though, just gave her shoulders a slight lift, which she hoped rode the fence nicely. "All right, then," she said, "I guess that about wraps it up."

Dinwiddie nodded and followed her to his office door. "Come

by Wednesday, and we'll have those employment papers ready for you to sign."

"I can't wait," she said and held up Mary Bridget Washburn's file. "Filing this will be my last official act as a public defender. Glory!"

Dinwiddie rewarded her with a smile. "It'll be good to have you on board."

Bridie put her arm around Samantha, who pressed close. "Look," Bridie said, "the Lord decorated the churchyard just for your mama's funeral." They walked through the budding crab apples and cherry blossoms toward the small crowd of parishioners who waited at the grave.

"I'm glad you decided to do this, Alasdair," Lorna said, giving her brother a squeeze on the arm.

"Anna deserves it," he said. "I should have done it long ago."

Winifred was silent for once. Fiona dabbed at her eyes with a handkerchief.

The new headstone was beautiful, carved with the face of an angel, who even looked a little like Anna, surrounded by three small cherubs.

Anna Ruth Williams MacPherson
Free from every bond
She rests with all the saints in the joy of her eternal home

The service was short but sweet. There were tears. Samantha sobbed quietly on Bridie's shoulder. Lorna wept, wiping away her tears against Cameron's shirt. Bridie cried, too, for everything lost. For mothers and childhoods, for time that would never be regained.

Alasdair read some Scriptures, then prayed. His face was tired but finally peaceful. No more tortured eyes peering out from the chained soul.

"Father, we entrust Anna to you. She has returned to the One who formed her out of the dust of the earth, now surrounded by that great cloud of witnesses beyond all time and space. We thank you that Christ himself welcomed her as she went forth from this life. May He, the Lord of Glory, who was crucified for her, grant her freedom and peace. May He show her the glories of His eternal kingdom as she sees her Redeemer face-to-face. Amen."

He closed the Bible, then knelt by the grave. The people filed by one by one, each leaving their offering. When they were finished, a bank of fresh flowers mounded at the foot of the marble stone. Afterward they went back to the parsonage, and Bridie was glad to have the task of serving and pouring to keep her busy. Finally they left, all but the family. Bridie went through the house, gathering up the empty cups and plates, and it might have been her imagination, but she thought she could feel a difference. There was a sense of peacefulness. Not happiness. Not yet. But the possibility that it could exist someday, even within these very walls. The cold presence that had haunted it for so long was gone.

ෳ *forty-two* ෳ

THEY WERE ALL WAITING IN the hallway when Alasdair returned home from the meeting—Winifred, Fiona, Bridie, and the children. He supposed their anxiety was to be expected. It had been a little unsettling to have the president of the denomination travel all the way from Richmond to meet with the congregation's pastor and ruling elders. Alasdair held the door open for Lorna, then followed her in.

They all looked at him, faces expectant. He thought about making a joke, but they were too intense. Each one wore a slightly different expression. Winifred was waiting to pounce. Fiona politely concerned. Bridie . . . It was hard to read her face, and hers was the one he was most interested in. He decided not to prolong their agony.

"Gerald Whiteman said that the persecution our family endured was inexcusable, and he would like to do whatever he can to make amends. The Big Three agreed. I have my choice of any open position in the denomination or a continued ministry here at the church with the elders' full support. It was a unanimous resolution. Even Edgar Willis voted yes."

Winifred gave a satisfied little nod. "I suppose they've come to their senses," she pronounced. Alasdair understood. This would soothe a little of the blistering she'd taken as a result of the newspaper article. It had hit her the hardest. Fiona had been slightly distressed, but mostly for him. Lorna had said it was good—get everything out in the open for once. Samantha said the picture made him look like a dork. He smiled.

"They're probably seeking to head off a lawsuit," Winifred continued. "I heard Bob Henry was fired."

"What did you tell them?" Samantha interrupted, earning a frown from Winifred.

Alasdair smiled broadly. "I resigned," he said, still hearing the wonder in his own voice.

"Yes!" Samantha exclaimed, jubilant.

"That's impossible!" Winifred burst out.

He ignored her.

"How do you feel?" Bridie asked, concern in her voice and on her face.

"Good," he said. "It feels right. I had to ask myself if I was doing it out of spite or anger, but I don't think so. I just have the feeling there's something else I'm supposed to be doing now. Whiteman said the denomination will buy the house and we can divide the proceeds. Given today's real estate prices, we should each end up with a nice little nest egg."

"What will you do?" Fiona queried. "Devote yourself to your radio ministries and writing?"

He shook his head. "I made the calls this morning. I've given up my radio program and magazine and told my publisher I'm taking some time off from writing."

Winifred had paled and looked as if she might faint. "But what will you *do*, then?"

He shrugged. "I don't know." How free he felt saying those words. How light and full of peace.

Winifred's face was a blank mask of disbelief. He took a quick glance at Bridie. Her face was pale but stoic. He could read no emotion whatsoever. He cleared his throat. "Another member of the family has news as well. She *will* be taking a position at denomination headquarters."

Winifred was truly outraged now. "Fiona, you never mentioned a word," she accused.

Fiona shook her head. "It's not I."

"I wasn't speaking of Fiona," Alasdair said. "Congratulations go to Lorna. Meet President Whiteman's new personal assistant."

"No!" Winifred's disbelief showed all over her face. Lorna's pinked with pleasure.

"It pays more than both my jobs combined, and he said I can work my way into administration."

Bridie clapped her hands with delight, and joy lit her face. When the moment passed it went back to the sober expression.

"What about you, Bridie?" Lorna asked, reading his mind. "What will you do? Have you decided?"

Alasdair tensed, the question taking him off guard. He'd had a scenario planned, and this wasn't how he'd worked things out. But there was nothing to be done for it now. He took a deep breath and waited to hear her answer.

Bridie paused before speaking, and those bright blue eyes filled with tears. But when she spoke, her voice was quiet and sure. "I want to go home," she said.

Alasdair felt his heart come untethered and softly float to the bottom, where it settled. Well, then, that was that. He looked down at the floor, willing his face not to betray him.

After a moment he looked up to meet her eyes, but instead of the matter-of-fact resolution he expected to see, or perhaps the detached decision, he was met with yearning—pure, raw, and undisguised. And that look had the same effect on him as a call to battle, the sound of a ram's horn being blown, the early morning whine of the bagpipe rousing the sleeping soldier. And whatever else was unclear, one thing became perfectly obvious. He could not lose her. He moved into the chaos without considering at all, and as he opened his mouth, the words that spilled out bore no resemblance to the eloquent speech he'd practiced.

"We'll take you there." The nonchalance of offering a ride, yet the meaning was lost on no one in the room. The silence was deafening and no less shocking than if, instead of mere words, he'd taken out a gun and fired off a few rounds at Mother's crystal chandelier. Winifred's jaw slacked open. Fiona arched one of her beautiful eyebrows and curved her mouth into a slight smile. Lorna looked as if she would burst with joy. Samantha began jumping up and down and shouting, "Yes! Yes! Yes!"

But the one face that counted was unreadable. Only the wideness of her eyes indicated she'd heard him at all. And suddenly he experienced a new emotion, one he hadn't felt in years. What if he had overstepped? What if she didn't want him along, complicating her life? An old man, after all, with tons of baggage, trailing along after her? What if she didn't want him?

It was as if there were just the two of them in the room. His mouth was dry. He swallowed. "If you would like that," he said, and then waited for her to answer, heart thumping in his throat.

The tears spilled out from the wide eyes. She bit her lip and gave her head a small shake, and Alasdair felt his heart scrape bottom. But just as he was opening his mouth to say whatever it would take to help her shake free of them, she came toward him. He opened his arms, and she stepped into them. He buried his face in the silky white hair, felt it slippery and cool beneath his hand, and smelled her fragrance, like summer air with a hint of honeysuckle. He still couldn't remember his speech, but it didn't matter. He kissed her, then let what was in his heart come out of his mouth.

"From the moment I got into that car to come and find you, I knew you'd been a gift to me, and I'd been too stupid to realize it. I love you, Bridie, with all my heart. Would you have me to be your husband?"

"Nothing would make me happier," she said, and suddenly everything seemed simple.

Bridie took one last look around her. The parsonage was polished and gleaming inside. Even its grim, forbidding exterior looked graceful and welcoming. The two big maples were in full leaf, the lawn lush and green, the new boxwoods fragrant and glossy, the white trim fairly sparkling. She had positioned a huge clay pot of pansies just outside the wrought-iron gates, now painted a glistening white, to welcome the new minister and his wife.

She and Alasdair loaded all their earthly belongings into a tipsy U-Haul trailer. The cooler in the back of the old station wagon was stocked for the journey with uneven peanut butter sandwiches and cartons of juice and chocolate milk. Alasdair had kept just their personal things, Winifred and Fiona being more than happy to relieve him of the rest of Mother MacPherson's antiques. That was fine, he had told them. A fresh start was just the thing he needed.

Winifred hadn't been as problematic as Bridie might have thought. Alasdair had taken her into his study the day he'd proposed. Bridie had no idea what he'd said, but Winifred had emerged red-eyed and meek.

"You may wear Mother's ivory satin wedding gown," she had pronounced. She'd nearly been apoplectic, though, when they'd told her they'd chosen to be married by the pastor of the neighboring congregation in his study, and she was critical of their plans to move the family to Woodbine. "It's the most ridiculous idea I've ever heard," she was still muttering last night when they said good-bye. The Ladies' Circle had a bazaar meeting this morning, and Winifred could not afford to miss it, lest Audrey Murchison take over the refreshments as she had last year. "Absolutely absurd," she'd offered as last words, "taking off for who knows where, with no idea where you'll stay or what you'll do when you get there."

"Abraham did no less when he left Ur of the Chaldees for the promised land," Alasdair had answered.

But Abraham hadn't had AAA and a road atlas, Bridie thought, looking at him as he leaned over the hood of the car, examining the map and plotting the course. And they had a place to stay, at least temporarily. Grandma had been beside herself with joy that Bridie was coming home and bringing her husband and children with her. She was in heaven.

"I want to do one more thing," she said to Alasdair.

He nodded, raised his head long enough to flash her a smile. Already his face looked easier, had lost that pursued look. "Take your time."

She crossed the cool lawn to the church. When she passed the house, she could hear Samantha and the children calling to Alasdair. She quickened her pace, climbed the brick stairway once more, and stepped into the cool narthex, remembering how its dim calm had been such a welcome haven to her. She saw the bulletin board with the falling sparrow, this week's prayer requests tacked underneath. She smiled, remembering, and went into the sanctuary.

The shutters were open and the bright morning sunlight poured through the old glass windows. It rippled and streamed across the red velvet cushions and landed in shimmering waves on the crimson carpet. She didn't feel tempted to linger, though, just walked down the center aisle and out the back door.

She passed through the bower of crab apples to the churchyard, but this time she didn't stop at the ancient grave she used to visit. She continued walking until she stood before her destination. This marble headstone looked bright and clean compared to the weathered tablets surrounding it. The grass, sprinkled with tiny daisies, had been neatly trimmed at its base. She rested her hand on the cool white stone and did what she had come to do.

"Blessed are the dead which die in the Lord," she murmured. "May she rest from her labors, and may her works follow her into eternity," she said and realized she was praying for herself as well as blessing Anna. She felt redeemed, clean, and for the first time, she thought perhaps she, too, could rest under such an epitaph someday. "I'll love them well, Anna," she whispered. "Thank you, Lord."

Feet thunked on the brick walkway, the crab apples shook, and a fresh shower of blossoms rained onto the grass. Samantha emerged with Cameron and Bonnie at her heels.

"Bridie, let's go." Samantha's warm hand clasped her arm, pulling on her like a child would, eyes bright.

"I'm coming," she said, pulling Samantha close and kissing the top of her head. It was sweaty and damp, and her hair was a wad of tangled curls. She was a little girl again, at least for the moment. Bridie took Cameron's hand and Bonnie's, and all of them went to join Alasdair, waiting at the car. They said good-bye to the small knot of people who had come to see them off, and Bridie's last sight was of Lorna, waving and wiping away tears.

Lorna waved until the car disappeared, then mopped her face and blew her nose. Again. It hurt to let them go, but it was a sweet pain and mixed with joy. A few of the diehard MacPherson supporters went back to the church to commiserate over stale cookies and coffee.

"Are you coming?" Fiona asked.

"No." She shook her head and offered no reason.

"Good-bye, then," Fiona said, and that was that. Lorna smiled in amazement. *No* was such an easy word to say once she'd gotten used to it. She turned and looked toward the parsonage, that house that had loomed so large in her life and imagination. She was leaving it now. Finally. Cutting free from it like a ship from an anchor. Ready to sail the wide sea. Tomorrow she would leave for Richmond, and who knew what awaited her there? Her heart thumped a little with anticipation as she walked back toward the house.

She opened the front door and went inside. Everything was squeaky clean, pretty and new. She went upstairs to her old bedroom. It looked very small. Passing through the hallway, she looked inside doors, remembering when each one had belonged to Father and Mother, Alasdair, Fiona, Winifred. She went downstairs and walked through the bare hallway, through the living room that had undergone such a transformation, to the kitchen. She finally stopped before the sink.

She rested her hands on the edge of the counter and looked at the wall, clean and white instead of covered with dingy orange mushrooms. This is where she had prayed. She closed her eyes, and there they were again as they'd been in the vision. Alasdair, face open and happy. Samantha, smiling, looking like a child again. The twins, loved and cared for. Just as they'd looked this morning when she'd said good-bye. *This is what I'm going to do,* He had said. *And you may help.*

She opened her eyes, overcome with joy, and suddenly this old house, this tiny place, was too small to contain it.

"Thank you, Father," she said out loud in a strong, clear voice. "Thank you that you always keep your promises. You always do what you say you'll do."

She smiled, looked around one last time, and then without turning back, she locked the door, slipped the key underneath, and left home.

Ɛ

They drove the morning away, babies chattering behind them, Samantha back to being a teenager now, listening to music on her headphones. Bridie leaned her head against the headrest and gazed out the window as the station wagon ate up the miles.

"What was the name you chose?" Grandma had asked, knowing full well she'd taken Mama's.

"Bridie," she'd answered.

"Mary means bitter, sorrowful. Your mama's name means strong and wise. I wonder if you knew what you were doing when you picked it," she had said with a smile.

She glanced over at Alasdair now. That piece of hair was falling down on his forehead again. He must have felt her eyes, for he looked toward her with a tender expression, as if she was something precious he'd almost lost but found again. He reached out his hand, and she took it, and the fingers that curled through hers were stained with blue.

"You're almost home," he said, nodding toward the sign that said seven miles to Woodbine.

She nodded back, too full of emotions to speak, and realized what she had always known somewhere deep inside. You can't run away from God, no matter how far you go. No matter how hard you try. He'll come after you, not resting until He brings you back. She drank in the sight of the smoky blue mountains in the distance, and the truth was as beautiful and as eternal as they were. She had never been alone. His eye had always been on the sparrow. He'd been watching over her all along.

If You Enjoyed *Not a Sparrow Falls,* You May Enjoy:

Sarah Graham is living life hard fast when it comes to a screeching halt. Now the only way to find her future is to make peace with her past.

Home Another Way by Christa Parrish

A marriage on the brink. A man scarred by war. A baby in need of a family. Can Ben and Abbi overcome the past before they lose each other forever?

Watch Over Me by Christa Parrish